"What are we going to do with an abandoned baby on Christmas Eve?"

"I suppose one of us could drive her to San Antonio," suggested the police officer who'd come to the scene.

"And do *what* with her once we get there?" Heather asked.

Shawn thought he detected an edge of panic in her voice and discreetly narrowed his eyes on the local foster mother.

Yes, there it was. She was afraid for this baby. So was Shawn.

"I just can't help but feel this baby was sent to us, to our town, to this church," he said.

To me. He wasn't about to say those words out loud, but he was certainly thinking about them.

"If we're not going to take Noelle to San Antonio tonight," the officer said, "then what are we going to do with her?"

Shawn took a deep breath and stepped out onto the high wire, knowing there was no net below him. He stared into the stormy blue-eyed gaze of baby Noelle.

"I'll take care of her."

A *Publishers Weekly* bestselling and award-winning author of over forty novels, with almost two million books in print, **Deb Kastner** enjoys writing contemporary inspirational Western stories set in small communities. Deb lives in beautiful Colorado with her husband, miscreant mutts and curious kitties. She is blessed with three adult daughters and two grandchildren. Her favorite hobby is spoiling her grandchildren, but she also enjoys reading, watching movies, listening to music (The Texas Tenors are her favorite), singing in the church choir and exploring the Rocky Mountains on horseback.

Gail Gaymer Martin is a multi-award-winning novelist and writer of contemporary Christian fiction with fifty-five published novels and four million books sold. *CBS News* listed her among the four best writers in the Detroit area. Gail is a cofounder of American Christian Fiction Writers and a keynote speaker at women's events, and she presents workshops at writers' conferences. She lives in Michigan. Visit her at gailgaymermartin.com.

Yuletide Baby

Deb Kastner

&

A Husband for Christmas

Gail Gaymer Martin

LOVE INSPIRED
INSPIRATIONAL ROMANCE

LOVE INSPIRED®

INSPIRATIONAL ROMANCE

Recycling programs for this product may not exist in your area.

ISBN-13: 978-1-335-28495-2

Yuletide Baby & A Husband for Christmas

Copyright © 2020 by Harlequin Books S.A.

Yuletide Baby
First published in 2014. This edition published in 2020.
Copyright © 2014 by Debra Kastner

A Husband for Christmas
First published in 2015. This edition published in 2020.
Copyright © 2015 by Gail Gaymer Martin

This edition published by arrangement with Harlequin Books S.A.

For questions and comments about the quality of this book, please contact us at CustomerService@Harlequin.com.

Love Inspired
22 Adelaide St. West, 40th Floor
Toronto, Ontario M5H 4E3, Canada
www.Harlequin.com

Printed in U.S.A.

CONTENTS

YULETIDE BABY

Deb Kastner

To Alex and Annie Baer.
May God bless your marriage in every way,
and may your love for one another grow stronger
every day. Love to you both, and Izzie, too!

Through the Lord's mercies we are not consumed,
Because His compassions fail not.
They are new every morning,
Great is Your faithfulness,
"The Lord is my portion," says my soul,
Therefore I hope in Him.
—*Lamentations* 3:22–24

Chapter One

Silent night. Holy night.

Pastor Shawn O'Riley pulled in a deep breath, savoring the rich combination of scents. Poinsettias and evergreens.

Christmas.

He relished the deep peace of the now-empty chapel and was grateful for the blessed evening, although he was equally glad it was finished. Christmas Eve for a pastor could be rather stressful, especially for a simple cowboy preacher who worked on the land for a living and pastored the little church part-time. He'd mended as many literal fences for the neighbors as he had spiritual ones, but he loved every second of it—all of it. Especially, on a night like tonight.

Not many knew of all the behind-the-scenes effort needed to pull the more complicated church services together. The children's nativity pageant had gone off without a hitch—give or take a few easily distracted preschool-aged angels and a donkey who couldn't stand still long enough to recite his single line. The parents had loved it and the children had enjoyed performing, and that was all that really mattered to Shawn.

Following that had been the Christmas Eve midnight service, which was one of his favorites, starting with beloved carols and ending in the tranquility of candlelight.

All is calm. All is bright.

And it was. The atmosphere couldn't be more silent and serene. So why did he have a niggling deep in his gut that something was wrong?

He scoffed softly and shook his head. It had been a long week, between preparing some of his animals for the big stock sale coming just after the first of the year and organizing the Christmas Eve festivities. He was overtired, it was as simple as that. There wasn't any deeper significance to whatever unease he was feeling. If he had any sense he'd stop standing here straining for sounds that didn't exist and head back to his ranch so he could get himself to bed where he belonged. Settle in for a long winter's nap, and all that.

Before heading out, all he had left to do was make sure all the lights were off, the candles blown out and the doors locked, and then he could go home.

Alone. To an empty house.

Was that the real reason he lingered?

It wasn't the first time he would be spending Christmas Eve on his own, and he was sure that it wouldn't be his last, but for some reason he was feeling it more than usual. He hadn't spent Christmas with his family since— Well, he didn't want to think about that.

He shook his head to unsettle the disturbing sense of melancholy. He *wasn't* alone. He might be feeling a little lonely, but the Lord was always with him. God had seen him through many a Christmas past.

With a weary sigh, he flipped all seven switches on the light plate, plunging the vestibule into darkness and leaving only the soft flickering of candles beckoning from the warmth of the sanctuary. He'd forgotten to extinguish them.

Shawn grunted and combed his fingers through the short tips of his reddish-blond hair and ran a hand across the five-o'clock shadow on his jaw. Just as well that he had to head back into the sanctuary to take care of the candles. It would give him a moment to refocus and shake this unexpected despondency, remind himself that feelings weren't everything. God was always his comfort and consolation, whether Shawn could feel Him or not.

The light beckoned him. He removed his cowboy hat from his head as he passed through the familiar arch that marked the entrance to the sanctuary. Reverently, and with a catch in his throat, he approached the altar.

He'd been given so many blessings. His health. A little spread of land he was proud to call his own. His six-year ministry at a chapel he adored in a town full of folks he loved. He hadn't been born in Serendipity, and yet the community had welcomed him with open arms as one of their own.

He had so much for which to be grateful. How could he possibly complain when many people were blessed with far less?

As he reached the foot of the altar, he knelt, his eyes dropping from the large wooden cross centered on the wall to the straw-stuffed manger the children had used during the pageant. He grinned as he recalled squalling

Baby Jesus, Eli and Mary Bishop's newborn son. The little nipper had squirmed so hard the entire manger—

Something moved within the straw.

Shawn blinked and rubbed his eyes. What *was* that?

He must be more exhausted than he'd realized. For a moment there he was positive he'd seen—

There it was again.

From the manger. Just the tiniest quiver within the stalks of hay, as if a whisper of a breeze had passed over it.

Only there was no breeze in the chapel.

A shiver ran up his spine as he bolted to his feet and took an involuntary step backward. The candlelight was no help, casting shadows across the walls and floor. His heart hammering in his throat, Shawn approached the crèche.

When he leaned in to see what had caused the disturbance, his eyes widened and his breath tugged.

A *baby*.

A real-live newborn infant, loosely wrapped—not in swaddling clothes, but in a tattered Dallas Cowboys snug-wrap blanket. As Shawn watched, the infant's face scrunched as if it were about to break into a wail, but then just as swiftly its expression relaxed back into the peace of sleep.

Adrenaline surged through Shawn, erasing whatever fatigue and anxiety he'd been combating moments before. His mind went into overdrive with a brand-new kind of worry. He was fearful to move, even to breathe.

What was going on here? This couldn't be happening. Not in this little church, in a small town in the middle of nowhere, and not on Christmas Eve. He rubbed his eyes with his thumb and forefinger, but when he glanced back down at the manger, the baby was still very much present.

Real. Alive. And kicking.

The hair on the back of his neck prickled as his mind raced to take in the facts, what few there were. Where was the baby's mother? Shawn cast a glance around the sanctuary, but there were no additional movements in the darkness. Somehow, the woman had come and gone without him even knowing she'd ever been.

And she'd left behind the most precious of cargo.

He knew he didn't have any new or expectant moms in the congregation, other than Mary Bishop. To Shawn's untrained eye, all newborns looked like Yoda, but he was certain this wasn't the same little guy who'd played Baby Jesus. He'd watched Eli and Mary pack up their little bundle and exit the church an hour earlier.

Come to think of it, he wasn't even sure the baby presently lying in the manger was a little *guy*.

The infant's eyes popped open, revealing an unfocused smoky blue-gray gaze. Shawn reached out a finger and the infant grasped it, pulling his hand toward its tiny mouth. Despite all the tension he was feeling, Shawn couldn't help but smile softly as he slid his large palm underneath the baby's head and tenderly scooped it into his arms. Babies were blessings from God, plain and simple.

Only, in this case, the *plain and simple* part of it was a little more complicated. He hoped he was doing this "cradling the baby" thing right. He was hardly an expert on the subject. He was supposed to support the baby's head and neck—that much he remembered from christenings. With this little one, it wasn't hard to do. The infant was so tiny it almost fit into one of his large palms.

"Shh, shh, shh," he murmured gently to the whimpering infant. He rocked on the heels of his boots. "It's okay, little one. I've got you. Everything's going to be okay. I promise."

He frowned. That wasn't exactly right. Not that the baby could understand his words, but he was hardly in a position to make a promise like that. There wasn't one single thing about this situation that was *okay*.

Where was the mother now? How had she gotten into the church and back out again without anyone noticing her? Had she disappeared for good, or was she lingering around somewhere to make sure her baby was well cared for? Had she picked this chapel for a reason, out of all the places she could have taken the child?

And maybe the most pressing question of all—what was *he* supposed to do with an abandoned baby on Christmas Eve?

If he wasn't mistaken, there were safe-haven laws in Texas to deal with the issue of child abandonment, but Shawn didn't know the exact details. Would a church even be considered an acceptable drop-off point in such a situation? Perhaps allowances could be made, since the nearest hospital was over an hour away? And speaking of hospitals, he should call Delia Bowden, the town doctor, who would no doubt want to check the baby's health. Also, he would need to call the police immediately, to report what could potentially be considered a crime.

He forced a breath through his lungs. He had people who'd help him through this. That was a good thing. But the question remained—whom should he call first?

No matter how he tried to reason around it, he couldn't get over the fact that whatever motivations had compelled the woman to commit such an act, the distressed mother had chosen to leave her precious baby *here*, in this church, and not at the police station or firehouse as she might have done.

A myriad of emotions pressed upon him and he struggled to work them out, to untie the knots in his chest. There had to be a reason the baby was here. God didn't make mistakes, and though it seemed incomprehensible to Shawn, it was abundantly clear to him that *he* was meant to find this child.

But why?

Threading his fingers through his hair, he murmured a frantic prayer for guidance under his breath. What would the Lord have him do?

Jo Spencer. Owner of Cup O' Jo Café and second mother to half the town, she had a word of advice to give for any situation under the sun. She'd been a good listening ear and friendly adviser to him in the past.

It was a decision, at least, and a good one, at that. He sighed in relief.

Jo would know what to do in his hour of need. She was the resident expert on everything—and everyone. Shawn was reluctant to wake her at this time of night, but he knew she would want to be part of this. At the very least, she'd help him think through his options, and she'd definitely know who else to call in as reinforcements. She quite literally knew everyone in town. She might even have an idea who the mother was. If there were any women outside the church's parish who might be pregnant and close to delivery, Jo would know about them.

Shawn's heart ached for the woman who was desperate enough to leave her infant at a church on Christmas Eve. She must be feeling such a deep sense of anguish. No doubt her circumstances, whatever they were, had been dire.

He shifted and wrinkled his nose as an odd, pungent odor assaulted him.

"Yes, little person," he said, addressing the baby. "We need to call in the cavalry."

Along with everything else, Jo Spencer would know how to change a diaper.

He curled the infant into one arm and fished for his cell phone in the pocket of his black slacks. Fortunately, Jo was an active member of the faith community, and her number was on speed dial.

After several rings, a gravelly, sleep-muted male voice answered.

"This'd better be good." Jo's husband, Frank, was gruff on the best of occasions, and Shawn highly doubted that being dragged from a dead sleep even remotely qualified for that category.

"So sorry to wake you, Frank, but I've got a bit of an emergency here. This is Pastor Shawn, by the way."

"Yeah, I figured. When Jo's new-fangled cell phone rang, your picture came up on the screen."

One corner of Shawn's mouth rose. He heard a crackle and a thump on the other end of the line.

"Emergency, you said?" Jo didn't even sound sleepy, though he knew he'd wakened her from the same state that had Frank so grumpy. "What can I do for you, Pastor?"

Shawn released the breath he'd been holding, relief

rippling through his muscles as he continued to jiggle his arm to keep the gurgling infant happy.

"I have a baby," he blurted.

"Oh. I…" It was unusual for Jo to stammer. He'd clearly caught her off guard, and no wonder. "Are congratulations in order?"

"What?" Of all the things he expected Jo to say, that wasn't it. "No. I mean— It's not *my* baby."

Jo let out a big guffaw. Shawn wondered how anyone could sound so gleeful in the middle of the night.

"Well, young man, you'll pardon me for sayin' I'm relieved to hear it. Not that you wouldn't make a wonderful father, mind."

"Thank you for that," he responded, chuckling under his breath. "But I do have a problem. That baby I mentioned—I have it right here. At the church. I think someone abandoned it." He hated calling the baby an *it*, but he thought calling Jo was more expedient than taking the time to check to see if it was a boy or a girl.

"Oh, my stars," Jo exclaimed. "An abandoned baby? Well, why didn't you say so to begin with?"

Shawn grimaced and the baby startled, wagging his or her little arms in the air and breaking into a weak wail.

"I hear the dear little sweetheart. Is it a boy or a girl?"

Shawn shifted the wiggling bundle to his shoulder and bounced softly on his toes. "I don't know. I haven't checked yet. I called you first."

"And that was exactly the right thing for you to do, my dear. I'll be over faster than you can say *Jack Washington*. We'll figure it out together, you and I. I do be-

lieve I'll also get on the horn with Heather Lewis and
see if she can come out and help us."

"Heather Lewis?"

"She's a local foster parent. I imagine she'll be able
to give us some perspective on the situation."

With an inaudible sigh, Shawn crooked the phone
against his shoulder so he could pat the infant on the
back. Jo had no idea how very much he needed to hear
that help was on its way. What he knew about babies
was quite literally limited to the christenings he performed. He didn't have any children of his own, nor did
he have nieces or nephews. He'd never actually had to
care for a baby before, especially not in the plethora of
ways he imagined this little one would need.

Apprehension shot through him like a bolt of electricity, crackling and exploding along every one of his
nerve endings. He wasn't qualified to be in charge of
a child. He hadn't even been successful watching an
older kid, much less a newborn. He closed his eyes and
saw his younger brother David's face, red and sweat-
ing, his palms pressed against the glass of the car door
and his mouth open in a silent scream.

No. Not now.

Pain stabbed through his gut, and he opened his
eyes wide, gasping for air.

Please, Lord, let Jo come quickly.

"I can't tell you what this means to me. Thank you.
From the bottom of my heart." *And then some.*

"No need to thank me, son. That's what I'm here
for—helpin' people as the Lord sees fit to use me." He
knew she told the truth. It didn't matter that it was the
middle of the night or Christmas Eve. Jo was happy to
be everyone's go-to woman.

"Hey, Jo?" he asked when the infant's face once again scrunched, turning from peach to red to an alarming shade of purple.

"Yes, dear?"

"You think you could possibly rustle up a clean diaper while you're at it?"

Jo chuckled. "Don't worry, dear. I'll bring supplies. We're going to manage just fine. Mark my words—everything is going to work out. For all of us."

What Shawn wouldn't give to have Jo's faith right now. He wasn't quite so certain about how things were going to work out, particularly for this precious child. All he knew for sure was that this long night was about to get longer.

Persistent pounding drew Heather Lewis from sleep so deep that she thought she was dreaming the noise— or that perhaps the pounding was just the headache that had set in earlier. She groaned and rolled over, covering her head with her feather pillow. With all the excitement of Christmas Eve, she hadn't managed to get her little brood to bed until late. Exhaustion weighed down every bone and muscle in her body.

Though muted by her pillow, the hammering continued. *Rap, rap, rap.* Pause. *Rap, rap, rap.*

Suddenly she sat bolt upright, adrenaline pumping through her veins and bringing her to instant alertness as she thrashed around, trying to release her legs from the blanket she was caught up in.

She wasn't dreaming about those sharp knocks. They were real. Her mind shrieked in terror.

Run. Hide.

She clutched the neck of her flannel pajamas as her

pulse raged through her, her nerve endings screaming and shattering.

Adrian.

No. She shook her sleep-muddled head. *Not Adrian.*

Adrian was in prison in Colorado, and he had been for years. She had recently returned to her hometown in Serendipity, Texas—far, far away from the nightmare she'd once lived. She was safe.

She tucked her forehead against her knees and gulped for air, a sob of relief escaping her lips.

She was okay. She was okay.

She repeated the mantra even as the pounding on the door resumed.

"Heather?" The voice coming from the other side of the door was a woman's, and though she sounded urgent, there wasn't an ounce of threat in her tone.

Heather rolled to her feet and padded to the front door, taking a quick glance through the peephole for final reassurance before opening up.

"Jo?" she asked, surprised to see the boisterous owner of the local café on her doorstep in the middle of the night. "What's wrong?"

"I tried calling but you didn't pick up."

"I'm sorry. I mute my phone at night so it won't wake up the little ones." She pressed Jo's wringing hands. Something had to be seriously wrong for Jo to be here this late, and on Christmas Eve, to boot. "Do you want to come in?"

"Thank you, dear." Jo followed Heather inside. "I hate to impose on you, especially at this hour, but I'm in desperate need of your assistance."

"Sure. Anything. Whatever you need." Heather didn't hesitate. Growing up in Serendipity, she'd spent many happy hours at Cup O' Jo Café, leaning on the advice of the ever-wise Jo Spencer. Heather couldn't imagine why Jo needed her help, but it was a given that she'd do anything she could.

"A baby has been abandoned at the church. Pastor Shawn is quite flabbergasted by the event, as well you can imagine. Seeing as we don't have a social worker here in town, I figured you were the next best thing, being a foster mother and all. You'll come with me to see to the little one, won't you? I already phoned your next-door neighbor, and she'll be here shortly to make sure your kiddos are looked after while you're gone."

"We're going to the chapel?" Heather was truly ready to do anything—except that. The shiver that overtook her rocked her to the very core. She hadn't stepped through the door of a church in years, and she never wanted to do so again. Not for as long as she lived. Her stomach lurched with the thought, and the fear was paralyzing.

She opened her mouth to decline, but closed it without speaking, rubbing her lips together as she considered her options. There was a sweet, innocent baby to think about. She'd made a promise to herself that if she was presented with the opportunity, she'd be there for any and all children in need.

But this? She squeezed her eyes closed and swallowed her trepidation, searching for her resolve.

"Give me a minute to get dressed," she said to Jo before walking back to the bedroom. She needed the time, not just to change clothes, but to decide if she was really up to this.

She slipped into jeans and a blue cotton pullover and stooped to lace her sneakers, her mind still in turmoil.

Could she do it? Would she be able to overcome years of terror and defensiveness to help the little one?

For the baby's sake, she had to try.

Once her next-door neighbor had arrived to watch the children, Heather and Jo set off. The drive from Heather's house to the chapel was only a few short minutes, but to Heather the distance seemed agonizingly long. Jo bustled out of her old truck the moment she parked it. Heather held back, clutching her hands together in her lap as she gathered her courage. After what felt like an hour but was probably no more than a few seconds, she forced herself to exit the vehicle. A wave of dizziness immediately overtook her and she grasped at the rim of the truck to keep her balance.

Air in. Air out, she coaxed herself. When these panic attacks hit, her breath came in shallow gasps and she hyperventilated, resulting in the light-headedness she was now experiencing. She was so...*angry* that she couldn't control her reactions. It was embarrassing. Humiliating.

"Heather, are you coming?" Jo had made it up to the chapel's red double doors before she glanced back and realized Heather wasn't following her. The old redheaded woman's face instantly crumpled with concern. "What is it, dear?"

Suppressing a shiver, Heather straightened her shoulders and picked up the box of baby paraphernalia from the back of Jo's truck.

She forced a smile. "I'm sorry I'm being so slow. Don't worry. I'll be in right behind you."

While in essence, that was true, emotionally, Heather was lagging, and she was painfully aware of why.

The chapel is just a building, she scolded herself

sternly. If anything, this particular chapel was a place of happy childhood memories. But she couldn't seem to separate the structure from the experiences in her past. The thought of church—any church—was tainted by the thought of Adrian, who had been a beloved and highly respected deacon. No one had realized that it had all been one big lie.

This guy isn't Adrian.

Truthfully, she didn't know anything about the pastor she was here to assist. There was no reason for her to believe Shawn O'Riley would be in any way similar to Adrian, other than being a part of the active leadership of a church. It was wrong to judge all men on a single man's faults, but she couldn't seem to help herself. In her experience, men said one thing and did another. And what they did was bad. It was *bad*. All of her self-preserving instincts were screaming at her to run fast and far away from this situation.

She knew it wasn't logical. This place, Serendipity's little white chapel, was the church she'd grown up in, a place of warm memories and happy times. It was where she'd first learned to sing "Jesus Loves Me," where she'd been told she was His little lamb and that if she became lost, He would cheerfully leave all of His other sheep to come and find her.

Only, when she'd become lost, no one had come to find her, not even the Lord.

And that was just one more grudge to hold against Adrian—one more way in which he'd hurt her. This place, that used to stand for security and love, now just made her anxious and uncomfortable. There was no safety to be found here. Not for her. Nor was there a chance of trust on her part to be given to any man who had a hand in running it. Just the thought of meeting the pastor made her stomach twist.

If she had a lick of sense she'd turn right around and go home. This wasn't her battle.

If it weren't for this baby…

But there *was* a baby. That infant *made* it her battle. She'd promised Jo she would help, and that alone would have been enough to keep her walking forward. But more than that, she'd made a personal vow that she would help children in need wherever and whenever she found them. She couldn't make up for what Adrian had done—and she could never fully forgive herself for what she had stepped aside and *allowed* him to do— but maybe, just maybe, she could help someone else's child, like this tiny gift of humanity who had apparently been horribly abandoned by the very people who should have loved him or her the most.

She'd help the baby, she'd do whatever Jo needed her to do—and then she'd leave the chapel, and the pastor she had no interest in knowing, behind.

As she entered the church and was greeted by Pastor Shawn, it was all she could do not to recoil from his handshake. Oh, he appeared pleasant enough with his Irish good looks—reddish-blond hair, a kind expression on his face and laugh lines fanning from his light blue eyes. Both his gaze and his smile were welcoming. He was obviously relieved that support had arrived. But Heather knew how easy it was for a man to put on a mask for the world and hide his true nature. A charming smile no longer had the capacity to fool her. Especially not on a preacher.

"Jo. Ma'am." He tipped his head toward Heather. "Thank you both for coming in the middle of the night."

"This is Heather Lewis," Jo said by way of introduction. "She's our resident expert, seeing as she has a house full of foster children. She also has a professional background in child care, which I suspect will be invaluable to us."

As small as Serendipity was, Pastor Shawn had probably heard her name, just as she knew his, but up until now they'd had no reason to cross paths. He wasn't a native of Serendipity and had become the pastor of the small congregation a couple years after Heather had left town for college, where she'd met and eventually married Adrian. And she'd certainly never even remotely considered darkening the door of his church upon her return.

"Thank you, thank you. I'm happy for any help I can get. I couldn't believe it when I found— Well, here. Come with me and I'll show you."

Shawn's stride was long and confident as he led them up the sanctuary aisle to where a life-size crèche beckoned. Heather's heart leaped when she saw the tiny infant lying in the manger, swaddled in what looked to be a tattered football blanket. She wondered if the baby had been left that way by the mother, or if the blanket was Shawn's touch.

"Oh, the poor little dear," Jo exclaimed, wasting no time in scooping the baby into her arms.

"He fell asleep, so I placed him back in the manger. Or her—I don't really know yet. It seemed like a safe spot, as close to a crib as I have available. As you can see, I'm way out of my league here."

"I can't even begin to imagine how you felt when you discovered the babe," Jo agreed, kissing the now-squirming infant's forehead. "And this is how you found him? Er—her? All wrapped up in this blanket?" Jo turned and thrust the baby toward Heather. "Heather, dear, can you help me get this poor little thing's diaper changed and get the boy/girl thing settled for us? I am already weary of referring to him/her in a double-gender fashion."

Heather accepted the infant and sat down on the front pew to change the child. It wasn't the most ideal of conditions, but at this point the baby's needs and comfort were more important than the propriety of the church setting.

"It's a girl," she informed them as she reswaddled the infant, this time in a soft, clean pink receiving blanket she'd brought along in her stash of baby things, leftovers from her previous career as a day-care provider.

"A girl," Shawn repeated, his gaze tender and his voice full of wonder. "How about that?" From the bemused expression on his face and the way his warm voice dipped in awe, she might have thought he'd never seen a newborn baby before. Maybe it was just the shock of the situation that had thrown him.

"The poor mother," Jo breathed, placing an empathetic hand over her heart. "I can't imagine what she must be feeling right now, to have abandoned her own flesh and blood on Christmas Eve, of all times. What kind of circumstances must she be under to prompt her to such an action?"

Heather bit the inside of her lip until she tasted copper. She could easily imagine such a situation—any number of them, actually.

"I agree," Shawn said in a low whisper so as not to startle the baby. "I was thinking the same thing. It's awful even to consider."

"It's the infant we need to worry about right now," Heather stated, her tone threaded with pain. "That's what the mother would have wanted." She believed the baby's mother had taken this drastic step for the sake of her child, and her heart flooded with compassion for both. She could do no less for the unknown woman than to make sure her baby was safe and well cared for.

Shawn's eyes slid to her, then shifted back to the infant. His gaze softened as he stared down at the tiny bundle. "Yes, of course."

Heather rummaged through the box of supplies and produced a bottle of formula she'd mixed together before leaving the house. While she didn't have any infants in her care currently, she'd never managed to get off the formula-makers' sample lists, and she was now glad of it, for the expiration date had not yet passed. "Getting her changed and fed is a good first step, but it's not going to solve the real problem."

Shawn brushed his palm over his jaw, which was taut with strain. "Right. We need to call in the appropriate authorities and decide what needs to happen next. I'll phone the police station first, and then we'd probably better get Delia Bowden on the line to make sure the poor little thing doesn't have any pressing medical problems."

He scoffed and shook his head. "What a mess. I really hate having to disturb everyone in the middle of the night, especially on Christmas Eve."

"It can't be helped, dear," Jo reminded him. "I don't think it's anything we can wait on. The police will probably want to start looking for the baby's mother sooner rather than later. She hasn't had that long to have gotten out of town. We don't know anything about her circumstances—she might be injured. And while she looks fine to me, we can't assume sweet Baby Girl here is healthy until Dr. Delia has had the opportunity to look her over."

Shawn's gaze narrowed and his lips tightened into a straight line. "If you ladies will stay with the baby, I'll make the calls."

He stepped out of the sanctuary, and Jo slid into the pew next to Heather, holding her arms out for the baby. Heather gently transferred the fragile bundle into the older woman's arms.

"What's your take on all this?" Jo murmured.

Heather shivered, masking it as a shrug. "I can't begin to guess. I feel in my gut that something truly terrible must have happened. It's got to be just horrible for the mother, whoever she is. *Wherever* she is."

"When Shawn returns we should all say a prayer for her," Jo stated with a firm nod that sent her red curls bouncing.

"Mmm." Heather acknowledged Jo's suggestion without agreeing to it. Jo Spencer was a woman of faith, and they were in a church, after all, so Heather supposed it only made sense that prayer would be part of the equation. It wasn't that she had anything against prayer, per se, but it seemed to her like an exercise in futility. Her prayers—not that she'd said many of them lately—seemed as if they bounced off the ceiling and came right back at her. They were certainly never answered.

"I know the police will want to look for her, but I have a feeling she's not of a mind to be found. Chances are she's out of Serendipity by now, though she couldn't have gotten far. Or possibly she's in hiding."

Shawn approached, sliding his cell phone into the chest pocket of his shirt. Heather didn't know how long he'd been listening, but he'd clearly caught Jo's last statement, at the very least. "Can either of you hazard a guess as to who the mother might be? I'm fairly certain it's no one here at the parish."

Heather shook her head. She'd only been back in Serendipity for a few months, and the truth was, she hadn't been overly social during that time. She preferred to spend all her time taking care of her three foster children, attending the older boy's sports games, mentoring her little girl's second-grade class in reading and volunteering for the preschool library day with little Henry. She'd crossed paths with some old friends at the grocery store or the gas station, but she made sure the chats were brief, and any plans to "get together and catch up" were kept deliberately vague. Frankly, she didn't have much time or use for adult company.

She glanced at Jo for the answer to Shawn's question, expecting that she would know something, but to her surprise, the older woman was likewise shaking her head.

"It's the strangest thing," Jo conceded. "I'm not aware of any women in the area who are bursting at the seams to be delivering a precious little bundle of joy—inside or outside the parish."

"So probably not a local, then." Shawn crouched before Jo and wiggled his fingers in front of the baby. The infant grasped his forefinger and pulled it toward her mouth. "She's a strong little thing. A real fighter."

"From the looks of things, she's going to have to be," Jo responded soberly. Both Shawn and Heather agreed with a nod.

Heather's heart physically ached for the baby girl. So sweet. So helpless. The world was harsh even to the tiniest and most innocent of God's creatures.

It wasn't fair. It wasn't *right*.

"So what's next?" Heather asked, clasping her hands in her lap. She wanted to scream and rail at the air with her fists, but she knew that wouldn't serve any purpose. It wouldn't make her feel better in the long run, and it certainly wouldn't help the baby.

"I just got off the phone with Captain James. He's sending Slade and Brody over to meet with us and give us their take on the situation. They should be here any minute now. Oh, and Delia is on her way, as well. She'll be able to give us a better idea if Baby Girl here needs special medical attention."

They didn't have long to wait—one of the blessings of living in a small town. Less than five minutes later, police officers Brody Beckett and Slade McKenna arrived in rumpled uniforms and with sleep-tousled hair. Though they were similar in build, both with the muscular stature of weekend bull riders, Brody was as blond as Slade was dark. Yet their half-asleep expressions matched perfectly. The police station in Serendipity on Christmas Eve was minimally staffed, and Heather guessed the two men were on-call rather than on duty and had been wakened to take this request.

Delia arrived immediately on their heels and went right to work on the baby, fussing over the infant while she checked her with her stethoscope, took her temperature, got her weight with the infant scale she'd brought and looked at her eyes and ears.

"My guess is that she's about three days old," Delia said, looping her stethoscope around her neck. "Eighteen inches and six and a half pounds. Someone's taken adequate care of her and she's not malnourished, although we'll need to keep a close eye on her weight to make sure she doesn't lose any more."

"Did the mother leave anything else behind?" Slade asked, directing his question to Shawn. "A note, maybe? Something that might clue us in as to why she left her baby in a church?"

Shawn frowned. "I don't think so, other than that tattered Cowboys blanket I found her wrapped in." He gestured toward the altar. "She was in the manger, all alone. It completely freaked me out. I'm sorry. It didn't even occur to me to look around. All I could think about was what I was going to do with the baby."

"That's understandable, and probably just as well," Brody assured him as he and Slade moved toward the crèche. "It may be better that the area was untouched until we got here to investigate."

"Are you considering this to be a crime scene?" Heather asked, shock skittering through her. How could they even think such a thing? Anger welled in her chest. The mother of this baby, whoever she was, needed someone's compassion and assistance, not condemnation and a jail sentence.

Slade glanced her direction. "No. Not yet, anyway, though it's always a possibility. Abandoning a child is a felony in the state of Texas. But we're reserving judgment until we can piece together what really happened here."

"What about safe-haven laws?" Jo asked. "Isn't there anything in the law to protect the mother if it turns out that she can't keep her child?"

"Technically, Serendipity doesn't have an official

drop site for a safe haven," Brody explained, his jaw tightening. "We're just too small. We don't have a hospital. An argument could be made that the fire station might be considered an alternative, but even that's kind of iffy."

"Add to that the fact that the mother might not have known what the laws were, or she may not have been in a reasonable state of mind to be able to sort all that out," Heather pointed out, feeling a need to champion the unknown woman. Delia had been holding the infant, but now Heather reached for her, coveting the comforting feeling of the baby in her arms. "She could have been thinking only of the baby's safety. We don't know what circumstances she's facing. Maybe she's poor and can't feed the little darling. Maybe she was being chased by someone. Or she could be in an abusive relationship."

Heather's throat tightened around the words and her stomach lurched at the thought. She struggled for a breath as drops of cold sweat broke out on her forehead.

"Any of that could be true," Slade agreed. "Then again, she could be a hopped-up crackhead who doesn't even care that she's dumped her baby into a stranger's hands."

"At a church," Shawn reminded him gravely. "The mother left her child at a church. Surely that tells us something—it suggests the woman was cognizant of her baby's needs, that she wanted the best for her. She could have abandoned the baby anywhere. I've heard horrible stories of babies left in Dumpsters or parking lots. That's not what happened in this case. The fact that the mother chose to leave the child here— on Christmas Eve, no less—must mean that she was appealing to our Christian duty to step in and help. Right?"

Heather was surprised to receive help from that quarter. Pastor Shawn was sticking up for the absent mother?

"We shouldn't speculate until we've gathered the facts," Slade conceded. "We don't know what we're dealing with."

"I think I've found something." All eyes turned to Brody, who was crouched next to the manger, sifting through the straw. He withdrew his gloved hand to present a small bundle tied with a dirty red strip of cloth, a seam that looked as if it had been ripped from the bottom of a cotton shirt.

"What is it?" Jo asked as they gathered around.

Brody shifted from a crouch to his knees and set the small bundle on the floor in front of him. Gingerly, he worked the knot in the cloth until it loosened.

"There's a bit of cash here," Slade said, sifting the contents. "And a crumpled piece of paper. Maybe it's a note?" He dropped it into an evidence bag.

"Can you use fingerprints from the letter to identify the woman?" Shawn asked, moving closer to Slade.

"It's a possibility, but not a great one. If the mom has a criminal record—maybe."

The men appeared to be more interested in the money as Brody rifled through the bills. Heather's attention was on the scrap of paper within the clear plastic evidence bag Jo plucked away from Slade. Heather, Delia and Jo all hovered over the mysterious missive.

"What does it say?" Heather asked, scooting closer to Jo as the older woman carefully handled the evidence bag. Heather's breath caught and held when she laid eyes on the delicate handwriting within the letter. The loops and curls were carefully formed and ornamented, so much so that Heather had the distinct, immediate impression of youth.

"I think we may be dealing with a teen mom," she speculated aloud.

Jo met her gaze, her eyes warm with a mixture of compassion and sorrow. "Unfortunately, I think you might be right, dear. Though for the life of me I still can't place any woman in Serendipity who looked to be in the family way, most especially a *young* lady. Teenage girls these days keep themselves so blooming skinny. I feel sure I would have noticed if one of them had been expecting."

Heather laid a reassuring hand on Jo's arm. From the tone of the older woman's voice, Heather could tell Jo was taking a good deal of the responsibility for the abandoned baby upon herself. The townspeople often joked that Jo was the first to know everybody's business. In this case, she was clearly calling herself to task for *not* knowing, likely believing that she could have helped the mother if she'd been attentive enough to spot the situation in time. Heather saw no reason for Jo to take any of the blame.

"It may very well be that you don't know her at all. It seems to me that, given the circumstances, it's far more likely that the mother wasn't a local."

"Serendipity is hardly the kind of place one just passes through, especially a teenage girl on her own. And on Christmas Eve, no less. This town is miles away from anywhere significant."

"If she is a stranger, somebody here is bound to have seen her. Or maybe there's a clue in the note."

Jo nodded and held up the missive, adjusting the range to support the farsightedness that came with age. "Wish I had my reading glasses with me," she mumbled, then cleared her throat and began reading aloud. "'Please take care of my baby. She is not safe with me. Her father must never find out I had her. This money is all I have to give.'"

The note was not signed, but there was a hastily scribbled postscript at the bottom of the letter that caught Heather's attention. "'P.S. Her name is Noelle.'"

The men approached just in time to hear the baby's name. Shawn smiled and reached out to brush the palm of his hand over the baby's silky black hair. "It's beautiful. A Christmas name for a Christmas baby."

Heather stiffened. Shawn was close enough that she could smell his spicy aftershave, and though he didn't actually touch her, she knew his palm fell just short of the small of her back as he leaned over to murmur nonsense syllables to Noelle.

"Any clues as to the mother's identity or whereabouts in the note?" Brody asked, leaning forward to see for himself.

Jo shook her head and handed the evidence back to the officer. "Nothing definitive. Heather and I are guessing she's a young mother and not local."

"It sounds like she is running away from the baby's father," Heather added, then hesitated. That wasn't quite right. She, of all people, knew how difficult it was to break free from an abuser's hold on her life. "Or maybe she's staying with him and she's just trying to protect the baby from him," she amended hastily.

"In any case, she's made it perfectly clear that she's not coming back for little Noelle, at least not at present. I think we can work off the assumption that she's gone." Slade frowned, his brow creasing.

Heather was glad that baby Noelle had so many people here concerned about her future, folks who Heather knew would help this child get a running start at life. That was more than many others had.

"There's roughly thirty-five dollars here, mostly ones," Slade informed them, holding out the crumpled wad of cash. "It's not going to get the child very far."

Heather sniffed as tears burned in her eyes. The sound evidently caught Shawn's attention, for he laid a gentle hand on her shoulder and his compassionate blue eyes flashed to hers. Their gazes locked for a moment and he seemed to be probing her thoughts and measuring her feelings, all without speaking a word. She shuddered and physically jerked from him, refusing to be taken in by whatever kindness he was showing her.

This wasn't the time to think of herself, or about Shawn. The baby needed all of their attention. "I believe that was all that the mother had to give."

Chapter Two

All that the mother had to give.

Shawn acknowledged that Heather was probably correct, and his chest squeezed with sympathy. He anxiously wondered where the mysterious young mother was and what she must have been feeling to leave her precious baby in the care of strangers.

He would make this right. He had to. Although he couldn't fathom a reason for it, God must have His reasons for depositing the baby into Shawn's care. He could do no less than follow this thing through to the end. It didn't matter that he had no training in infant care or that he hardly even knew which end of a bottle was up. God willing, he'd figure it out.

He'd been having a running conversation with God ever since the moment he'd first seen the small movement in the hay, and he wasn't about to stop praying now, not when he was facing the possibility of walking a tightrope with no safety net underneath him.

"So the question remains," he said, knowing even before he asked that he was committing himself to something far beyond his scope of expertise. "What are we going to do with an abandoned baby on Christmas Eve?"

"I suppose one of us could drive her into San Antonio, if we can rustle up an infant car seat somewhere," suggested Brody, although with the catch in his voice, he didn't sound particularly warm to the idea.

"And do what with her once you get there?"

Shawn thought he detected an edge of panic in Heather's voice and discreetly narrowed his eyes on her.

Yes, there it was. The flare in the black irises of her eyes, which were surrounded by a beautiful hazel color. She was afraid for this baby. So was Shawn. They all were. Every person in the room knew what taking Noelle to San Antonio in the middle of the night on a holiday would mean—dropping her into the inhospitable hands of an aloof system where she would have no one to be her personal advocate.

But Noelle *had* an advocate. Shawn.

"Do we have a legal obligation to make a permanent decision about her situation tonight?" Shawn piped up. Maybe with a little time they could figure out a better plan.

Slade raised his dark eyebrows. "Well, eventually we'll have to report her to the proper authorities. Texas social services will want to know about her. But that does not necessarily have to happen tonight. If I'm not mistaken, we have somewhere around one business day to bring her to the attention of the state. The fact that it's Christmas Eve works in our favor, if you're wanting to hold off a bit. *Is* that what you want? And if you don't mind my asking, why? What do you have in mind?"

"Yes, dear," Jo urged, patting Shawn's forearm. "Tell us—what's your plan?"

"I'm not— That is, I don't have a plan. I just can't help but feel this baby was sent to us, to our town, to this church."

To me. He wasn't about to say those words out loud, but he was certainly thinking about them.

"I agree," said Jo. "We know our good Lord. He doesn't make mistakes. Somehow this baby is part of His good and perfect gift to us."

"Amen to that," Delia agreed, adjusting the stethoscope draped around her neck.

Shawn's heart welled even as his stomach tightened. Jo had the extraordinary ability to see the good in everything and everyone, along with the uncanny ability to be able to remind others of God's hand in their life circumstances.

But how could an abandoned baby be a gift from God?

Shawn acknowledged in his heart that the Lord could turn even the worst of circumstances into blessings, but he was struggling to wrap his mind around it. Whatever God had planned for them and for this child, it was beyond his ability to see.

"If we're not going to take Noelle to San Antonio tonight," Slade said, his even tone indicating the statement was a fact and not so much a question, "then what are we going to do with her?"

Shawn took a deep breath and stepped out onto the wire, knowing there was no net below him. If he looked down he knew he would take a mental nosedive, so instead he stared into the stormy blue-eyed gaze of baby Noelle.

"I'll take care of her."

* * *

Shawn taking baby Noelle overnight sounded like a reasonable enough plan, at least until four o'clock in the morning came and went and he hadn't gotten a single moment of sleep. The small gathering of neighbors had loaded him up with suggestions on baby care, wished him well and then gone home to catch a few hours of shut-eye before Christmas morning dawned, where they would celebrate with their own families.

Shawn had mistakenly thought he had everything under control. How hard could it be, really?

Ha! The joke was on him. The Lord certainly had a sense of humor.

He groaned and smothered a yawn. Instead of enjoying a happy snooze with sugarplums dancing in his head as he would have done if he'd gone home alone, he was pacing the hallway with an unappeasably fussy baby.

Holding her close to his heart, he gently patted her back in a slow, steady rhythm. The little *bundle of joy* wasn't the least bit happy, and he hadn't a clue what to do for her. He wished he knew what was wrong so he could fix the problem.

After a bottle of formula and a diaper change, Noelle had initially drifted off to sleep. Shawn had thrown together a makeshift bassinet from a shallow plastic bin and some blankets and placed it by the side of his own bed. All was calm—and bright.

For about five seconds.

No sooner had he laid his head on the pillow than Noelle started to wail. And wow, but the kid had a pair of lungs.

He shuffled through his mental list. Diaper changed.

Warm bottle. Patting her back to help her remove any lingering bubbles in her tummy. Swaddled. Multiple attempts at a pacifier, although he'd qualified that as a fail, since he couldn't even get the baby girl to keep it in her mouth.

Nothing seemed to work. If anything, the more attention he paid to Noelle, the harder she cried, and now she was making little *hic* sounds when she breathed. He was afraid she was hyperventilating.

Could babies hyperventilate? It frightened him that he didn't even know the answer to that question.

What if she passed out? What if something was seriously the matter with her? Had Dr. Delia missed something critical when she'd examined the baby?

Noelle scrunched up her tiny face and sneezed. Shawn reached for his cell phone, then stopped and shook his head, laughing at how easily flustered he was getting.

Who was he going to call? Emergency services? And say what?

Hello, can you help me? My baby just sneezed!

"I'm overreacting, aren't I, little darlin'?" he murmured to Noelle. Her face relaxed, and she quieted, appearing to respond to the sound of his voice. Well, that was good, right? He kept talking. "Let me tell you, sweetheart, I have a brand-new appreciation for the parents of infants. Is this what Eli and Mary are going through every night right now? Huh? You think?"

Noelle sneezed again.

"Uh-oh. I hope you're not getting sick. Dr. Delia was pretty thorough when she was examining you, and she pronounced you good to go, at least for the time being. But I suppose there's always the possibility that she missed something. Are you coming down with a cold, little darlin'? Or am I just being a worrywart?"

He chuckled softly when he realized Noelle had stopped crying. When he gazed down at her, he realized she was looking at him expectantly, sucking contentedly on her tiny fist.

"So that was all you needed? A little man-to-baby conversation? Well, I don't mind talking to you, sweetheart, but wouldn't it be great if we could table this discussion for now and pick it up in the morning?" From the expectant look on her face, it seemed the answer to that question was no.

Well, if all he had to do was talk, he supposed he could handle that. He was a preacher, after all. Words were his livelihood.

Just not in the middle of the night.

He took a seat on his plush easy chair and kicked back the footrest so he could settle Noelle on his shoulder. He'd heard young parents joking about how their babies had their days and nights mixed up, but he'd never quite understood what that meant.

Now he got it, and got it good.

If nothing else, taking care of Noelle over the Christmas holiday would be a tremendous learning experience for him. After what he'd experienced tonight, he had all kinds of ideas on how to be a better pastor to the parents of newborns in his congregation. Up until this point he realized he'd kind of missed the mark. For one thing, he'd be more sympathetic, and he'd be sure to look for ways to make the transition into parenthood easier. He'd never envisioned the type of sacrifice parents made on a daily—and nightly—basis, and he imagined a strong support system would make all the difference in the world for them.

Noelle gurgled, and Shawn rubbed his fingertips against her tiny back. "What are you here to teach me?" he murmured, offering his heart to God and to the child. "I'm your student now. You've got me in the palm of your sweet little hand. So why don't you tell me, young lady—what am I here to learn?"

In a more innocent time of her life, Heather's favorite time of the year had been Christmas. Peace on earth, goodwill to all. She recalled participating in joyful caroling parties with hot apple cider and eggnog afterward. Joining in the throng of busy shoppers as they scurried around trying to catch seasonal deals for their loved ones. The anticipation as she wrapped presents and created pretty, elaborate homemade bows to tie around them. And most of all, she remembered the joy of celebrating God made Man in the person of Jesus. The nativity.

All of that had been part of her best childhood memories.

But her parents had passed on, and all the goodness associated with the season had gone by the wayside during her years with Adrian. Oh, they'd attended their fair share of Christmas parties, but Adrian was in the habit of secretly imbibing on the side. Then afterward, he'd cross town to where no one knew him and hit the bars until he was stumbling drunk.

He despised Christmas, and he'd mocked her attempts to give their house a personal touch for the season. He'd insisted on professional decorators and expensive ornaments, and eventually she'd just stopped trying. She hadn't even bothered to give any input—it wasn't like anyone listened to her wishes, anyway. It was just more work for her to do and there was no one but her to enjoy it. There wasn't much joy in her life to celebrate. Adrian would complain about the twinkling lights and the space it took up and failed to appreciate the tree and Christmas decor for what they represented.

Church services became exercises in deception. So many people loved and respected Adrian, an active leader and deacon in the church. To members of the congregation, she strived to appear to be the happy, faithful wife of a charming man, with a seemingly perfect marriage and not a care in the world.

What a lie. A whole pack of them, as a matter of fact.

Well, no more.

But even though she no longer carried the weight of the lies on her shoulders, the damage they had done to her still remained. Some days it was all she could do to rise out of bed and go about her daily activities. Her foster children—nine-year-old Jacob, seven-year-old Missy and three-year-old Henry—gave her the strength to face life again. Their precious hugs and sweet laughter made even the worst of days bearable.

This year she'd purchased a freshly cut Virginia pine tree from a tree farm. No artificial trees in her house. If she was being honest, it was as much for her as for the children. It filled her heart with great joy to see the children's excitement as they spotted the perfect tree and hauled it inside. Little hands helped as much as the big ones did.

The tree filled her home with the crisp, refreshing scent of evergreen. She'd helped the kids decorate it with a string of lights and candy canes, and then they'd threaded popcorn and cranberries and draped them over the branches for the final touch. Every cent she made from the state for fostering went straight back into caring for the children, and on the tiny salary she made as a virtual assistant, she was barely making ends meet. It was unfortunate that her finances didn't stretch nearly as far as she would have liked, and this year, at least, she wasn't able to afford the shiny new glass ornaments displayed in the window of Emerson's Hardware, but if her years with Adrian had taught her anything, it was that fancy decorations didn't make for a better holiday.

Simple pleasures were worth treasuring. She was surviving and taking care of the children, and for now, that was enough. She'd budgeted every spare dime to purchase at least one gift for each of the kids from their wish lists, and it was important to her that she followed another old Lewis tradition, so their stockings were overflowing with tokens of her affection, small and inexpensive though they were.

The scene this Christmas morning was picture-perfect. All that was missing was the pitter-patter of feet and the happy squeal of children.

She didn't have to wait long before she heard stirring from down the hall. She promptly attuned her practiced ear to the sound. Muffled whispers emanated from the shadowed spot where the hall met the living room.

"Come out, come out, wherever you are," she called, infusing gaiety into her voice. "Who wants to see what Santa brought this year?"

Heather closed her eyes for a moment and simply savored the lovely sounds of Christmas. Children.

Laughing, happy, excited little voices. She allowed the cheerful clatter to penetrate and fill her empty heart and warm her icy spirit.

Her eyes snapped open and her pulse quickened at the sudden shrill buzz of her cell phone. She'd turned the sound back on as she did every morning, but she wasn't expecting a phone call, especially at this time of the morning and on Christmas Day.

She put a hand to her chest to still her galloping heart. She was sick and tired of her first reaction to the phone or doorbell being a spike of terror. It had been several years now since Adrian had been incarcerated, and still she dealt with this. She'd thought moving back home would help. How long would it take her to relearn the basics, replacing her automatic fear impulses with healthy responses?

"Wait for me, my sweethearts. Don't go looking in your stockings until I'm off the phone," she admonished the children playfully. She reached for the phone in the pocket of her bathrobe. It was a long-standing habit of hers to keep her cell close by, even while she was sleeping. Better safe than sorry.

She glanced at the number. She didn't recognize it, but it was local.

"Hello?" She hoped her voice didn't sound as shaky as she felt.

"Heather? This is Pastor Shawn O'Riley. I apologize for interrupting you on your Christmas morning."

"Shawn?" *The baby.* Heather's adrenaline spiked along with her anxiety. "Is something wrong with Noelle?"

"No—no," he answered hastily. "Well, maybe. I'm

not sure. I think perhaps it's just that I don't know what I'm doing. I've never been in charge of a baby before."

Heather pinched her lips and shook her head at the irony. A pastor, a man used to directing others, had in one single night discovered that caring for an infant offered a completely different set of challenges. Even a natural leader couldn't make a baby do what he wanted her to do.

But there were some men who would try.

She shoved out a breath. Shawn had given her no reason to suspect he might fall into that category. "Can you be more specific?"

"Let's see…I've changed her diaper, fed her, burped her—repeatedly, as a matter of fact. It's a never-ending cycle, it seems."

Welcome to parenthood, Heather thought. She'd never had children of her own, but for a while just after graduating from college she'd found great happiness working in a day-care center. In her heart of hearts she'd desperately wanted a baby of her own, but the idea of Adrian fathering any children she might bear had left her frightened beyond words at the prospect of conceiving and bringing a child into her terrifying and hopeless world. She hadn't dared to have a child, who'd have been immediately put at risk.

"Sounds like you're doing everything right," she assured Shawn, forcefully shifting her thoughts to the present. To Noelle.

"I hope so, but I sure don't feel like it. She's a little darlin', but I'm beginning to think I've bitten off more than I can chew, so to speak. I've tried everything. I've done bathing, swaddling, attempting to coax her to take a pacifier—which, incidentally, is much more difficult in practice than it looks at first approach."

Heather chuckled. "It takes some getting used to."

"Yes, but here's my problem. The one thing I cannot get her to do is *sleep*. She'll only doze off for a few minutes at a time, and even then, it's only if I'm rocking her in my arms. The moment I try to lay her down on her own, her eyes pop back open and she starts wailing in earnest. Then the whole process begins again." He sighed deeply.

It sounded as if the poor man was sleep-deprived in a major way. Heather imagined it was hard enough to care for a newborn when there were two parents in the house to tag-team on getting some rest. She had to admire Shawn for taking such immense responsibility on his own shoulders, even for one night. It wasn't something she would have expected from a single man.

But why was he calling her?

"Is there something I can help you with?" she asked, her breath catching in her throat as she waited for his answer.

His groan was one of utter defeat. "No. Not really. I guess I just wanted to hear the sound of someone's voice, an adult someone, that is—and maybe be reassured that I'm doing everything I need to be doing for Noelle. I don't want to mess this up. Jo Spencer considers you the resident expert, since you raise foster kids and have worked in day care and everything. I figured you were the one to call. I would hate to think I accidentally overlooked something important that I could have done to make Noelle more comfortable. Anyway, thanks for listening. I appreciate it."

"Do you have anyone who could come over and spell

you for a while so you can get some sleep?" Heather didn't know why she asked. It wasn't as if this situation had anything to do with her. Not directly. She wasn't Shawn's friend, and she didn't want to be, thank you very much. But this concern she felt wasn't truly for his sake, was it? No, it was for Noelle. The sweet baby deserved loving, capable care. And while Shawn seemed to be earnestly trying his best, he was unpracticed at child care even when he *wasn't* sleep-deprived. "A friend? A neighbor?"

"No. This is all on me. I wouldn't want to pull anyone away from sharing Christmas with their families." He stifled a yawn. "I'm sure I'll make it...somehow."

"I can't leave my foster kids."

"Of course not." He sounded genuinely surprised. "I wouldn't expect you to, even if you could."

"My parents are no longer living, so I don't have any help from that quarter." She didn't know why she felt the need to rationalize her actions to him, but there it was. "I'm single. I have no one else to watch them."

"Seriously, Heather. I'm not asking for you to go out of your way for me and Noelle. I guess I shouldn't have called. I didn't mean to bother you or to put any kind of pressure on you."

"You aren't bothering me," she replied, which was half true. It would be a good long time, if ever, before she was completely comfortable around men—particularly those who claimed to be men of faith. But this was about the baby, and making sure the tiny infant was taken care of could never be a bother.

She squeezed her eyes closed and took a deep breath—in through the nose, out through the mouth—as she'd learned through many, many months of therapy.

Be calm. Relaxed. Composed.

She knew she was going to regret the next words coming out of her mouth, but she'd made a promise to herself and God that she'd help children in need whenever and wherever she found them. It was, in a sense, her penance for all of the mistakes she had made.

And at this moment, that meant she was going to help Noelle.

There was nothing she could do for the two children who'd died instantly after being sideswiped by Adrian's car as he swerved all over the road in a drunken haze. She couldn't turn back the clock and keep Adrian from walking out the door on that fateful day, even though she'd known he'd had too much to drink and that he was going to get behind the wheel and drive. She'd only been thinking about herself at the time. She'd wanted him gone, and she'd let him walk away.

She wished she could make things right, but she couldn't. However, she *could* do something for the tiny baby who'd been abandoned by her mother on Christmas Eve. She could—and she would.

"I know I said I can't leave my kids alone in the house, but that doesn't mean you can't come over here. I will set an extra plate, and you and Noelle can join us for Christmas dinner. I'm sure the kids would love to have extra guests at the table. I'll be happy to watch Noelle for a bit while you catch a power nap. Unless you have other plans, that is."

"No. No other plans. But are you sure I won't be imposing on you?" Relief was evident in his voice.

"No." *Yes.* "Not at all."

"Well, then."

Why was he hesitating? Could he hear the tentativeness in *her* tone?

"Oh, that's right. You don't have a car seat, do you?" She slung out a guess.

"That's not a problem. A car seat isn't necessary. It's not an immediate issue, anyway. I'll have to procure one eventually, I suppose, if I'm going to be the one taking Noelle to the authorities in San Antonio. But today, we can walk."

Her shoulders slumped in relief and she dragged in a silent breath. He hadn't noticed her uncertainty, then. *Good.*

"Then it's settled. I'll set an extra plate for you. Come over whenever you're ready. Oh, and be sure to bundle Noelle up really well. There's a bit of a chill in the air."

"You're sure you don't mind the extra company?"

No, she wasn't sure. She would never be sure. Probably not for one single day for the rest of her life. And she wished he would stop asking, or she was liable to give in to her doubts and capitulate.

"I'm absolutely certain," she reassured him for what she hoped was the last time. "I'm looking forward to seeing that precious little blessing of yours."

At least that was the truth.

Chapter Three

Shawn had never been so uncomfortable in his life. Being the kind and thoughtful woman she was, Heather hadn't said as much out loud, but it didn't take a rocket scientist to figure out that he was intruding on her personal family time—and that she was only allowing it because he was entirely inadequate to the task of caring for an infant.

From the moment he'd stepped into the house, Heather had swept Noelle into her arms and taken over all of the baby care. How quickly she had put the poor little infant's world to rights. Heather had also fixed *his* most pressing problem, insisting he head straight into Jacob's bedroom for a quick nap.

He'd dropped into a dead sleep but had been wakened shortly after by a phone call from Jo, inquiring how he was faring with Noelle. She hadn't even sounded a little bit surprised when he revealed he had come to Heather's house for help. Probably because Jo already suspected how hopeless he'd be with an infant.

Why no one had bothered to inform *him* that he wasn't up to the task was beyond him. No one had uttered a single word of warning. Instead, every last one of them had played right along last night when he'd unwittingly offered to care for the infant. No one had laughed. No one had even seemed startled by his hasty proposal. They'd let him dive right off the side of a cliff without testing the depth of the water first.

How could he have known what he was letting himself in for? He was a simple cowboy preacher. He knew ranching and he had the gift of gab. He was a single man and lived alone. His needs were few.

Noelle's needs were apparently many, or at least they were a mystery to him, and he was clearly lacking in his ability to take decent care of her. At least here with Heather, he could be assured that Noelle would have everything she needed. Though the downside was that he'd have Heather as a witness to see exactly how inept he truly was. He grinned, not bothered by the laughter that was bound to come at his expense—and if there wasn't yet, there soon would be. Christmas Day wasn't over. He had a while yet to display the stunning depths of his incompetence.

He didn't really care if other folks caught a laugh or two over his present circumstances—he was laughing at himself. It was pretty funny, when he thought about it.

Chuckling, Shawn assured Jo that all was well for the time being. It was all good *now*—because of Heather's generosity and help. Jo laughed with him and agreed with his assessment of Heather and then promised she'd check in on him later. Shawn tucked his cell phone into his shirt pocket and stretched to get the kinks out of his shoulders. Now that he was awake, he wasn't sure what he should be doing.

Probably leaving. He didn't want to take advantage of Heather's kindness, particularly on what he understood to be her first Christmas with her foster children.

But when he padded back into the living room and spied Noelle and Heather looking so comfortable and contented together in the rocking chair, he couldn't find it in his heart to break them up. And truth be told, even considering how awkward he felt right now being the third wheel, he wasn't yet prepared to go off on his own and face another night of single-parent foster-daddy duty.

He shuffled toward the corner of the living room, his hands stuffed into the pockets of his blue jeans. He probably should at least offer to do something to help, but he hadn't the faintest notion of what assistance he could give. He wasn't family. He wasn't technically even a guest. He didn't know where she kept the silverware. His cooking skills were marginal. And though he could probably manage to keep the older kids occupied, he was totally useless with the baby.

"You don't have to hold up the wall," Heather commented with a gentle smile, brushing a long strand of mahogany-brown hair behind her ear. "Feel free to sit wherever you can find a free space, although it looks like you may have to move something to find a seat. I usually have a rule about putting away toys before new ones get taken out, but I'm being a little lax today, since it's Christmas."

He smiled and nodded to acknowledge her offer, but he was too fidgety to sit down just yet. Besides, standing gave him a better view of the kids. There was nothing like the sight and sound of jubilant children on Christmas morning to raise a man's spirits.

Crumpled wads of bright-colored Christmas wrap, now ripped and forgotten, lay balled underneath the glittering tree. Heather's three foster children were busy with their new toys. The boys, nine-year-old Jacob and three-year-old Henry, played together, pushing their shiny cast-model race cars around a plastic track. Seven-year-old Missy held a new doll in the curve of her arm and mimicked Heather's sounds and movements as she held Noelle. It was a heartwarming sight, especially since just yesterday he'd imagined he'd spend the day as a lonely bachelor.

What a difference a day could make. Here he was, enveloped in the warmth of a child-filled house. He hadn't realized just how wonderful it would be after having been alone all these years. It filled his heart with great joy to realize how little it took to make the young ones happy. He needed a little bit more of that innocence in his life. If only adults had the same capacity to give and receive as generously as the youngsters.

Heather hadn't gone overkill on the number or size of the gifts—whether because she couldn't or she chose not to, but there was no shortage in the amount of joy she'd given her children in what they *had* received. It was abundantly clear to anyone observing the scene that she knew each of her foster children intimately and was mindful of what they wanted and needed.

Shawn was envious of that quality in her. *He* apparently hadn't been able to anticipate Noelle's needs at *all*.

It was a good thing for the baby that he wasn't going to end up being her permanent foster parent. She would no doubt go to a wonderful home with a foster mother like Heather, who had the knowledge and capacity to care for her. All of her needs would be anticipated and met without Shawn's doltish stops and starts. She was such a sweet little girl, and he was certain she'd eventually be adopted by a nice Christian family with a mom and a dad who loved each other. Maybe she'd have other siblings to play with and a dog and a cat and a yard with a fence.

All he had to offer was the dog and the cat and the yard and the fence—and pigs and goats and horses and ranch land.

Not good enough. Not by any stretch of the imagination.

He shifted his attention back to Heather, who watched over her brood from an old-fashioned wooden rocking chair laden with colorful floral cushions. She hummed a Christmas carol as she rocked. She had a lovely, rich alto voice that enthralled Shawn as much as it did Noelle, purring through his muscles until he felt thoroughly relaxed and yet completely alert at the same time. It was an odd paradox, but true nonetheless.

To his utter astonishment, he discovered that Noelle, who was contentedly curled in the crook of Heather's arm, wasn't asleep as he'd first assumed she must be. Instead, she was staring up at Heather, her chubby fist in her mouth and her eyes just beginning to focus on the woman holding her.

What she *wasn't* doing was crying. Not wailing, not squalling, not bawling, not even a whimper.

Go figure.

Shawn was amazed by how quickly Heather had made everything right in the tiny baby's world. He didn't know if it was because she was experienced in caring for infants or the fact that she was naturally suited to be a mother. Maybe it was a combination of both, but Noelle responded to Heather in a way that made Shawn feel especially incompetent, a fact which, while impressive, grated against his distinctly male pride. *He* wanted to do it right, get things done the first time and in an expedient manner—not stumble over his every move.

He watched in awe as the baby took a bottle from Heather without a fuss. Adding insult to injury, Noelle fell asleep while Heather was in the midst of patting her back.

Heather definitely must know some tricks of the trade that he didn't. Or maybe the tiny tyke was plain old worn-out from her self-appointed task of keeping Shawn awake all night. She had to sleep sometime, right?

Just not on his watch.

Shawn shifted his weight and smothered a yawn behind his fist. The catnap he'd taken was a drop in the bucket after the past twenty-four hours. It wasn't just the fact that he'd had to stay awake, although there was that. It had been quite a few years since he'd pulled an all-nighter. But there was a great deal more to the fatigue weighing him down—like the stress of being singularly responsible for a tiny human life, completely helpless and dependent upon him.

"You still look thoroughly exhausted," Heather commented. She tilted her chin and blinked up at him with her big hazel eyes that softly glimmered from the lights of the tree. "I think maybe you need to sleep a little bit longer. There's no rush, you know. I don't mind watching the baby this afternoon."

Caught up in her gaze, Shawn's stomach did a little

flip and he barely stanched the urge to clear the catch out of his throat.

"Jo woke me when she phoned to check on Noelle. I attempted to go back to sleep but my mind started spinning with all that's been going on and that was the end of my nap. As tired as I am, I don't think I could sleep any more."

"That's a shame. Maybe you should have put your phone on mute." She smiled, though it looked a bit forced. "Well, in any case, you don't have to stand in the corner. You look like a hat stand—or else like someone put you in time-out."

Shawn chuckled. "It wouldn't be the first time."

"And probably not the last. Seriously—please come sit down on the couch and take a load off. You make me nervous when you hover that way." Despite her kidding tone, he almost got the sense that she truly *was* nervous. But that couldn't be right, could it? What reason would she have to be nervous around him?

"I don't even mind if you put your feet up on the coffee table—well, the storage bench that serves as the coffee table—either," she continued. "As far as I'm concerned, that's what it's there for."

"Not for decoration? It's a nice-looking piece of furniture." The bench looked as if it fit with the rest of her decor—not that he was any kind of expert on matters of decorating. The padded corners were a little worn, but it exhibited the same lived-in look as her other furnishings. He liked lived-in.

She chuckled. "No fancy furniture in this household. *Decorative* would last about a day. With three kids running around, functional is the name of the game here."

He groaned in delight as the plush cushions on the

chocolate-colored couch enveloped him like gentle arms. True comfort. Everything about Heather's house suggested it was the genuine article. Her entire home expressed her heart—and it was all about the children.

Her home was far more comfortable and welcoming than the more perfectly kept, sanitized houses of some of his congregants, where he found himself tiptoeing around, afraid to stand near the furniture, much less sit on it. He felt ill at ease in too-clean houses. As a pastor, visiting his flock was one of his favorite tasks, but as a cowboy who lived and worked on a ranch with horses and goats and pigs, he wasn't always dust- and dirt-free. Heather certainly didn't need to apologize for her furniture. He wished everyone kept a house like hers.

She was literally encouraging him to put his feet up. *Sweet!*

All he needed now was a cold soft drink and a football game on television—although of course he'd never suggest such a thing. He'd already probably put enough dents into her holiday without bringing sports into it.

"I can't believe how worn-out I feel," Shawn said, running a hand across the stubble on his jaw and belatedly realizing he hadn't shaved that morning. Now that he thought about it, he hadn't combed his hair before he left, either—and then he'd gone and taken a nap, which could only have served to worsen his already disheveled appearance. He must look like the abominable snowman's twin brother, and yet Heather hadn't blinked an eye, not when he'd appeared at the door, and not when he'd shuffled out after his nap. "I don't know how new parents do it, but I'm certainly too old to try to pull all-nighters anymore."

Heather raised a brow and huffed a breath through

her teeth. "You're not exactly over the hill. What are you—twenty-six? Twenty-seven?"

"Twenty-nine, although at the moment I feel more like I'm sixtysomething. Was it only a few years ago when I was in seminary that I could stay up all night with ease? Seems like forever. Me and my buddies used to get lost in these deep theological debates. They'd last for hours, many times the whole night, and then I would go straight to my classes the next day without so much as a yawn. I studied for finals that way, too. Pulled all-nighters and managed to do well on my tests without much more assistance than a stout cup of coffee or an energy drink to back me up. Now look at me." He chuckled and hung his head with a dramatic groan. "One night with a baby and I'm as good as gone."

She laughed. "It might be the stress that's really taking it out of you, you know. Watching a baby isn't for the weak of heart. I've never been the parent of an infant myself, but I saw plenty of them during my experience as a day-care director. If I don't miss my guess, all new parents go through this no-sleeping stage, at least to some extent. I remember my first few nights as a foster parent of these three sweethearts—hovering over the kids' beds when they were sleeping just to check and make sure they were all breathing. I was hypervigilant for the entire first month, I think. And my kids aren't even infants."

Shawn groaned and shoved his fingers through his hair. He appreciated the way Heather was trying to make him feel better, but he still believed he'd epically failed in something that up until last night he'd simply and erroneously assumed was easy. He apparently lacked the entire skill set for being a father. "Thankfully, I'm not a real parent yet. I always thought I'd have a family someday, of course, but now I've got to admit I'm questioning how smart that would be. I'm not sure I can handle this *daddy* business. Unless maybe it's different when it's your own kid."

Heather shrugged and dropped her gaze from his, but he thought he detected sadness in her gaze before she looked away. "I wouldn't know. It might be. Do you regret agreeing to care for Noelle through the holiday?"

Regret? No, that wasn't the word he would use to describe what he was feeling about fostering Noelle.

Heather's soft-spoken question jarred him to the core. Despite the lack of sleep, Shawn's heart went out to baby Noelle in a way he couldn't even explain. He believed God had His hand in placing Noelle in the manger at his little chapel instead of at the police station or firehouse. Sure, he missed the sleep he would have gotten. But the regret would be a hundred times stronger if he hadn't made the choice to take the baby in.

He shook his head. "No. I'm glad for the opportunity. And I do believe God put Noelle into my life for a reason. I won't soon forget her. She's stolen a piece of my heart. If nothing else comes of this, the experience will give me a better pastoral understanding for new parents in my little parish."

Shawn didn't miss the way her jaw ticked when he mentioned God. He had a feeling there was a reason why she didn't attend church, but even though he was curious, now was hardly the time to press her on the issue. She was virtually a stranger to him, and yet she'd opened up her home and her holiday to him, and even more important, to Noelle. She had a good heart and acted on her kindness.

She brushed a kiss across the baby's forehead. "I think you're right about her making a difference in people's lives. She's affected me as well, the little dear. I just hope Noelle's mother finds the help she needs. Whatever circumstances led her to giving up her baby, she has to be hurting right now."

"I've been praying for her nonstop," Shawn agreed. "We may not know where she is, but God does. He can help her in ways we never could."

There was that tic again, only this time Heather narrowed her eyes on him. She was clearly scrutinizing him, but for what? What did she think she was going to see in his gaze?

Suddenly uncomfortable, he started to get to his feet, but Heather beat him to it, covering the distance between them in two steps and sliding Noelle into his arms. "I think she's going to sleep for a while, especially since she was so restless last night. If you can hold the baby and keep an eye on the kiddos for me, I'll go see if I can get our supper ready. The ham is probably done but I've got some side dishes to finish. In the meantime, let me pull out some appetizers. I've got a veggie snack tray and ranch dip in the refrigerator, or I can put together tortilla chips and some salsa if you'd prefer."

Her queries were coming a mile a minute and though Shawn repeatedly tried to answer her rapid-fire questions, he couldn't get a word in edgewise. She appeared to be trembling—both physically and emotionally. He didn't have a clue what had caused this sudden alteration in her mood. Was it something he'd said?

If Heather was flustered, Shawn was now doubly so. All his pastoral training deserted him in a flash. Something about Heather set him off-kilter in a way visiting with his parishioners and hanging out with his neighbors normally did not.

He shifted Noelle so she rested on his shoulder, careful to keep a hand curled around her neck to give her extra support. Silently he took a mental step backward and scanned his recent conversation with Heather, filtering it for clues as to where he'd gone wrong. Somewhere along the way they'd taken a detour.

His reference to the Almighty was bothering her— of that much he was certain. Beyond that, he couldn't say, although he sensed it was more than just the one thing that had gotten her so upset. He made a mental note to back off speaking about anything religious for now, although he acknowledged that was going to be difficult for him to do.

It wasn't so much that he was a preacher with the deep desire to press his religion on everyone. The only truth he wanted to preach was how he lived his life. That was his faith message, much more so than the words he spoke. His real problem was that since he didn't have a family, his pastorate pretty much summed up his life. Try making nonreligious conversation over that. He didn't even have any notable hobbies to speak of, other than his ranch and the animals he kept, and he doubted the ins and outs of his pig-breeding program would interest her.

He belatedly realized she'd suddenly stopped hammering him with questions and glanced up to see her waiting with an expectant look on her face, one fist propped on the delicate curve of her hip as she waited for his response.

He cleared his throat and stared back up at her. He was absolutely lost. Heat started at the tips of his toes and crept all the way up to his ears. What had she been talking about?

Oh, yeah. Right. Food. Appetizers. Vegetables or chips.

"Either one would be fine," he answered, stammering over his words. "Whatever works for you works for me. I'm easy. When I was a kid, my mama used to say I'd eat anything as long as it wasn't moving."

She chuckled. "Well, I think I can promise you that."

He swallowed, knowing he needed to acknowledge her teasing, but his amusement had dissipated the moment his mother's face flashed through his mind. Regret stabbed his gut, thinking of his mom—his dad.

And David.

Holidays were especially difficult for him, but he didn't like to dwell on it. He pressed the blackened, charred ruins of his family memories to the back of his thoughts and forced a smile for Heather's sake. "Whatever you and the kids would rather have."

She nodded crisply. "I'll put the vegetable tray out, then. The kids all like the carrot sticks. Would you like me to turn a game on the television while you wait? I'll try not to turn the volume up too much so it doesn't wake Noelle, but I definitely want to hear what's happening, especially with the Texas game. I'm a die-hard Longhorn fan."

"You like college football?"

"Doesn't everyone?" She sounded genuinely surprised. "I've been a fan since I was knee-high to a grasshopper."

Shawn didn't know why it shocked him to discover that about her, but it did. It wasn't as if Heather was the first woman who'd expressed an interest in football. He'd been to countless Super Bowl parties in mixed company. But Heather's voice held an excited, nearly fanatic died-in-the-wool tone, and he sensed a kindred spirit, college-football wise.

"I'm a Baylor fan, myself."

She wrinkled her nose. "I'll forgive you this once. But only because I'm feeling especially generous, today being Christmas and all."

They shared a laugh. Shawn felt better, and for the briefest moment, the tension in Heather's expression dissolved. He caught a glimpse of the true beauty in the woman, which until that moment had been hidden behind the mask of whatever burdens she silently carried. He didn't know what troubled her, but he knew those burdens were there. His breath caught as her hazel eyes, green irises shadowed with flames of burnt orange, locked with his. Her gaze shifted, turning anxious, and then he saw it all—those things of which she had not spoken.

Love. Loss. Pain.

His throat bobbed as he searched for words of comfort, anything to let her know that he got it. He might not know the details, but he didn't have to know what or who had hurt her to sympathize with her.

But before he could speak, the doorbell rang.

Heather's breath returned with a fevered gasp as the peal of the doorbell severed the magnetic draw of Shawn's gaze. Her adrenaline-shocked pulse hammered relentlessly as waves of panic washed through her. She closed her eyes and concentrated on evening out her breathing. Meanwhile, she fought the anger and resentment that rose to the surface, unwanted and uninvited, knowing stress would only make her reaction more pronounced. Fighting the anger, at the circumstances and at herself, was hard. She hated that she had no control over when and how these episodes occurred. Her panic attacks weren't always rational, nor were they necessarily based entirely on emotion. Sometimes they just appeared out of nowhere, for no good reason whatsoever. She'd been warned it might happen, yet she still couldn't get used to having such strong physical responses she couldn't control.

For the first time in many months, it wasn't initially or even primarily the doorbell that had startled her. She couldn't have been more stunned than she was to find the first thing that popped into her head when she closed her eyes wasn't the nightmare of being chased down by Adrian.

Confusion reigned, and she knew it showed outwardly in the flush of her cheeks. But how could she not be perplexed as she frantically sorted through her feelings? She was absolutely floored to find that among the myriad of emotions she was currently experiencing, fear was surprisingly low on the list.

When Shawn had looked at her, she felt as if he'd really *seen* her—glimpsed into her heart at the woman hiding deep within. That should have scared the socks off of her.

It hadn't. Shawn hadn't frightened her, at least not in the way she'd been accustomed to in the past. He'd thrown her for a loop. She suspected he'd seen more of her than she wanted, and that was cause for panic. But he hadn't frightened her.

What *had* happened? These days, she was always so careful not to let her guard down. Not ever. Most especially not with men. Shawn was a pastor, but that was hardly a recommendation to Heather. It certainly didn't procure any kind of confidence in him. She didn't trust church leaders as far as she could throw them. For all she knew, Shawn was the worst kind of charlatan, profiting off unsuspecting folks in the name of God.

And yet—there was something different about Shawn. There had been no judgment in his gaze, only compassion for whatever he read in her eyes. Not many men in Heather's life had ever bothered to look beyond the shell of her physical appearance. Any outward beauty she possessed was a curse, and the have-it-all-together woman she presented to the world was a counterfeit. She sensed that Shawn had not only seen that which she strove to keep hidden, but had somehow reached out to her and touched her inner person.

That rattled her more than any physical contact ever could.

"Don't move," she snapped a little more harshly than she intended. "You've got the baby. I'll get the door."

Relieved to be away from Shawn's probing gaze, she rushed forward and swung the front door open wide, forgetting even to check through the peephole to see who it might be. That *moment* with Shawn had shaken her up to the point where even her common sense had rocketed out of her reach. She supposed it was also possible that she wasn't as concerned over who was at the door because she was bolstered by Shawn's pres-

ence in the house, but she wasn't ready to go down that
path, even if it was only in her mind. The last thing she
needed or wanted was to be dependent on a man—for
anything. And she would certainly never depend on a
man to make her feel safe.

Besides, facts were facts. Adrian was in prison, and
he was going to be in there for a good long time. She
had nothing to fear, though her psyche sometimes forgot that. Maybe she was finally getting used to the
truth. Maybe eventually she could put all her fear behind her and move on with her life.

"Merry Christmas, my dears," Jo Spencer exclaimed
the moment the door was opened. The stout redhead
stepped inside the foyer without waiting to be invited.
Her arms were laden with parcels—a plate of cookies
and several festive gift bags.

"Comin' through," shouted a scratchy voice from
behind Jo as her husband, Frank, entered the house. "Jo
brought me along to be her packhorse," he grumbled.
"Where do you want all this stuff?"

Like Jo, Frank had his arms full, mostly of canvas
bags with the Sam's Grocery logo on it, filled with
what seemed to be baked goods and baby clothes.

"Head straight back to the kitchen, Frank," Heather
instructed with a chuckle. She didn't take the least bit
of offense to Frank's curtness. Few in Serendipity did.
He was a lovable old man for all his guff. "I haven't
set up the table for the meal yet, so you can place all
your parcels there."

"Chance and Phoebe told us to make sure to wish
y'all a happy Christmas, as well," Jo continued, ignoring her husband's griping. "Naturally all the stores
around here are closed for the holiday, so we've got

nothing new to offer you, but Phoebe dug through a few boxes of their baby things and managed to find a few pieces to help clothe Noelle. Nothing pink, I'm afraid, seeing as their youngest is a boy, but they found a few one-pieces and such in green and yellow that I think will do nicely."

Heather's heart welled, as did the tears in her eyes. Her throat constricted, and she found herself at a loss for words.

Her nerves snapped to attention when Shawn's voice came from directly behind her. "That's very kind of y'all to think of us on Christmas day, and especially to go out of your way to help out baby Noelle."

"Nothing exceptionally out-of-the-ordinarily kind about being neighborly," Jo said, bustling around the table, removing a couple of glass casserole dishes and a cherry pie from the pile of bags. "Did you remember to grab the whipped cream, Frank?"

The old man snorted. "What do you think? You only reminded me about it three times before we left."

"So in other words you're tellin' me you forgot it, then?" Jo chuckled and bussed Frank's scruffy cheek.

"No, old woman, I'm tellin' you that you're a nag." He reached into one of the canvas bags and withdrew a large tub of whipped topping, then tossed it to Shawn without warning.

Heather was impressed by Shawn's quick reflexes. He caught the bucket easily with just one hand and with a single smooth move deposited it into the freezer.

"You see there, son?" Frank continued, wrapping an affectionate arm around Jo's ample waist. "You'd better be a hundred and ten percent certain before you go and tie the knot, 'cause this is what you'll have to put up with."

The words were as grumpy as usual. If Heather had been going only by those, she would no doubt have found herself smack-dab in the middle of another panic attack. But it wasn't about the words. It was the looks the couple shared between them. The actions and affection that set them apart. Frank and Jo Spencer exemplified what Heather had once believed marriage could be. Love conquers all. It didn't matter how different Frank and Jo were from each other—and they were about as different from each other as two people could be. But it was perfectly obvious to Heather, and no doubt to everyone else who had ever met the old couple, that love bridged that gap.

She didn't know how they did it. Whatever their secret, it was clearly beyond her understanding. She'd made every mistake a woman could make, one right after the other, leading not only to heartbreak, but the death of innocent children.

Heather blinked against the burning sensation in her eyes and turned her gaze away, fighting to breathe around the lump of emotion in her throat. She couldn't stand it. She really couldn't stand it.

Even in the face of kindness, why did life have to be so hard?

Chapter Four

Shawn leaned over the sink to splash his face free of shaving cream, careful not to drip water onto the little bundle of joy strapped to his chest by a baby carrier. He hummed as he dried his jaw with a hand towel, partially because Noelle seemed to appreciate either his voice or the vibration of his chest, and partially out of sheer gratitude as he remembered the outpouring of love and generosity parishioners had given him— *them*—on Christmas Day. Even though he'd been the pastor of his small congregation for several years, remembering the incredible scene at Heather's house still sent him reeling with thankfulness for so many blessings.

Good people. Wonderful, amazing friends and neighbors.

After Jo and Frank had come and gone, he and Heather had been visited by at least a dozen other families, all bringing supplies for Noelle and extra food and gifts for Heather and her kids. He knew he shouldn't be stunned at how quickly the word got around town that there was a baby in need, nor the amazing way people responded when they heard.

Serendipity was like that. Folks cared for each other, even to the point of interrupting their own holidays to make sure little Noelle had what she needed. Of course it wasn't enough that everyone had had such open hearts toward the baby. They'd been thinking of Heather and her children as well, which Shawn considered far more than merely the icing on the cake. He had a whole new appreciation for living in Serendipity.

Since Christmas Day was on a Friday, Shawn had been able to spend the whole weekend with Noelle, and he was glad for the opportunity. His sleep deprivation hadn't lessened, but that was to be expected. He was proud of how well he'd managed to adjust to the role of foster father. Of course, it helped knowing Heather was no more than a phone call away. He experienced far less pressure with Heather as his right-hand woman, and he had, in fact, made use of her expertise several times over the past two days.

There was definitely a steep learning curve where infants were concerned, at least for him. Someone had slipped him a copy of a baby-care book in one of the bags, which probably would have been a tremendous help to him—*if* he'd had nine months to prepare and memorize every line in the manual. It wasn't as if he had time to sit down and read *any* book cover to cover between feeding and diapering duty, and yet that was probably exactly what he needed to do. Somehow. In his nonexistent spare time. As it was, he was grateful for the index and the table of contents that allowed him to turn to specific pages for assistance.

But as nice as the book was, it was nothing close to

the advantage of having Heather on his side. She was infinitely patient with him, and didn't seem to mind his endless string of clueless and sometimes brainless questions, nor the fact that he phoned her quite literally every couple of hours, even in the middle of the night. She'd been a great deal more than a shoulder to lean on. She was practically holding him up. She'd offered to spell him again if he needed her to take the baby for a while and gracefully let him know he could avail himself of the charity of her home should he need a bit more shut-eye than he was getting on his own.

He'd considered her invitation and more than once had been on the brink of accepting it, but thankfully, he and Noelle seemed to be hitting a stride with each other and he hadn't had to put Heather out any more than he already had. He was certainly bothering her enough just with the numerous phone calls and questions. No need to further complicate matters by becoming a mainstay at her house.

She already had her three kids to take care of. She didn't need two more.

Now that it was Monday, they'd made plans to take Noelle to San Antonio to meet with the social worker who was the point person for Heather and her three children. Heather had arranged for a neighbor to take care of Jacob, Missy and Henry so she could accompany him, giving him even more reason to be grateful for her. He was racking up quite a bill of kindnesses given to him, and he knew he'd never be able to repay her. Not only was she encouraging him by her presence and her connections, but she'd even offered to drive him to town. He was glad she was going along, if nothing else, to remind him of what a really good foster parent looked like—and to underscore the fact that he wasn't that person.

With every minute that ticked closer to their appointment time, he found himself more urgently needing the reminder that he was *not* the right person to see to Noelle's care on any kind of permanent basis. And what kind of crazy was that for him to even consider? Noelle deserved better than a cowboy pastor with zero parenting experience.

He would have thought that as much as he'd struggled to care for Noelle, especially at the beginning, he'd be anxious to put her into decent care with people who knew what they were doing. So why was this so hard? It shouldn't be, practically speaking, but his heart wasn't listening. It was going to be difficult for him to hand her off to a stranger.

Painful.

Maybe it was his lack of sleep, or maybe it was that he'd had two days with no one to talk to except Heather and the tiny infant, but he had bonded with Noelle. It was the strangest thing. He felt as if his large heart was tied to her tiny one by a delicate thread—a string that would snap the moment Noelle was lifted from his arms.

If he had a wife by his side to mother the infant, he knew he wouldn't think twice before volunteering to foster Noelle, maybe even adopt her. But he didn't. And even with a woman by his side, he wasn't sure he'd ever be father material.

His own family was a train wreck of gigantic proportions. Shawn acknowledged that he was the cause of all his family's ills. A mother hospitalized under permanent psychiatric care. A father who loved the bottle more than his life. His brother…

He couldn't let himself think about David.

There was no way he could ever put another human being in that kind of jeopardy. He didn't trust himself, and never would. As much as his heart went out to Noelle, he couldn't be responsible for a child's life.

He brushed a blue terry-cloth towel down his face to remove traces of aftershave and stared at himself in the mirror, but he didn't see his own reflection. Instead, he saw his younger brother's face.

Little six-year-old David, his ginger hair sticking to his sweaty forehead, his fair, freckled skin burned and red. His palms flat against the surface of the car window, fingers spread. His mouth open wide in a silent scream, pleading for Shawn to reach him.

To save him.

Shawn shuddered and turned away from the mirror. He hadn't been able to rescue David, and he hadn't been able to salvage what was left of his mother's sanity after her younger son had died. His father had never picked up a drink in his life until he'd watched his younger son being lowered into the ground.

Shawn had done that. He had failed his family on every conceivable level.

Noelle needed better than that. She needed safety. Security. Someone who knew what he or she was doing, someone confident around an infant and able to make the kind of permanent commitment the baby required.

She needed a good family who would give her the love and care she deserved.

Please, God, let it be so.

His prayer was shortened by the sound of a car horn.
Heather.

Shawn didn't want to keep her waiting. He grabbed
the infant car seat off the kitchen table on his way out,
thankful that Zach and Delia had been willing and able
to temporarily loan it to him for Noelle's one-way trip
into San Antonio. He swallowed back the emotion that
burned his throat. There was no point in his buying a
car seat for her when he'd only need it for today. Her
new foster parents would no doubt purchase one for her.

Ignoring the ache in his chest, he exited the house
and waved to Heather as he approached her silver mid-
size SUV. She hurried around to the passenger side and
opened the back door while he unfastened Noelle from
the baby carrier on his chest.

"The car seat goes in the middle," she informed him,
gesturing toward the interior. "Why don't you let me
hold the baby while you get it snapped in?"

He nodded and handed Noelle to Heather, giving his
shoulders a mental straightening as he turned to meet
this new challenge—strapping in a car seat. It couldn't
possibly be that difficult, right? Besides, he'd looked
up the directions online, although he probably wouldn't
admit that part aloud. It was a first for him, but he
didn't want to look incompetent around Heather, and
he wanted to get it right for the sake of Noelle's safety.

Five minutes turned into ten. The metal clip that was
supposed to be used to keep the shoulder strap stable
was next to impossible to thread onto the seat belt, and
it had to be perfectly positioned to keep the backward-
facing baby seat tight. Just as he was about to give up
and let Heather have a go at it, the lock clicked.

He uncurled himself from the backseat with a sigh

of relief. He thought Heather might be amused by his amateur attempt at securing the car seat but her expression was serious.

He flashed a self-effacing grin, hoping to lighten the moment. "Wow. That car seat really gave me a run for the money there, didn't it? My lack of experience is showing again. Is there anything about caring for an infant that is easy?" he joked.

She started to shake her head and then stopped, tipping her chin so her hazel eyes met his. "Love. Loving them is easy."

He felt her words like a swift uppercut to his jaw.

KO. Knockout.

Yes. Loving Noelle was easy. But it wasn't simple, because right now loving Noelle meant letting her go. And that was as complicated as it got.

"Yes, it is," he agreed through the catch in his throat. He reached for Noelle and fastened her into the car seat. Then he moved around to the front driver's side to open the door for Heather, allowing her to take her place behind the wheel before he moved around to the other side of the SUV. "I really appreciate everything you're doing for me," he added as he slid into the passenger seat.

"For Noelle, you mean," she responded without looking at him, her voice barely above a whisper.

It felt like a rebuke to Shawn's already raw heart. This day was getting tougher by the moment. But she was right. It wasn't about him.

"For Noelle," he agreed, hoping she couldn't hear any telltale grief in his tone.

The hour-long drive to San Antonio was made almost entirely in silence. Twice Shawn tried to make small talk, and twice the conversation quickly lapsed into stillness. It wasn't an easy silence between them, either. The air felt prickly. Shawn didn't know how Noelle managed to sleep so peacefully through it. Heather kept her attention on the road, but Shawn sensed there was more to it than good driving habits. She kept both white-knuckled fists clutched onto the steering wheel. The smooth skin at the corner of her jaw occasionally twitched with strain.

What bothered him most wasn't just that she was acting withdrawn in general, although there was that. This day wasn't going to be easy on anyone, Heather included. It was more the sense that she was purposefully withdrawing from *him*, and he didn't know why.

It had been her idea to accompany him, after all. She was here to help him, or rather, as she'd so succinctly pointed out, to help *Noelle*. But it appeared she didn't want to share any more of herself than was absolutely necessary. Shawn didn't even know how to begin to address the issue. Every time he spoke up, he ended up floundering to an awkward halt.

So much for being a friend to her. And his pastoral training was no help whatsoever, completely deserting him when he most needed it.

Heather seemed to relax as they entered the city. Her posture changed. Straightened and softened. She lost her stiffness and her eyes gleamed with anticipation.

Shawn, on the other hand, was a bundle of tense muscles and overactive nerves that twitched and tightened more and more with every mile they drove closer to their destination. He wanted to tell Heather to turn around and drive back to Serendipity…but he knew that wasn't an option. No matter how he felt about it personally, this thing needed to be done. It was the only way, the logical and rational conclusion to everything that had happened since the moment he'd first found Noelle in the manger.

But the knowing didn't make the doing any easier. Not for Shawn.

"You'll like Maggie," Heather remarked softly as she turned the SUV into the parking lot of the government building. "She's very down-to-earth and quite practical, but you can tell she really cares for the kids. And at the end of the day, that's what it's all about."

"I'm looking forward to meeting her." *No, he wasn't.* Shawn rubbed his palms against his khaki slacks and then reached for the door handle.

"Shawn?" She reached for his shoulder, her touch hesitant and her voice quivering with emotion.

Swallowing back emotion, he turned and appraised her. She gave him an encouraging smile, but her gaze was filled with doubt.

"It's going to be okay," she murmured.

"Yeah." His voice dropped an octave and turned the consistency of harsh gravel. He wasn't sure he believed her. He didn't even know if *she* believed her own words.

She slid her hand down the length of his arm until her palm met his. Her hands were tiny and fragile and her fingers shook as they squeezed his. Here she was trying to make him feel better when she was probably struggling herself. This wasn't easy for either of them. Suddenly he felt as though he ought to be the one doing the reassuring. Somehow that thought infused him with courage. His hand closed over hers and she tightened her grip. Their gazes met and locked, giving and taking.

Abruptly, she broke the moment, snatching her hand from his and practically tumbling out the door in her haste to put distance between them.

"We're going to be late," she said, her voice sounding high and squeaky.

He slid a hand over his hair, feeling oddly as if something precious had been taken away from him. He didn't know what had just happened, but it had nothing to do with needing to get to the social services office. Yet what else could he do but go along with her?

"Right. I'll get the baby."

Thankfully, it was easier to remove Noelle from her car seat than it was to put her into it, and soon they were approaching Maggie Dockerty's office, such as it was. There was no receptionist at the front desk, only a clipboard with a lined sign-in sheet dangling off the front counter by a worn chain. A felt-tip pen was attached by a piece of Velcro.

Shawn glanced around. A couple of raw, informal cubicles were sectioned off by gray partitions that looked as though they'd seen better days. Hand-me-down office equipment littered the area. The whole place felt old and decrepit, not at all what Shawn would have expected from an office dedicated to finding children good homes.

A middle-aged brunette with short, spiky hair popped her head around the corner of the nearest partition. "Heather? It's good to see you again. And you must be Shawn O'Riley," she continued, nodding his direction. "Come on back and take a seat here. I'm anxious to meet that precious little baby girl Heather has been telling me all about."

Maggie's tone and words set Shawn's mind at ease. At least she appeared to genuinely care about Noelle, to acknowledge her as a person needing care.

That was something, wasn't it?

They entered Maggie's cubicle, and Shawn offered Heather a seat before taking his own, careful not to disturb Noelle, who was sound asleep in the curve of his arm. His gaze darted from place to place and finally settled on Maggie's desk, which was littered with paper. He couldn't look at Noelle or he would simply lose it, and he didn't dare meet Maggie's eyes, afraid his distress would show. He hadn't shed tears since the day they had buried David, but right now his eyes were burning like hot coals, and it took every ounce of his will to screen his emotions.

"I've already got the papers drawn up for you, Shawn," Maggie informed him, pushing a stack of papers across the desk and into his view and waving a ballpoint pen under his nose.

"Papers?" he echoed, confused. He took the pen from her, but only because she wouldn't leave off waving it at him.

Why would they need him to sign anything? He wasn't the child's guardian. Was it because he was the one who'd found her?

"Naturally, we'll have to schedule a home visit so I can make sure you've got everything baby-proofed, but it's mostly just a formality. We don't have nearly enough foster parents, and it certainly isn't every day that a man steps up for a child the way you are right now."

Steps up? What was Maggie talking about?

He shifted his confused, questioning gaze to Heather, whose hazel eyes widened in dismay. She grimaced, her hand flying up to cover her lips.

"Oh, I'm sorry, Maggie," she blurted out. "You must have misunderstood me. Shawn was gracious enough to take care of Noelle until we could get to San Antonio, but he can't keep her. Not permanently."

"I see." Maggie pinched her mouth around the edges and tiny lines formed on her upper lip. "I beg your pardon, Shawn. I was under the impression that you'd come in today to apply to become Noelle's foster father."

"I—I can't," Shawn stammered, heat rising to his face and his throat tightening, cutting off his supply of oxygen. "I would, but I—"

"Of course. I understand." Maggie cut him off before he could finish the sentence, and he was glad of it. He didn't know how he *would* have finished that sentence if Maggie hadn't taken pity on him and interrupted when she did. It wasn't so much a matter of "wouldn't." It was a matter of "couldn't." He couldn't take care of baby Noelle. He couldn't risk it. She deserved so much better than anything he was capable of offering.

"As Heather well knows, it's difficult to foster children when you're single," Maggie continued. She smiled gratefully at Heather, but Shawn noticed the stress lines that had formed on her forehead. He imagined it wasn't an easy job for her, finding homes for all the tough foster cases she dealt with every day. No wonder she looked taxed. "Heather told me you're a pastor in addition to being a rancher, Shawn. I com-mend you for that, and I'm sure you're far too busy with your congregation and your ranch work to care for an infant."

"No," Shawn snapped back immediately. "It's not that at all."

Both women looked at him as if he'd grown an extra eye on his forehead, and he grimaced before apologizing for his tone. He was better than this. Taking a deep breath, he focused his attention on his voice, leveling it out to something less...*frantic*.

"What I mean to say is it's not my job that prevents me from offering my services as a foster father to Noelle. I've come to care for her, and honestly, there is nothing I'd like more than to keep her with me. It's just that—"

For a man who made his living off words, he was having difficulty forming anything remotely resembling a coherent sentence clarifying why he couldn't take Noelle. The rationalization for his choice was murky in his own mind. He only knew that he couldn't risk Noelle's safety, never mind her happiness, on his potential inabilities.

"You don't have to explain," Maggie assured him. "It's completely understandable. Believe me, I was completely aware that what I was asking you to do went far above and beyond what most folks could muster." She wheeled her office chair over to the file cabinet in the corner of her cubicle and opened the third drawer down, riffling through several multicolored folders before she selected an olive-green one. "Let me just find the papers we need to get Noelle enrolled in a state home and I'll take her off your hands."

"A state home?" Shawn repeated, his heart suddenly

coming alive in his chest, beating a wild, irregular tattoo marked by rapid shots of adrenaline. The fight-or-flight instinct was kicking in, though he wasn't sure why. "I thought— That is, I assumed she'd go to a nice foster home. With someone like Heather."

He heard a little gasp from Heather but he didn't look at her. His gaze was focused entirely on Maggie, who was frowning and shaking her head.

"As you can well imagine, there aren't enough people like Heather in the world. I'm afraid we have a serious overflow of foster children right now and not nearly enough homes for them. The procedure is that kids are temporarily assigned to state facilities until we can find potential foster families for them or they get permanently adopted, which doesn't happen nearly enough. Noelle being a newborn plays in her favor, though. Folks are more interested in adopting newborns than the older kids like Heather's taken. There's that working for her, at least. She may not have to stay in the state home for long."

"How long are we talking?" Shawn asked gravely. "A few days?"

"Weeks, more like. Sometimes months. It's hard to say. Noelle will have to be formally evaluated by one of our physicians. Often in cases of abandonment, the baby has been exposed to illegal substances in utero, which makes placement more difficult due to the medical issues drug babies face."

Shawn was stunned into silence, but his mind was screaming. Noelle in a group home with a bunch of other kids? What kind of care would she receive? How many adults would be there? Who would love her?

"A drug baby. Well, that might explain a lot,"

Heather murmured. "About Noelle, I mean. It could be that she's crying so often because she's in physical withdrawal from her mother's drug or alcohol habit."

"It's definitely a possibility," Maggie affirmed. "I'll make a notation in her file and we'll get her a checkup immediately so we know what we're dealing with. Now, if I can get some information from you, Shawn, I'll get this new paperwork in motion."

"No."

Maggie's green eyes snapped to his, her dark, contoured eyebrows displaying a high arch. "I beg your pardon?"

"No. I don't want Noelle going into a state facility."

Heather placed a hand on his forearm, which was a measure of comfort against the anxiety coursing through him that had him feeling as if he was about ready to jump out of his skin. Somehow she seemed to understand what was happening to him. Maybe she could see it. Every muscle in his body was crackling with energy. He was walking the proverbial plank with his hands tied out in front of him and manacles bound to his ankles.

But what else could he do?

"I'm afraid we don't have any other options," Maggie informed him crisply. "Group homes are an unfortunate by-product of the system, but I assure you that we'll do all we can to make sure Noelle is well cared for. Texas has a strong support system. Her potential problems notwithstanding, I'm optimistic that she'll eventually be placed in a permanent home. There's nothing for you to worry about."

Nothing for him to worry about?

The lady was clean out of her mind if she thought

Shawn was capable of *not worrying* after handing an innocent baby off to her with no guarantee of where Noelle would land. It wasn't as if he could simply walk out of the office and forget he'd ever found the infant in the manger Christmas Eve. As if he could somehow put it all behind him and go on with his life.

"'Eventually' isn't good enough for me," Shawn informed her, adjusting Noelle in his arms so his hold on her was even more secure. Right next to his heart, where she belonged—at least for now. "I'm taking her home with me."

Heather's pulse jolted to life at Shawn's words. He was going to step up and foster baby Noelle, after all?

What man did that—set aside his own expectations, his own lifestyle, to care for the needs of another, especially one as innocent and helpless as Noelle?

None that she'd ever known. He was a rarity, for sure.

Shawn had already surprised her a number of times over the past weekend, beginning with the moment he'd volunteered to take Noelle into his care rather than pawn her off onto someone else on Christmas Eve. It would have been easy enough to hand her off to the police, or try to find someone else in town to take the baby on temporarily. But he hadn't done that. He cared enough to sacrifice his own comfort to do the right thing, even when the going got rough. And then later, after being exposed to the truth about parenthood, he hadn't broken. No matter how tired and sleep-deprived he'd been, he had never once lost his temper, yelled or complained—at least that she had heard.

And now, even after learning firsthand how difficult

taking care of a newborn could be—very possibly a newborn with unforeseen medical problems—he was going to take the ultimate leap into foster parenthood.

What kind of man would make such a sacrifice?

Apparently, she was looking at him. She just couldn't believe her eyes. Or her ears. Never mind what her heart was telling her.

Shawn was a man whose actions spoke louder than his words. He was a man who saw the worth in a tiny bundle of humanity who'd been thrown out to be eaten up by the big, wide, nasty world—and he not only noticed, but stepped up to do something about it. When Noelle had been abandoned, Shawn was there to protect and defend her.

In short, he very much appeared to be the kind of man Heather had once hoped and believed existed somewhere in the world but had long since given up on finding in reality. At least, *her* reality.

The jury is still out, she reminded herself sternly. She winced inwardly. She knew better than most that what a woman observed on the outside was not always what she got on the inside, not when push came to literal shove.

"Give me a pen," Shawn said, his voice a deep, rich hum. "I'm ready to sign whatever legal documents are necessary to keep Noelle with me."

"Excellent," Maggie said. Unlike Heather, Maggie didn't sound surprised that Shawn had changed his mind—or rather, made up his mind. But then again, thinking back over Maggie's comments, Heather wondered if Maggie had been pushing Shawn that direction all along.

"Are you sure?" Heather couldn't help but ask the question aloud.

Did he realize what he was getting himself into?

He'd come with the intention of handing Noelle off to another foster family, which of course was to be expected. Why should he change his whole life because he'd found a baby inside his church? Noelle wasn't supposed to be his problem.

But now she would be. He was making her his problem, legally and officially. And Heather couldn't imagine why.

She was well aware of why *she* fostered children, or at least why she'd taken Jacob, Missy and Henry in the first place. Her motives had shifted over the months she'd had the kids, as she'd fallen in love with the three little sweethearts. But that didn't negate the fact that originally she'd signed up as a foster mother as a meager form of penitence. She wasn't kidding herself about her motivation. While she would never be able to make up for the lives lost due to her negligence with Adrian, she could and did make her foster children's lives better.

They were happy. She was as content as she'd ever been. And she loved her kids more than she'd thought possible.

But what were Shawn's motives?

God presumably knew, but Heather certainly didn't. If the pensive expression on Shawn's face was anything to go by, she doubted even Shawn knew.

Shawn patted Noelle's back in a gentle rhythm. "You mentioned baby-proofing my house." He grimaced, cleared his throat and flashed a weak grin. "How do

I do that, exactly? Do you have an instruction guide? Diagrams?"

"The best I can offer you is a policy-and-procedure manual," Maggie said with a laugh. "We offer weekly parenting classes, but I'm not sure how feasible that would be for you, living as far out of town as you do."

"I'll manage," he said. The corner of his lips twitched with strain.

"I'll help," Heather assured him, even though it went against the grain to make the offer. She had enough on her plate without getting more involved in Shawn's drama, but even though she didn't feel entirely comfortable with him, who else would be there to help him prepare his living situation for Noelle, if not her? "It's really not that complicated. We'll need to cover all the open electrical outlets and put child-locks on the cabinets. You'll definitely want to move any harmful chemicals out of the reach of little hands and make sure any medicine bottles and firearms are well-protected."

"I'm not a hunter, so I don't have any weapons in the house. And I'm as healthy as a horse, so I don't have any prescription medicines around."

"Any over-the-counter painkillers? Vitamins? Antacids?" Heather probed. "They're all dangerous if ingested by an infant. Childproof caps are all well and good, but they certainly aren't fail-safe."

Light dawned in his pale blue eyes, along with a flash of panic. "Oh, yeah. Right. I didn't think. What if I... That is... I don't want to miss anything." Shawn stroked his face, drawing Heather's attention to the strong line of his clean-shaven jaw. He was taking this very seriously, she had to give him that much. It made her want to reassure him.

"You won't. I remember how overwhelmed I felt when I first brought my three kids home. Just remember you aren't alone. I'm here to help, just like I've been since Noelle came into our lives. Just a phone call away, day or night."

"You will never even begin to comprehend how much that means to me," he replied, brushing a kiss against Noelle's dark hair.

"Oh, I think I do," Heather murmured. She couldn't help but smile at the admittedly adorable picture Shawn made, his expression as helpless as the baby in his arms.

"Is it all right if we stop at a discount store before we leave San Antonio? I'm going to need to buy a crib and a car seat immediately, and then you can help me make a list of the other supplies I'll be needing."

Heather chuckled. "Put diapers at the top of that list. Lots and lots of diapers."

The neighbors who'd visited on Christmas Day had provided enough diapers, bottles, packages of formula and changes of clothes to get Shawn and Noelle by for a while, but Heather knew there would be numerous challenges in the days ahead, and she knew she would be able to help, even if it pained her to do so.

"Diapers. Right." Shawn made a face. "Guess it goes with the territory."

"Give it a week," she advised. "Soon it'll come second nature and you won't have to think about it."

He didn't look convinced, but the glow in his eyes exhibited his resolve. He was clearly going to make a go of it on willpower alone, if nothing else.

"We can make a quick stop at Emerson's Hardware once we get back into Serendipity. They carry all the baby-proofing items we'll need. Right now Noelle is too small to get into too much mischief, but it's only a matter of time before she'll be crawling around your house. You'll need to evaluate with an eye to what a baby might get into or be harmed by. Glass furniture, sharp edges, potentially hot surfaces, even the toilet bowl. That kind of thing."

"And that will be the purpose of my visit, as well," Maggie added. "Simply to ensure Noelle's long-term well-being—not that I have any doubts, mind you. I already have a really great feeling about this particular matchup."

Shawn glanced down at Noelle and a smile played at the corners of his lips. "Blessed by the Almighty's hand."

"Perhaps," Maggie agreed mildly. "It certainly looks that way."

"I don't know why He picked me."

That statement was somewhat enlightening. Was that what this was about? Shawn having some kind of guilt complex because he'd been the one to find Noelle? Was he doing this because he thought God had somehow ordered the circumstances, practically depositing Noelle in Shawn's lap? How long would that conviction last—and what would it mean for Noelle in the aftermath?

"In any event, I assure you it's not my intention to judge you or your home in any way except to make suggestions on how to keep Noelle safe and sound. I hope you'll consider me your partner in this."

"Safe and sound," Shawn repeated with a nod. "My primary goal."

Heather's stomach turned over but she managed a

light laugh despite her misgivings. "And surrounded by love. Don't forget your main concern as a foster father will be to love her."

His eyes widened on her, his shock evident. "I didn't forget," he assured her. "Loving Noelle—well, that's just a given. It's not going to slip my mind or anything. I don't have to work on that part."

"No, I don't think you do," Heather agreed, and she was astounded to find she actually believed him. This guy was quite literally putting his life on hold for this child. Perhaps there was good in the world after all.

Chapter Five

Shawn jammed a pitchfork into a bale of hay and tossed it into the nearest stall, then repeated the process for the three stalls down the line. His Shetland sheepdog, the Queen of Sheba—Queenie, for short—followed at his heels, barking. It was a little more complicated to pitch hay and carry feed with an infant strapped to his chest, but he hadn't figured out what else he could do with Noelle while he worked, and the animals had to be fed.

Morning and evening, he and Noelle were out in the barn doing chores.

In addition to his three horses, he owned a brood of chickens, seven stubborn, lawn-mower-worthy goats, six sows—and at the moment, a dozen piglets. It didn't pay to own a boar, so he just borrowed one from the neighbors when the time was ripe.

He loved his work as a pastor, but ranching was in his blood. And while he didn't have time to care for a herd of cattle, his pigs and goats brought in a tidy hobby income and he had plenty of opportunities to ride and rope and mend fences helping friends, neighbors and congregants with their stock. Still, on a regular daily basis it was fairly lonely work. He actually liked having human company, even that of a little human. Over the week since he'd officially become a foster father, he'd learned to adapt all the components of his busy lifestyle to the baby's needs.

It was a mild day, and he'd bundled Noelle in long-sleeved terry-cloth pink pajamas, complete with footies. His kid was cute. Adorable. His breath crammed into his throat every time he looked at the little darlin'.

He had just finished slopping the pigs when Heather's silver SUV turned into his long driveway. He waved to her and she returned the gesture with a jerky nod.

Shawn's breath caught. There it was again. That gut *feeling* he had—as if something was amiss between the two of them, only it was all on Heather's side and he didn't know why. Had he done something?

"We have company, baby darlin'," he informed Noelle, who noisily sucked her fist in response. He grinned and tossed the feed bucket into the barn, hurrying to help Heather get the kids out of the car.

"I'm glad you brought the kiddos along with you," he said as she rounded them to her side. "I think they'll like the ranch."

"It was your idea, remember?" she reminded him with a dry chuckle.

"I know, right?" he agreed, joining his laughter to hers. "I figured it would be easier for you to bring them along than try to find alternate care for them."

"Easier for me, perhaps," she agreed, "but I'm not going to guarantee it will be easier for you. These kids are a handful and a half." She didn't sound as if it bothered her—only that she believed it might bother him.

Shawn didn't think it would be a problem. He liked kids, and they usually seemed to take to him. He'd gotten along with Heather's kids on Christmas Day just fine. He knelt to the children's level. "I have a surprise for you. Do you want to see what it is?"

Missy immediately nodded and slipped her tiny hand into his, her smile eager and trusting. Little Henry looked from him to Heather and back again, seeking direction on whether or not it was okay to go with this man. He stared at Shawn with wide brown eyes, his thumb in his mouth, and then opted to crawl into Heather's arms instead of taking Shawn's other hand.

Jacob's demeanor was also less than enthusiastic. He frowned and slinked back at Shawn's words, shifting his attention from Shawn to the barn to his shoes, but not before Shawn thought he glimpsed the hint of interest in the boy's eyes. Shawn prayed silently for the poor kid. He imagined Jacob had been through a lot in his young life. It was no wonder he was hesitant.

He knew firsthand what it was to be a young man with no one to depend on but himself. After they'd lost David, Shawn's mother hadn't been there at all, and his dad had been mostly out of the picture with his drinking habit. At least Jacob had Heather now. She provided the love and stability Shawn had never had as a child. For whatever reason, Heather had dedicated herself to these three foster kids, and they were blessed to have her. He hoped they'd someday realize what they had.

"Come with me and we'll grab a baby bottle out of the barn," he said, regaining his feet and pointing toward the large red structure.

"You keep your baby formula in the barn?" Heather asked, her voice an even mixture of astonishment and horror.

Shawn laughed and shook his head. "Not exactly. Although, come to think of it, I imagine Noelle will be ready to eat pretty soon here, too."

"Too?"

Shawn raised his eyebrows and flashed Heather what he hoped was a mysterious grin. "It's easier for you to see what I'm talking about than for me to try to explain. Why don't you all follow me and I'll show you what I mean."

He led the way into the shadow of the barn, scooping up the bottle he'd prepared off a shelf just inside the door, and then glanced over his shoulder to make sure Heather followed. She was just behind him, holding three-year-old Henry on one hip and tugging a reluctant Jacob along with her opposite arm.

"Have you spent any time on a ranch? Do you like farm animals?" Shawn asked, directing his question at nine-year-old Jacob.

The boy shrugged noncommittally and didn't quite meet his gaze.

"Horses?" Shawn prodded. "Goats? Chickens? Pigs?"

"Piggies!" seven-year-old Missy exclaimed, tugging on her blond ponytail and twirling on her toes like a tiny ballerina.

"Piggies it is, then," Shawn agreed, his grin widening. At least the little girl seemed excited about her day. He'd have to work on the other two.

Heather wrinkled her nose. "I was raised on a ranch

here in Serendipity, but I can't say taking care of the animals was one of my favorite chores."

"No?" Her statement caught Shawn off guard, and he shuffled to a stop, tossing a look over his right shoulder to see if she was teasing him. Her lips were pinched together in a straight line that accentuated the crease in her eyebrows. She was far too young to have the kind of worry lines she displayed.

He had to admit his surprise. He would have pegged her for an animal lover. She had that sensitive nature about her. She was a small woman with a delicate physique, so it wasn't as if he expected she would go all-in for heavy ranch labor, but for some reason he'd supposed she would enjoy spending time around the animals. In fact, he'd banked this whole day on that assumption. "So you're not a fan of farm animals, then?"

"No, not really. Is that a terrible thing to say? I was incredibly jealous of my older sister, Havanah. All she had to do was wash dishes every evening, while I was responsible for getting up at the crack of dawn every single day to milk the dairy cow. Rain or shine, hot or cold, in school or on summer vacation, three hundred sixty-five days a year." She scrunched her lips in distaste.

Shawn chuckled. "That bad, huh?"

"Considering I am not, never have been and never will be a morning person? Yes. Definitely *that bad*. It wasn't the milking I minded so much, or the cow, for that matter. Hershey, our milk cow, was my confidant. Free therapy to go along with the benefits of calcium."

"And chocolate milk?" he teased.

She chuckled. "I wish. It's been a long time since I

thought about my life back then. Those were definitely the good old days."

He laughed. "You are far too young to have 'good old days.'"

"Well, thank you, but you're wrong about that."

Her eyes met Shawn's, and for the briefest beat he had a glimpse of her vulnerability—and her pain. She did look older than her age, but only in the depths of her gaze. He suspected she'd seen too much, lived too hard.

She shook her head and scoffed, and the moment passed.

"Listen to me going on as if my high school years were something special. I had as much teenage angst as anyone—as Hershey well knew." Her laugh was forced and unnatural, but the sigh that followed after was real enough. "I couldn't stand the daybreak part of the equation. Some mornings I wanted to pelt something at those roosters when they started their annoying crowing. Ugh. Country living definitely has its pitfalls."

He'd never thought of it that way. He liked the roosters and God's brilliant sunrises. He saw happiness in the start of a new day, where she observed the drawbacks.

Everything positive in his life that made it the joy it was centered around country living. The seven years he'd spent in the city going to college and seminary were the longest of his life. He'd enjoyed school, but he missed the clean air, the hard work—and the animals.

Where ranching was concerned, he supposed it didn't hurt that he was a morning person. He'd never thought twice about rising before dawn to care for the stock. He would be up even if he didn't have to be. It was easy for him. Enjoyable.

But not so much for Heather. He got that, and he felt bad that he'd already evidently brought back unpleasant memories for her. He didn't want to make it worse. But what were they really talking about? He could feel in his gut that there was much she was not telling him, and whatever the subtext was, it had little to do with small-town living or even getting up in the morning. He wished he could read between the lines, understand what she was *not* telling him.

The fact that she'd come back to live in Serendipity after moving away for whatever reason was telling in itself. She obviously didn't dislike sprawling ranch land enough to stay away—although the fact that she lived in town and didn't own a cow that needed daily milking might have been a factor, as well. Yet now she was caring for children. As he had learned with Noelle, children ran on their own timetables. What made that more palatable to her than the timetable of ranch life?

He wondered if he'd made a tactical error inviting her into his barn. Baby-proofing the house was one thing. Stomping around with the animals was quite another.

Maybe she'd think his operation was lame, or worse, it would remind her of not-so-happy days. He hesitated, rethinking his options, but in the end, he plunged into the shadow of the barn, passed the three horses and then turned left into a stall that was…*otherwise* occupied.

No horses here.

The children would like his surprise, he was certain of it. And whether or not it was precisely what she would have chosen, he suspected Heather would be pleased with the outcome, simply because he expected it would include seeing her kids all bubbly and full of joy.

Inside the stall, lounging on a fresh bed of hay, were a plump mama sow and twelve little black-and-white-spotted piglets. Just a few days old, they were only just beginning to sprout hair. Most of them were grunting and rooting for their mother's milk, but one little piglet, the tiniest of the bunch, was consistently squeezed out, no matter how often he attempted to dive into the middle of the fray.

"See this little fellow here?" Shawn asked, dropping to his knees before the pigs and scooping the runt into his hand. "His big brothers and sisters aren't letting him have a turn for a meal. How fair is that? We're going to help him out a little bit so he can grow big and strong like his siblings."

Missy cheered, clearly delighted with the idea. Both boys leaned in to see what Shawn was going to do next. He was happy all the kids were interested, but his eyes were on Heather's reaction.

"You're feeding the runt of the litter?" She squatted down beside him. Even though the hay was clean and freshly tossed, she didn't actually kneel in it. He noticed how carefully she chose her footing, despite the fact that she was wearing cowboy boots that looked as though they'd seen their fair share of use. She'd spent the past several years in the city—a country girl who'd possibly been displaced a little too long? Was that why she was so uncomfortable with her surroundings?

Shawn forced a grin and winked at her, hoping to ease the tension between them. "I figure everyone ought to try to help the weak ones among us."

Heather gave a surprised gasp and her hazel eyes

widened on him. It was the oddest look, and it made him uncomfortable.

"That's so...wonderful," she murmured.

Shawn lifted a brow. It was just a pig, after all.

Or were they no longer speaking of barnyard animals? She was staring at him as if he'd just said he was single-handedly conquering world hunger. He couldn't mistake the admiration shining from her gaze, and for some reason it simultaneously choked him up and revved up his ego, which was going to swell to the size of Texas if he didn't avert his eyes from the smile softly forming on the curve of her mouth. Her lips didn't need gloss or color to shine—just happy thoughts.

"Do you want to do the honors?" he asked Missy, pressing the bottle into the little girl's hands. Anything to get his mind away from the myriad distractions of Heather's outstanding facial features.

Eyes. Lips. Straight, narrow nose. Good grief. He was getting carried away.

The seven-year-old gripped the bottle tightly, her small, pink tongue pressing out from between her lips as she concentrated on aiming the working end of the container at the piglet's snout. What a cute little darlin' she was.

The girl. Not the pig. Well, the pig was kind of cute, too. And the other children, including his precious Noelle.

Okay, the woman was pretty decent, as well.

Aaand there he went again.

"I named him Hammie," he told Missy as the piglet rooted for the nipple.

Heather snorted. "Hammie? Really?"

Heat crept up Shawn's neck. "All right. I'll admit

that's not the most original name I could have come up with."

"Of course it is. H-Hammie. For—" The end of her sentence was cut off by another sputter of laughter. She pressed her thumb and forefinger to her eyes. "And I suppose you've also got Bacon and Pork Chop somewhere in this bunch."

She snorted. *Snorted*. And Shawn didn't think he'd ever heard anything so adorable.

"Honestly, I think it's cute that you named him."

Cute?

Well, at least he had her laughing, and it was the real thing, for once. Their eyes met and held. She grinned at him, a genuine smile that made his gut spring into a series of gymnastic flips he found difficult to tame. What was it about this woman? He'd never felt so off-kilter in his life.

"I've named all my animals," he admitted, wondering just how silly he must look to her. His ego shriveled. "I know that sounds kind of dumb, but it helps me keep them straight in my mind. Otherwise the goats just blend into a mass of spots and I don't know who's been fed and who's still hungry. Although with the goats, they are always hungry." He chuckled at his own joke.

"I would imagine so," she said, smothering a laugh with her palm. "I seem to recall our goats eating anything and everything. Grass. Clothing. Shoes."

"Right? The goats keep my grass nice and trimmed, but I've got to watch them or they get into mischief."

"Me feed Hammie?" Henry asked, lisping the words around the thumb he hadn't bothered to remove from his mouth before he spoke. "Me do it. Me want to feed the piggy." He'd gone from a simple "May I" question to downright insistence in less than one second.

"Sure you can, big guy," he said, trying to counter the sudden turning of Henry's emotions. The boy looked as if he was about one step short of a tantrum. Shawn wasn't quite sure what to do with a three-year-old, and he shifted his gaze to Heather for help.

"It's 'May I,'" Heather corrected, her voice equal parts firm and soothing. "Missy, will you please allow Henry to have a turn?"

Shawn prepared himself for Missy to have an equally volatile temper. Seeing the gentle way she cradled the piglet in her arms, he expected her to have some trouble sharing this experience, but the little girl immediately nodded.

"Guess so," she said, sounding only a little bit disappointed.

"I'll tell you what, Missy," Shawn said, not liking the way his own heart dipped upon hearing the little girl's reluctance to give up the task, "you and your foster brothers can come over to visit the piggies whenever your mama says it's okay."

He helped the two children facilitate the transfer of the piglet and bottle between hands. Heather shifted sideways to come between Missy and Henry, ready to lend a hand if necessary. A whiff of roses reached Shawn's nostrils, a startling contrast to the sharp tang of barn smells. He struggled not to lean in toward Heather and discover whether the scent was coming from her shampoo or her perfume. Either way, it knocked his socks off. Way better than the smell of horses.

"Jacob?" He didn't want to press the boy, but he also

didn't want him to feel left out. "If you'd like a turn then you're up next, after Henry."

Jacob grunted and shook his dark head. "That's okay. I don't want to." He scowled, and for a moment Shawn thought he was about to let loose on all cannons. Then he shrugged and turned away from the adults. "No, really. Let Missy and Henry feed it. No big deal."

Jacob sounded as if he wasn't having any fun at all, and Shawn's heart gave a little tug for the boy, who not only carried wisdom beyond his years in his gaze but also had to step up to the plate for his younger "siblings," displaying a maturity quite remarkable for his age.

"I can see what a good foster brother you are, looking out for Missy and Henry all the time," Shawn said, laying a hand on Jacob's shoulder. "Your mama must be very proud of you."

Jacob shrugged his hand away, trying to look as if it didn't matter to him one way or the other what anyone thought, but when he shook his dark hair back, Shawn could see his blue eyes were alight with pleasure from the commendation.

"I depend on Jacob for the big jobs," Heather assured him.

The boy stubbed his toe into the ground, his hair falling across his forehead.

"He's the regular man of the house. I couldn't do without him."

Shawn didn't have to be particularly observant to see how much Heather's praise meant to Jacob. Pride was flashing there in his eyes for everyone to see. His shoulders straightened and he stood up a good inch taller, his gaze full of strength and determination. He was the *man of the house*.

Shawn grinned, but he was sad for Heather. Jacob was a good boy, but he was nine. He couldn't be protector and provider for her or his younger foster siblings, and he shouldn't have to be. Shawn understood more than most the weight of responsibility that came with caring for a sibling. He wondered how Heather carried such a burden, and if she sought God for help. Even if her relationship with the Lord was rock-solid, being a single foster mother to three children would be tough for any woman.

"Got to watch over the little ones," Jacob stated with a resolute nod. "Otherwise they won't have anyone."

Heather absently brushed Jacob's black hair off his forehead with her fingertips. "See? That's exactly what I'm saying. You're a good boy, and you know better than anybody that you kids need to stick together. I'm so proud of you, Jacob. You children mean everything to me." She sniffed, and Shawn thought she might have brushed a tear aside with a casual flick of her hand.

Jacob colored and made a big production out of stooping down to pet Queenie, who barked with a high-pitched yap that startled Noelle. Shawn gently bounced her with the palm of his hand, coaxing her back to sleep. Queenie nipped at the boy's heels with the natural instinct of a herding breed. Shawn noted the glassy appearance of Jacob's eyes, and he hid his smile. Heather was clearly not the only one sniffling over the emotional discourse. Even Shawn's throat felt a little rough with emotion.

Time to take the conversation in a new direction. The last thing Shawn wanted was for Heather to burst into tears. Even in his pastoral duties, he never had been good at handling a crying woman. And she wasn't the only one he was worried about.

He well remembered what it was like to be nine years old and having to man-up against his father's perpetual drunkenness and his mother's absence from his life. He knew the last thing a young boy like Jacob would want would be to be caught with tears in his eyes, especially since Heather had just singled him out as being the man of the house. At least with Jacob that title was an honor and not a curse.

"You know, it sounds like I'm the exact opposite of you." Shawn pulled Heather's attention toward him so Jacob would get the heat taken off him and have a moment to pull himself together.

Henry's attention had already wavered, and the piglet rolled out of his lap and onto the hay. Missy had wandered off to follow Jacob and Queenie, leaving poor Hammie to squeal and squirm.

"Really? How's that?" Heather asked, taking pity on the piglet. She scooped it up and cradled it in her arms, much as she did when she was holding Noelle. The woman had nurturer written all over her, from her body language to her expression to the soft, sweet gaze in her eyes.

"This baby pig is outright adorable," she commented. "Look at him. He's wagging his little tail just like a happy puppy."

He'd mistakenly thought she wouldn't want a turn holding Hammie, seeing as she was so skittish around the barn. She wouldn't even put her knees into the hay—and yet she was willing to cradle a pig?

Shawn didn't understand women, and he was especially thick where Heather was concerned, but he was happy to relieve Henry of the bottle and pass it to her, especially since Henry was now completely distracted and caught up playing with Queenie, just as the other children were.

"We were discussing ranch chores before," he explained. "You mentioned you never much liked the early-morning rooster calls and the need to get up and milk the cow, whereas I've always found great solace in taking care of the animals. Granted, I didn't enjoy mucking stalls any better than any other boy or girl of my acquaintance," he said, gently adjusting the angle of the bottle in Heather's hand so Hammie had better access to it. Babies and pigs were slightly different in that respect. "But I didn't mind getting up in the early hours. I still rise before the sun—and probably would even if I didn't have stock to attend to."

It was true that he hadn't ever talked to his animals the way Heather apparently had as a teen—not out loud, at any rate—but he suspected more than one of the cows and horses from his childhood had known the secret pain of his teenage heart. Hadn't he spent many hours in the saddle as a child trying to escape the reality of his life? "I've always found it rather peaceful, out there all alone in the barn, just me and the animals. You know?"

He paused, shook his head and laughed at himself. "What am I saying? Of course you know—from personal experience. Like I said, we're opposites."

"We may not be as different as you think. Granted, there are things I'd rather be doing at that time of day," she acknowledged. "Like catching some extra z's, for example." Her lips tipped up at the corners, but amusement didn't quite reach her gaze. "It wasn't that I hated it, exactly. I'll admit there's something to be said about having had regular chores growing up. Ranch work taught me responsibility at an early age, which is never a bad thing. And I learned that sometimes it was necessary to perform my duties even on those days when I wasn't real keen on it. Those lessons have served me in good stead now that I have to work for a living. You can't exactly call your boss and tell him you don't want to go to work today because it's too early and you don't feel like it, right? I work at home as a virtual assistant, so some days I have even more of a challenge motivating myself to get the job done. And that's before getting into what's involved in being Mama to these busy, energetic children. They don't ever take a day off. I definitely can't decide to walk away from my obligations with them, nor would I want to."

Her gaze shifted back to Jacob and the corners of her lips dropped into a frown. "Perhaps I should have given the idea of buying a ranch more than a passing thought when I moved back to Serendipity. It occurred to me, but I didn't spend too much time thinking about it. My little house is relatively easy to keep clean, or at least as neat as a home with three children can be, but it would have been nice to have something more physical to offer my kids, especially Jacob. I think he could use something challenging to dig into. He's got so much energy, and I'd like for him to have something positive and constructive to do with his free time."

A thought occurred to him, but he wanted to be able to discuss it with Heather before sharing it in front of the children. He wanted to offer her the opportunity to bring the kids over on a regular basis to interact with the animals and learn ranching skills—if the idea appealed to Heather.

"Kids, I've also got kittens. Two doors that direction," he said, pointing to a corner on the other side of the barn. "Little gray tabbies. Only a couple of weeks old. You ought to go take a look."

"Look, but don't touch," Heather amended. Shawn appreciated how she was always on top of the parenting thing. He wasn't certain he had that same ability. Observing Heather at work was better than a college course in parenting skills.

Jacob took Henry's and Missy's hands and led the way across the barn to where Shawn had indicated. He smiled when he heard their mutual exclamations of delight. Even Jacob sounded excited at the furry find.

Heather smiled, as well. Still in a crouch, she shifted her weight so Hammie was more safely entrenched in her arms, then lost her balance and fell forward onto her knees in the hay. A lock of her glossy brown hair escaped from the low clasp of her ponytail and fell over her forehead. Her arms were full trying to restrain the wiggling piglet, so she tweaked her chin and blew at the stubborn strand in an unsuccessful attempt to get it out of her eyes.

Without pausing to give it any real thought, Shawn reached forward to brush her hair behind her ear for her. His fingertips barely grazed her temple, but she tossed the bottle and jerked backward as if he'd physically slapped her, her heels raising dust and hay from the ground. She lost her air in an audible huff when her bottom hit the solid floor of the stable. Hammie squealed and squirmed out of her grasp.

"I'm so sorry. I—" Shawn stammered. Heat rose to

his cheeks as he scrambled to his feet and reached for the woman sprawled across the hay in an undignified heap with one hand, cradling Noelle with the other. His arms and his expression pleaded with Heather. "I didn't— I wasn't trying to—"

Heather shook her head violently and scuttled backward until her back met the stable door. She inhaled again, another audibly terrified sweep of air. Her hazel eyes were wide and glassy. She was staring straight at him, but it was almost as if she were looking through him. Shawn had the distinct impression it wasn't his face she was seeing.

His breath felt glued to the inside of his lungs and anxiety banded around his chest.

Lord, help me. What had he done?

She reminded him of a frightened doe cornered by a mountain lion. That he was the mountain lion in this scenario made him sick to his stomach. She was frozen in place and yet visibly quivering, ruffling Shawn to the core of his being.

He became intensely aware of his every movement, afraid he was going to make things worse. Slowly, carefully, he lifted his hands in a gesture of surrender so she would recognize he was no threat to her. He waited silently as she visibly took control of her thoughts and her breathing. Gradually, the bright beacons of alarm faded from her gaze. Slowly, she released her clenched fists and uncoiled herself from her defensive position, wobbling slightly as she regained her feet. She snatched Hammie from the floor and held him close to her heart, whispering comforting nonsense syllables to the tiny, wiggling piglet. Shawn suspected the reassurance was more for her than it was for the pig.

He searched his mind for the right thing to say but came up blank. He sensed that they were at a defining moment in their dubious friendship.

If he said the wrong thing now, she'd be out of his life so fast his head would spin. And then where would he be? As selfish as it sounded, he was absolutely positive he wouldn't be able to be a good foster father to Noelle without Heather's assistance.

But never mind how it might affect him. His primary concern right now was how *Heather* was feeling. What had happened in her past to make her have that marked and painful of a reaction to his touch?

And how could he help?

Whatever it was, it must have been horrible. It had to have been a man who had hurt her at some point. Fury rose in Shawn's chest. He wanted to grab whoever had done this to her by the collar and shake him senseless. Tension rippled through his body, and he had to force himself to relax and not clench his fists.

Deeply aware of how any violence in his actions would look to her, he jammed his hands into the back pockets of his jeans and rocked back on his heels, waiting for her to make the first move. He was glad the children were two stable doors down so they weren't witnessing their foster mother's distress. He was certain they would have picked up on the fact that she was shaken to the core. Kids were sensitive that way.

"I, um—" Her voice wobbled. She ran a hand down her face, then pinched the bridge of her nose and sighed. "I imagine you're probably wondering why I completely freaked out on you just now."

"I wouldn't put it quite that way," he corrected gently.

"No? What would you call it, then? I just made a

complete and total spectacle of myself in front of you. I've never been so humiliated in my life."

"Heather." How could he comfort her without touching her? "I don't want you to worry about me. You have absolutely no reason to feel embarrassed. None whatsoever. I'm not judging you at all—I promise. I care. I really do."

Her gaze snapped to his. He stood absolutely stock-still as she cautiously took his measure. After an extended pause, she nodded and then reached a tentative hand toward his forearm. Her fingers quivered and she tightened her grip. "You're right. I know this about you. I do."

"You know...*what* about me?" he asked, not certain he was following her train of thought. In fact, he knew he wasn't keeping up to the recoil of her emotions. She'd gone from scrambling away from him to resolutely touching him. "I don't, um— That is—"

Stammering was not helping this situation, but he felt as if his tongue was in knots. Deep down, he experienced an agonizing physical yearning to wrap his arms around her and protect her from whatever it was that had her so rattled. It took every bit of his strength of will not to do so, and only because he knew that would be the absolute worst possible move he could make right now.

His mere touch had her both physically and emotionally somersaulting away from him. If he tried to hold her in his arms—well, that would only make things worse. He wasn't going to do that to her. He wouldn't do that to anyone, but Heather wasn't just anyone. He couldn't explain it any more than he could explain where his faith in God came from, but he felt differently about Heather than any of the other women of his acquaintance, present or past. She was special, somehow, and he was attracted to her. But she was a package deal, three kids included.

Which was all the more reason for him to be mindful of his actions. He needed to tread extra carefully where Heather was concerned. He was hardly adequate as a foster father to Noelle. He'd never measure up to the challenge of three more needy children. They deserved an experienced hand to guide them, and he was not it.

Her eyes dropped to the piglet in her arms. "You don't understand why I'm acting so skittish," she finished for him.

He shrugged and bent his head until he could capture her gaze once again. "I'm a good listener."

"Right. Because you're a pastor."

"No. That's not why. Or at least, that's not all of it." How could he explain that his reaction to her distress had less to do with him being a pastor and a great deal more with him being a man? If he tried to convey that his feelings at the moment went beyond Christian charity, he was fairly certain he would send her running for the hills as fast as her legs could carry her. Yet he knew conversations about faith made her uncomfortable. If she felt that he was only there for her as a spiritual leader, he knew instinctively that she would clam up rather than explain her problems and fears to him.

He didn't know how much she would actually share with him, if anything, but the barn was hardly the place for a serious conversation. Much better that he invite her back up to the house, where she could sip a cup of coffee and compose herself.

"Kids?" he called, loud enough to be heard across the stable. "Anyone up for some ice cream?"

The last thing Heather wanted to do was follow Shawn back to his house. Shame filled her at the way she'd treated him, at the reactions she couldn't seem to be able to control even after all this time. He hadn't deserved her going off on him the way she had.

He'd graciously accepted her fumbling apology, but he'd closed up on her. And it was no wonder.

If it weren't for the fact that Shawn had offered the kids ice-cream sandwiches—their favorite special-occasion dessert—she would have come up with some lame excuse for why she had to leave immediately. Never mind that she wouldn't be fulfilling her obligation to do what she came here to do—namely, checking Shawn's progress on baby-proofing his house before the social worker made her official visit.

Let it go. Let it go.

Heather's heart continued to reel from the memory of Shawn's gentle touch and her own outlandish reaction. Her thoughts and emotions made her equal parts alarmed and angry. Angry that Adrian had ruined even the possibility of her responding well to a kind touch, or ever knowing love in her life, and the fear that—

Well, there it was. She'd been around Shawn enough to believe that the man he presented to the world was exactly the man he continued to be behind closed doors. With Shawn, what a woman saw was what she got. Like seeing the way he cherished Noelle, pretty much acting as if the sun and moon rose in her tiny face. He was the kind of man any normal woman would be thrilled to have a relationship with.

But she wasn't *normal*, now, was she?

Adrian had never in his life dealt with another human being the way Shawn treated virtually everyone with whom he crossed paths. Lost in the throes of his addiction, Adrian only had room in his life for one person—himself. And his scotch. The few times she'd tried to interrupt the relationship between the man and his booze had resulted in a broken wrist. Broken ribs.

Dead children.

Was it any wonder she still reacted negatively to even the slightest touch from a man? No one could blame her if she did.

But she hated it. Really, really *hated* her inability to live a normal life. She'd give anything not to have to explain to Shawn why she'd responded the way she had.

Not to live in perpetual fear.

"Food first, and then a tour of the house," Shawn said, breaking into her thoughts. Nothing about awkward explanations. He unstrapped Noelle from his chest and kissed her downy forehead. "Ice cream for the older kids, and it's a bottle of formula for you, Little Miss Noelle." He gestured to Heather and pointed to the freezer. "I've got two flavors—of ice cream, that is. Strawberry and vanilla. The children can choose whichever they like. You, too, Heather. And there's coffee in the pot by the sink. Now if you'll excuse me a moment, I have to take care of somebody's wet diaper."

Once Shawn was out of her line of vision, Heather busied herself serving ice-cream sandwiches to the children. Her stomach was too raw to take one for herself, but a warm cup of coffee sounded good. She located the pot and then went in search of mugs.

She wasn't snooping, but it was quickly evident that

Shawn's cabinets were as bleak as his decor—which was to say, he had nothing. Or almost nothing.

Four mismatched glass dinner plates in one cupboard. A couple of large, fluorescent-green plastic cups graced another. She finally found two unadorned white coffee mugs in the cabinet over the sink.

"I take it you don't have many guests around here," she said to Shawn when he returned. She poured two cups from the carafe. "I could only find these two mugs for the coffee. I hope they're okay."

"They're fine. As you observed, they are our only choice."

"I thought pastors did a lot of that. Entertaining, I mean."

He plunked Noelle into the bassinet and then rummaged through the walk-in pantry, reappearing with a baby bottle in hand. Then he opened the refrigerator and removed what Heather assumed was a jug of baby formula.

"I can offer you sugar for your coffee. Sorry, no milk—unless you want a drop of this." He hefted the container of formula and chuckled. "I'm not guaranteeing how it would taste in coffee."

"Eww." She wrinkled her nose. His teasing put her at ease. "No, that's okay. I think I'll pass."

"It's exactly like you said. I don't get visitors. I don't drink milk, so I don't buy the stuff. I suppose that'll change if I have Noelle for more than a few months." A flash of melancholy crossed his gaze, but only for a moment. Then his expression cleared and filled with so much joy Heather wondered if she'd imagined the sadness in his eyes.

"I'm sure you'll adapt," she assured him, taking a

seat in the nearest kitchen chair and leaning her forearms against the table, which was littered with an assortment of baby-proofing hardware. "Look at you. You already are."

Shawn's red-gold eyebrows danced. He zapped the contents of the bottle for a few seconds, removed it from the microwave and tested the temperature of the formula against the inside of his wrist.

"See? You're a pro."

"I'm getting there. Even diaper duty isn't too bad anymore." He settled into the chair opposite her, cradling Noelle in one arm. She couldn't believe how much more comfortable he appeared with Noelle compared to the first few days he'd had with the baby.

Noelle was likewise a great deal more complacent, taking her bottle from Shawn without even a whimper of protest.

It didn't take long for Heather's kids to finish their ice cream, nor for Noelle to drain her bottle. Heather and Shawn kept up insignificant chatter, but to her, at least, there was a gigantic elephant in the room, one she knew she'd eventually have to address.

The questions were there in his eyes, even if he didn't voice them aloud.

Why had she bolted like a branded calf when he touched her?

Like the gentleman he was, he didn't press her for answers. He was clearly letting her set the pace.

"Why don't you kids go out onto the back porch and throw a stick for Queenie?" Shawn suggested as he tucked a now-sleeping Noelle into the bassinet.

"Stay where I can see you," Heather added. The sliding glass door wouldn't make it difficult to monitor the kids from where she sat in the comfort of the kitchen.

Her heart softened as she watched Shawn fuss over the baby. It was incredibly cute how he took extra care to make sure she was tightly swaddled and resting comfortably, and the nonsense syllables he babbled at her were beyond adorable. Heather suspected Noelle might nap better in the crib in her bedroom—the Jenny Lind crib she'd helped Shawn pick out the day they were in San Antonio. But from all appearances, Shawn didn't want to let Noelle out of his sight, not even for a minute.

So sweet. So loving. The man had father written all over him.

Her own father had died when she was just ten, but to her as a child, he had been a shining example of all that a man could be. She remembered him leaning in close to her mother and tickling her ribs just to see her giggle. Her father's laugh had been hearty and frequent. She idealized him, and consciously or unconsciously had been looking all her life for those qualities her father had possessed in abundance—qualities Adrian had initially seemed to share. She'd realized only too late that it was all an illusion.

A man like Shawn—handsome, clean-cut, responsible, a man of faith and a pastor—why, he ticked off every item on any woman's hypothetical Qualities to Look for in a Man list. So why hadn't some nice Christian woman come along and taken him off the market?

She didn't like how uncomfortable the thought of another woman in his life made her feel. She lifted her chin and shifted her gaze away from him. Better that she keep her eyes and her mind on her children, who were having a raucously good time throwing sticks for

Queenie. The dog was plenty energetic enough to keep up with all three of them.

Silence reigned in the room, hot and thick and heavy. This was beyond awkward. Shawn had just seen her at her worst out there in the barn, panicking at his mere touch even though he'd done nothing to deserve her distrust. She could feel his gaze upon her but didn't have the heart to turn back to see what he was thinking.

Coward.

No, she was not a coward—not anymore.

Elephant in the room? She was going to tame that beast right now, before the circus began.

She cleared her throat and turned her attention to him. He was, indeed, staring at her, but it didn't unnerve her the way she expected it to. He kept his full attention on her face. That was something else she'd noticed about Shawn. He looked people straight in the eye. Not so much challenging her, but stepping up beside her and comforting her without words or a physical touch.

She swallowed hard to remove the lump of emotion choking the breath from her lungs and forced the words from her mouth. "I'm sure you're wondering why I did the—er—Texas Two-Step out in the barn earlier."

He didn't even pretend not to understand. He acknowledged her statement with a brief nod, and compassion flooded his gaze. His tenderness nearly undid her. She could not—would not—come unhinged while talking about Adrian. Her past was just that—her past. There was no way around the pain and discomfort except to plunge forward, right through the middle of it, and no amount of time or therapy would ever quite take away the sting.

"I wondered," Shawn murmured. "But I don't want to push you. If you're not ready to talk about it, that's okay. I'm here for you if you need me, but I don't want you to feel I'm pressuring you."

"Is that your pastoral training talking?" She didn't know why she said it that way. The question sounded dismissive and off-putting even to her ears. She couldn't imagine how it sounded to him.

His eyebrows shot up in surprise. "No. I don't think there is training for situations like this one. I want to be your friend, Heather, not your pastor. If you'll let me."

Could she let him?

Her heart said yes, but she didn't trust her emotions anymore.

"You probably know I was married before," she began, stumbling over her words.

He nodded but didn't interrupt.

"Well, what you don't know—it's something I don't usually talk about." She paused and squeezed her eyes shut, praying she could get through this and say the words aloud. "My ex-husband is serving time in prison."

"Is he?"

"Yes. It's where he belongs. Adrian is not a nice man, but he puts on a surprisingly effective facade. I'm embarrassed to admit I fell for it. I thought I was marrying a charming, faithful man. It was only after we'd exchanged vows that I discovered I was married to a monster."

"He was physically abusive," Shawn concluded. It hadn't taken much for him to fill in the blanks. "Which explains a lot."

"That was the least of it." Heather couldn't keep the disgust from her voice, nor the fear and pain.

"Don't say that." Shawn started to reach across the table, then abruptly stopped himself and leaned back in his chair, crossing his arms.

His gaze said it all. He believed in her. How little he knew.

"It kills me that he hurt you," Shawn said through gritted teeth. He clenched his hands into fists, and his biceps pulsed, but oddly enough, she didn't feel threatened by his posture. She felt safe. "What makes this infinitely worse is that I can see the lasting effects his abuse has had on you, showing me that he's *still* hurting you even though he's not around anymore. Honey, you're worth more than you know. To God. To your kids. To me."

Her breath scratched against her throat. She so wanted to believe his words, but he'd spoken in haste, before he'd heard the whole story. Once he had, she had no doubt his opinion of her would take a nosedive. She was too far beyond God's grace for easy redemption.

She paused. Maybe she should stop right here and not say any more. She'd said enough to explain her peculiar reaction to him in the barn. She could leave off and he'd never have to know the woman she really was.

But she wanted—well, she didn't even know what she wanted. Or at least, she couldn't put it into words. But she was certain playing the pity card wasn't going to get it for her.

Shawn had extended a genuine hand of friendship. She couldn't accept it under false pretenses, no matter how much a part of her wanted to sweep her past under the rug. No, her memories were something she would have to live with for the rest of her life.

"I need to tell you why Adrian is behind bars."

Shawn's lips quirked and his gaze flashed with anger. "If you'd like to tell me, I'll listen."

Heather shoved out a breath and squeezed her eyes shut.

"Homicide."

Chapter Six

The word hung in the air like an icicle between them. Sharp. Jagged. Dangerous.

Shawn pursed his lips, searching for words. What was there to say?

"He killed someone." It wasn't a question, and Shawn didn't phrase it as such.

"Three people." Heather's complexion turned a pasty white. Shawn couldn't blame her. He felt a little nauseated himself. "A mother and her two children."

Oh, dear Lord, comfort her, he prayed silently. What a heavy burden Heather was carrying.

Shawn had already suspected that Heather was the victim of physical abuse, and there was no shortcut out of that camp. But the fact that Adrian had somehow killed people? That was heaping misery upon misery.

"How did it happen?" He approached the question with caution. Bringing these memories to the surface was clearly painful for Heather, but at the same time, he suspected sharing her burden with someone—with *him*—might be the first step in her healing process. He experienced a deep, burning desire to be the bridge that reconnected Heather with God and helped her find peace within herself.

"It was an automobile accident—if you can call it an accident. He ran a stop sign and sideswiped the vehicle."

"That's terrible." His chest ached so hard he thought it might burst. And if it was this bad for him, he couldn't imagine how Heather could even stand it. He wanted to do something, anything, to ease her pain. He'd never felt so helpless in all his life. His very ministry was built on his ability to come alongside people and comfort and strengthen them, guide them back to the gentle fold of God.

He searched, but he had nothing.

"It was terrible," she said, pressing her palm to her temple. "The police showing up at our door. Adrian being arrested. Finding out that children had died because of his actions. The whole thing makes me sick. And the worst part is, I was an accomplice." She swept in a breath that was half a hiccup, half a sob. "God forgive me, I let it happen."

"That can't be true." Shawn could see the shades of guilt in her gaze, but he didn't understand it. How could this sweet woman, who had done nothing to deserve the physical and emotional abuse she'd endured, blame herself for the accident? Didn't she realize that she was as much a victim as that poor family Adrian had hit?

"You see, I let him walk out the door that day. I knew he was going to get behind the wheel of a car. And he'd been—"

The doorbell rang, bringing her sentence to a grinding halt, but Shawn knew what she was about to say.

He'd been *drinking*.

This time the sharp ache in his gut was all too familiar. He knew all about alcoholism and the helplessness those who lived with such addicts felt. Surely she realized she couldn't have stopped Adrian even if she'd tried. Couldn't have stopped him from drinking, and couldn't have stopped the reckless behavior once the alcohol was in his system.

Thoughts shot through his head like bullets as he excused himself to answer the door. He wasn't expecting anyone. As he'd told Heather earlier, he rarely had visitors. He was often invited to his parishioners' homes to share a meal with them, but it was unusual for someone to come by the ranch.

Maybe someone was in the midst of a crisis. His curiosity ramped as he swung the door wide-open.

"Dad!"

"Took you long enough." The white-haired, sixtyish man with a deeply lined face and skin wrinkled beyond his years stumbled past Shawn and into the house without waiting for an invitation. "Sh-pected you'd be happy to see me, at least."

Shawn's stomach tumbled and he sent a horrified glance toward the kitchen, where Heather sat waiting for his return. Noelle was with her. The kids were playing in the backyard. This had the makings of an all-out catastrophe.

Dad's timing could not have been worse. What could he do with him to keep him from causing an unnecessary and very likely excruciating ruckus?

Shawn had been anticipating—and dreading—this confrontation with his father for a long time, but he'd never in a million years imagined circumstances like these. His father's health had been heavy on Shawn's heart for a while now, but he'd expected, or at least hoped, that he would be able to deal with this outside the watchful eyes of Serendipity.

And Heather—if she were to encounter his father...

Shawn didn't even want to know.

He took his father's shoulders and guided him toward the hallway. Maybe if he could get Dad into a back bedroom the situation would resolve itself. As soon as his father saw a bed, Shawn knew he would pass out within minutes.

"Shawn?" He heard Heather's curious voice coming from behind him and pressed harder on his father's back.

A few more feet and he could breathe easy.

He didn't anticipate his father's next move. Kenneth O'Riley planted his feet and then spun around, slipping under Shawn's grasp and staggering back toward the living room. "Didn't tell me you had company," his father cackled. "Of the female per-shway-shun."

Shawn cringed at the sound of his father's slurred words. He couldn't imagine how this episode would affect Heather—and just as he'd believed she was beginning to trust him.

Why had God let this happen? There must be a reason, but Shawn was too numb with horror to think it through.

It was bad enough that he was going to be forced into an impromptu intervention with his father, but he was far more concerned about Heather's reaction. After all, an alcoholic man had dragged her through the pit. For her to witness his father like this...

Heather rounded the corner between the kitchen and the living room, a polite, slightly strained smile on her lips. "I didn't realize you were going to have company. I'll just gather the children and leave."

Shawn scowled and stepped in front of his father, doing his best to shield Heather from seeing him. "Sounds like a plan. We'll talk later."

She wasn't buying it. Her eyes filled with curiosity, and Shawn knew why. His behavior at the moment wasn't exactly falling into the normal category as he physically blocked his father from advancing. His heartbeat pounded through his head.

Go, Heather. Please. Just go.

"Shawn?" Heather asked, her voice hesitant. "Is everything okay? Do you need me to stay?"

He met her gaze and was stunned at the strength he found there. Only moments before she'd been practically falling apart as she relayed her own horrific story, cringing away from his touch; but now she was reaching for him, gripping his forearm, offering him the support she somehow sensed he needed.

If only he could make this all go away. The feel of her palm against his skin helped calm the panicked racing of his mind, but even as he straightened out his thoughts, he realized there was no easy way out of this mess.

"Who-sh the young lady?" his father asked with a laugh that made Shawn's hair stand on end. "Aren't sha gonna introduce us?"

Shawn's eyes met Heather's, and he shook his head almost imperceptibly. He hoped she'd understand what he meant and head for the hills.

Don't get involved. Take the kids and run.

But no. She stepped forward and offered her right

hand in greeting. Her jaw was tight but her expression was resolute. She wasn't backing down.

"I'm Heather Lewis, a friend of Shawn's. And you are?"

Heather didn't have to wait for the inebriated man's answer to guess who he was. Shawn's likeness to his father was as unquestionable as the fact that the man must have started drinking near breakfast time for him to be as intoxicated as he was now.

Shawn had never said—but then, he hadn't really had the chance. Their conversation had been interrupted by the arrival of this…person.

"Kenneth O'Riley," the man said, wrapping his clammy hand around hers and pumping it vigorously. "Sh'my pleasure."

It certainly wasn't Heather's, and it definitely wasn't Shawn's. She didn't know whether the worry lining Shawn's face had more to do with his father showing up here smashed and presumably unannounced, or whether it was because he was concerned about how she was going to handle it, but either way, she was determined to step up and come to his aid.

She could handle it. And she could help Shawn with his father.

The situation might have overwhelmed her not so long in the past, but to her astonishment, today it didn't. Maybe it was because Shawn was here with her. She knew that no matter how belligerent or out of control his father might get, Shawn would keep her safe. Perhaps it was because Shawn looked as if he was out of his element and needed her assistance.

She wasn't out of her element. Not a bit. This was

home turf for her—dealing with a drunk man. Bring it on.

"Why don't you sit down, Kenneth, and I'll grab you a cup of coffee from the kitchen?" she suggested mildly, gesturing toward the couch.

Shawn nodded and clasped his father's arm, carefully leading him toward the sofa at the far end of the living room. Heather scrambled for the kitchen, taking time to check on Noelle and check on her children, who were, thankfully, still entertaining themselves throwing sticks for the Shetland sheepdog to retrieve for them. Since there were only two mugs in the house, she quickly rinsed out the one she'd been using and poured a fresh, hot cup of coffee for Kenneth. Curling her fingers around the warmth of the ceramic, she paused, closed her eyes and offered a quick prayer.

She didn't know if God would listen—not because she believed He wasn't there or couldn't be bothered, but because she wasn't worthy of approaching His throne to make requests in the first place. But she hoped for the best. After all, she was praying for Shawn, and he *was* a good, God-fearing man. Surely the Lord would hear and take account because of Shawn.

Blowing out her breath to steady her nerves, she returned to the living room and pressed the mug into Kenneth's hands. His head lolled back against the forest-green cushion, and Heather was a little worried he would spill the hot liquid into his lap.

Then again, she supposed that would get him sobered up right quick.

Shawn crouched before him and placed a hand on

his knee, shaking him gently to gain his attention. "Dad. What are you doing here?"

The answer was long in coming as Kenneth attempted to focus his bleary eyes on Shawn. "Came to stay with my shon," he mumbled.

"You can't stay here. Not until you're sober. We've talked about this." Shawn's voice was gentle but firm.

Kenneth came alive, slamming his cup on the coffee table and spilling the dark liquid across the wood. "Look at this house. You're all by yourself here, and you've got plenty of room," he roared.

Shawn didn't budge, but Heather jolted backward, an instinctive and unconscious act of self-preservation. This was what she knew.

Violence.

Shawn grabbed his father's shoulder with one hand and held up the other to Heather, palm out, reassuring her that he had control of the situation.

"I'm not backing down on this, Dad. I've done some calling around and I've found a nice place in San Antonio that has an opening. They're experts. They can help you find a way out of your addiction."

Heather waited for the denial she knew was forthcoming.

"I don't see why you're pressuring me." Kenneth glared at Shawn, but to Shawn's credit, he didn't budge or capitulate. "I've said it before and I'll shay it again— you're looking at this all wrong. I'm not an alkie. I don't have to drink. I like to drink. There's a difference."

Shawn's soul-weary sigh moved the depths of Heather's heart, but Kenneth remained unfazed.

"No, Dad, that's where you're wrong. You drink to mask the pain, and until you deal with the underlying causes—David's death, Mom's illness—you will never find peace. It certainly isn't at the bottom of a bottle."

Kenneth growled in protest. "Don't you preach to me, kid. Remember who you're talking to."

Shawn shook his head. "Unfortunately, it's not something I can forget. And I'm not preaching at you. Just stating facts. Now, are you going to let me get you some help, or aren't you?"

Heather was certain no one breathed as she and Shawn awaited Kenneth's answer. For an instant the man's expression changed. He looked old, tired, weak. But then resolve took hold and Heather braced herself, hoping Shawn had also seen the subtle shift in his father's demeanor. Kenneth wasn't going down without a fight.

"I'm jush fine the way I am. Butt out of my business."

Shawn's jaw tightened and his shoulders firmed as he stood and yanked his father up with him. "Then you are no longer welcome in my house."

Heather could see the pained look in Shawn's eyes and knew just how difficult it was for him to stay strong in this. But no matter how hard it was, it was the right thing to do. She was impressed by Shawn's display of fortitude. Kenneth might be a drunk, but he was Shawn's father, and it was obvious that Shawn loved him. It was equally apparent that he refused to be an enabler—something Heather had never known how to do.

"David would never have treated me thish way," his father slurred. "You are not a good son."

Shawn winced and his expression froze. "I guess

we'll never know about that, will we?" His voice was so ice-cold that Heather shivered.

Kenneth mumbled and protested as Shawn physically escorted him to the back bedroom, but Shawn was larger and stronger than his father, even without the benefit of Kenneth having had too much to drink. Shawn opened the door and deposited his father on the bed.

"Sleep it off. When you wake up, I want you to leave. You know where to find me if you change your mind." He closed the door with a firm click and turned and leaned his shoulders against it, scrubbing his hands down his face as he shoved out a breath.

"Heather, I'm so sorry for that."

"There's no need to apologize," she assured him.

"I would have told you, especially after what you've been through, but I didn't get the chance. And I certainly never expected that Dad would actually show up here in Serendipity." His shoulders slumped, the first sign of succumbing to the intense pressure he'd been under. "I don't know. I guess I should have realized it would happen eventually. He's been calling me for weeks, asking for money, mostly. I should have figured if he couldn't get at me one way, he'd try another."

"You can't anticipate what an addict will do," Heather responded, wishing there was more she could say to take the burden from him.

Their eyes met and held. His gaze was a mixture of gratitude and vulnerability, the boy he used to be dealing with his unruly father. Truly heartbreaking.

She brushed his hair out of his eyes and smoothed his temple with her fingertips as she did to soothe little Henry from his nightmares. But Shawn wasn't a child, and the action that had started as a comforting gesture transformed into a caress across his scratchy cheek. Their breath came in unison, their hearts beating as one.

He held his arms out to her. Not demanding, not forcing. Not even begging.

Just asking.

She answered by stepping into his embrace, curving her arms upward as her palms grazed the firm planes of his shoulder muscles. His hands found her waist.

For several seconds she stood immobile, working through her irrational fight-or-flight instinct, acknowledging it and letting it flow through her. Warmth and peace nudged fear out of her heart and she relaxed into his arms.

Shawn was her safe place. There was no threat here, only a man who needed the comfort of a woman's embrace and the reassurance of her words.

"You're very brave," she said.

He scoffed and leaned back so their eyes met but didn't release his hold on her waist. "Am I? Because right now I feel like a world-class jerk."

"You're not. I know it's hard now, but you did the right thing. You can't let him think he's got you fooled or he'll continue to take advantage of you. You wouldn't be doing him any favors by ignoring his addiction. At the end of the day, the best thing you can do for him is force him to see himself as he really is—locked into substance abuse. He needs to look in the mirror and understand he needs help. He's got to want it. Until that happens, there is nothing more you can do for him."

"I know." He tightened his embrace and lowered his

head, his breath warm on her ear. Her heart thrummed. "But it isn't easy to say no to him. And I do wonder sometimes..." His sentence drifted into a strained silence.

"What?" she whispered when he didn't continue.

"How different things might have been if David were here."

Who was David?

The words were on the tip of her tongue to ask when they were interrupted by the clamor of children barging inside like a herd of elephants, followed by the high-pitched wail that signaled Noelle was awake.

Even though the kids were in the kitchen and couldn't see them, Shawn snapped his arms to his sides and stepped away from her. He attempted a weak smile but it didn't reach his eyes. "We're up. It sounds like our kiddos need us."

Heather regretted that the moment had passed before she could receive answers to the questions she had yet to ask. As she watched Shawn gather Noelle into his arms and shepherd the other three children toward the living room, her emotions swelled into her throat, cutting off her breath.

There was so much to learn about this man, a man whose heart was big enough to care for farm animals, a church full of people and a tiny baby girl.

He'd experienced heartache, too, and plenty of it. She'd just scratched Shawn's surface with what she'd seen today.

She wanted to know more.

Chapter Seven

Who was David?

Heather mulled over the question as she knitted a sweater for Noelle and watched her children racing from room to room playing Follow the Leader. Jacob was currently in front, and he tended to play a little rougher than his foster siblings, so Heather kept a close eye on them.

Was David Shawn's brother? And what had happened to him?

The questions haunted Heather, but despite the fact that she and the kids were now regular visitors to Shawn's ranch, she'd not been able to find an appropriate opportunity to ask. Instead, the time was spent with the children helping Shawn take care of the animals. He was a mentor and a role model for the kids, showing them how a good man thought and acted.

But he was careful never to be alone with Heather, and he never offered any further explanation as to who David was, or what had happened to his mother that had sent his father seeking solace in a bottle. It wasn't the kind of thing one just blurted out, so she did the only thing she could do—play by his rules. He'd completely avoided talking about what had happened that day between him and Kenneth.

She understood why he didn't want to draw attention to the situation, and she didn't want to add to his sense of shame and vulnerability by bothering him about it.

She ought to just let it go—and yet she couldn't quite put it out of her mind. Whether she was playing with the children or knitting a scarf for one of the kids or answering email for a client, thoughts of Shawn would creep in. She had curiosity about his family situation, but if she was completely honest, that wasn't all there was. Her mind kept drifting to the way her emotions had skyrocketed when she was wrapped in his muscular arms.

She'd felt safe. Secure—feelings that had been foreign to her for so long. That was part of the reason why she couldn't stop thinking about it. But there was something else, something she'd never experienced before, not even when Adrian was courting her.

Her stomach tumbled with butterflies. It was the nicest of feelings. The warm glow of a fireplace on a cold night couldn't even begin to compare.

She scoffed and returned her attention to her knitting. She was dropping stitches. And for what? Silly notions?

She needed to nip that kind of whimsical nonsense right in the bud. Even if she wasn't completely physically and emotionally scarred after Adrian, Shawn was not and could never be the man for her. He was a pastor. He had the love and respect of the entire community.

She was the beat-up, badly used and tossed-away plaything of a convicted killer. Hardly a perfect match.

A shrill scream suddenly rent the air, and Heather bolted to her feet, tossing her knitting aside. Jacob sprinted out of the hallway, his hands waving wildly and eyes wide with fright and gleaming with moisture.

"Mama, Mama, come quick," he said, grabbing her arm and urging her down the hall. "Missy hurt herself."

With her heart in her throat, Heather followed her older foster son into her bedroom, where Missy lay wailing, curled up on a pillow with her face buried in her hands. Heather's breath cut out when she heard what she immediately recognized as Missy's pain cry.

The child was really hurt.

"She hit her head," Jacob explained on a sob as Heather gathered Missy in her arms, expecting she'd need to comfort the poor little girl for getting a bump on the noggin. It wouldn't be the first time such an accident had occurred. One of the more painful lessons she'd learned as a new foster parent was that she couldn't shield her kids from all harm. Children were bound to get a few bumps and bruises along the way as they explored their world.

But when Heather rolled Missy over to pull her into the curve of her arm, she was shocked by the amount of blood covering the little girl's forehead.

Lots and lots of blood, coming from a gash that was a good half inch long and just as deep.

"Jacob, what *happened*?" she demanded, trying and failing to keep the sharp edge from her voice. It was no good panicking, and her going off would only upset the boys more than they already were. She took a deep breath and tried again. "Get me a clean towel from the linen closet, please."

Jacob dashed out and returned a moment later with

a freshly bleached white towel, which Heather pressed to the wound. Poor Jacob's blue eyes were flooded with tears that ran unheeded down his face.

"It's all my fault," he wailed, clinging to Missy's hand.

"What happened?" Heather asked again in a gentler tone.

"We were jumping on your bed," he admitted miserably, not meeting her gaze.

"You know you're not allowed to—" she started, but then quickly brought her sentence up short. Jacob knew he'd broken the rules, and he was clearly distressed over what had happened to Missy. He was learning a painful lesson today and didn't need her to rub it in.

The hand towel was soaked with blood within a minute, and Heather felt a moment of panic. She was all alone with an injured child and two more who needed her care. This wasn't a scenario she'd imagined when she'd signed the papers to become a single foster mother.

She needed help. *Now.*

"Jacob, bring me my cell phone. It's on the end table next to the sofa."

He was out and back with it in a jiffy. She pressed the phone log, wondering if she had Dr. Delia Bowden's number stored. In hindsight, she realized that was something she ought to have done—put the doctor's number on speed dial. But it was too late now to rectify that oversight.

Instead, it was Shawn's number that popped up first on the list. Not surprising. He still called nearly every day needing advice on parenting Noelle.

This time she was the one who needed *his* help. She pressed his number and waited, her breath in a knot.

He answered on the first ring. "Hey, Heather. Are you and the kids going to meet me at the ranch later to help me feed the animals?"

"Missy had an accident," she said, cutting right to the chase. "She hit her head and she's got a big gash on her forehead. I tried using direct pressure, but I can't seem to get it to stop bleeding."

"It probably needs stitches," Shawn surmised. "But don't worry, honey. Head wounds tend to bleed a lot. Doesn't necessarily mean it's serious."

"I know you're right, but it looks awful."

"I'm at the church now. Get the kids buckled up in your SUV and I'll be right there. I'll drive you to see Delia."

She breathed a sigh of relief and tears pricked at her eyes. She hadn't even had to ask for his help. She'd simply shared her problem, and that was enough to prompt him into action on her behalf.

Now was not the time to wonder why calling Shawn had been her first impulse after she realized she didn't have the doctor's number.

"Jacob, grab your coat, and get Henry's while you're at it. Just to be on the safe side, we're going to take your sister to the doctor."

The boy nodded and ran for the jackets. Heather wrapped Missy in a quilt and continued to apply direct pressure to the girl's forehead as she led the kids outside to her SUV.

"Jacob, why don't you sit in front? Pastor Shawn is coming to drive us over to the doctor's office. I'm going to sit back here with Henry and Missy, okay?"

It was only after she'd managed to get Henry buckled into his booster seat that she realized she needed to make room for Noelle, but when Shawn arrived a few moments later, he was alone.

"Where's the baby?" she asked as Shawn climbed behind the wheel.

"Jo Spencer has her. Apparently 'Auntie Jo' wants to show her off to all of her customers today."

Heather expected that statement to be accompanied by one of Shawn's frequent and heart-stopping grins, so she was surprised when the corners of his lips turned down. That wasn't like him.

"How's our little patient doing?" he asked, glancing in the rearview mirror as he started the engine.

Hmm. Maybe that was all it was. He was worried about Missy. But something niggled in the back of Heather's mind, and her gut feeling was that there was more he wasn't saying.

"It's quite a large gash. The bleeding has slowed some but it hasn't stopped yet. She'll probably have a nice scar to remember this day by."

"How'd it happen?"

"Certain little monkeys were jumping on the bed when they weren't supposed to be."

"And one fell down and bumped her head," Shawn added.

"Exactly."

"That's why you need to listen to your mama, kids," he admonished. "She knows what she's talking about, and she's trying to keep you safe."

"Now you sound like a preacher," she teased, and the back of his neck grew red. "Or a father."

He shot a look over his shoulder that Heather had

a hard time identifying. Almost as if she'd—well, not insulted him, exactly, but definitely called him a name he didn't want to hear.

Which was what? *Preacher? Father?*

Nothing new there. No startling revelations. Shawn was both pastor and parent.

Shawn pulled the vehicle up in front of Delia's office before she had the opportunity to question him about his odd reactions. He was out and around the vehicle, opening the door for her before she'd even had the opportunity to get unbuckled.

"Come on, little lady," he said, scooping Missy into his arms, careful to keep her wound covered. "Let's go see Dr. Delia and get you all patched up." He was incredibly gentle for a man his size, and once again Heather marveled at his kindness.

And she wasn't the only one who thought so. Missy gazed up at Shawn as if he were her knight in shining armor. In a way, Heather supposed he was, quick to come to their rescue when she'd called him.

Missy reached up and placed her little palm on Shawn's whisker-roughened cheek, and Heather's chest could barely restrain the swelling emotion. Such an innocent display of love and trust—and Shawn, she knew, wouldn't betray that trust. *Ever*.

Delia greeted them at the door and immediately ushered them to the back room, where she instructed Shawn to place Missy on the nearest bed. She made quick work of examining the girl. Shawn didn't leave Missy's side, and the little girl clutched his hand.

"It's not as bad as it looks," Delia assured them. "No signs of a concussion, and the wound itself is superficial. I'll clean it up and we'll use some glue and a butterfly bandage to seal it up tight."

"I like butterflies," Missy inserted, looking hopeful.

Delia laughed. "Well, Missy, I'm afraid the bandage isn't actually a butterfly, but I'll bet I have some princess stickers around here somewhere."

Missy's excitement immediately turned to fear when Delia dabbed the wound with an alcohol swab.

"It hurts. It hurts," she wailed, fresh tears brimming in her bright green eyes.

Heather hated this part of motherhood—the part where she had to put on a brave face for her children when she was quaking inside. Shawn, however, didn't flinch.

"I know it hurts, darlin'," Shawn told the girl, pressing his palm against her cheek. He didn't try to dismiss her pain or marginalize her fear. No wonder he was such a good pastor. "You're being such a brave girl. I think cookies are called for after this, don't you? Just let Dr. Delia get you all glued up and I'll take you over to Cup O' Jo's for a treat. All of you," he added, his eyes on Jacob.

Heather wanted to hug him for including the boy, who was still huddled in on himself in guilt. She probably would have launched herself at Shawn, if it weren't for Delia being in the room.

The doctor worked quickly, cleaning and gluing the wound, then covering it with gauze and tape. "Keep the wound clean with soap and water," she advised, "and call me if you see any signs of infection—redness around the gash or oozing from the wound. Otherwise, come back in a week for a quick follow-up."

Delia allowed each of the kids to pick out a sticker

from a bucketful of choices, but she allowed Missy to have three, since the little girl couldn't choose between princesses. She liked them all, so she got them all.

Heather was relieved that Missy was all patched up and the accident had resulted in nothing more than a gash that could be fixed with a little glue. Missy seemed to have forgotten that she'd been the one on the doctor's table at all. She was the first one out the door, racing down the clapboard sidewalk with her brothers right behind her, heading toward Cup O' Jo's on the corner.

The only one who looked as if he'd been negatively impacted by the day's events was Shawn. As long as he'd been in Missy's line of sight, he'd been all smiles and strength, but now he looked as if he'd swallowed something bitter and was fighting to keep it down.

She followed Shawn out of the doctor's office and couldn't help but admire the view of the cowboy preacher replacing his straw hat and loping along after the children, but she wondered at his distracted mood. She caught up with him and laced her arm through his, half expecting resistance. He glanced at her, surprise evident in his gaze, but he slid his hand over hers and slowed to match her pace.

"No more monkeys jumping on the bed," he teased, but his attempt at a smile was faltering at best.

"Do you want to tell me what's wrong?" She applied pressure to his arm, stopping him before he could enter the café.

"I—" he started, then stopped and shook his head. "No. It's nothing. The kids are waiting for their cookies, and I'm sure Jo is plenty ready to be done with baby duty. She's had Noelle all day."

Heather highly doubted the truth of that statement. Jo Spencer loved babies above all things. She wouldn't be in any great hurry to part with darling Noelle. But Heather knew a brush-off when she heard it, so she reluctantly turned loose of his arm and allowed him to enter the café.

Jo looked up from the register when the bell rang over the door and bustled out to greet them, her red curls bobbing with the same energy that radiated from her friendly smile. There was no sign of Noelle, but with Jo at the helm, there was no immediate cause for concern. Curiosity, perhaps, but not concern.

"Now, Pastor, I told you it wouldn't be a problem for me to drop Noelle by the church when I was finished with her."

Shawn swept off his hat and combed his fingers through his hair. "I was afraid if I waited until you tired of her you might not ever give her back. Besides, we were just down the road from here."

"We?" Jo's gaze flitted from Shawn to Heather and a wide smile spread across her face. "Ah. I see. I'm glad you two are spending time together."

Heather's face suffused with heat. Jo was jumping to all the wrong conclusions here. She'd just as much as proclaimed loud enough for half the restaurant to hear that she was seeing a couple where there were actually two single individuals with a brood of foster children between them.

"You all out for a day at the park or something?" Jo laughed as Henry pressed his nose and palms flush against the glass of the pastry case. "Looks like somebody is hungry for a cookie."

"I promised them a treat," Shawn said.

"We've just come from Dr. Delia's office," Heather explained. "Missy fell and hurt herself. Got a little gash on the head."

"Poor dear. Is she okay?"

"Delia glued the cut," Shawn said, his tone incredulous. "I didn't realize doctors don't sew you up with stitches anymore—at least not with a wound like this. Delia said she might end up with a small scar from this little incident, but three princess stickers and the promise of a cookie and I think she's forgotten her big owie already." He barked out a dry laugh. "Kids. What are you going to do with them? What kind of cookies did Phoebe bake today?"

"Chocolate with chocolate chips," Jo said, reaching in to retrieve the cookies. She removed five rather than three, and after handing out the treats to the kids, she offered the remaining cookies to Heather and Shawn. "Trust me, y'all don't want to miss these, and you two look like you could use a little pick-me-up. Chocolate cures all ills, you know."

Heather glanced at Shawn. A muscle ticked in the corner of his jaw and his mouth tightened with strain. She doubted chocolate would do anything to help what was ailing him—whatever it was.

"I'm a little remiss not to have asked where Noelle might be," Shawn said, scanning the café for his foster daughter.

Heather followed the trail of his gaze. The inside of Cup O' Jo would come as a surprise to anyone not formerly acquainted with it. The café, like all of the buildings on Main Street, had a nineteenth-century feel to its exterior, like something straight out of an

old Western movie. Cup O' Jo's even boasted a hitching post out front.

But the inside of the café was a different ambiance
altogether. Open and friendly, it was decorated in a
contemporary, modern-coffee-shop style. Individuals
hunkered over the computers lining the back walls.
Several families and small groups enjoyed an early
dinner. It was *the* popular spot for folks to gather in
Serendipity. Chance Hawkins served up the best home-
style food in Texas.

Jo threw her hands up and cackled in delight. "Why,
I can't get that baby out of the back room. Chance and
Phoebe are so taken with her I wouldn't be surprised
if they decided it was time to start working on growing their own family again. Let me get them for you."

She hustled to the serving window and leaned her
head and shoulders into the kitchen. "Chance. Phoebe,"
she hollered, making Heather laugh. With Jo's voice
she could have stayed right where she was. She didn't
need to be at the serving window to be heard. "Pastor
Shawn is here for his daughter."

It warmed Heather's heart to hear Noelle referred
to as Shawn's daughter, but Shawn didn't look altogether pleased by the reference. The crease between
his eyes deepened.

Phoebe, brandishing a spatula in one hand, was the
first out of the kitchen. Her blue jeans and light green
pullover were dusted with flour, and she had a wide
streak of white on her nose, as if someone had purposefully dabbed it there. She was quickly followed
by Chance, a rugged-looking cowboy with a white
apron draped haphazardly around his waist. He held
the baby in the crook of his arm and was murmuring

nonsense to her. She clutched his thumb and kicked at her swaddling.

"She's a strong little thing," Chance said as he deposited her into her foster father's arms. "I bet she'll be a real handful when she gets a little older—and you probably don't even want to think about her teenage years. Sweet darlin'. You're gonna be needing a baseball bat to fend off all the boys."

Shawn blanched, but no one other than Heather appeared to notice that, or the tightening of his jaw.

"It's hard to believe Aaron was ever that small," Phoebe said of her now school-aged son. "And Lucy is graduating from college this year."

"We're getting old," Chance teased, his dark eyes gleaming as he brushed Phoebe's hair in a familiar, affectionate caress.

Squealing, she wriggled away from him and wielded her spatula like a weapon. "Speak for yourself, mister. I've got a few good years in me yet."

"All right, then, I guess I'll hold off on trading you in for two twenties."

"Take that back, you!" Phoebe swatted at Chance, who easily ducked out of the way.

"Make me," he said, laughing and dodging around her.

Phoebe perched her hands on her hips. "Don't tempt me. You know I can."

Chance grinned at Shawn. "You see what I have to put up with, Pastor?" He nodded toward Heather and winked. "So much to look forward to, you know?"

"I don't see you wearing any chains around your neck forcing you to stay," Jo admonished her grinning nephew. "You wouldn't change a single thing about your life with Phoebe and you know it."

"No, ma'am, I wouldn't, and that's a fact."

"There, then, you see?" Jo crowed, delighted that the conversation had turned in her favor. "The married state is a great place to be, no question about it."

Once again, heat flared to Heather's face. Subtlety definitely wasn't one of Jo's prime virtues. Shawn's flushed cheeks signaled that he hadn't missed the not-so-delicate intimation, either.

"I've got to be going," he said, backing toward the door.

"But you came in my car," Heather protested.

"I'll walk. My truck is at the chapel, along with Noelle's car seat. See y'all in church on Sunday." He planted his hat on his head and tipped it, then was gone without another word.

"Well," said Jo as the four of them stood staring at the empty doorway.

Well, indeed. That was beyond awkward. Heather felt as if she needed to say something to explain Shawn's odd behavior, but how could she when she didn't understand it herself? Who knew what ran through a man's mind?

Clearly something was stuck in his craw. The only question was *what*?

Or maybe *who*?

Had she inadvertently done something to offend him?

The familiar sensation of panic trickled down her spine before she mindfully pressed it away. Shawn wasn't the kind of guy to react spitefully. If he had a problem with her, he would talk to her about it, not hold it over her head and leave her wondering.

As if intruding on a private moment, Chance and Phoebe awkwardly excused themselves to return to the kitchen. No doubt they felt the tension in the air, so thick a person could slice it with a knife.

Heather tried for a smile and missed the mark by a mile. "I ought to be going, as well. Let me just round up my kids and we'll be out of here. Oh." She suddenly remembered Shawn had not paid for the cookies. "How much do I owe you for the treats?"

She reached for her wallet but Jo waved her away. "Don't you dare even think about it, dear. The cookies are on me. Poor Missy deserves a little TLC after having such a scary day. Besides, my dear," she said, nodding toward the door where Shawn had just made his rather overdramatic exit, "I think you have more pressing matters to deal with."

"Yes, I certainly do." Heather didn't question why Shawn's odd behavior would be her problem. He was always there for her when she needed him, so how could she not step forward when he needed help? First, she needed to figure out what to do with her kids, and then she'd find a way to help Shawn.

"Let me feed the children a good meal for you," Jo suggested, almost as if she'd known the direction Heather's thoughts would be taking. She gave Heather a friendly pat on the back and turned her toward the door. "Go. Don't worry about your young'uns, they'll be happy as little larks here at the café. Take care of your man. I think he needs you right now."

Heather wasn't worried about her children as long

as they were in Jo's care. Shawn wasn't her man, but she didn't bother to correct Jo.

Because she agreed with her on the most important point of all.

Shawn needed her.

And she would be there for him.

After leaving Cup O' Jo's, Shawn didn't bother returning home right away. It was tempting to return to the ranch. His first inclination under stress was to go out riding. Sitting in the saddle and cantering across fields was his favorite form of prayer. But he had the baby to think of, and he still had a sermon to finish, so he went back to the chapel instead.

After the great deal of excitement he imagined Noelle must have had being passed around to all his doting neighbors, he figured with a diaper change and a bottle she'd be down for the count, and he was right. In less than ten minutes the baby was sound asleep. He settled her in her car seat, which he often used to haul Noelle around with him both inside the building and in his dual-cab truck.

His unfinished sermon, scribbled on a yellow legal pad, was taunting him, but after sitting at his desk for five minutes without writing a single word, he gave up. He couldn't keep his mind on his message—he couldn't even get it there in the first place.

He needed to refocus or else he wasn't going to have two words to share with his congregation come Sunday morning. Scooping up Noelle's infant seat, he carried her into the sanctuary, where he flipped on only enough lights to illuminate the altar. He approached and knelt reverently, his gaze lingering first on the cross and then on the sleeping baby.

Had it only been a few weeks ago that this sweet little darlin' had come into his life? Right here, in this very sanctuary, his world had been forever changed. By Noelle, and by the woman who'd come to his and the baby's rescue—Heather Lewis.

He remembered how helpless he'd felt when he'd heard Noelle cry for the first time. Now that he'd been with her for a while, he could distinguish between her cries—whether she was wet, hungry or just needing a little attention.

And hurry up with that bottle, Foster Daddy.

The smile that had claimed his lips when he regarded his baby girl disappeared when he thought about the future. He'd received a troubling phone call earlier in the day, just before the one from Heather that had sent him rushing off to help the family.

The news had him all in knots. Then all that combined with the incredibly helpless feelings he'd experienced at not being able to do anything to fix Missy's injury, other than taking her to the doctor. He hated feeling as if he couldn't do anything to help.

He was a mess, and the only thing he could think of to do was to give it all to the Lord and seek His guidance. How could he lead his congregation into faith and good works if he was struggling just to plant one foot in front of the other? This was getting way beyond him. Maybe he ought to step down for a while or take a sabbatical, do a little cow-poking and spend some time on the range, under the stars.

What did God want of him?

"I'm listening," he said aloud, acknowledging his need for the Almighty.

"Good, because I'm fairly certain I have something to say."

Shawn jerked to his feet, his heart hammering. He'd thought he was alone in the chapel. He lifted his arm to shield his eyes from the glare created by the lights above the altar, but he couldn't see into the shadows.

Yet he didn't need to see to know who was there. He recognized that rich, warm feminine voice almost as well as his own.

"I didn't expect an answer," he said with a chuckle.

"No, I don't suppose you did. I'm sorry if I startled you."

"That's okay. I'll live. Did you need something, Heather? Has something happened with Missy?"

"Missy is fine. She's taking supper with the boys and Jo Spencer."

Shawn cast about for a reason Heather might be here at the church but came up empty. The only time he'd ever seen her in the chapel was the night he'd discovered Noelle. He'd gathered from talking to her that church wasn't really her thing—thanks at least in part to Adrian. So it was unlikely she'd dropped by to pray.

"The doors of the church are always open," he said, sweeping his arm out in a welcoming gesture. What else could he say?

His statement was met with a dry laugh. "Funny you should say that."

"Oh? Why?"

"I have this thing about churches. You can probably chalk it up to one of those doesn't-make-any-sense emotions, like many of the others I'm slowly working my way through. Feel free to laugh at me if you'd like."

How could he possibly make fun of her for her confusion when his own thoughts and emotions were so ruffled?

"You know I won't do that. Go on."

"It's another by-product of my time with Adrian. I'm slowly working on my own personal relationship with God, but for some reason church buildings continue to give me pause. I must have stood outside for five minutes trying to talk myself into the courage to come into the chapel tonight."

"Why?"

"Who knows? Maybe it's because attending church was absolutely the most awful experience for me when I was with Adrian. It was horrible mixing with good and honest people when my whole life was a lie. Pretending I had the perfect marriage and a charmed life, never letting on that Deacon Adrian was anyone other than the upstanding man he presented himself to be in the public light."

She shivered and crossed her arms. Shawn closed the distance between them in a second, offering her the shelter of his arms and, crazy as it might sound, desperately wishing he could protect her from the pain of her past. Wishing he could change it for her. She was defenseless against the onslaught of her memories and he couldn't step between her and her dragons. He didn't even have a sword for this fight.

She stiffened in his embrace and then relaxed into him with a sigh, clutching his shirt and resting her head on his shoulders. That alone was enough to remind him that Heather wasn't entirely at the mercy of her past experiences. She fought against them every day, but each time she took a step in the right direction she conquered more of her fears.

Whereas *he* tended to simply stuff his anxieties into the back of his mind and slam a mental door on them. He counseled people to acknowledge and work through their issues, all the while ignoring his own.

Talk about a hypocrite. She was braver than he would ever be.

"I think everyone tends to present his or her best self at church. It's natural for us to want people to like us. But let's face it—we all have issues we'd rather other folks not know about. Every one of us. What you see is never quite what you get. There aren't any truly perfect people, which is why it's such a good thing that God's mercies are new every morning."

She sniffled. "I think you come pretty close. At the very least, you're a good man if I've ever known one."

He scoffed inwardly but held his tongue. If only she knew just how wrong she was. She wouldn't be so quick to be praising him, that was for sure.

"I didn't mean to interrupt your prayer time," she said, slipping out of his arms to check on Noelle, who stirred briefly and returned to her slumber. "She's so sweet in her sleep."

"She's sweet all the time," he agreed. "And don't worry about interrupting me. I don't think I was ready to hear any answers yet. My problems are still rumbling around in my head too much. Bumping off all the rocks, you know?"

They both laughed. He was glad he could lighten the mood a little. Heather didn't look quite so uncomfortable being in the chapel now—not as she'd been when she'd first walked in. Which reminded him—she must have come here for a reason, and he had yet to find out what it was.

"I don't think you ever answered my question," he prompted. "Why'd you stop by? Is there something I can help you with?"

"Not this time," she said, sitting on the front pew, where she could easily lean over the baby. The pacifier had popped out of Noelle's mouth in her sleep and Heather gently replaced it. "I don't know how to approach what I'm about to say, so I think it's better if I just come straight out with it."

He tensed at both her words and the tone of her voice. This didn't sound good. "I value straightforwardness and honesty. Have at it."

"I want to thank you for all you've done for us today. You made a frightening situation far less so, and you are now Missy's new favorite person. You're a regular hero in her book, and in mine, too."

He scoffed and shook his head.

"Now, see, this is what I'm talking about. I know something's bothering you. Don't try to deny it. You were a total superhero with Missy, but the rest of the day? Not so much. You've been pulling back. Acting distant. Frowning when you usually smile."

"That bad, huh?" He grimaced. "I didn't think I was being so obvious."

"You cut out of Cup O' Jo's like your tail was on fire. Everybody noticed it."

Ugh. He'd hoped he'd behaved with a little more finesse than that. He slumped onto the pew next to her, pressed his face into his palms and groaned. "I got some news today."

"Bad news? I'm so sorry. If you don't want to talk about it…" Her touch was incredibly light and tender against his shoulder, but it brought him instantly alert. Even in the midst of his turmoil, or maybe *especially* in the middle of it, he was hyperaware of her proximity to him. The warmth of her breath and the soft floral scent that wafted around her. Roses.

"Not bad news, exactly, and I think you need to know about it," he replied, reaching for her hand as it drifted down his arm. He turned her palm over and brushed his lips against the spot on her wrist where her pulse beat, then threaded their fingers together. She gave his hand a reassuring squeeze. "Some of it is bad news. Some of it's good, I guess. Maybe. It could be. Or maybe not."

"You're rambling. And so far you haven't said anything."

Great. His confusion made manifest to the one woman in the world he'd most like to impress. There was danger in being this close to someone. He wanted to share his innermost thoughts and emotions, but those very same feelings made him vulnerable.

"Right. Um—" He hesitated, then plunged forward. "I got a call from Maggie Dockerty at social services. Noelle's mother has been identified."

Heather's gasp was audible. She clenched his fingers so tightly she was cutting off his circulation, but he didn't attempt to remove himself from her grasp. "That's good news, right? Or is it? What happened to her? Is she okay? Does she want to reclaim Noelle?"

He barely knew where to begin answering the questions she'd peppered him with. "Her name is Kristen

Foxworthy. She was in an accident. Hit-and-run on a highway where she wasn't supposed to be walking."

"That's awful. How serious is it?"

"Unfortunately, it's very serious. She's currently in a medically induced coma, and the doctors don't give her a lot of hope. They're monitoring her brain function, which at the moment is nil. They're planning to remove the respirator. From there, I guess it's up to God what happens. It's very sad, though."

"And how do they know she's Noelle's mom?"

"Apparently she was lucid for a little while right after she was hit. She gave the emergency technicians enough information to help social services identify who was who in this case."

"So Noelle has a family, then? Someone who might want to take her?"

"Not that they can find. They think that's why Kristen was wandering the streets, poor girl. She must have been devastated—and desperate—to leave Noelle the way she did. I've been praying for her nonstop. I guess that's all we can really do."

"Yes. We should pray," Heather agreed, her voice breaking. "That's probably most important. Are you going to go see her?"

Shawn's gaze shot to hers. She looked back at him with a clear and determined focus he'd not seen before.

With faith.

"Yes. I'm planning on it."

"I thought you might. Where does that leave Noelle?"

"Right now? Nothing's changed. But when they take Kristen off the ventilator…well, she's not expected to make it."

"Then Noelle becomes a ward of the state."

"Yes."

"And then you can officially adopt her." Heather's voice built in volume along with her excitement. "You'll be able to give her a permanent home. Watch her grow up."

"That's just it. I'm not sure I'm going to be able to do that. The whole adoption thing—I've been thinking about it since the day Noelle entered my life, and I don't believe I'm cut out for it. I mean, I've wondered, you know, if I could be a father."

"What do you mean *if* you could be a father? Of course you could. You *are*. You're doing a great job with her. You've adapted to being a daddy a lot better than many of the natural fathers I know."

"I won't be enough for her. I grew up with only my dad watching over me. My mom, she—" He paused a beat. "She was out of the picture."

He didn't think it was necessary to add that his dad hadn't been much of a father. Heather had met the man and seen him in action. Kenneth O'Riley was an addict. His affection had been misplaced. Shawn had had nothing positive to draw on, no role model to grow up with.

And that was before even considering what Shawn himself had done—or failed to do, with David. Was it fair or safe to put Noelle into his care permanently?

"That must have been rough for you."

"I'm not looking for sympathy. It was what it was, and anyway, I deserved it. But even if there wasn't my lack of background in good family dynamics, I'd still worry that I'm not suited to parenthood. Today with Missy solidified it for me."

"I'm not following. You were wonderful with Missy."

"Maybe on the outside it seemed that way. Inside my gut was turning over like a combine and I thought my heart was going to beat out of my chest. What I mean is—well, I don't want to freak you out or anything, but what if her injury had been worse? What if I had made the wrong decision and she'd ended up in serious trouble? I didn't know whether we should have called the paramedics. I made assumptions when I probably shouldn't have. I'm no expert."

"It could have been worse," Heather acknowledged. "But it wasn't."

"And then I thought about Noelle, and what would happen if I adopted her. Something bad could happen to her and I would be powerless to stop it. And what if I made the wrong decision in the aftermath, and made things worse? I don't think I could handle it if something serious happened to one of these kids. Yours or mine."

"Do you hear yourself? That's an incredibly defeatist attitude—and coming from you. You've jumped off the bull before it's even out of the gate."

"I know it seems that way, but—"

"But what, Shawn? Help me to understand. I see your reluctance. Feel it, even. It's no small commitment you and I are considering, and our circumstances are far from ideal. It's only natural that we'd be scared of the responsibility. But at the end of the day, we aren't really in control of anything, are we? We don't know what is going to happen from moment to moment. Every breath is a gift. Some of what happens to us and to the kids is going to be bad. Yes. But some of it will be good. Really good."

She gestured to the sleeping infant. "Remember that amazing feeling you had the first time this sweet baby girl smiled at you? Well, there's more to come. She'll take her first step. It'll happen before you know it. And she'll say her first word, which I can tell you right now is going to be *Dada*."

He grimaced.

She smiled. "I don't know about you, but I accept the bad things that have happened to me. I hate that they happened, and I don't know that I'll ever completely recover. But those circumstances led me to having the heart to foster Jacob, Missy and Henry, and I wouldn't miss that for the world."

"You're thinking of adopting them?"

"More than thinking about it. I've started filling out the paperwork. These kids have become everything to me—and I can't imagine my life without them."

She absently rubbed her thumb over his. He thought she probably wasn't even aware of the motion, but for him, it was as if his skin had grown millions of little nerve endings, each one full of electricity.

"I know it's not the traditional way of things. Us being single parents depending on help from friends and the community rather than spouses and family. And I do want the best for them. But these kids…" Her voice broke. "If they didn't have me, they'd have no one."

"They deserve you. And you deserve them. Don't ever doubt yourself. I'm happy for you."

"But that's not how it's going to be for you and No-elle." It was a statement and not a question, and although he was certain Heather didn't mean it that way, it almost felt like an accusation. It was the dark shadow of his own guilt lingering over him.

"No, I don't think it is." He could barely get the words out from between his clenched teeth, but it was all he could do to control the emotions thundering through him like a herd of wild horses—anger, shame, guilt, longing.

"Is it because of your pastorate? Are you afraid you won't have enough quality time to spend with her? You know the people of Serendipity are going to gather around you and support you. Noelle will have more female role models than she knows what to do with. She'll have me."

"I know—you're right about that. And I appreciate that you'd be there for Noelle. But I just can't be responsible for another human life."

"What did you say? Another?"

"That's right." His gaze met Heather's and time stopped. He forgot to breathe. How quickly her curiosity would turn to aversion once he told her about David. But it was time for her to know the truth. "I was responsible for my brother's death."

Chapter Eight

"David." Heather hoped her voice didn't waver. Her mouth had suddenly gone as dry as the Texas plain in the middle of summer. It was all coming together. She could now make an educated guess as to who David was, and she wished she couldn't. She wasn't sure she wanted to hear Shawn's next words.

His face said it all.

"How do you know about David?"

"I don't, really. I heard you talking about him when you were speaking with your father, but I had no idea he was your brother until now. What happened?"

She clung to his hand. Whatever he was about to say, she wanted him to know that she still believed in him. Cared for him, more than she wanted to admit, and definitely more than she should.

"I was eight years old, just a little bit younger than Jacob, and David was six," he began, his lips quirking with anguish at the memory. "We were on vacation. At the beach off the coast of California. It's the only time I've ever been to the ocean. Before or since."

His eyes took on a faraway look, and she knew he

was seeing the moment as if it were happening again. She wanted to put her arms around him but feared that might be too much for him. She knew how it felt to need to get something out without drowning in emotion. So she did the best thing she knew how to do. She listened.

"We were playing in the waves. My brother, he had this Irish complexion. As ginger as they came. You know—bright red hair, fair skin, freckles. The sun was roasting him as red as a cherry. Mom forgot to bring the sunblock out to the sand, so she sent us back to the car to get the bottle."

He groaned and shook his head, his fingers biting into her palm.

"I was only distracted for a second. There was this sand crab on its back. I was watching it struggle to turn over."

"Sounds like something any eight-year-old boy would be doing." She tried not to tense, knowing he would feel her stiffen, but her pulse was beating rapidly as her mind filled in the blanks. Even without all the details, she knew what was coming. Her stomach lurched.

"I unlocked the car door and David crawled into the backseat, digging for the lotion in one of Mom's canvas swim bags. I threw the keys on the front seat, Heather. I don't know why I did that. How stupid could I be?"

His voice broke and his gaze broke away from hers. His struggle was evident in his rigid jaw and the tense lines of his neck.

She wanted to tell him it was all right, but of course it wasn't, and would never be. She was afraid if she spoke she'd only make things worse for him. So she waited, silent, for him to finish his tragic story.

"He was goofing around, pretending to drive. Pushing all of the buttons and pulling at the wheel. I yelled at him to knock it off but he wouldn't listen to me. I kept thinking of how Mom was going to be mad at me for letting David push the buttons, like maybe when she started the car and the windshield wipers would go on or something."

"It wasn't the wipers you had to worry about," she guessed.

"No," he growled, agonized and angry. "It wasn't the wipers. Or the air conditioner. Or anything else on the dashboard. He hit the door lock."

"Goodness," Heather said in a breathy voice, hardly able to absorb the incredibly tragic story. And to think Shawn had carried it around on his shoulders all these years. Her heart ached for him.

"It was so hot that day. I didn't know what to do. I didn't realize how quickly hyperthermia could set in."

"Of course you didn't. You were only eight."

"He begged me to help him." Shawn's face turned as white as his shirt. "He screamed for me. I didn't know what to do. I tried to talk him through it, to get him to unlock the door, but he didn't understand what I was trying to tell him. All of those buttons. I couldn't get him to push the one that unlocked the car."

Heather was so deep in her own imagination, picturing the event, that she nearly started out of her skin when Noelle let out a wail. Shawn immediately disengaged from Heather, jamming his fingers through his hair, clearly as dazed as she was. But she intensely missed his touch when he walked away from her.

Glad to have something constructive to do, she scooped Noelle into her arms, shushing her mildly and rocking her back and forth. She wished it was as easy to comfort Shawn in his grief.

"David was rapidly overheating," Shawn continued. "I didn't know all the ins and outs of what was happening to him, but I could see the changes in his face. I can still see him staring at me, terrified, his palms pressed against the glass. I was his big brother. He depended on me to save him, and I couldn't. Lord forgive me, but I couldn't."

"It's not your fault, Shawn. It was a terrible accident, to be sure, but you weren't the cause of it."

"No, maybe not directly, but I could have stopped it from happening. I should have been more careful. I should have held on to the keys and put them in my pocket instead of throwing them on the seat of the car. I shouldn't have gotten distracted with that stupid crab. I should have recognized how serious the circumstances were as soon as I realized he'd locked himself in the car. Maybe if I'd run for my mother straightaway things might have turned out differently. By the time I comprehended that I needed adult help, it was too late for David."

"Could the adults have done anything to save David if you'd brought them in earlier, do you think? Your mom, I mean? Did she have an extra set of keys? What could she have done in that short space of time that you didn't do?"

"I don't know. I don't know." He slumped back onto the pew and covered his face in his hands.

"Then how are you at fault? Explain that to me?" She hated to push him, but she needed him to see the truth—that it was a terrible accident for which no one was to blame.

"Do you know what David's death did to my mom? She's institutionalized, Heather. She completely lost her mind thanks to me. She needs psychotic meds and constant supervision just to make it through the day, even all these years later."

He scoffed in disgust. "You want to know why my dad drinks so much? Well, there you have it. Because of me."

The hard edge to Shawn's voice upset Noelle, who protested and squirmed in Heather's arms. The baby wasn't used to having her daddy use that tone of voice.

Heather thought Shawn was lost in his own world, but he immediately noticed how his reaction had affected his baby.

"I'm upsetting her." He held his hands out and Heather transferred Noelle into his arms. "I'm sorry, little darlin'. It's all right. I'm here, baby. Nothing's going to hurt you while I'm around."

Heather wished Shawn could see himself through her eyes. She wanted him to see what she saw—a man who had beat nearly insurmountable odds to become a pastor. He'd spent his life helping other people and didn't think twice about putting his own convenience on the line for the sake of the abandoned baby girl.

Most men would have passed Noelle off to the system. But not Shawn. He'd given the baby his very best. He gave everyone his very best. And it *was* enough, even if he couldn't see it right now.

"I still see David's face when I close my eyes," he continued in a soft, carefully modulated tone of voice.

"Forever reaching out to me. Calling for help. Not only in the daytime, either. I have nightmares."

"I know where you're coming from with the nightmares. Not a night goes by that I don't wake up drenched in a cold sweat."

Even in the midst of his own turmoil, Shawn's gaze flooded with compassion. "Because of what Adrian did to you."

"No," she countered in surprise. "I mean, I suppose I still think about that sometimes, but my nightmares are of the family Adrian hit with his car, the children I could not save."

Shawn grunted and shook his head. "You can't blame yourself for what happened. That was all on Adrian."

"But looking back on it, I feel like I could have stopped him from walking out the door in the first place. I should have tried harder. I knew he was drunk, and I knew he was going to climb behind the wheel. Hindsight is twenty-twenty. Like with you throwing the car keys on the seat instead of putting them in your pocket. We can't stop the regrets over the things we'd do differently if we had the chance to do it all again."

"But there aren't any do-overs in life."

"No. No, there aren't. There's no going back. But we *can* move forward, and that's where I think you've got it all wrong."

Shawn stiffened. The woman certainly didn't mince words. She didn't hesitate to point out that he was wallowing in his own misery. If he was being brutally honest with himself, he had been wallowing for years.

And Heather was calling him on it.

Resentment built for exactly one second before he took in Heather's demanding hazel-eyed gaze, challenging him to push his pride aside. His respect for her grew with every beat of his heart. Every time he was with her, he grew to appreciate her more.

Respect, appreciation and…something more. If things were different for him—for them—he might have pursued that line of thought. But circumstances being what they were, he consciously pushed his feelings aside. Heather had just said she was in the process of permanently adopting her three kids. She didn't need him and Noelle to further complicate her life.

"Would you answer a question honestly if I asked you to?" she asked.

"I'm always honest, but whether I answer or not depends on the question."

"The day we were in San Antonio. You were prepared to hand Noelle over to the state, and then suddenly you weren't. Why not? What changed?"

"That's two questions." Shawn laughed, trying to shake off the tension between his shoulder blades, but it remained, fierce and tight.

"I don't know. I guess I had it in my mind that she'd be going straight into a loving home."

"Mom, dad, two-point-five kids, a dog and a white picket fence?"

She got him. Again.

He quirked his lips. "Something like that."

"But?"

"But the reality was sobering. I hadn't realized that Noelle was probably going to end up in a state home, at least at first. I know after I got her tested that she was negative for drugs, but who knows what would have happened if she'd become a ward of the state. They might have labeled her a possible drug baby even before the testing, which would mean she'd never get a fair shot. Or—well, I don't know where she might have landed."

"And you still don't. That's the real point here, isn't it? You *didn't* know where she would end up and so you stepped up to make sure she had a soft, safe landing."

"I suppose. I didn't have a lot of time to think about it. It was more a reaction than an action."

Heather smiled, and Shawn's heart jumped into his throat. She stroked his arm where Noelle was cradled and sleeping, and then she shoved out a breath.

"Now, Pastor Shawn O'Riley, you have the opportunity to change that reaction into an action. A very important, thoughtful and loving action."

"That's what *you're* going to do, isn't it? Adopt your kids?"

"Yes, I'm going to try. When I originally agreed to foster my three, I was driven by a sense of guilt over the children Adrian killed, but now…"

"Now it's all about love." He could see it in her eyes, hear it in her voice. Even the rose-laced scent of spring in her perfume hinted at new beginnings.

He wanted that. He wanted what she had. She carried this deep, abiding assurance that she was doing the right thing. And it hadn't come easy to her. He knew how hard she'd worked for it, how much she'd overcome, and that only made him want it more.

He had every confidence that Heather would succeed with whatever she put her mind to, up to and including adopting her three children. He just didn't know if it was possible for him to do the same.

He settled Noelle back in her car seat and buckled her in. Heather reached for his elbow and turned him around.

"Promise me you'll think about it, at least," she whispered. "That you won't make any rash decisions without talking to me first."

He couldn't help but doubt himself, although seeing Heather's courage in the face of conflict somehow infused his spirit with a new energy. And when he looked into her eyes, he saw what she'd been trying to say all along but that his ears and his stubborn heart refused to hear.

She believed in him.

It was right in front of him—her faith, her strength, her hope for the future, and…

His entire being warmed with what he saw in her gaze. It wasn't that he'd never thought about this—he had. Many times. But she had so many emotional walls up, and rightly so, that he'd never considered it might actually come to pass.

He never thought… He never imagined that he might be the man to break down those barriers. He'd put up his own walls as well, but the second he looked into her eyes, he forgot what they were.

He didn't move. Didn't breathe, even. Didn't want to be the one to ruin this moment with a misplaced word or wrong movement.

She was the one who closed the distance between them. She stepped forward and reached for his hands, wrapping them around her waist, and then she laid a tentative hand on his jaw. It was the lightest of caresses, but he was a goner. Shawn leaned into her touch. His gaze dropped to her full lips. She was smiling as she tilted her head up to his.

"Heather, I—" he started, but she brushed a finger across his mouth, silencing him before he could continue.

"Please, Shawn. No words. Just please—kiss me."

His heart slammed into his ribs and it took every bit of his self-control for him not to do just that. There was nothing in the world he wanted so much as to taste her lips and drink in the strength and tenderness of this wonderful, magnificent woman.

But he had to be sure—that she was sure. He was caught up in the moment, and she might be, too. If she was, she might not really be ready, and she might not know how to put the brakes on. He couldn't begin to imagine everything she'd been through, and so he didn't know quite how to proceed.

"There are only two people in this room right now," she said, the timbre of her voice a low purr. She clutched his shirt and pulled him forward, closing whatever distance had been left between them. "Well, except for the baby, and she's asleep."

She chuckled against his lips. It was the laughter that relieved Shawn of any anxiety he was feeling.

He kissed her slowly but thoroughly, softly exploring every inch of her lips. He let her set the pace while he simply reveled in her—her touch, her taste, the smell of roses.

This woman was meant to be cherished, honored and loved by a man with his whole heart. She was all that was good and right in the world, and the fact that she had chosen him, at least for today, that it was *his* arms she'd allowed to shelter her, made him feel honored and blessed, as well.

And when she sighed and deepened the kiss, time stood still.

Chapter Nine

Heather opened the hatch to her silver SUV and let Will Davenport handle loading her groceries so she could concentrate on getting the children buckled into their seats. Sam's Grocery was located on the corner of Main Street with a designated lot in the back for the customers to park. And fortunately for Heather, it also provided a handsome ex-military man who was married to the owner and guaranteed her customers got first-class service.

Getting personalized assistance was one of the perks of small-town Serendipity that Heather liked and appreciated—the special service at Sam's Grocery, for example, where her groceries were not only bagged for her but toted to the car, making shopping that much less of a hassle, especially when she had the children with her.

"Thank you so much, Will," she said out the window when he tapped her hood in the universal sign for "good to go."

"My pleasure, Heather. We'll see you next week."

Heather glanced at her reflection in the rearview

mirror and smiled softly. Little did Will and his wife, Samantha, know they would be seeing her sooner than that. She was planning to shock everyone—herself most of all—when she attended church on Sunday morning.

It was high time her children started Sunday school, especially since she now intended for them to stay in Serendipity on a permanent basis. It was her new opinion that every child should be brought up in a church—as long as it was the kind of church pastored by a man like Shawn O'Riley.

She touched her lips, remembering the tender way he'd kissed her. In the chapel, of all places—which might have been shocking were it not so sweet. They'd been interrupted by Noelle's fussing before long, anyway.

Her heart flared to life every time she thought about his lips on hers—thoughts that had occurred with striking regularity in the two days since she'd last seen him. But doubt quickly extinguished the flames.

When she'd kissed Shawn, she'd been absolutely, 100 percent certain of what she was doing. She would not have approached him otherwise. In the years since her divorce, she hadn't had the least bit of desire to be held by a man, much less be kissed by anyone. If anything, she was revolted by the mere thought of it. And yet with Shawn it was different.

With him, everything was different.

She was a little embarrassed at the enthusiasm with which she'd initiated that particular string of events. It was so...*forward*. Especially for her.

And it wasn't as if she'd missed the fact that he'd hesitated.

More than once.

The more often she replayed the scene in her mind, the clearer it became. He'd verbally tried to stop her, or at least slow her down, but she hadn't even let him speak. She'd quite literally thrown herself at him, taking his arms and placing them around her waist. He hadn't fought it, but she wasn't sure he would have taken that step on his own.

She'd so desperately wanted to feel his strength that she'd given no thought to the awkward position she'd placed him in—or the awkwardness she herself would face in the aftermath. Her cheeks heated with shame even thinking about it.

What must he think of her?

She didn't know for certain, but it didn't take a rocket scientist to speculate on the issue. He hadn't called her in two days. He was probably avoiding her.

Granted, she hadn't tried to get in touch with him, either, but it wasn't because she didn't want to see him. Quite the opposite, in fact.

There was no going back for her. All she wanted in the world was to step right back into the warmth and safety of his strong arms and feel the tenderness of his embrace. But she'd already made a fool of herself once. She was in no hurry to repeat the humiliating ordeal.

The confidence that had propelled her into Shawn's arms had faded quickly once the kiss was over, replaced by her usual insecurities. Was she fooling herself to believe she and Shawn might have a future together? Was it even fair of her to ask him to take her on, given his lack of confidence in his parenting ability and her commitment to her children?

Better to give them both some room. Let the air cool between them.

"Mama, you drive?" Henry asked from the backseat.

Heather laughed. "I suppose I ought to be driving, since we're sitting here in the car and all. We'd best get home and unload these groceries."

She turned the key in the ignition and took another quick glance in the rearview mirror before backing out of her parking space.

She didn't know why she noticed the man parked at the far end of the lot, leaning on a nondescript white sedan.

A subtle movement, perhaps? Leftover survival instinct?

Despite his shaggy hair and unkempt beard, Heather immediately recognized him. Cold blue eyes turned her stomach. Lightning flashed before her eyes, thunder rumbled in her chest and her breath twisted as if caught up by gale-force winds.

"Oh, God, save us," she whispered, her words very much a prayer. She ducked out of sight before she'd given it a second thought.

Adrian.

What was he doing in Serendipity? He was supposed to be in jail.

Had he seen her? Recognized her? How had he found her? A lucky guess that she'd gone back to her hometown?

He'd probably seen her. He'd appeared to be looking right at her when she'd spotted him.

What to do? What to do?

The children. She'd inadvertently put them in danger. If they were with her, Adrian could harm them.

She had a permanent restraining order against him. Technically, he wasn't legally allowed to get as close to her as Sam's small parking lot afforded. But a restraining order was nothing more than a piece of paper when it came to an angry, drunken man. Adrian had never been much for following the law even before he'd gone to prison, and she had no reason to believe he'd do so now.

She locked the doors and scrambled to locate the cell phone in her purse, all without lifting her head above the height of the dash.

"Kids, we're going to play a little game right now," she said, trying to keep her voice calm and steady. She closed her hand around the phone and hiccuped in relief. "Everyone duck down in your seat until I say 'peekaboo.'"

"What's wrong?" Jacob asked, ever astute and sounding slightly offended. He was too old to be playing peekaboo with his mother.

"Please, Jacob, just do as I say. I'll explain when I can."

Her breath lodged in her throat and her heart hammered as she dialed 911 and waited for the operator to pick up.

What if Adrian approached the vehicle? How would she keep the kids safe? She didn't dare even spare a backward glance to see if he was coming toward her. If somehow by the grace of God he hadn't already seen her, she didn't want to accidentally tip him off.

"What is the nature of your emergency?"

"I think I'm being followed. My ex-husband is out of prison. I have a permanent restraining order against him but I don't feel safe."

"What is your location?"

"Sam's Grocery. The parking lot. I'm in a silver SUV. I have my three children with me. Please hurry."

"A unit has already been dispatched. ETA less than a minute."

Another reason to be grateful for small towns. But a lot could happen in a minute.

"Mom?" Jacob spoke again. "Who is following us? Did you just call the cops?"

"Yes, honey, and they are on their way to help us. I'll explain it all to you, I promise, but right now we need to stay low and wait for the police to get here."

She jumped when someone rapped on the driver's-side window but was relieved to see Slade McKenna nodding at her. She'd never been happier to see red and blue flashing lights.

She rolled the window down a crack. "Slade. Thank you for coming so fast."

"Where did you see your ex-husband?" Slade cut straight to the chase with no formalities.

"He's directly behind me, at the far end of the lot. Blond hair. Beard. He's driving a white sedan, although he was out of the vehicle when I saw him."

Slade glanced in the direction she indicated and frowned. "Keep your doors locked and your head down. Stay right where you are until I return."

Tension crackled through the air as Heather counted every heartbeat. Her own breath sounded painfully loud. In what seemed like hours later but was probably only a matter of minutes, Slade returned and once more tapped on her window.

He pressed his lips together before speaking. "I'm sorry, Heather, but there's no sign of him."

"What? No," she disputed, regaining her seat and turning to look over her shoulder. "He's right—"

But the space where the white sedan had been parked was empty. She scanned the lot, hoping to point him out so the police officer could arrest him, but Slade was correct.

Adrian was gone.

Had she been seeing things? The Adrian she knew had always taken great pride in his clean-cut appearance. It was one of the ways he fooled everyone. But the man she had seen, unkempt and bedraggled, had looked every bit the criminal he was, and for that reason was that much more intimidating.

No, she wasn't mistaken. She'd seen him. And if he'd seen her, then not only her safety but the safety of her children was at stake. How could she ever possibly have thought of adopting these precious children and putting them in danger?

"I didn't imagine him." She couldn't have.

"No, of course not, Heather. I totally believe you. He was here. I've radioed the station and put out an APB on the guy. He's not going to get very far. We've got all our eyes watching for him. And we have a patrol car scheduled to run down your block on an expedited basis, okay?"

That Slade believed her—that the *police* believed her—gave her a measure of comfort but no real confidence. Adrian was a smart man. If he wanted to confront her, he'd find a way to do it. He'd get around the police somehow.

"I'm sorry I couldn't nab the guy for you today. Is there anything else I can do for you? Just name it."

"I appreciate your help, Slade, and there's no need

to apologize. You got here as fast as you could." Other than assigning her a 24/7 police escort, which was completely beyond the scope of Serendipity's police department, there was little Slade could do.

Or maybe there *was* something. "There is one thing. Is there any way for you to find out when and why he was released from prison? I thought he still had at least a few more years to serve before he'd be eligible for parole, which is why I was doubly shocked to spot him here."

"Where was he imprisoned?"

"Colorado."

"I'll get that information to you right away. We'll pick him up as soon as we see him and get him locked back up again. He's already violated your restraining order, and if he's out of a prison in Colorado, it's a good bet he's broken his parole."

If they caught up with him. *If* they could catch him. Those were pretty big *ifs*.

Adrian had contested their divorce when she'd filed, but there was little he could do about it from prison. She hadn't wanted anything from him and she hadn't taken anything other than her clothes and what was left of her dignity.

He was frightening when he was angry. And if he was here—in violation of his parole and his restraining order—then he was angry.

But she wasn't the same woman Adrian had intimidated for all those years. She had found a renewed sense of strength, hope and faith, thanks in large part to her relationship with Shawn.

All the angst and awkwardness she'd been feeling earlier over their kiss dissolved with the gravity of these new circumstances. She had some serious decisions to make about her life, and there was one person in this world who'd had a real glimpse of the depths of her heart, one man who would truly understand what Adrian's abrupt arrival in her life meant for her and the children.

Already more than halfway home, she turned her car around and headed for Shawn's ranch.

Shawn had picked up his phone to call Heather at least a dozen times in the two days since they'd had their *moment* and he'd replaced the phone without actually making the call every time.

He'd never been in this position before. He'd never expected he would come to feel the way he did about Heather, and he didn't want to scare her off with the intensity of his emotions. And the worst of it was that he wasn't sure he could mask how he felt. And even if he could, he still wasn't certain he would be able to step up and be the man Heather needed him to be.

He did what he always did when he needed to think—went out to the barn to tend the animals. He might not talk out loud to them the way Heather had done in her youth, but there was a certain amount of comfort in the routine of pitching hay and even in mucking the stalls. Noelle seemed to like being strapped to his chest and contentedly watched what he was doing.

At least he was learning how to please one of the women in his life.

How was he supposed to hide his feelings for Heather when he wanted to shout them from the mountaintop? If he had his way, he'd scoop her clear off her feet, swing her around and laugh and hug and sing.

Well, okay, maybe not sing. He didn't want to send her off screaming with her hands over her ears.

Heather had done such a number on him that he felt as if he were floating. Walking on clouds. Who knew that all those overly romanticized stories about falling in love were actually true?

Kissing Heather—now that was a game changer.

For him, at least.

For her? He couldn't begin to guess.

She'd taken his hand and pulled him through his past, helped him to finally acknowledge all that had happened. Hopefully he would finally be able to start working through it. The problem was, he didn't know how to perceive the kiss that had followed that wonderful talk. She was such a generous and compassionate woman. Was that why she'd kissed him? Had she just so completely empathized with his situation that she'd got caught up in that whirlwind?

She'd certainly given him enough food for thought where permanently adopting Noelle was concerned—and she'd made him promise not to make any rash decisions. Nothing compared to a good woman challenging a man to step up and face adversity head-on. He was definitely thinking about it now, opening his mind to the possibilities of the future.

All the possibilities. He just didn't quite know what his life would look like yet. He felt as if he were on the verge of a discovery that hovered just out of his reach. There were blank spaces he had yet to fill in.

The sound of car tires crunching on the gravel in his driveway not only surprised him, but also gave him a moment's hesitation. He wasn't expecting anyone, and the last time he'd had an unanticipated visitor, it had been his father.

Just what he didn't want to deal with today.

Steeling himself for the worst, he tossed one last pitchfork of hay into the nearest horse's stall, shifted Noelle to fit more firmly against his chest, adjusted his hat lower on his brow and exited the barn. If it was his dad, it was better just to get the confrontation over with.

But it wasn't his father's beat-up vehicle that had pulled up in front of his house. It was Heather's SUV, and she had all her kids with her.

He didn't care that she'd come unannounced. In fact, he was relieved. If she was here then she wanted to see him. And if she wanted to see him…

A smile split his face and his pulse burst to life, and he knew exactly why. He was seeing his favorite people. Heather and her children made his life here on the ranch complete.

He'd been trying to fill in the blanks in his life, but until he saw Heather, he hadn't realized that the missing pieces of the puzzle were the people who'd come to mean more to him than anything in the world.

He rushed forward to open the door for Heather, trying not to give away the gymnastic backflips his heart was currently performing. He wanted to tell her everything he'd learned about himself—and how he felt about her—but this wasn't the right time or place. They had their little tribe with them right now, and that was what was important.

The right time would come. He just knew it.

His smile widened even more, if that were possible.

His whole world was opening up. It was as if the day had suddenly dawned on him and he could see everything around him, crystal-clear and sparkling.

Until he saw Heather's face.

She wasn't smiling. Her eyes were glassy and red. Her complexion had faded to a pasty white. And she was visibly shaking.

The ground dropped from under him as he reached out his arms to steady her. "Heather, honey, what's wrong?"

Her lips thinned and she shook her head. "Not here."

The children. Of course. Whatever was bothering her, she didn't want to share it with the kids around to hear.

He opened the back door and unbuckled Henry while Heather used the opposite door for Jacob and Missy. With his heart in his throat, Shawn herded the three out to the back to play with Queenie, and then he settled Noelle in her crib. Thankfully, she was sound asleep and probably wouldn't waken from her nap for a while.

He wasn't sure he wanted to hear what Heather had to say. Both grief and determination were evident in her gaze, and she hadn't yet said a word.

This was serious.

He joined her in the kitchen and poured each of them a cup of coffee, and then slid onto the chair opposite her. Neither one of them spoke, and tension was thick in the air between them.

She was unhappy. It sliced his heart into tiny pieces to see her this way. Especially if he was the cause of it.

Maybe she was trying to figure out a way to let him

down easy. Had she spent the past two days wondering how to gently tell him to take a hike?

He couldn't stand to see her this way. He wanted to reach out to her, to thread his fingers with hers, but he was afraid that would be exactly the wrong thing to do in these circumstances—whatever they were.

He should just make it easy for her.

"About the other day…" he started, then stopped and tried to clear the huskiness from his throat. How did a man apologize for a moment that he considered one of the best in his life?

"I saw Adrian."

Her declaration hung in the air for a beat and then plunged into his lungs and gutted his rib cage.

"What did you say?" He must have heard her wrong. "I thought Adrian was in prison—for a long time yet to come."

"Yes, well, evidently not." Her voice was laced with sarcasm, anxiety and, above all, anger.

"Tell me." Shawn didn't think twice about reaching across the table and taking her hand. Not now. Her fingers clung to his like a lifeline.

She related the story of how she'd seen Adrian in the parking lot of Sam's Grocery. How he'd been staring straight at her but hadn't approached. How she'd called the police but the man had disappeared.

How she knew he'd be back.

Shawn's determination to protect her grew with every word she spoke. If this Adrian guy thought he was going to stalk Heather or intimidate her—or worse—he had another think coming.

Shawn wasn't about to let Adrian anywhere near the woman he loved.

"Why do you think he's here?" Cold settled into Shawn's gut and the muscles across his shoulders tightened. With the amount of adrenaline pumping through him, he hoped she wouldn't feel him quiver.

"Honestly, I have no idea. I didn't think he'd be out of prison so soon. It's in his best interest to stay as far away from me as possible."

"You'd think."

"But he's not. Which means he's got a real problem with me. Who knows what a man in that state of mind might do? He's already broken his permanent restraining order, and probably violated his parole, as well. I requested advanced warning for his parole hearings, but somehow I didn't receive that notice. Maybe there was a glitch in the prison system. And the most frightening part of this whole experience was that I had the kids with me in the car. To think that their being with me might put them in any danger— It makes me sick to my stomach."

She wasn't the only one feeling that way. Shawn's gut was roiling.

"What are the police doing about it?"

"Everything they can. Slade said they put out an APB on him, and I was able to give them quite a bit of information as to what they're looking for. They're scheduling a patrol car to run by my house on a regular basis. If they see him and pick him up, he's going straight back to jail."

"That's not good enough." Shawn shook his head vehemently. "You and the kids aren't safe as long as that guy is lurking around."

"No," she agreed. "We'll never really be safe. Not ever. I thought after the divorce I wouldn't have to see

Adrian again, but now I realize I'll never be rid of him. Even if they send him back to prison, he'll eventually get out again. Everything has changed now."

For the worse.

Shawn wasn't about to let Heather lose everything she'd worked so hard to gain.

"I can't have someone watching over me 24/7, so I'm really out of options. I feel like I ought to hold off on signing those adoption papers." Her hazel eyes flooded with tears. "He's going to be a permanent nightmare for me."

Adrian's threat would haunt her for the rest of her life.

Shawn couldn't let that happen.

"There's another way."

The revelation didn't dawn on Shawn—it knocked him over. The solution was simple. Right before his eyes.

"Yeah? What's that?" She sounded unconvinced, but he supposed he would, too, if he were in her position.

"Marry me."

"What?" She practically choked on the word.

"Marry me," he said again, emphasizing each syllable.

She made a sound halfway between a chuckle and a sob. "Nice try, mister. Thank you for your attempt to lighten the mood."

Lighten the mood? Did he not look serious?

She wasn't getting it. For a man who communicated for a living, he was doing a poor job of it. Marrying him would fix everything. He had to make her see that.

He stood and moved around the table without releasing her hand. He didn't want anything between them.

Not now. He wanted to be near her, to touch her and make her believe. He took a seat in the chair next to her and placed her palm on his chest, over his heart.

"I'm not joking, Heather. Think about it. It makes sense for us."

"You think?"

"You and the kids would be able to stay with me, where I could watch over you all. You wouldn't be alone at night or vulnerable to an ex-husband who doesn't know when to quit. You wouldn't have to worry anymore. Not now. Not ever."

She sniffed and shook her head. "I've got to admit you make it sound tempting. But I didn't come here this afternoon expecting a marriage proposal."

Shawn wondered if she could feel his heart slamming in a mad rhythm against her palm. The proposal was more than him protecting her from Adrian. So much more.

"Think about the children."

"I *am* thinking about the children."

He'd made her mad. Why was she mad?

"We can be a family. All six of us, and eventually we can have more of our own, if you'd like, or even keep adopting. The kids love the ranch. They'll be able to grow up here, learn all about raising animals and taking care of the land. It makes sense for us."

She pulled her hand away and dragged it down her face. He'd never seen her look so bone weary. It pulled at him.

"Can I think about it before giving you my answer?"

"Of course. I'm not trying to pressure you. All I'm asking is for due consideration that you'll take me seriously."

"You've got that. I promise."

"I've got pastor friends in the area. We should have no problem finding someone to hitch us up on short notice."

"Short notice?"

"The sooner the better, don't you think? With Adrian in town, who knows what will happen. We don't want him catching up with you when you're alone."

Way to not pressure her, you jerk.

Shawn wanted to kick himself. If he was trying to scare her off, he was doing a mighty fine job of it. Reminding her that Adrian was a present threat instead of assuring her that he would protect her and the kids.

"Do you have someplace you can stay until we get this sorted out? A friend or neighbor?"

She stood and moved to the coffeepot, pouring herself a fresh cup and then checking out the window on the children before returning to the table. She leaned her hip against the edge of the wood and crossed her free arm over her waist instead of returning to her seat.

"I don't want to impose on anyone like that," she said. "You know how much of a handful the kids can be. Besides, I need to face this." She sounded as if she was trying to convince herself. "I'm not a victim any longer, and it's high time I stopped acting like one."

Was that a *no*?

Shawn's heart twisted as he waited for her to elaborate. Surely she wasn't turning him down, not without taking more time to think about it.

Please. Not a *no*.

"I'm going home."

That was even worse. "Think about what you're saying. It's not safe there. He probably knows where you live." She might not be ready now—or ever—to make a commitment to him, but he wasn't going to step aside and let her walk right into the vortex of danger.

"I'm not an idiot."

"I didn't think you were."

"I'll take every precaution," she assured him. "I'll keep the doors locked and my phone on me. And I'll call the police the moment I see him. Adrian is a mean drunk, but he's only as intimidating as I let him be. He's used to a shell of a woman who won't fight back. I think he's going to be surprised to find that's not who I am anymore."

"He's been in prison. Who knows what kind of man he is now? He could be truly dangerous, Heather. Worse than he was."

"You're right. I don't know what kind of man he is now. But if I run from this, I will be running my whole life. Don't you understand? I can't do this anymore."

"If he shows up at your house?"

"I'll call the police and he'll be arrested. At least then I'll be able to rest easy again—for a while, anyway."

Shawn thought it was a bad plan. The most awful one he'd ever heard, in fact. For starters, he wasn't part of it. And he could count on two hands the number of things that had the potential to go wrong.

And yet—it seemed that Heather had turned a corner. Her weariness and the desperation she'd worn like a cloak for as long as he'd known her had disappeared.

Replaced by determination.

Strength.

Belief in herself.

How could he take that away from her?

She hadn't come here to have him solve all her problems. She'd come to regroup and solve her own. And she had.

He loved her enough to let her see this through, but he couldn't completely let go. He had to do all he could to protect her.

"My number is on speed dial, right?"

She smiled softly. "Number one."

"Good. Don't be afraid to use it. For any reason. Day or night. Whatever you need, I'm your man."

"Thank you for that." She blushed, making her countenance even more lovely.

His pulse heightened, and he wanted to take her in his arms and kiss her senseless, prove he meant every word he said in his proposal. Convince her she really should be with him. It was all he could do to hold himself in check when she brushed the back of her hand against his cheek.

"I'm going to round up the children. It's time for us to go home."

"Heather?" His arm snaked out to capture hers. She turned, an unreadable look on her face.

"Yes?"

"I just wanted you to know…my offer still stands."

Chapter Ten

My offer still stands.

Heather looked in on her sleeping children, tucking their blankets up under their chins and brushing a soft kiss on each of their precious brows. She triple-checked the locks on all the doors and windows and then settled down on the couch with a cup of tea, drawing her legs up beneath her.

Had Shawn really offered to marry her? She couldn't help but feel she'd somehow coerced him into making such a rash proposition. She hesitated even to call it a proposal. Heather scoffed and shook her head.

Adrian hadn't only muddled her life and potentially put her children in danger, but now he was messing with Shawn's head.

Shawn O'Riley didn't deserve to be a part of this drama, and yet in typical Shawn fashion, he'd willingly thrown himself right into the middle of the storm to help her.

He had already changed his whole life around for the sake of little Noelle—and all without a single complaint, which just magnified his goodness and strength.

And now he was ready to embrace her and her children and make them a permanent part of his life for no reason other than to keep them safe. Even though they'd never talked about it, she knew Shawn well enough to know he took marriage seriously. Shawn was a forever kind of guy.

But marriage to her? How could he even imagine it? Of course he wouldn't think of her children as a burden, as she expected most men would. He might worry that he wasn't good enough for them, but he'd never consider them a problem.

But dealing with an abusive and criminal ex-husband and stalker who posed a certain threat to their lives? No one would want to take on that kind of responsibility.

No one but Shawn.

She'd really believed he was joking when he'd first brought up the subject of marriage. A pastor marrying the local divorcée. Yeah—*no*. They would be the talk of the town, and not in a good way. She couldn't imagine how his congregation might respond to him allying himself to her in such a serious and irrevocable way.

Impossible. Outrageous.

But the fact remained that he *had* asked her to marry him—in earnest—and he'd reiterated that offer before she'd left.

He'd even run down a thorough and practical list of reasons why their getting married was a good idea. To protect her from Adrian. To be able to formally adopt all their children. To create a more stable home environment for them.

If she married Shawn and moved to his ranch, the children would all have a mom, the best dad ever, a yard with a fence—split-rail and not white picket, but a fence—*and* a dog. Oh, and however many other animals Shawn happened to be keeping. She'd seen pigs, goats, horses, cats and chickens.

The picture-perfect family.

She choked on her tea.

Marrying Shawn would be anything but picture-perfect. He had enumerated every potential benefit of their possible *collaboration*—except for one, and in Heather's mind it was the most important aspect of all.

Shawn had said nothing about love.

Glaring red flag there. Heather had never imagined she would be in the position of receiving a marriage proposal ever again in her life—nor did she believe she'd ever want one. But a marriage without love?

She'd already been there, and with disastrous results.

Not that there was any comparison. Adrian was all about himself and his own needs and desires. He thrived on hurting people. Shawn never thought twice about willingly sacrificing his own convenience for the good of another person. The proposal itself was just further proof of that.

But marriage?

That was asking too much of him. She couldn't allow him to sacrifice *that* much for her, no matter how tempting it sounded. No matter that his idea—when viewed purely pragmatically—had merit to it.

She couldn't look at marrying Shawn as anything more than a practical consideration even if she wanted to.

The truth dawned on her with such clarity that she couldn't believe she hadn't seen it until now. Her fingers were shaking so fiercely that she was rattling her teacup and had to set it on the table before she spilled the hot liquid on her lap. She placed one palm against her racing heart and the other over her lips.

She couldn't marry Shawn—not because there was no love between them, but because there *was*.

She was in love with Shawn.

When had it happened? Somewhere along the way Shawn had stealthily tripped the switch that opened her heart to trusting again—feeling again. She didn't just appreciate Shawn for all the things he'd done for her—she had fallen in love with him.

Wow. How had she not seen this one coming?

She'd been preoccupied with Adrian, that was how. She still was—sitting here in her living room, half afraid to sleep for fear Adrian would try to break into the house after dark. Assuming he knew where she lived and that he would slink around in the dark. Adrian's usual MO was to face up to situations right in the light of day and charm his way through them. But prison could have changed him, and she had no way of knowing for sure.

She wouldn't be worried if Shawn were here. His strong arms and warm embrace were her safe spot.

She suddenly wanted to accept his offer of marriage more than anything in the world. Which was, of course, why she couldn't.

A platonic relationship wasn't ideal, and it certainly wasn't anything she'd ever seen in modern America, but it could work. Might work. Maybe—if they were both committed to adopting and raising their children with only feelings of friendship and respect between them.

But living with the man and loving him when he didn't return the sentiment? That was just plain crazy.

Rap. Rap. Rap.

Heather jolted to instant alertness, her heartbeat pummeling her rib cage as adrenaline surged through her.

Was someone at the door?

No, it wasn't the door. At least not the front door.

She must have drifted off daydreaming about Shawn—or rather, mulling over the reasons the two of them could never be together.

What time was it?

She fished the cell phone out of her pocket, but before she could check it, she heard the noise again.

Rap. Rap. Rap.

It definitely wasn't the front door. It sounded like the sliding glass door in the back through the kitchen.

Adrian.

He was here. It was time to end this nightmare.

She dialed the police with shaky hands. As she waited for the emergency operator, she jogged down to the end of the hallway where the kids' rooms were located.

She spoke in quiet tones as she explained the situation to the emergency operator and rattled off her address.

"Please hurry," she ended, hoping she didn't sound as frantic as she felt.

She slipped into Missy's room and scooped the sleeping girl into her arms and then brought her into Jacob and Henry's room and deposited her in bed next to Henry.

"Jacob, honey, wake up." She shook her elder son's shoulder.

"Mama?" he asked sleepily. "What's wrong?"

"That bad man we talked about? He's here. Mama needs to go talk to him. The police are on their way. I want you to watch over your brother and sister. Stay in this room and lock the door when I leave. Don't open it for anyone but me. Do you understand?"

Jacob's eyes went wide but he squared his shoulders and nodded.

"Yes, Mama. I'll take care of them."

"I know you will, my brave boy." She took his face in her hands and kissed his cheek. "It's going to be okay, honey. The police are going to get this guy and put him back in jail so he can't bother us anymore."

She hoped—prayed—that the words were true.

Please, Lord. Watch over the little ones.

She should have listened to Shawn when he'd suggested she not return to her house, or at least she should have found somewhere else for the kids to stay. But she really hadn't believed Adrian would come here. Not in the middle of the night, anyway.

She wouldn't let the regrets take over. The truth was, she was tired of running away. She wanted to confront him and get it over with. If he realized she wasn't afraid of him anymore, he would no longer have any power over her. That moment couldn't come soon enough.

She pressed her cell phone into Jacob's hand. "I've already called the police, but I want you to hang on to this, just in case. Dial 911 for an emergency, all right?"

"Mama?" Jacob's voice was shaky and his lower lip quivered. Heather's heart turned over.

"We're going to be fine, honey." They were. They *were*. She was going to make it happen.

She closed the door and waited until she heard Jacob turn the lock. She wished she believed her own words—that she knew for sure it would be okay. But she didn't know. Only God knew.

She concentrated on evening out her breathing. It wouldn't help for her to hyperventilate and pass out in front of Adrian. He needed to see her at her best so he'd know for certain that she wasn't afraid of him.

She'd come to Serendipity to start a new life, and her nightmare had followed her here.

It was time to put that nightmare to rest once and for all.

She shoved out a breath and turned the corner from the bright living room to the darkened kitchen. She pressed forward, hugging the wall, trying to see outside the glass door without giving her position away. There was no more than a sliver of pale moonlight, just enough to cast ominous shadows across the lawn. She strained her ears to hear anything out of place, but all she could hear was her own breath, which sounded incredibly loud against the silence.

She frantically filtered through her options. Adrian was lurking somewhere around her house. She was fairly certain he'd been trying to open the doors rather than knocking on them, which meant he was attempting to sneak into her house under the cover of darkness rather than announcing himself in the daylight.

But where was he now?

Even if she knew his location, she had no clue what her next move should be.

She wished she'd thought to borrow Queenie from

Shawn for a couple days. Having a dog around the house would be a detriment to stalkers.

The police couldn't possibly be far off. She just needed to stay quiet until they arrived and pray that the younger children didn't wake up. They would be so frightened. Poor Jacob had put on such a brave face for the sake of his foster siblings, but she knew he was hunkered down in the bedroom scared half out of his wits.

She despised Adrian for that—for harming her children.

"Heather!"

Adrian's voice sounded as if it was coming from the vicinity of the kitchen window, which she confirmed when he banged his fist against the glass.

"Heather. I know you're in there. I can see you."

Her hair stood on end and alarm skittered like an icy finger down her spine. She struggled to keep hold of her shredding composure.

He yelled and slammed his fist into the glass once again, hard enough to make the pane rattle. That had to hurt his hand, but he didn't flinch. Which meant he'd been drinking. If he kept it up, he'd not only break the window, but he'd wake up the children for sure.

She'd given her cell phone to Jacob, so she couldn't check the time. How long had it been since she'd called the police? Surely they should be here by now. Hadn't they said they were going to keep a cruiser running by her house on a regular basis? Even if they weren't in the neighborhood at the moment, this was a small town. How long could it take?

Where were they?

Adrian had seen her, so there was no sense hiding any longer. She stepped out from behind the wall and looked straight into the window over the sink, glaring at the man who'd single-handedly made her life so miserable.

The face looking back at her through the cloudy, opaque glass reminded her of a dark, fairy-tale version of the evil queen's magic mirror. Adrian's sunken eyes burned into her, his scowl black and menacing. His wild hair and beard combined together to form something truly ghastly.

She should have been terrified. There was a time when she would have been. And though she was not foolish enough to discount the wild-eyed, not-quite-sane reflection in his countenance, she was not afraid.

Not of him. Not anymore.

He reached up to pound his fist into the window again and she didn't even hesitate. He was going to wake up her children, and then she was going to get really angry.

Adrian wasn't here about the children. He wanted her—and he was going to get her. Without considering where her actions would lead, she marched to the sliding door, flipped the lock, flung it wide and stepped through, closing it tightly behind her.

"You want to see me? Well, here I am. What is it you have to say to me?"

She'd heard of people's jaws dropping in surprise, but she'd never literally seen it. Not until now. Adrian was staring at her as if she'd sprouted wings.

"Well?" she challenged, instinctively going on the offensive. "I'm waiting. What are you doing here?"

He stood gaping for another beat before he regained his senses. Then his brows lowered over cold blue eyes.

"No," he countered, his voice low and menacing.

He craved fear almost as much as booze, and he was searching for it now. Trying to provoke her. "The real question is what *you* are doing here. Did you really think you could just walk away from me, Heather?"

She had. And she'd been mistaken in that. She couldn't hide from her past. He was staring her right in the face. Icy dread curled around her stomach but she ignored it.

"We're divorced, Adrian. And I have a permanent restraining order against you." She strained her ears for the sound of sirens but heard nothing.

Adrian sneered. "You think a piece of paper is going to stop me, you little piece of trash?"

Heather braced herself. She'd once believed all the names he'd called her. She hadn't seen her true worth until she'd viewed herself through another's eyes. Shawn's eyes. He saw her as God saw her. Her chin rose.

Adrian couldn't take that away from her no matter what he did, but she suspected he was going to try.

He stepped forward, looming over her, using his height to try to intimidate her. She stood tall and maintained eye contact with him. Inside she was quivering, but outside she stood strong.

"You're going to come home with me. Now."

She scoffed. "Not in this lifetime."

Where were the police? What was taking them so long?

The fact that she'd talked back to him appeared to fluster him.

"I'm going to teach you a lesson you are never going to forget," he promised, his voice rising with the excitement of hurting her. He raised his hand to slap her.

"I wouldn't count on that." Shawn stepped out of the shadows, large and aggressive, the brim of his straw cowboy hat pulled low over his eyes. If Adrian was intimidating, Shawn was doubly so.

Adrian took a surprised step backward and pulled his fists up in a defensive stance against Shawn.

Heather had never been so happy to see anyone in her entire life. Not even the police could have topped the relief she felt at the appearance of this cowboy preacher.

"I don't know who you are, mister, but this isn't any of your business."

"I'm making it my business." Heather had never heard Shawn's voice so cold and hard.

"You'd poach on another man's turf?" Adrian asked snidely.

Heather's stomach lurched. That was how Adrian had always seen her. As his property and nothing more.

"I happen to love this woman," Shawn informed Adrian coldly. "I've asked her to be my wife, and will be grateful until the day I die if she accepts me."

"You can't do that," Adrian growled. "I'm her man."

"You're not a man." Heather's throat closed around the words, nearly choking her. "You never have been."

"Shut up," Adrian spat.

"You speak to her like that again and you won't be standing on your feet," Shawn warned. His voice was low and surprisingly steady, but there was no doubt he meant what he said.

"I can speak to her any way I please. She's my *wife*."

"I'm not your wife," Heather countered, her voice high and strained. "I haven't been for years. You may not want to accept it, but the state does. Get out of my life."

"I told you to shut your trap," Adrian yelled, raising his hand to her once more.

Shawn's fist came out of nowhere, connecting with Adrian's jaw with a satisfying crack. Adrian grunted and went down. Out cold.

Shawn shook his fingers out and shrugged down at the man on the ground. One side of his mouth curled up and he winked at Heather. "I warned him."

"Yes, you did." Heather started giggling and couldn't stop, so great was her relief.

He opened his arms to her and she sagged into him, clutching his shirt, nestling as close to him as she was able. He was so strong. Safe. Steady. She wished she could stay forever in his embrace, listening to the rhythm of his heart, but sirens broke through the silence, and Adrian groaned at their feet.

The police had finally arrived, and Adrian was waking up.

Heather excused herself to check on the kids while Shawn saw Adrian handcuffed and shoved into the back of Slade McKenna's patrol car.

"Sorry we were late to the party," Slade apologized, crossing his arms over his chest and leaning his hip on the hood of his cruiser. "Serendipity is as quiet as a mouse and just as boring, until it's not."

Shawn grunted. That was for sure. Like when an abandoned baby showed up in a manger at his chapel. Or a hazel-eyed beauty entered his life and turned it upside down and backward.

"We had a bit of an emergency at Jo's house. Her

hip gave out again. You'd think after all the surgeries she's had that the doctors could keep her on her feet."

"Is she okay?"

"Sure. You know Jo. She wouldn't let anyone fuss over her, and taking her to the hospital was completely out of the question. But she does like drama. She had everyone on duty at the fire department, all the paramedics, the cops and Dr. Delia swarming around her house like bees."

"With Jo as the Queen Bee," Shawn guessed.

"Exactly. So it took me and Brody a minute to unravel ourselves from her when the call came in. Of course, once she understood the situation, Jo was the first one pushing us out the door. We came as fast as we could."

"It's all good. I was here before Adrian got too far out of hand."

Slade laughed. "Yeah. It looks like you saved the day. Nice work, you decking him, Pastor. I would've done the same."

"I'm not a fan of physical fighting," Shawn admitted. "But I'm not ashamed of what I did tonight. The jerk was about to slap Heather. That's not going to happen while I live and breathe. Not ever."

"He won't be here to bother her again anytime soon. He violated his parole by coming here, so he's going straight back into the can."

"I'm glad to hear it. Heather has enough on her plate taking care of her kids without having to worry about Adrian lurking about."

"Hopefully he'll learn his lesson this time."

"I'm not holding my breath. He's not beyond the

Lord's help, but that's what it's going to take to get through to him."

"How did you know to be here, anyway?" Slade asked, his lips quirking into a lazy smile and his eyes gleaming with amusement. Shawn could see he already had his own theories as to the reasons Shawn might be near Heather's house so late at night.

Shawn still held out hope that Heather would accept his marriage proposal, but whether she did or not, he didn't want anyone spreading gossip about her reputation.

"Nothing shady, I promise you," he said, shoving Slade lightly.

Slade laughed.

"No, really. Jacob called me. Heather had told him to watch over the younger kids and keep the bedroom door locked. Apparently she gave him her cell phone. He got kind of freaked out and called me. I came running."

"Yeah. I'll bet you did."

"Yes," Shawn agreed, narrowing his eyes on Slade. "I did."

"Just teasin' you, buddy. It's all good. I'm glad you were here."

"Shawn?" Heather called, returning to the sliding glass door. "Did you want to come in for a bit? I've got Missy back in her own bed and Jacob all tucked in. And I just made a fresh pot of coffee."

"Pour me a cup, will you? I'll be right in," Shawn replied, before turning to shake hands with Slade. "Thanks for your help."

"You've got it. Tell Heather I'm sorry we didn't get here sooner."

"Will do."

Shawn dragged his fingers through his hair as he stepped through the door and slid it closed behind him. He was still experiencing a mild sense of unease and he wasn't sure why. Adrian was going to jail. Heather and the kids were safe.

All's well that ends well, right?

And then, there it was—the lingering problem. All *wasn't* well for him. Not until Heather answered his question. Would she agree to be his wife?

The present threat was over and Adrian was on his way back to prison, but that didn't change a thing as far as Shawn was concerned. He would marry Heather yesterday, if he could. Or tomorrow. Or next month, or next year, as long as she said *yes*.

He found Heather on the sofa in the living room, her legs pulled up beneath her and a mug of coffee in her hand. She'd set another mug on the opposite side of the table next to the armchair, but Shawn slid it toward Heather and sat down right next to her with his arm across the back of the couch.

She wouldn't even look at him. She sipped her coffee in total silence, her gaze fastened on the black liquid in her mug. The easy camaraderie they'd shared just minutes earlier had vanished, replaced by an uneasy tension.

What was she thinking? He waited for the silence to prod it out of her, but she was stubbornly quiet.

"Heather, honey, talk to me," he said at last.

"I guess I should thank you for rescuing me." She laughed, but she'd never sounded so apprehensive before.

How could she think he was waiting for an expression of gratitude? Didn't she know him at all?

"There's no need for that, you know. Of course I came when I was called. I would have been there earlier if I had known. I'll always be there for you."

"Wait—what? I didn't call you."

He chuckled and brushed her hair back behind her ear with the pad of his thumb. "Not directly. Jacob did."

"Jacob? I gave him my phone, but I didn't expect him to use it."

"Mmm. I'm glad he did. Poor kid was frightened half out of his mind."

"I didn't know whether I should wake him up or not when Adrian arrived. I should have thought it through better and left him sleeping. I've probably scarred him for life."

"Naw. Don't beat yourself up about it. I made sure he knew he was a hero for protecting his brother and sister—and protecting you by calling me."

"But I want him to be able to be a child as long as possible. I feel like I've ruined it for him, forcing him to man-up before his time."

"Boys appreciate a little responsibility. He got the chance to show you that you can depend on him. That's a good thing."

"I'm still taking him out for ice cream tomorrow."

Shawn chuckled. "Sounds good. I'll buy."

She made a tortured sound from the back of her throat. "Shawn."

Concerned, he narrowed his gaze on her. "What is it, honey? Talk to me. Please."

She smiled at him, but there was so much agony in her eyes that it went straight to his gut, knife-sharp and stinging. She brushed the back of her fingers down his jaw as if it were the last time she was going to touch him.

Tension rippled through him as he waited for her to speak.

"Adrian is on his way back to prison."

Right. Nice to know, but not exactly news. "Yes. And?"

She still refused to look at him, her gaze going no higher than his mouth.

"And you don't have to pretend anymore." The words came out in a rush, stumbling over each other.

"I'm sorry?" What was the woman talking about? How was he pretending?

"It was so sweet of you. You'll never know how much I appreciate your help. Really. And I understand why you said what you said to Adrian. But now it's just you and me, and I'm letting you off the hook, so you can relax."

She was *letting him off the hook*? What did that even mean?

He filtered through recent events, trying to figure out what he'd said to Adrian that Heather believed hadn't been entirely truthful. From what he could remember, there hadn't been many words in their altercation. Mostly it had been his fist on Adrian's face. Nothing dishonest about that, as far as he was concerned.

"You want to tell me what you're talking about?" Maybe if he had a hint.

She seemed to shrink into herself. "You said you loved me."

Why did she make it sound as if he'd said that he thought she smelled like apple cider vinegar?

"Yes," he agreed. Not like this was some great revelation, either. "I did. And?"

"I understand why you said it. But now that it's over—well, I just don't want you to feel obligated to continue the charade."

What *charade*?

"I feel like I've missed something," he admitted, running a hand across his jaw.

Something major, apparently.

"I know why you asked me to marry you, Shawn. And that makes you the best kind of man there is. I'll never be able to find words to tell you what that means to me. You were ready to sacrifice everything for me and the kids."

"Well, of course I was. Am," he corrected himself, frowning.

The woman wasn't making sense. What good was a husband if he wasn't willing to sacrifice everything, even his own life, for his wife and children?

"I want to thank you, and tell you I appreciate it."

"You already said that."

"But it's over."

Over? After everything that had happened, she could just walk away from what they had together? Or had he been so wrapped up in his own emotions that he hadn't realized she didn't return the sentiment?

He reached for her chin, gently tipping it his direction so she had no choice but to look at him.

"Are you trying to tell me you don't love me—that there's no chance you ever will?"

Her eyes widened to epic proportions. Her mouth moved, but no words came out.

"I—I—" she stammered, trying to turn her head away, but he wouldn't let her, not holding her with his hand, but with his gaze.

"You...what?"

"I love you."

He nearly sagged with relief, but his love for Heather flooded through him, bringing every nerve ending to life.

"That's good to know."

"But I don't see how that changes things."

Shawn shook his head. "Woman, if you don't stop talking in riddles, you're going to send me right off the deep end of crazy."

"I love you," she reiterated. "I can't deny it. But you don't love me, and I can't live like that. I thought about it—a lot. But I can't. I just can't."

"But I said—"

"That you loved me. Under duress, to protect me from Adrian. I get it. But I'm not holding you to it."

"I did not say I love you under duress."

"What do you call it, then?" She didn't allow him to answer, but answered for him. "I call it self-sacrifice. Thinking of other people before yourself. And I applaud you for it."

"Okay, I'm obviously slow, so you're going to have to lead me to water by the nose. I asked you to marry me. So how is it that you don't think I'm in love with you, exactly?"

She laughed through her teeth, a dry hiss. "You didn't say so when you proposed, for starters."

"What do you mean I didn't—" He stopped dead in the middle of the sentence as the realization hit him like a bullet in the chest. "I didn't." He rubbed his hands down his face and groaned. "I didn't, did I?"

Heather drew back.

He slid off the sofa and crouched in front of her,

framing her face in his hands. "Honey, I'm an idiot. Forgive me."

Her hazel eyes clouded with tears and Shawn felt like the biggest dolt in the world. He'd clumsily trampled over her feelings and now was at a loss as to how to undo his mistakes. He'd already caused her enough pain as it was.

"I'm so, so sorry. I was busy trying to prove to you that I could keep you guys safe, and then I go and neglect to mention the most important thing of all—that I love you."

Hope flared in her irises, burnt orange turning gold, the color of sunrise.

"In my defense, it wasn't that I forgot to mention it, exactly. I am so crazy in love with you that it was a given in my mind and I thought it was written all over my face. For some reason I believed it was coming out of my mouth, when clearly it wasn't. My heart was doing backflips when I asked you to be my wife."

She rubbed her lips together as if they'd suddenly become dry. She ran her hand over his eyes, down his nose, over his jaw, as if she were trying to memorize his face.

"I blew it before, but hear me now. There is nothing in this world I want more than to put a ring on your finger. Not because I have to, but because I want to. I offer my protection, yes, and my provision. But most of all I offer you my heart. You and the children. You're already my life. I hope I can be yours."

She stared at him but didn't speak.

He couldn't swallow around his emotions. Love. Hope. Fear of rejection.

"You don't have to answer if you're not ready. And

I know I pushed you too hard earlier today about setting a date. I was thinking about Adrian's threat to you, but he won't be bothering you any longer. We can take our time. Just—just please don't say no without thinking about it."

She smiled then, and to Shawn it felt like the swelling of a symphony. "You silly man. You think I'm going to turn you down?"

"Well, you did say—"

"That was only because I thought you were asking out of a cockeyed sense of obligation to me."

"Oh, I'm obligated, honey. Obligated to kiss your pretty lips. Often and thoroughly. I'm obligated to say 'I love you' instead of rattling off my to-do lists. Obligated to give you my heart and my life." He lowered his head to hers, hovering just above her lips. "But there is one thing I need from you in return."

She wrapped her arms around his neck. He'd never felt anything quite as perfect.

"Name it," she whispered. "It's yours. *I'm* yours."

"Yeah, that's the thing," he said back, kissing her, and then kissing her again. "You never really answered me."

Their foreheads met and she smiled into his lips.

"Then I'm answering now. *Yes.*"

Epilogue

*R*ap. *Rap. Rap.*

Heather's pulse jumped, but it wasn't because some-one was knocking on the door, or even because of who was on the other side.

Today was the day.

"Heather? You about ready?"

When Heather turned in her bustle to move to the door, Alexis gave a little squeal of distress and launched herself for the train of the white gown. Heather had thought a different color might be more appropriate, but Shawn had talked her into white. She had asked her new friends from church—Samantha Davenport, Mary Bishop and Alexis Haddon to stand up with her today.

"Sorry," Heather said as she giggled, swinging the door open. They were tucked into one of the Sunday school rooms for final preparations.

Shawn's father beamed back at her. Six months sober and counting. He was still in rehab but had come out for the wedding today. To their delight, Kenneth had come clean after Shawn had called to tell him of the engagement. He'd said he wanted to be there for all of his grandkids, and so far, it appeared he was serious about the endeavor.

"Shawn sent me to tell you that curtain call's in fifteen minutes." He wagged his eyebrows. "You're certain you're ready to get hitched to my son?"

"More than you could ever imagine," she assured her soon-to-be father-in-law. "Is everything good to go on the other end?"

"I don't know about that," Kenneth said with a laugh. "Shawn's practically jumping out of his skin, he's so anxious to tie the knot with you. I'm afraid he's going to pass out from too much adrenaline. You don't happen to have a paper bag on you, do you?"

"Sorry, no."

"Just teasing, love. I'll get him to the altar, don't you worry none about that."

"I appreciate it." She smiled. She hadn't really been worried. "Tell Shawn I'll see him soon."

Meeting Shawn at the altar couldn't come soon enough for her. She'd been dreaming about this day for months now. Shawn had insisted she plan every little thing. She would have been happy with just the two of them standing up in front of one of his pastor friends, but he'd insisted she have a "real" wedding, whatever that was. He wanted everything to be perfect for her on her special day. Before she knew it she was caught up in colors and caterers and floral bouquets.

All she cared about was having a real *marriage*, and she knew she was going to get that with Shawn. She was glad, though, that they'd waited, if only because the extra time meant she'd had the opportunity to start attending church, reacquainting herself with old friends and neighbors and meeting new ones.

They were all out there now, waiting to see their beloved pastor marry the love of his life. She supposed it was about time she made that happen.

It was only when she stood in the vestibule just outside the sanctuary that her nerves kicked in. She was more than a little anxious about stepping on her dress and falling on her face in front of everyone, but not a bit worried about joining her life to Shawn's.

There was no fear in love.

Samantha and Mary helped Henry, in a little white tux with his blond hair carefully slicked back, start up the aisle bearing the pillow on which their rings were bound. Next went Missy in her precious red flower-girl dress and carrying a basket of rose petals. Shawn had insisted on roses—it was the only real opinion he had on the wedding details other than the color of her dress.

With final giggles and well wishes, Samantha, Mary and Alexis drag-stepped down the aisle. Heather strained to see if she could catch a glimpse of Shawn, but he was standing off center and she couldn't see him. She knew once she looked into his eyes all would be well in her world.

She carefully released a breath and smiled at Jacob, who was pacing the vestibule and looking uncomfortable in his classic black tuxedo. Like Henry, he'd slicked his dark hair back, but a stubborn lock fell over his forehead. Jacob, like his future father, preferred life in jeans and boots to dressing up, but he was trying to be a good sport about it. Just for today.

"Ready to do this?" she asked him.

The boy's eyes gleamed. He stood tall and offered his arm to Heather.

"You look beautiful," he murmured with an awkward grin.

"And you, sir, are unbelievably handsome. I'm so proud to have my son walking me down the aisle today." The three children's adoptions were set to be finalized just after the first of the year, but in Heather's heart it was already a done deal.

The bridal march started and the congregation rose. Heather scanned the room, seeing a tidal wave of the joy-filled faces of her friends packing the entire sanctuary. The place was full to overflowing. Standing-room only.

Nerve-racking.

Thank You, Lord, for seeing me to this day, but please don't let me trip over my dress. Or my feet. Or my tongue.

She stepped into the aisle, straining to see Shawn. Where was he?

Fresh Christmas trees with twinkling lights from Emerson's Hardware lined the outside walls and poinsettias graced the altar, creating an intoxicating mixture of scents. The Christmas season would always carry a special place in their hearts, even without their anniversary falling deep in December.

Shawn stepped forward, into the middle of the aisle, and reached out his free hand to her. In the other he held Noelle, who'd grown considerably over the past few months. She was saying simple words and was near to taking her first step. Her little red dress matched Missy's, and she had roses threaded through her black curls.

Shawn's gaze met hers and she forgot to breathe. He was handsome in his work clothes—khakis and dress shirts—and even more so in jeans and boots and sporting that straw cowboy hat of his. But today, in a classic black tux and bolo tie, his black boots polished and shining, he was magnificent.

She reached his side and he wrapped his large, warm hand over hers. Kenneth took Noelle and deposited her into her birth mother's arms. Kristen had made a full and complete recovery, a blessing the doctors could not explain. She was now enrolled at a community college and had a job and an apartment, all of which Shawn and Heather had helped her acquire. It was wonderful and satisfying to see the teenager get on her feet. She'd asked—begged—for them to adopt Noelle, and so they'd met with a lawyer to see about an open adoption. Kristen visited them on weekends to get to know her daughter, and they were happy to have her.

After all the years of not wanting to wake up in the morning, Heather now couldn't wait for each day to begin. Holding the hand of the man she loved, surrounded by her family and friends, every day was an adventure, every second filled with love and joy.

The ceremony was kind of a blur to her. She couldn't think. She could only feel—overpowering love and emotion for the man standing at her side. She didn't hear a word anyone said until it was time for her to turn to Shawn so they could speak their vows to each other. He recited his vows to love and cherish her in the stout, persuasive voice of a natural-born orator, but she didn't need his words to be convinced.

He proclaimed his love for her with every smile, every gesture, every expression. And when she looked into his eyes, she could see forever.

* * * * *

A HUSBAND FOR CHRISTMAS

Gail Gaymer Martin

Many thanks to the helpful residents and store employees who answered questions and welcomed me to Owosso, Michigan, the setting of this novel series. Much love to my husband, Bob, who supports me in this career in a multitude of loving ways. He is my inspiration for the love, joy and faith found in my novels.

She became his wife. Then he went to her,
And the Lord enabled her to conceive,
And she gave birth to a son.
—Ruth 4:13–14

Chapter One

"Why did I say yes?"

Nina Jerome looked out her front window at the neighbors toting folding tables and chairs or picnic tables for their annual end-of-summer block party. She'd tried to refuse the invitation, but her neighbor Angie Turner wouldn't listen, and Angie didn't give up.

Retracing her steps to the kitchen, she opened her refrigerator and eyed her pasta salad. It looked a bit bland so she sprinkled sliced ripe olives and slivers of red peppers on top for color. She would attend whether she wanted to or not so no one would think of her as antisocial.

She shrugged. Who would care? In the few months she'd lived on Lilac Circle, she'd gotten to know very few people, but she preferred it that way. Or did she? "Face it, Nina. You can't be a recluse. You need to meet your neighbors." She spoke aloud to herself, and then chuckled. She had become a master of having great conversations with herself—or should she question her sanity?

The sound of the doorbell drew her from the kitchen.

When she opened the door, she wasn't surprised. "Hi, Angie. I—"

"You're joining us, aren't you?" Technically it was a question, but Angie's expression was only allowing one answer.

"I sure am." She tried to brighten her voice. "I just put some finishing touches on my salad. It's ready." She opened the front door wider.

Angie stepped in. "Can I help you carry something? You don't need a table. You can share ours, but you might want a lawn chair."

Nina motioned for Angie to follow her to the kitchen. Angie carried her salad, and she grabbed a lawn chair in one hand and a plate of cookies in the other.

Angie led the way across the street and down the block. Cars lined her end of the street where they'd been moved to make space for the food tables.

Angie's soon-to-be stepdaughter, Carly, played on their front lawn with three other children. One girl, Nina suspected, was the niece of the single guy she'd heard about. It was probably that information which had discouraged her from attending the event.

When she'd first met Angie and admitted she was divorced, Angie had mentioned the single man who was caring for his young niece. Nina sensed an ulterior motive, and any reference to matchmaking stopped her cold. She'd had enough of men. Todd had walked out of their marriage at the worst time in her life without an apology or even an attempt to offer a sensible explanation. She had to provide one for herself. And she didn't like what she'd come up with.

"You can put your food down there on the tables."

Angie pointed toward a row of long tables behind the sawhorses. "We'll be eating soon."

Following Angie's direction, she worked her way around the lawn chairs, giving a nod to those she hadn't met. When she found a spot for her pasta salad and shifted items to make room for her cookies, an elderly gentleman appeared beside her. "You've made a friend today, neighbor."

She looked up and couldn't help but smile, a real smile, at the man's glinting eyes and friendly greeting.

He extended his hand. "Everyone calls me El."

"El must stand for something." She grasped his palm.

"Elwood Barnes." His eyebrows lifted. "And you are...besides being the lady who brought cookies?"

"Nina Jerome. Everyone calls me Nina." She chuckled, captured by the smile in his eyes. For the first time since she'd moved, she felt comfortable with a stranger. "I also brought a pasta salad." She pointed toward the selection of dishes. "With olives and red peppers on top."

"I'll be sure and try some." He motioned toward a man sitting alone on a lawn chair. "Come meet my neighbor across the street."

While he steered her closer, she tensed, suspecting she was about to meet the single man on the block. He was good-looking with light brown hair and one of those five o'clock shadows that gave him an attractive rugged look, yet he appeared bored, as if someone forced him to join the party. She almost chuckled, aware of the similarity to her attitude.

"Doug, this is another new neighbor, Nina." El shifted his focus. "Jerome, is it?"

Doug rose and jammed his hands into his pockets, his expression polite but stoic.

She eyed him without making a move.

"Nina, Doug Billings and little Kimmy over there." El pivoted and motioned toward the children. "They moved here a month or so before you did if my old brain recalls."

Doug glanced toward the children. "I'm sort of caring for my niece."

She pressed her lips together, hoping not to laugh. "Sort of caring?"

He shook his head, as if waking from a bad dream and finally looked at her. "I do my best."

He looked more uncomfortable than she felt. "Nice to meet you, Doug." She detested the meaningless phrase. "I'll head back before Angie thinks I ran off. Thanks, El, for introducing yourself and for…" She motioned toward Doug. "I'm sure I'll see you both around." She strode away, monitoring her legs to keep from running.

Avoiding meeting people had become a new problem. Though never outgoing, she knew how to be civil and welcoming. And she liked El. He was a sweet grandpa-type.

"There you are." Angie looked at her, a hint of coyness in her grin.

Nina grasped her lawn chair and pulled it open. "El is a real gentleman. He introduced himself." She slipped into the chair.

"He is." She arched a brow. "Meet anyone else?"

The telltale look on Angie's face gave her away, and Nina squirmed. "You must have seen El introduce me to Doug Billings."

Angie grinned. "I wondered where you'd gone so long, and then I noticed you with him."

"He's worse than I am, Angie. Either he's very shy or he's preoccupied."

Angie shrugged. "I suppose he's worried about his sister. It has to be hard on Kimmy to be away from her mom so long. It's already been over a month. I think Doug had planned to watch her for a week or so while his sister and her friend went on a trip, and then the accident happened. Now she can't travel or do much for herself with her injuries. Two broken legs plus he mentioned something about a torn retina."

Nina shook her head, unable to imagine what it would be like in that situation and stranded from her child.

Stranded from her child. She felt that way at times. Having a physician tell her she could never carry a child to term and, in fact, might never get pregnant again sliced through every nerve. Her husband's lack of compassion, his turning his back on her and walking away at a time she needed his love, had destroyed her trust and hope of being a wife, let alone a mother.

"Nina?"

She jerked her head upward. "Sorry. I was empathizing with Doug and his sister, I guess." She shifted her gaze, wanting to drop the topic. "The kids seem to be having tons of fun."

Angie nodded. "I hate to stop them." She motioned toward the tables. "But it's nearly time to eat." She swung back, a question in her eyes. "Did you receive your wedding invitation?"

"I did. Thank you." Envy stabbed at her heart. "Sorry. I should have mentioned it."

"No need to apologize. A cousin called a couple days ago and said hers hadn't arrived. I know I sent it so I'm a bit antsy now."

"It was most likely a fluke, Angie. Mine came three weeks ago. I wouldn't miss the wedding. Carly's your flower girl, right?"

A glow filled Angie's face. "She is, and she'll look beautiful. I adore that little girl."

"I know you do." She swallowed. "I'm ashamed to say that sometimes I envy you."

"Why? It could be you one day, Nina. Love happens even when you least expect it, and it covers all the flaws and fears we've carried into our lives. Everything worthwhile deserves a second chance."

Angie's words sank in, and though she loved the idea, it seemed impossible. "You might be right." She scrutinized the tables overflowing with casseroles and platters. "I think you're definitely right about the food. I see people heading that way."

Angie looked again. "Then we should round up everyone, I suppose."

"Can I help?"

"I was thinking about inviting El to sit with us." Angie gestured toward his house. "Do you mind asking him?"

"Not at all." She bounded from the chair and retraced her steps toward El's front yard. As she approached, Doug crossed the street with a dish, set it on the table and approached her.

"Hi." He gave her a hangdog look. "I'm afraid I hadn't been very welcoming when Mr. Barnes introduced us." He tucked his hands into his pockets again.

Was that a nervous habit or a way of binding his

hands to keep them out of mischief? She grimaced at her thought. "You're forgiven. What's in your dish?"

A faint grin curved his full lips and she spotted a different side of him emerging. "Baked beans. You know. I open a can, pour them into a casserole, add a dash of Worcestershire sauce, dice up onions and cocktail wieners and bake. It's one of my limited bachelor dishes."

Her pulse skipped, wondering how this nice-looking man escaped getting caught up in wedding bells. She often wished she'd made a wiser choice. "I don't think marriage is for everyone."

His eyes narrowed slightly until he shrugged. "Maybe, but in my case life got in the way, I suppose."

Digesting his words, she realized life had got in her way, too. "And you have Kimmy to care for. You must be a special uncle."

"Not really. Love motivates." He looked downward as if embarrassed. "Speaking of Kimmy, I hope she's at Angie's. I forgot the beans and went inside for a few minutes." He shrugged.

"She was playing ringtoss in the front yard."

He craned his neck to check for himself. "She's in good hands. When you go back would you ask her to come home? It looks about time to eat."

"Sure will." She turned toward El, noticing he had a card table sitting with two chairs on his front lawn.

El smiled as she arrived.

"Angie asked me to invite you down to her table to eat."

He gave her a wink. "Tell her thanks, but I've already made plans with Birdie. Angie'll understand."

"Birdie?"

He grinned as if she were in on a joke.

"Okay, I'll tell her. See you later." She headed back to Angie's, curious about El's sudden friendship to Birdie.

When she told Angie, her eyes widened like a full moon. "You are kidding."

"No. He said you'd understand." She anticipated an explanation, but Angie only stared at her with her mouth agape.

Finally Angie chuckled. "Birdie has been one of those neighbors everyone's tried to ignore." She released a long breath. "But you realize El has a loving heart. One day, he asked me to befriend her because he suspected part of her problem was loneliness."

"He asked you?"

"Me." Angie rolled her eyes.

"Why?"

She shrugged.

"I'm not sure since I was the one who called her a gossip. I felt ashamed, but I did it because he asked. I baked cookies, of all things, and went to visit, but she wasn't home. I praised the Lord for the reprieve."

Nina couldn't help her chuckle. "And then what?"

"Birdie appeared at my door a couple days later saying she'd heard I'd been snooping around. When I told her why I'd come, she actually apologized in her own way, and softened a bit. She even had a bounce to her step when she left." She lifted her shoulders. "Maybe she's been thinking about her behavior and realizes she's chasing people away rather than making friends. I have no idea but something happened."

"Good for you."

"Have you met Rema?"

Nina checked the direction of Angie's gaze and spotted a woman heading their way. "No, I don't think so."

"Then it's time you two meet." Angie flagged her over. "I thought you were missing the party?"

"No, I goofed. I thought my casserole was warming in the oven." She shook her head. "But I'd forgotten to turn it on." She lifted the cover. "I hope I'm not too late."

"People have just begun to eat." Angie motioned toward Nina. "Rema, I don't think you officially met Nina Jerome."

Nina extended her hand, and then recalled Rema was holding a heavy casserole so she let her hand drop. "I'm glad to meet you."

Angie rested her hand on Rema's shoulder. "If you have no other plans, please join us. We have lots of room here." She motioned to the picnic bench and the long table she'd butted up next to it.

"No plans. I'm just being neighborly." She gave a shrug. "Thanks for the invitation." She tilted her head toward the food. "I'd better get this to the table before everyone's eaten." She turned and hurried down the street.

Nina eyed the food line and spotted Doug standing alone in front of his house. A lonely feeling crept through her. She'd been doing the same thing since Todd had turned his back on her. Alone. Her memory kicked in, and she snapped her finger. "Doug asked me to tell Kimmy to go home so she can eat."

Angie eyed the line and then turned toward Rick. "Time to eat." She pointed down the street.

Carly bounded across the grass with Kimmy on her

heels. "Can Kimmy eat with us? We have room." She gestured to the long folding table.

Angie looked down the road. "Kimmy, you need to ask your uncle Doug first. If he says yes, tell him we have plenty of room at our table and he's invited, too. I don't want him eating alone. Okay?"

Kimmy nodded, and Carly jumped in on the task.

Angie grinned. "Okay, you can both go, but wait down there. We're going to get in line, too."

"I'll go with them." Before Angie responded, Nina followed behind the children. As she neared Doug, she scrutinized him in a way she hadn't before. When they met earlier, she'd noticed his good looks but not his physique. He had to be nearly six feet with a lean waist and a great set of shoulders. She liked his executive haircut that seemed to have a mind of its own.

Doug stood as she neared, and she hoped he hadn't noticed her steady gaze. By the time she arrived, the girls had already given him the invitation.

"I'm sorry, Doug. I almost forgot to deliver your message, but here she is." She chuckled, hoping he would smile. "You might as well join us."

He hesitated, a thoughtful expression growing.

"I'm sitting with them, too. Makes it more of a party."

"Please, Uncle Doug." Kimmy's plaintive urging did the trick.

"Why not?" He shrugged, and again his hands vanished into his pockets.

Nerves or a habit? She longed to know which.

When Angie arrived, the kids joined her, and then she and Doug fell into line.

When Nina spotted Doug's baked beans, she took

a big spoonful and he gave her a smile. Surprised, she grinned back, liking that he'd finally let her see a new side of him. The man was too attractive to not smile. She completed her plate with a slab of ham, but chuckled when the girls headed for the hot dogs. Kids and hot dogs.

"I'll check out desserts later." She tilted her head toward the array of goodies and maneuvered her way back to Angie's table with Doug's smile the sweetest treat of all.

Doug stared at his plate, wishing his appetite would return. He'd become overwhelmed by too many things. He'd always been a responsible person, sure of his decisions and able to roll with the punches. Not lately. He'd weighed the reasons, and the best answer he found was Roseanne's accident and feeling unprepared to be a temporary father figure. Though he could handle a multifaceted career, he had no idea how parents kept up with a child's energy and needs. No wonder he'd hesitated looking for a wife.

He looked at Nina. Something about her captured him. Although nice looking, she wasn't a woman most men would call beautiful, yet he saw a kind of beauty. He admired her long wavy hair, the color of a chestnut, sort of brown with hints of red. She tied it back, and he longed to see it flowing around her shoulders. Her eyes tilted downward, and though she held a direct gaze, something in her eyes seemed haunting. She had an appeal that went deeper than physical beauty.

Delving his fork into pasta salad, he stopped his musing. Women hadn't penetrated his hardened mind for years, so why now? His job kept him busy, and he'd always tried to be there for his sister, whose life hadn't been the smoothest. And then sweet Kimmy. That broke his heart.

He swallowed hard, forcing the pasta down his throat and following it with a long drink of iced tea.

"You're quiet."

Nina had leaned close enough for him to smell her fragrance, like fresh-picked fruit. "Sorry." He managed a grin. "My mind got tangled somewhere. I think in your scent. You took me away to an orchard. I could almost hear birds singing." A flush grew on his cheeks. "Sorry, I got carried away."

Nina grinned. "It was a lovely compliment." She paused while a question flickered in her eyes. "What kind of birds?"

He laughed and it felt odd. "I'll have to think about that."

When she chuckled, his spirit lifted. How long had it been since he'd really laughed?

Though they had been talking drivel, his shoulders had eased, and a good feeling rolled through him. He glanced toward Kimmy to make sure she was behaving. But he had no need to worry. She and Carly were talking and giggling like old friends. "I'm glad the girls have each other. I moved here at a terrible time. I'd thought Roseanne would be back by the time moving day arrived, but with the accident…" He shook his head.

"Kimmy seems to have adjusted well. You're, apparently, doing a good job."

"I've misled you if you think that. Every day was a struggle until Carly came along. I was trying to balance my work hours with child care hours. Can you imagine my telling her bedtime stories?"

"I can." Her grin broadened. "You have a nice speaking voice, and I'm sure you can read." She added a wink. "And, most of all, you love her. I can tell."

His cheeks warmed with her compliment. "Thanks. I do love her."

"You'll make a good dad one day."

Her comment addled him, and not knowing what to say, he changed the subject. "What brought you to Owosso?"

"I work in public relations, and I was tired of traffic and high-priced apartment rentals. I couldn't afford a house in the city. So when I learned we had a branch in Owosso, and I could transfer, I jumped at the chance. Home prices are much better here. Payments are less than my apartment."

"I found that to be true, too. But do you like small town living?"

"I've only been here a few weeks, but I think I do. It's friendly. Have you ever had a block party in downtown Chicago? Or Detroit?"

He chuckled, but before he responded, Angie's voice cut through their prattle.

"What are you two laughing about?"

"The weather." Nina grinned. "About apartments in the city versus owning a home out here."

Angie's fiancé, Rick, nodded. "I'm with you on that one. Not so much the price but the space and freedom. Carly loves the yard. My apartment doesn't have one."

Angie rose. "Anyone ready for refills?"

Rick eyed the girls. "More food, ladies, or dessert?"

Kimmy bounced beside him. "Me, too, Uncle Doug?"

After he gave her permission, Angie and Rick left for the food table with the girls while he and Nina stayed behind, making small talk, but he enjoyed it. For so long he'd feared that a woman might think he was coming on to her and not just being friendly. But Nina had a way about her that gave him no worries that she was looking for romance.

More at ease, he returned to their discussion. "I'm guessing our places are similar. Mine has three bedrooms and a good-sized dining room." He doubted she cared, and he disliked small talk, too, but that's all he could come up with.

"Mine's similar. Would you like to see it?"

"Sure, but let me check on Kimmy first." He rose and spotted Angie returning with the girls. "Will you keep an eye on Kimmy for a few minutes? I'm going—"

"No problem." She flashed a playful wink. "Have fun."

Nina arched an eyebrow. "It's only… Never mind." She brushed her words away and rose. "We don't need to explain, do we?"

"Not at all." He enjoyed her lighthearted spirit and joined her on the sidewalk, heading to her home. Though he'd passed her house often, he'd never really noticed its homey look. It had a porch on half of the front and the other side, an overhung alcove with attractive wide windows. His home lacked the warmth and was more streamlined. Too much like him. "It has a friendly feel, Nina. Like you."

"Me?" Her voice rose. "I'm just boring."

"To yourself maybe, but not to me." Hearing his honesty startled him.

"Thank you, Doug." Her stunned expression set him back.

She opened the door, and they stepped inside. "This is the living room, naturally."

The size surprised him. "It's like a great room. I like the corner fireplace."

She didn't comment. "Dining room." She made a sweeping gesture.

He slipped his hands into his pockets, uneasy that he had no awareness of what she was thinking. He noted the wide archway added even more space to the already-large living area.

Nina gestured to the doorway leading from the dining room. "And the kitchen."

She stepped inside and he followed, noting numerous cabinets but minimal counter space and a pair of folding doors. "Is this a pantry?"

"I wish." She folded back the doors to expose a washer and dryer. "This is my laundry room." She gave a shrug. "No basement."

"Mine is a small room off the kitchen." He leaned his back against a counter and studied her a moment. "You have lots of room for one person. Are you anticipating finding someone to share it with?" He cringed. Why not just ask if she was engaged or dating someone?

"I'm not anticipating anything." Her tone had an edge. "I like the space."

He wanted to undo the damage. "You never know about the future."

A frown shot to her face. "No marriage plans in my future, if that's what you mean. None. Not interested."

He drew back, wishing he'd kept his mouth shut.

"I'm sorry, Nina. That sounded crude and too nosy. I have no plans at the moment, either. Once Kimmy's back with her mom, it's just me. That was an ignorant comment."

Her frown faded, replaced by an unreadable expression. "Doug, I've been married once. I don't think it's meant for me. Once is enough."

Though he reacted as if he understood, her sharp response sent a sliver of disappointment through his chest and left him even more curious.

"Back to the tour." She strode through the kitchen doorway to a short hallway on the opposite side of the house. "Three bedrooms. Right now the smallest is sort of an office with my computer and some exercise equipment. The middle size is a guest room." She raised her eyebrows. "Now all I need are guests. And the master bedroom is large and faces the back with a walk-in closet and master bath."

She didn't step inside but raced through her descriptions, gesturing as he glanced into the three rooms. Her manner had changed since he'd stupidly asked the personal question about her future plans. He'd messed up, but then he'd done that before. He mumbled something about the attractive rooms and watched her edge toward the front door.

Obviously she wanted out of the situation. He decided to give her a solution. "Thanks for the tour. I should get back to Kimmy."

She didn't say a word but headed for the door.

He followed her into the great room. "You have a nice place here, Nina."

She only nodded and opened the front door.

His chest constricted. He had no doubt this was

the end of their amiable relationship. And he knew it was for the best. He had nothing to offer except his preoccupation with his sister's horrible situation and Kimmy's needs. Then he had his own feelings, ones he disliked more than he wanted to face. *Inadequacy* had never been a word in his life until now. But when he'd opened his mouth to repair the damage he couldn't even put a patch on it until he got himself and his head in the right place. Obviously a repair job was pointless. He'd made a mess of it, and of all things, he liked her.

Chapter Two

Despite her declaration to remain uninvolved, Doug's image dangled in Nina's thoughts like a mule's carrot. His smile, his lost look, his fleeting glances rolled into a tempting nugget in her imagination. She opened her computer to occupy her mind with something other than Doug but when she stared at the monitor, her mind segued back to the block party. For someone who could evaluate promotional programs and manage entire brands, she failed when it came to her own life.

Spending the morning with her thoughts spinning motivated her to break down the steps she used in her work to evaluate her own needs and goals. But the big question was how? How did she look with fresh eyes and see anything that wasn't tangled in her past?

She scooted her chair back and rose. Why did she waste time reliving her last conversation with Doug? She'd got in a huff, and when he left her house, she'd ushered him to the front door without a kind word, and the poor guy had no idea why. And she couldn't explain it, either. Yes, he'd brought up a bad time, but that had been years earlier. Nothing could be done, so why dwell on it?

She strode to the kitchen and poured coffee into a cup. The strong odor curled her nose so she poured it out, rinsed the cup and found a tea bag. Microwaves came in handy for a single cup of tea. Waiting, she opened the sliding door and gazed into the yard. Even though the season was late, she'd wanted to add some perennials that would come up next year. Angie's yard looked lovely with fall blossoms.

The buzzer sounded, and she headed back to her makeshift office with her cup of tea. Yet the tea didn't help, either. Her mind flew from one idea for a client to the block party. She'd met a few neighbors, saying hello or responding with "Yes, I'm new on the block," but still it was a beginning. She especially enjoyed meeting El. He embodied a rare spirit filled with wit, kindness and wisdom.

El had an innocence about him—a man who trusted his instinct and didn't question his decision to be friendly or look for motivation. That's where she had failed. Any question that delved too deeply into her personal hang-ups or sorrows invaded her comfort level and she assumed the person was nosy or prying. Doug's question had been general not probing.

Draining the last of her tea, she rose and set the empty cup in the kitchen, grabbed her house key and stepped outside. The quiet of the street spilled over her, as empty as her teacup. The block party had resounded with voices, children laughing and music playing on a speaker somewhere. A few people had danced in the circular area of the street.

How long had it been since she'd danced? Forever.

She recalled Doug saying life had got in his way. She stood on her sidewalk, her eyes closed for a moment, picturing the friendly atmosphere of the Friday block party.

As she walked, she spotted El sitting on a wooden glider in his front yard. Though she regretted not having a treat to offer him, she headed that way. Flowers bloomed in his flower beds, and she wanted to ask about them. Maybe he could offer her ideas on what would be good to plant this time of year.

Thoughts returned again on her rudeness to Doug. She'd startled him as well as herself. Nearing El's, she realized her motivation for coming was feeling alone. El had mentioned loneliness once, and today it overwhelmed her, a strange emotion with no solution other than to seek company. For years, she'd avoided company after Todd left, saying she didn't care.

Her heart skipped as she neared Doug's house. His car sat back in the driveway signaling he was home, but she saw no sign of him. She should be relieved to avoid a confrontation, but instead, a guilty sting burned through her. She'd behaved terribly.

El saw her coming and raised his hand in greeting. She waved back, glad for the distraction. As she stepped onto his lawn, he rose, planting his feet on the ground while hoisting himself from the glider without losing his balance.

He grinned. "How are you this fine Sunday?"

She nodded at his welcome and ambled toward him, hoping to look casual and not unnerved. "Beautiful day, isn't it?"

"Couldn't ask the Lord for better."

The reference helped her understand El's ways. He

lived by the rules that people of the church took for granted. She'd known a few things about faith once, but she'd let her curiosity die. Had her divorce triggered her hopelessness? She couldn't recall what ended her interest. Yet she sometimes envied those who had faith. They lived with the philosophy that life never ended. This world was only a stepping stone to something better. The idea that life held more than the here and now, though strange, had a comfortable ring to it. A spark warmed her again.

El patted the seat on the swing. "Join me a minute." He grasped the arm and sank back onto the slats.

With her growing curiosity, she did as he suggested and sank beside him. "You have pretty flowers, El." She twisted on her hip to face him. "You don't mind that I call you El?"

"Mind." He tossed his head back with a chuckle. "That's my name, and I'm hanging on to it."

He made her grin. "Okay, then. In case you forgot, I'm Nina."

"Pretty name. I wouldn't forget that one." He gave her arm a pat. "Thank you for mentioning the flowers. My wife always urged me to plant flowers. I was smart enough to learn that urging was one of those things that women did rather than just demand their husbands do it."

This time she chuckled. "Did your wife have favorite flowers?"

"She sure did. She loved the ones that came up year after year. That's mainly what you're looking at—daisies, coneflowers, asters, and those purple ones are called catmint. I added a few geraniums. They're faithful flowers, growing in nearly every environment." He winked. "They're not fussy."

"That's one of the few flowers I know by name. But now I recognize the white daisies."

"Coneflowers are the colorful ones there." He pointed to a bed of daisy-like blossoms. "Pretty things in so many colors."

"I want to do some planting. I have a few clumps of flowers in the front. I'm not sure what they are, but…" She relaxed against the seat back. "I finally have my new house organized." She eyed him. "Sort of."

He chuckled, his gaze washing across her face as if he had questions but didn't ask.

"How did your meal go with Birdie on Friday?"

"Fine. I think she appreciated the company and that I accepted her invitation." He chuckled again. "She asked if we could eat together, but she didn't have a table or chairs. That means she sort of urged me to ask her." His eyes glinted with his joke before he leaned forward, his elbows on his knees, hands woven together. "Birdie's been standoffish until recently. That's a lonely life for a woman who still has years to enjoy each day."

His words swept over her. "To be honest, El, I've been somewhat that way, too."

He nodded while a faint crooked grin grew on his face. "I sensed that, Nina. You know, whatever happened in your past is just that. It's passed. Ahead of you is a future, but you have to participate in it." He stopped and shook his head. "This is just ramblings of an old man, but sometimes I see things and…" He sat a moment his head hanging. "I see you and sense you have regrets and sorrows that you're clinging to. Ask yourself if they're worth it."

Worth it? Though his first words rankled, she forced herself to listen, and a sense of possibility hung over her, nebulous but there.

"Please forgive me. How you live your life is none of my business. Birdie got in trouble nosing around other people's lives, and I'm doing the same thing."

She touched his arm and squeezed. "El, you're not a gossip. You're not spreading rumors. You're talking to me like a father might. That's something I never had." The admission spilled ice water through her body. "You're right. I had a bad marriage, and I have other issues that formed my judgment. Marrying again is basically not a possibility. I guess the reality makes me a little empty...and what you just said. Lonely."

"Nothing could be so bad it stops you from falling in love again. Are you sure marriage is out of the question?"

His tender look rent her heart. "I'm sure. I'm sorry, but I don't want to talk about it. I know how I feel, and I think that's how it will be." Without warning, her gaze flashed back down the block toward Doug's. Her pulse skipped when she spotted him outside with Kimmy.

"Then I'll pray for you to find an answer to your problem, Nina. Do you pray?"

His question stopped her. She almost felt ashamed to answer him. "I've never learned to pray."

"You don't learn it, Nina. What are we doing right now?"

She eyed him, trying to decipher what he meant. Thoughts surged. They had talked about the flowers, her attitude toward marriage. "We've talked about a lot of things."

"Yes. That's it."

"That's it?" Her head spun. "Talking?"

"Yep. Prayer is just talking to God. Tell Him about your day. Ask Him for answers to your questions. Thank Him for His blessings. And then listen."

"Listen? That's the thing about prayer I don't understand. God doesn't speak. They say He's there. You know, sort of like the wind is there. We can't see it, but we feel it or we can see what it does."

"Yep, you got it. You can't see Him, but you can feel Him if you open your heart, but then that takes trust."

"It's hard to trust something or someone you don't know." She brushed a curl from her face.

"But it's not impossible. Think about things that you trust even though you don't know why or don't have the details. You trust your employer will pay you. Why? Because he said he would."

She shook her head. That was a given. Wasn't it? Maybe not. "You trust the sun will come up in the morning. Even if it's behind a cloud, you know it's there."

"But that's nature. It's always been that way."

"So has God, Nina. He was there before the sun was made."

A frown wrenched her face even though she tried to stop it.

"Do you have a Bible?"

Her back tensed. "No."

"I have Margie's. I think she'd like you to have it."

"Margie?"

"My wife's name. Marjorie. Most people called her

Marge, but she was always Margie to me." A tender sweetness spread across his face.

The look touched her. "El, I couldn't take your wife's Bible."

"Why? She doesn't need it, Nina. She's sitting up there listening to the Lord, and He tells her all she needs to know. She's in her glory." He chuckled. "In her glory in Glory." He nodded as if he'd settled on an agreement with himself.

"But it's precious to you. A keepsake."

"It's more precious to me if someone's using it." He shifted on the seat, causing it to glide back and then forward. "Now I know you're not a Bible reader, but if you have questions or if you're curious, you can check the concordance and look up the exact topic you'd like to know about."

"You mean an index?"

He pushed himself forward again but this time he rose. "You can call it that. It's right inside. Hang on a minute."

Before she could react, he headed toward the house on a mission. She'd never seen him move so fast. She lowered her head, sorting through all that had happened. Somehow she'd moved from flowers to faith without knowing how. Maybe that was one of those God things people talked about.

Guilt rattled up her spine. If she took his Bible, realizing she had little choice, what would make her read it? The possibility wavered over her.

"Here you go."

She jerked, unaware El had returned.

He extended the worn-looking Bible, and not knowing how to refuse, she grasped it. Hoping to make him happy, she opened it to the back and flipped through the topics with verses listed underneath—hardship, loyalty, prayer. She turned the pages back. Faith. She eyed the long row of verses. The first she spotted was Matthew 17:22. She eyed the preview. *He replied, "Because you have so little faith. I tell you the truth..."* The example stopped her cold. What? What was the truth?

"Is something wrong, Nina?"

She drew her head upward. "No. Not at all. I was thinking, I guess."

"Nothing wrong with that. I'm not rushing you. You have God's Word in your hands if you have any questions, and though I don't have all the answers, you're always welcome to ask me anything."

She rose, clutching the book, and gathered her wits. "Thank you, El. And I feel bad taking your—"

"It's an honor, Nina. Margie is smiling in heaven." His face brightened. "I know she's smiling."

How could she refuse his generous gift? "Thank you, El. May I kiss your cheek?"

"I'd love that, Nina."

She leaned forward and pressed her lips on his soft cheek. "Thank you for everything. I'll take your flower advice, and I promise... I'll keep the book handy. I'm sure one day—"

"I'm sure you will." His smile broadened. "I'm anxious to see those flowers, too."

The best part for now was the flowers. She was anxious to get to a nursery. Most plants were probably on sale, she hoped, and she'd save money as well as adorn her flower beds.

Hope. That had been a rare word in her vocabulary, but El's certainty that she would read the Bible made her grin. That was hope. And she had faith, too, but different. If she planted flowers in the fall, she had faith they would blossom in the spring or summer.

She tucked the Bible under her arm and headed down the sidewalk, aware that Doug and Kimmy were on the other side. Although her mind was as ragged as it had been when she stepped outside, a sense of peace had sneaked into her being. Though it would be short-lived, something about El gave her a sense of security and hope. Hope? She'd had so little, but today she had a touch of it.

As she drew closer to Doug, her peace sank into confusion. She could hardly ignore him, but what could she say? She marched along, wishing he wouldn't notice her.

Doug sat on a porch step keeping an eye on Kimmy working on her first school project collecting bugs. Offering science classes seemed a little early for second graders. But what did he know? He shook his head, hoping Kimmy didn't get stung or bit by something, but her search was in the name of homework so he didn't say a word.

Trying to be a good father-type for Kimmy, he usually joined her in projects, but today his thoughts weighted him down. He'd done something to upset Nina. His questions had been too personal for her, he guessed. Something…

When he looked up, his heart stopped. Nina appeared across the street like a vision, but he knew she was real. Her long hair hung to her shoulders in waves. It fluttered in the breeze, and he longed to brush it from her cheek. He faltered, unsure of what he wanted to do.

When she glanced his way, he raised his hand, a natural instinct that he hadn't monitored. Anticipating she'd ignore his greeting, his chest constricted when she crossed the street. Though curious where she'd been, he wouldn't ask. That question could be too personal, also.

"I noticed you outside with Kimmy. How are you?"

He wanted to tell her he was confused, but he changed his answer to something safe. "Good. The weather motivated me to come outside."

She strode up to Kimmy. "What are you looking for?"

"Bugs." She grinned.

"Bugs. Hmm? Any special reason or are you just curious?"

"School started and I'm in the second grade."

"Second grade. And you have to find bugs." Nina tilted her head.

"Homework." Kimmy's face glowed. "It's for our science class."

"Did you find any ladybugs?" Nina looked at the insects in Kimmy's jar.

"Those ones who fly away home 'cuz their house is on fire?"

The girl's face lit with a smile, and Nina grinned. "I'm sure those are the ones."

Kimmy shook her head. "I only found two ants, a fly and something with lots of legs." She held up her jar with air holes punched in the lid.

"I have ladybugs at my house. They like flowers, and even though I have only a few blossoms, I see insects there."

Doug watched, amazed at Nina's lighthearted banter with no hint of anger. Still, she was talking with Kimmy, not him. But she'd stopped by and that was something.

"Uncle Doug, can I go to Nina's and get some ladybugs?" She gave him a beseeching look.

He couldn't hold back his grin. "I don't want to hinder research. I suppose you can if Nina doesn't mind."

Nina tousled Kimmy's hair. "Come down whenever you'd like. I'm home for the evening."

He opened his mouth but sat speechless.

"Doug." Nina closed the distance and sat beside him, running her fingers through her hair. "I owe you an apology. I'm sorry for the way I acted on Friday."

"You don't owe me—"

"I owe you respect and friendship. You've been kind, and I enjoyed your company until my fortress rose to shield me. It does that sometimes without my realizing it. You didn't deserve to be treated that way."

Although her fortress aroused his curiosity, relief flooded him, and he released a strangled breath. "Thank you. I don't need to forgive you, but I will. We all let our protective devices appear sometimes. I've done it myself. You know I question my ability with…" He feared Kimmy would hear her name so he tilted his head. "I would love to have confidence in my parenting skills. Women seem to have those built in."

Nina's crooked grin preceded her head shake. "We are frightened, too, Doug. Women know they're supposed to have inborn motherly instincts, but that's a myth. We cover up our worries and plow ahead. We read books and ask friends who won't think we're silly. In a way, it's like anything new. We do the best we can. Whatever you've done, Doug, has been right from all

I see. Kimmy seems happy and healthy. You can't ask for more."

As if she'd heard her name, Kimmy came skipping toward them. "Can we go now?"

"We have company, my girl."

"But we can take her along." She beckoned to them.

Nina grinned. "Thank you for inviting me to join you."

Missing the point, Kimmy gave her a big smile. "You're welcome."

He gulped down his chuckle and patted Nina's hand. "Sorry. I think it takes a few years for a sense of humor to develop."

"It's funnier that way." Nina rose and extended her hand. "Friends."

"Positively."

"Good. Now I'd better go home since I'm expecting company." She stepped toward Kimmy, but he stopped her.

"What's in your hand?"

She glanced down as if she'd forgotten.

"It looks like a—"

"Bible." She took a step closer. "It was El's wife's. He wanted me to have it since I don't own one."

His back straightened. "Did you mind?"

She shook her head. "I would expect nothing less from him. He lives his faith. I've never learned what that is, and I suppose he thought he would help me understand."

He didn't know what to say so he just gave a nod.

"I'll see you later, right?"

"For sure. Kimmy has her heart set on it." So did he.

Nina gave a wave and returned to Kimmy's side.

She gave her a pat and whispered something in her ear before heading home.

He watched her go, both relieved and confused. He couldn't be happier to see her with the Bible, and he prayed she would look inside and grow in faith. He should do the same with all his doubts and worries. And maybe his new concern was one of those useless worries. Though something about Nina was lovely and intriguing, something else still blocked her from living fully. That's what he sensed, and it saddened him.

Chapter Three

Kimmy skipped along the sidewalk and paused when she reached Nina's. Doug caught up and faced the house, hoping his big mouth didn't result in another problem as it had at the block party. Though she'd apologized, he realized his question about the possibility of someone living with her had been blunt. Rude, really. It had been none of his business. On top of that, his ulterior motive was also inappropriate. Why not just ask if she were seeing someone? Or was that also blunt? Women confused him.

"Come on, Uncle Doug." Kimmy skipped halfway up the front walk and beckoned to him.

Before he took a step, Kimmy had already turned her attention to a few clumps of flowers in the beds along the house. He gazed at her creeping around the leaves, loving her curiosity and eagerness to do homework, hoping her attitude would last a lifetime. Having a good work ethic helped a career. He shook his head, realizing how far in the future he'd gone. Instead he should focus on his own future.

"Coming in?"

He faced Nina standing in the doorway. "Stay right here, Kimmy, and then let me know when you've finished.

Nina swung the door wider, and again he wished he had a larger living room. When he stepped in, she motioned toward the sofa, her only seating besides the recliner.

Still in the doorway, Nina leaned out. "The door's open, Kimmy. Come in when you're done."

His senses heightened. "Something smells delicious."

"Good." She turned from the door. "I'm making enough for all of us, but it'll be a while. It's in a slow cooker. Are you starving?"

Even if he was, he wouldn't admit it. He shook his head.

"Good." She sank into her recliner. "I thought if I have leftovers, I'd take them to El later tonight so he will have a surprise home-cooked dinner."

Doug couldn't imagine having home-cooked meals delivered to his door. His own simple recipes didn't thrill him. "You're a good person, Nina."

She lifted an eyebrow. "Thanks. I wish—"

What did she wish? His mouth opened, then closed. He had to learn not to ask questions or make comments. She'd made it clear her life and problems were not up for discussion. "We ate lunch before we came so we're good." His eyes shifted from her to the Bible beside her.

Nina studied him, as if noticing his distraction. "You asked about the Bible earlier." She rested her hand on the black leather book sitting on the table. "I'm not a religious person. Never brought up that way." She shrugged. "El must have thought I needed to take a look. I couldn't say no, but it's all rather difficult for me."

She looked away a moment, and though he sensed he should respond, he was at a loss for words.

"I will admit that El had some solid attitudes about God and faith. Things I'll ponder, I think."

"Faith is different for each person. I think it happens in its own way. I grew up in a home where church was a normal Sunday activity. I went to Sunday school and sometimes the adult services. I believe, but even I find it easy to skip church sometimes, especially since I moved. I need to look for a home church." A rivulet of guilt ran through him. "I've passed so many here in Owosso. I think there's one on every other corner." Though he chuckled, his discomfort didn't fade. "I try to go most Sundays when I have a church family."

"Family?" She shrugged.

"It feels like a family and it's a meaningful break in the week."

"I imagine it is. Music and readings. Those things can draw a mind away from day-to-day troubles." She patted the Bible and pulled her hand away as if it had burned her. "Any news from Kimmy's mom?"

He drew his focus from the Bible to Nina, noting a look of discomfort on her face. "I talked with her yesterday." A pang of sadness whipped through him, mixed with concern. "She's in therapy now, but I don't think she can stay by herself yet even if she comes home. It sounded as if she'll go into an inpatient rehabilitation facility for physical and occupational therapy before they release her." His throat caught as he absorbed the issues continuing to grow. "Our mother lives a number of miles away but she wouldn't be much help, and I work every day."

"I'm sure a facility would be the best for her, Doug. She'll get good treatment." She searched his face, her own growing taut before she glanced out the window. "Doug, you've never mentioned Kimmy's father. Is he anywhere in the picture?"

His mood darkened. "Never. He's never seen Kimmy. I don't know if he ever knew about her. Roseanne never talks about him."

"She'd never married or—?"

"That's right. She took a chance, and Kimmy happened. She won't talk about it so I don't know a thing about him."

"That's hard." She appeared thoughtful. "Does Kimmy ever ask about him?"

He shrugged, hoping to hide his dark feelings. "I guess she has but Roseanne concocted some story. I think she said he died."

"One day when she's older Kimmy will want details. How he died. When? Did he love her? All those things we all want to know about our parents."

"I agree, but Roseanne only shakes her head and ignores me. She'll do what's right when Kimmy's older, I hope."

"I think she will. Truth from a mother with her child is important."

Letting the subject fade seemed his best move, and he gazed out the window and a grin broke the tension. "Kimmy's chasing something in one of the bushes."

Nina craned her neck to look outside "She seems to be doing well. She's adjusted. It's better for her to stay with you." Nina looked away a moment. "And you know, Doug, Kimmy's a bright little girl, and I fear she might feel too much responsibility and even guilt if she went home with her mother still needing care. I don't suppose you want to hear that."

"I've thought about that, too." He forced his eyes to stay connected with hers. "But I'm worried how to work it out. I can't take a leave, Nina. It's not feasible. Yet I'm the only one Roseanne can count on."

"I wish I had the answers." A distant look filled her eyes, but then she brightened. "I realize we've only met, but she's a sweet girl and… I'd be willing to help in any way I can."

Her concern for Kimmy touched him, and he wondered why she didn't have children, but he knew better than to even hint at the question. "I'm sure you're right, and thanks for your offer."

The subject weighed on him, and he opened his mind to allow another thought to slip from his memory. "Isn't Angie and Rick's wedding soon? I overheard something on Friday. For a while, I thought they were already married, but obviously they're not. He always goes home at night."

Nina laughed. "They're ones who follow their religion, I think." She shook her head. "But that's wise."

She quieted again, and he wished they could recapture the easy, casual relationship they'd had when they first met.

Finally she broke the silence. "I was surprised when I received a wedding invitation. We've only known each other a short time, but we clicked, I guess. I like Angie and Rick. Carly's a doll, too. She'll be their flower girl."

"I thought flower girls were toddlers who cry and run back to their moms."

She laughed. "Sometimes, yes, but this is a wonderful way to include her in the ceremony."

"It is. I was being silly." He grinned, glad his remark had broken the tension.

She studied him for a moment. "Do you get upset by personal questions?"

He managed to lasso his laugh, recalling her idiosyncrasy. "Not usually, but I'd say it depends on what kind of personal question."

She sent him a half grin and glanced out the window again. "I know you're single, but I can't help but wonder why."

"I ask myself the same question. I mentioned once that life got in the way. And there's truth to that. My dad was ill for a long time, and I did what I could to help my parents. Mom wasn't that healthy either, and Dad needed to be lifted or helped to stand. He lost both legs to diabetes." Those horrible days resurfaced, bringing pain with them. "Dad was a man's man. Wouldn't listen to my mom or the doctor's warnings. He thought he could beat all illnesses, but he couldn't. Strange how we do that, isn't it? We know what's best, but we ignore it."

Her face darkened a moment, and he feared he'd done it again. "Nina, I'm sorry if I—"

She held up her hand. "No. It wasn't what you said. There's truth to that. I've been bitter for years over my failed marriage, and yet when you said we know what's best but we ignore it, it struck home. The divorce was probably for the best under the circumstances."

Questions flew to his tongue but again he refrained

from uttering even a small question. Her marriage seemed to cause the last bugaboo, and he'd already spilled out too much of his life. He forgot they were virtual strangers. They'd met a short time ago, and yet it seemed as if it had been forever.

She eyed him as if wondering why he'd become silent.

He buried his question. "It's good sometimes to look back with fresh eyes. I think with most things, time clears our heads and we can face things differently. We let the blame go and focus on the result or the possibilities."

"Possibilities. That's sort of like hope, isn't it?"

"I suppose it is." He dragged his fingers through his hair. "I still hold out hope that one day in the near future I'll find the right person." What had he said? His mouth flapped without control. He'd spent much of his life preoccupied with everyone but himself. Where had those feelings come from?

And yet he knew. He studied her, admiring her light brown eyes that crinkled when she smiled and her intriguing wavy hair.

"For some people that's a real hope." She lifted a finger. "Let me check on the time. I still need to add something to the slow cooker." She rose and hurried away.

He watched her disappear beyond the door, as if she anticipated another question from him and was dodging it. He wished he could control his mouth and his heart. Nina looked uneasy, and he wished he knew what he could do to make their friendship as relaxed as it had been before.

He rose, perplexed, and wandered to the window, amazed that Kimmy spent so much time and patience in search of bugs. He shook his head. His patience ran amok more times than not. He should learn something from his young niece.

"I'm back."

He turned and was struck by how lovely Nina was. She walked with an air of confidence, yet she had an amiable aura. Despite her discomfort with personal subjects, she reached out to Kimmy in a sweet manner. That's what attracted him.

Nina joined him by the window. "I suppose we could go out and look for bugs, too."

"Or just watch. I don't want to ruin Kimmy's fun."

She chuckled. "Are you one of those men afraid of spiders?"

"I'm not talking."

With no other comment, she stepped outside to the porch, where two canvas chairs sat on the far end. He settled into one and Nina followed. "What do you do if Kimmy's sick or if you have to work overtime?"

He drew in a breath, hating to think of those situations. "Thank the Lord, they've been rare, but I had to take off work or see if I could get a neighbor to step in for me. In my previous home, I had an older woman close by who usually volunteered. She was a blessing."

"You know I can often work at home, Doug. If you ever need someone in a pinch—"

"I couldn't ask you to do that, but thanks for offering. I just pray that she stays healthy, and I can get off work on time. They have a latchkey program at her school so Roseanne had her in that program until she could pick her up. It was only for an hour or so."

"If you're sure, but just in case..." She rose and headed into the house.

His jaw sagged at her quick departure. In a moment, she reappeared and handed him a small card. He glanced at it, surprised she had a business card. "I see you're a public relations consultant. That sounds interesting."

"That's why I can work from home at times. It's a lot of computer work. As long as I get it done and it's good, that's all that counts."

"Can you find me a job like that?" Feeling relief, he sensed their relationship had smoothed out again. He tucked the card into his pocket, pleased to see her cell phone number on it.

"Look, Uncle Doug."

"I see you found a ladybug."

"Two of them. Look."

He slipped his arm around Kimmy and gave her a hug. "Your teacher will be very happy with all the insects you captured."

Nina glanced at her watch. "I think it's time to get cleaned up for dinner. The food should be ready soon."

Doug loved Nina's manner with Kimmy. He let the two go ahead of him before joining them inside, enveloped in a cozy feeling too often alien to him. The idea of being a family and having children wrapped around his mind and left him with a sense of wholeness. The sensation gave him pause. He'd become too enamored of Nina, and he needed to sort out his feelings. Was it her kindness to Kimmy that brought up these emotions? Or was he truly altering his attitude about relationships…and marriage?

Nina hit Save on her computer and rose. Her eyes burned from staring at the monitor. She'd worked at home all day, and in the quiet, she'd accomplished one large task for her new client, but she had more to do.

She sank into her easy chair. Though things had gone smoothly on Sunday with Doug, he hadn't contacted her since. Four days had passed with nothing. She'd thought their friendship had solidified with her apology and Doug's positive reaction.

When she lifted the footrest lever, she dropped back and closed her eyes, needing to sort her feelings. The word *friendship* struck her, but something deeper inched into her emotions. Getting involved again frightened her, and she'd set her mind to stay away from even a hint of commitment. Yet, Doug had come along and the idea of companionship cheered her. It aroused a sense of hope that Doug often talked about.

Since she'd moved to Lilac Circle, she had made friends with Angie and El and maybe that was enough. But as soon as she let the thought breathe, she knew the answer. She'd regret it if she and Doug didn't become true friends.

Friends, even good friends, could enjoy each other's company without calling it a date. Going to dinner together, talking on the porch, those were pleasant events without imposing two lives into one. That's what marriage was. The willingness to give of yourself and be one. She could stand on her own without anything more than an enjoyable friendship. The idea sent tension out the window. Good friends. Best friends, maybe. Platonic. That was the word. Platonic friendship. She blew a stream of air from her lungs.

Now to believe it and act on it.

As the friendship idea drifted, Angie's wedding came to mind. Though Angie had addressed it to her and a guest, she had mailed her RSVP indicating she would attend alone. Her shoulders heaved. Being alone at a wedding made her cringe. She would feel like an elderly maiden aunt who was parked in a chair and everyone had fun around her. What could she do to get out of it now? Illness? She could fake that, but it seemed so obvious. Her shoulder twitched again, and she veered her gaze out the window.

When she shifted her eyes, they lit on the bible. Margie's bible. El shouldn't have given it to her. Giving it to someone who would use it made more sense.

Yet her eyes remained on the book, and the verse she'd spotted at El's came to mind. She flipped to the back and turned pages until she spotted the reference, and then searched through the scripture until she found the verses—Matthew 17:20.

He said: "Because you have so little faith, I tell you the truth. If you have faith as small as a mustard seed, you can say to this mountain, "Move from here to there" and it will move. Nothing will be impossible for you.

But who was the He referred to in the verse? She moved her eyes upward and found her answer. Jesus. Jesus said with the tiniest bit of faith nothing was impossible. How could that be? She closed her eyes. A mustard seed was minute, but she couldn't claim to have even that amount of faith.

Her cell phone's ringtone sounded from a distance, and she slipped the Bible onto the table, dropped the footrest and hurried to the computer table in her office.

She viewed a number she didn't recognize. It persisted. She hit talk and said hello.

"Nina, this is Doug."

Her heart lurched. "Is something wrong?" Her head spun—how did he have her number? Right, the business card.

"Nothing horrible. I've been asked—that's a nice way to put it—to work overtime tomorrow. I have a meeting in the morning and a huge project to get ready. I hate to ask, but—"

"Doug." Her heart slowed to a trot, knowing Kimmy was fine. "I volunteered. I don't mind. I'm going to the office in the morning and I'll be working at home the rest of the day. Kimmy will be fine with me."

"Are you sure?" The question rang with concern.

"I won't indulge you with a response." She cleared her throat with as much drama as she could, hoping he recognized she was teasing him.

"Okay, I get you." Relief sounded in his tone. "I'll stop by tonight with the info you'll need, and I'll go into the school when I pick her up today and leave your name so they'll know I sent you."

"Good, because I don't want to be arrested for kidnapping."

He chuckled. "Thanks so much. By the way, I'm sorry I haven't seen you since Sunday. Once again life happened. I had to spend time with my mother on the phone, and then Kimmy and I went there one evening. She's having some health issues, and I'm trying to convince her to sell the house and move into an assisted living facility."

"Any progress?"

"Mom isn't the easiest to convince. It's frustrating."

She recognized the weariness in his voice. "I can imagine, and with her living a distance away, it's even more complex."

"Thanks for understanding." His contrite tone had brightened. "I'll drop by tonight."

The conversation ended, and she headed back to the chair, grateful that her work allowed her to spend time at home. And now with Kimmy, it answered Doug's need. A sense of purpose eased through her as she tilted back in her chair. She closed her eyes while visions of her new life spread around her. She'd see Doug tonight and spend time with Kimmy. What could be better? A platonic relationship seemed perfect.

Hearing the doorbell, Nina dropped the footrest again and bounded from the chair, startled that she'd fallen asleep. Confused, she eyed her watch as she opened the door.

"Hope I didn't interrupt." Angie grinned and took a step forward, anticipating being invited in.

"You didn't." She shifted back and beckoned Angie inside. "In fact, I'm glad you came." Nina swung her arm toward the recliner. "I'd fallen asleep in my chair."

"I'm so sorry I woke you." Angie frowned. "So what's stressing you out?"

Angie's questioning look caused Nina to shake her head. "Nothing. Why would you ask that? My eyes were tired. I've been staring at a monitor all day."

Angie chuckled. "It's a good excuse."

Nina ignored the comment and motioned to a chair. "Please have a seat."

She looked behind her and settled on the edge of the sofa. "I can't stay long, but I finally got around to checking the RSVPs and I noticed you only put down one person attending." She tilted her head, her eyes questioning.

"That's correct. There's no law, right?" Nina flashed a grin, though uncomfortable with Angie's reaction. "I'm not dating anyone, and I decided it was easier just to come alone."

"You can, but it's more fun when you have a friend with you. Do you like to dance?"

Angie's question stung. "I used to. It's been a long time."

"It's like riding a bike. You never forget how to do that."

Her attempt at humor failed. "I'll keep that in mind if the opportunity arises."

Angie rose. "I must have sounded pushy, Nina. Forgive me. I would love to see you have fun. I really like you."

"Thanks." She stood and rested her hand on Angie's shoulder. "But I think I'll come alone."

"Okay, but…what about Doug? He's a great guy and a neighbor. If we'd known him better, we might have invited him, too. In fact, there's your answer."

Whether she came alone or with someone wouldn't ruin the wedding reception. "Angie. I've already decided that I'm not asking anyone."

Angie studied her a moment as if ready to rebut. "Okay, if you're that determined, but I'll put you down for two just in case." She gave a one-shoulder shrug and turned toward the door before she wiggled her fingers in a wave. "See you later."

Exasperation bristled along Nina's arms as she said goodbye and watched her go. Maybe Angie was teasing, but why couldn't she make her own decisions without people pressuring her?

After stepping back through the doorway, she sank into her comfy chair. Bring a date? Angie assumed Doug was the only guy she knew well enough to ask. That was true, but she had never asked anyone for a date, and she wasn't starting now.

She shook her head. As for Doug, she already had concerns about her feelings. Asking him would be truly stupid.

As she tossed herself back, she hit the footrest lever. Maybe she could fall asleep again and awake convinced that Angie's visit was a bad dream.

Who was she kidding?

She closed her eyes, and her senses returned. What was she fighting? Angie hadn't suggested a date. She'd suggested an escort. Friends sometimes did that for friends.

Friends. The word rolled around in her mind. Minutes ago she'd thought the solution had been found. Platonic friends. Then what was the probem? She closed her eyes, releasing a sigh that rattled through her chest. She could fool others but not herself. Having Doug escort her, in reality, tempted her emotions. One day, he would face his own reality and want a family. If she fell in love with Doug, he could walk away as Todd had done when he learned she couldn't bear a child. Her chest constricted. And he should walk away if he wanted a family. She couldn't chance it.

After working without a break, Nina checked her watch. One. She needed to pick up Kimmy at school between three and three-thirty. Fatigued again, and not only from the monitor. She felt plain old tired. Her sleep the night before had been restless. She thanked Angie for that. Why had she made a big deal about attending the wedding alone? Yes, she would mess up the table seating. Most everyone attended as couples, so the tables usually seated eight or ten. She'd make it seven or nine. She managed a chuckle. Maybe someone's maiden aunt needed a seat.

She made her way to the kitchen, longing for something to distract her. The refrigerator didn't pose any invitation as she gazed inside. The few cookies still in the jar she'd kept for Kimmy. Crackers? With what? Peanut butter, but she ran out a few days before. Maybe a trip to the grocery store would do it.

Instead she opened the back door and stepped outside, her eyes grazing the landscape. She'd done nothing about the perennials, and soon it would be too late. She hurried back in, grabbed her cell phone and purse and slipped into her car, recalling a garden shop not too far away. Soon she was pulling into the parking lot. After studying two rows of flowers, she spotted the coneflowers and hoisted a plant into her basket while her mind slipped to Kimmy. Time was ticking away, and she didn't want to scare her or disappoint Doug by being late. With time on her mind, she spotted a sales clerk and caught her attention. "I'm in a new house without much landscaping, and I'm checking perennials but I want to make sure it's not too late to plant. Can you tell me?"

"Sure. You have coneflowers there. It's a good choice. They're hardy flowers, and in Zone 5 the fall months are perfect for planting."

She thanked the salesclerk and then asked directions to find the daisies.

The woman beckoned her to follow. With her guidance, she set three pots of daisies into the basket. Finally she circled back and grabbed three more colorful coneflowers to brighten her garden and her life.

She paid the bill, her mind everywhere but on her purchases. After she arrived home and unloaded, she realized Kimmy would already be waiting for her. Angry at her carelessness, she dashed to her car and headed down Oliver Street.

When she spotted the redbrick building, darkened with age, she slowed and pulled into the pickup lane. Only a few children were outside waiting, a couple others were getting into cars, but Kimmy wasn't among them. Panicking, she pictured Doug's frantic face and felt nailed to the seat. She sat a moment deciding what to do. Her only choice was to go inside. She drove to the parking lot and slipped out as her nerves set in. What would she do if Kimmy had been picked up by someone else. Kidnapped? Her carelessness rent her heart.

Breathless, she darted along the inside corridor, following the sign to the office. As soon as she reached the door, she spotted Kimmy. Her legs weakened as relief spread over her.

Kimmy's eyes widened as she ran to her. "I thought you forgot me."

"I'd never do that, Kimmy." The words reverberated through her chest. She gave her a hug, noticing tears on Kimmy's cheeks. Nina's heart wrenched. "I'm sorry, sweetie. I would never forget you." Her throat closed as she struggled to continue. "I went to the nursery for flowers and time ran away from me." She tilted her head. "But I'm here now." *Thank You* soared above her and stopped her cold. *Thank You.* Had she prayed? Warmth spread through her body as her fears flew away.

She pulled herself from the sensation, noticing a questioning look from the woman behind the counter. "I'm sorry I'm late. Doug Billings gave you my name, I think. I'm here for Kimmy. He had to work overtime today."

The woman gave her a frown and checked a list near the phone and nodded. "You are?"

"Nina Jerome. Doug and I are neighbors."

The woman nodded. "We have to be careful, and we also ask that you be on time."

"Yes, I know. It won't happen again. I guarantee." She meant every word.

The woman gave a faint nod. "Kimmy, you can leave now and have a good weekend, okay?"

Kimmy grinned. "Okay."

"And do you have all of your belongings?"

She nodded to the woman while Nina stepped away, wanting to escape before the woman had her scrubbing boards or banging erasers.

Kimmy caught up with her in the hallway "This weekend I have to find different kinds of leaves and things that grow on trees and bushes." She adjusted her backpack. "Can we find them in your yard?"

"We sure can." Nina slipped her arm around Kimmy's shoulders and guided her outside.

When Kimmy spotted the car, she bolted ahead, and Nina had a hard time keeping up. Like a father, Doug had put the booster seat into the back of her car, and Kimmy slipped in and locked the seat belt. Captured by the image of Doug with his arms embracing a child of his own, Nina's heart grew heavy. If only… Not wanting the thought to ruin her day, she headed for the driver's seat and turned the key.

On the way home, she thought about the cookies she'd saved for Kimmy, but other than those, she had no after-school snacks for her. Her mind drifted until Kimmy broke her train of thought.

"Can we plant your flowers when we get back? Carly got to help Angie plant the flowers. She told me."

Competition. Nina grinned. Though she liked the idea, today it wasn't practical. "It's late today, but let's plan it for another day—maybe tomorrow—and you can tell Carly you helped me plant flowers. Instead, let's do your homework. That will be fun, but first we'll stop at the store for a treat."

Kimmy's face brightened. "I like treats."

So did she, except for the calories. Again an image of Doug entered her mind, his smile the best treat she'd had in years.

She shook her head and pulled into a grocery store. Kimmy unhooked her seat belt, slipped outside, and they headed into the store. She guided Kimmy to healthy snacks and was pleased when she thought of string cheese. Kimmy liked those and peanut butter crackers. She selected multigrain. Another good choice.

In minutes, they were back in the car and pulling into her driveway. Kimmy lugged the grocery bag from the backseat, and they hurried inside for the snack and then the homework project.

Once in the yard, Kimmy slowed, her expression thoughtful. "Do you like my uncle Doug?"

Like? The question startled her, and her chest tightened. "I think he's a very nice man, and I like you, too." Her heart thudding, she studied Kimmy's expression. "Why do you ask?"

"He's happier since he met you. I'm glad you like him 'cuz I think he likes you…a lot."

Heat rushed up her neck and warmed her cheeks. "Thank you, Kimmy. It's always nice to be liked. I'm sure lots of people like you."

Kimmy looked thoughtful. "But I think you make Uncle Doug happier."

She made Doug happier? He made her happier, too, but this topic had to stop before she lost it. "Look there, Kimmy." She pointed to the grass, grateful she'd spotted the pinecone. "Do you know what that is?"

"An acorn?" Kimmy eyed the cone a moment before shaking her head. "It's the other one. A…"

"Right. It's a pinecone. People make Christmas decorations out of them."

Her eyes widened. "They do?" She picked up the cone and studied it. "How?"

Her brain went into gear. "I think they spray them with gold paint and tie a red bow on top. They can add artificial holly berries or other little Christmas symbols."

"Can we make some for Christmas?"

"Christmas?" Nina's heart weighted, doubting Kimmy would still be with Doug then. The old familiar loneliness spread through her. She drew in a breath. "We'll have to wait and see. You might be home and busy with your mom."

A shadow slipped across Kimmy's face. "But I could

come and visit Uncle Doug." Hope washed away the gloom. "Then we could make them."

"We probably could." Nina stepped away, needing to avoid the emotions barraging her. She'd never given the future much thought, and she didn't want to start now.

Her mind bogged with Kimmy's questions and especially her earlier comment. If a child noticed Doug seemed happier when she was around him, wouldn't everyone spot it? She hadn't known him long enough to notice a change in his behavior. Her heart pressed against her chest as if it were paper and could tear through. One thing she couldn't do was offer Doug empty hope. She bit the edge of her lip unable to face her own emptiness.

Kimmy dashed around the yard collecting leaves from shrubs and plants, even two blades of crabgrass that Nina needed to attend to. She watched the girl, caught up in her excitement and energy. Though she was only thirty-four, her energy had dropped a couple of notches each year. She'd be bedridden by fifty if she didn't perk up and find enjoyment in life.

A sound drew her attention, and she felt her pocket. She dug into it and pulled out her cell phone. This time she recognized the phone number. "Hi, Doug."

"How's it going? Did you pick up Kimmy?"

"Sure did." Her pulse kicked into a high gear. "We had healthy snacks, and now we're doing her homework."

Doug chuckled. "What is it this time?"

"Here, you can ask Kimmy." She beckoned to her, and she bounced forward, a smile brimming on her face.

"Hello."

Whatever Doug asked or said, Kimmy rattled on about the snacks and homework, along with a list of what she'd found.

Nina's cheeks warmed again, seeing joy in the child's face. She amazed her, rolling with catastrophes better than most adults. While her mother was miles away, badly injured, Kimmy had dealt with the situation like a professional, making the best of her time with Doug without complaint. Even without fear.

She longed to cope with upheaval as well as Kimmy. If she'd done so, today she would be ready to make changes in her life, to move on and find happiness once again. Instead, she'd clung to her pitiful past and feelings of abandonment in the way someone would cherish old pictures.

Kimmy returned the phone to her, and she lifted it to her ear. "We're doing fine, Doug."

"Good. I hope to get out of here by seven-thirty. Eight at the latest."

She pictured his face, his eyes crinkling at the edges as he talked, the lock of hair that sometimes dipped to his forehead, the five o'clock shadow she found so appealing. "We're fine, Doug. Really."

"I owe you one, Nina. Ask and it's yours. Anything."

His offer sent prickles up her arms. "You might be sorry you said that."

"Never. I'll see you later."

They disconnected, and she approached Kimmy with Doug's offer ringing in her ears.

Angie's insistence that she have an escort for the wedding had bugged her, and naturally Angie thought of Doug. But Doug had already been embedded in her mind since they'd spent so much time together. Everything had been innocent and mainly involving Kimmy. The wedding didn't involve Kimmy. In fact he'd have to hire a babysitter. She couldn't ask him.

I owe you one, Nina. Ask and it's yours. Anything. Anything. But escorting her to a wedding certainly wasn't what he had in mind. But...what had he meant? He said *anything.*

Her mind spun, and she closed her eyes. Truth was, the more she thought of it, she disliked attending the reception alone. A wedding service, maybe, but the celebration? A party? Alone would be a downer. Still asking Doug...that would take gumption on her part and even a bit of faith.

The idea settled in her mind. She'd already talked to God once today. Maybe, just maybe, another little chat might give her unexpected courage.

The whole idea spread through her like puzzle pieces. She'd always been good with them except the puzzles of her life. That was one she hadn't conquered yet. But maybe, just maybe...

Chapter Four

Doug leaned back in his office chair and eyed the stack of paperwork that he'd nearly conquered. He rubbed the back of his neck, kneading out the knots, and checked his watch with blurred vision. He'd stared at the computer too long, and though he still had portions of the documents, he couldn't face another moment. He had to consider Kimmy's needs.

Nina slipped into his mind again, and his pulse snagged. He'd never met a woman so unselfish with her time. Not only had she spent hours with Kimmy already, she had volunteered to spend more. What kind of woman did that?

A grin pranced to his lips. A woman who loved children. He nodded. That was it. He'd watched her with Kimmy, and she was a natural and very creative with her. He loved that. Again, his pulse stumbled as he faced the truth. He liked Nina. Liked her a lot. More than any other woman he'd known. But then she was easy to lov…like.

And now Angie had offered him an opening. Her wedding. He'd never expected to receive an invitation with the stipulation he escort Nina. All he needed now was the nerve to ask her. The wedding would be a way to know her better and to see her in a social setting. The neighborhood outdoor party had been the only social situation where they'd been together, and she seemed somewhat withdrawn. He had so much to learn about her. Only then could he really let his thoughts take flight. He drew in a breath as he admitted his failure. They'd already taken flight without his permission. So unlike him.

He shook his head to clear his thoughts and flicked through the documents, confident he could finish in the morning before his meeting. He riffled the pages and tapped them into a neat stack before slipping them into a folder and dropping them into his work tray. As he logged off the computer, his stomach rumbled, reminding him he'd rushed through a flavorless sandwich at noon, and now eating a good meal sounded great.

Tonight cooking was out of the question, but take-home was perfect, and Kimmy loved Chinese food. Tasty food with no work hugged his thoughts. He grasped his cell phone and located Nina's number. His heart lurched when she answered on the second ring.

"Nina, this is Doug."

She chuckled. "I saw your face on my phone."

His chest tightened. "My face?" He'd seen hers so often in his mind, but on his—

"I snapped a photo of you one day in the yard when you weren't looking. Now I can see your picture when you call."

A grin stole to his lips again. "Lucky you." He hoped he sounded lighthearted. Although in his ears, he sounded breathless. Exactly how he felt.

She chuckled. "How's work?"

"Done for the night. Did Kimmy eat dinner? I—"

"Doug, I'm sorry. We had a late snack and I haven't done a thing yet, but I can feed her for you if—"

"Don't be sorry. That's good. I thought I'd pick up Chinese." He hesitated before barreling ahead. "Do you like it?"

"Love it."

"Great. I always bring home too much for us, and I'd love to share. You won't have to worry about cooking tonight…unless you need a break from Kimmy."

"From Kimmy? Never."

"How about me?"

She laughed. "A break? Not at all. I look forward to seeing you…and the Chinese food, especially egg rolls."

"Our favorite, too." Though she'd stumbled over her words, he was glad he'd asked. His shoulders straightened. "You'll see me and the egg rolls soon, plus a surprise."

"Surprise? We'll be waiting. But you'd better hurry. Kimmy overheard me mention Chinese egg rolls, and she's dancing around the room."

"What about you?"

"I'm not dancing, but I'm looking forward to the surprise and to seeing you. We're both anxious."

"Maybe twenty minutes." He ended the call and cringed. His surprise comment sounded like something extraordinary. All he had in mind was a couple of their favorite entrées. He shook his head, frustrated with his silliness. Her tone had changed as if she ex-

pected something really special. Not entrées. Whatever she had in mind, he hoped he wouldn't disappoint
her too much.

Nina stared at her phone a moment before slipping
it into her pocket. Shocked by her own directness, she
steadied and sent up another warning to herself. She
knew more about his sister than about him. Why had
she admitted that she looked forward to seeing him?

Unable to retract her admission, she stepped around
Kimmy and headed for the kitchen. Chinese food didn't
take long to prepare, and Doug would be there before
she knew it. She opened a cabinet and pulled out three
plates and silverware, unsure of what she needed but
it gave her a distraction.

"Nina." Kimmy's voice piped into the kitchen from
the hallway, and she heard her skipping footfalls as she
bounded through the door. "What else is Uncle Doug
bringing?"

"Else?" She shook her head. "I don't know. He only
mentioned egg rolls."

"That's only a ap-tizer. We like wonton soup and
Chicken… I can't remember the name."

She grinned at Kimmy. "That sounds like a lot of
food."

"We like it." She spiraled and plopped into a chair.
"Uncle Doug will probably bring too much. He always
does, and today he'll want to make you happy." She
tilted her head. "You know why?"

The child's expression confused her. "Not really."

Kimmy giggled. "Because you make him happy."
Her grin sank to a frown. "Did you forget? I told you
that he's happier when you're with us."

Nina stopped herself from biting her lip. "I guess you did tell me, but I forgot." Never. She couldn't forget that. She ruffled Kimmy's head and gave her a hug. Kimmy rewarded her with a beaming smile and hopped off the chair. "I'm going to watch for him so I can help him carry in the bags."

"Okay, I'll be right here."

As Kimmy skedaddled through the doorway, Nina sank into the empty chair and caught her breath. She'd warned herself many times to keep her emotions in check, but it seemed she'd lost her ability to hang on to her heart. Kimmy had captured her from day one, and Doug's vulnerability was a close second.

He seemed to approach everything with caution when she first met him though he'd opened up a bit. Still, she had her own barricades too, and she'd tried to grant him the same privacy. Yet being on the other end, she disliked it.

Everything had a good explanation. Doug's life seemed to revolve around Kimmy, his sister and his mother. Everyone but himself. Since they'd met, his reaction mirrored a child finding a new friend or getting a new toy. He had something to entertain him for a change. She didn't have to worry about Doug getting romantic ideas. Neither of them were ready for anything. Now all she had to do was convince her prancing pulse and hitching heart.

"Nina." Kimmy's call jerked her from the chair.

She hurried to the living room. "Is he here already?"

"No. There's a lady coming here."

As the words left Kimmy's mouth, she saw Rema climb the porch step. Curious, she reached the door before she rang the bell. "Hi, Rema. What's up?"

She grinned with a shrug. "Nothing important. I thought I'd stop by and say hello again."

Though poor timing, she wanted to be sociable and pushed open the screen. "Come in. I'm waiting for our dinner to be delivered, but he's not here yet."

Rema stepped inside and spotted Kimmy. "Hi." She gave Kimmy a weak wave. "Isn't this Doug's child... niece. I think that's it."

"He's my uncle." Kimmy studied Rema's face. "Do you know him?"

"Not really. I met him at the street party we had at the beginning of September. I think you were playing with Carly."

Kimmy nodded. "Can I sit on the porch and wait for Uncle Doug?"

"Sure you can." Nina welcomed her request, fearing that Rema might say something about her friendship with Doug or ask questions.

Kimmy bounded to the porch, and Nina turned to her surprise visitor. "Would you like to sit?"

"I know you're busy so I won't stay." She checked the nearest chair and sat. "I hope you're learning your way around the city. I know you're new here."

"I've done quite well. That's what's nice about a small town. I have the city map and it's been helpful."

"And you seem to be very friendly with Doug. I'm sure he knows a lot, too."

"Yes, he's been very helpful. I'm helping him with Kimmy sometimes when he has to work late...like today."

"Ahh. I see." She grinned. "Still, if you need any directions or recommendations, just ask." She looked away and seemed to sink into thought. "I'm not sure how long I'm staying here. Maybe I'll get the house. It's hard to know with a divorce settlement coming up."

"Divorce. I'm so sorry." Her lungs depleted for a second, thinking of her own trials. "If you need any advice on that, I've been through one. Not pretty and not what I wanted."

Rema perked up. "Me, either. Far from it. I was blind to Trey's unfaithfulness much longer than I should have been."

Rema's eyes searched hers. "That must have hurt."

"Very. Plus I felt stupid. Then your divorce wasn't because of cheating?"

She drew back a moment, looking for words to explain but said nothing. "No, not that kind of unfaithful…" The statement made no sense to her so Rema couldn't possibly understand what she meant.

"People can be unfaithful in many ways. Dreams they ignore. Promises they don't keep."

Her eyes widened. "You understand. I thought I'd spoken in circles."

"No. I don't suppose you want to talk about it?" A frown rose on her face. "Sorry, I shouldn't have asked that question."

Though she might be able to trust Rema, she couldn't. She hadn't trusted anyone except Angie, and she hoped that Angie could keep that between the two of them. She wanted no one's pity for being childless. "You're right. He broke the basic promises of the marriage vows to love in sickness and health and in time of trouble. When that happens, doubt and questions smother the love that had been there. They're emotions I don't want to relive."

Rema rose and rested her hand on Nina's shoulder.

"I don't want you to relive any of it. I've been struggling with the same. You have a friend who understands." She gave her a pat and stepped away. "Doug will be here soon so I'll say goodbye. Remember if you need anything just ask."

"Thanks. I appreciate your stopping by."

"I enjoyed it." She gave a wave and stepped outside.

Nina returned to the kitchen and grasped the teakettle. She could make decaf coffee, but tea seemed more appropriate for a Chinese dinner. She turned on the burner so it would be ready and placed a glass on the table for Kimmy's milk.

Finished with all she could do until he arrived, she strode back to the living room, and as she entered, Kimmy let out a yell. "He's here."

Nina spun around and hurried toward the door but Kimmy swung it open, and jiggled behind the screen as Doug appeared on the porch. A strong cold wind followed Doug into the living room.

"It's getting nippy out there." He approached her carrying a large bag and wearing a broad smile. "We won't go hungry."

Nina shook her head. "Should I call around and invite the neighbors?"

Doug winked. "We look forward to leftovers." He turned his head toward Kimmy. "Don't we?"

She dragged her tongue over her lips and nodded.

Still astonished at the size of the sack, Nina reached toward it, but he gave a quick head shake. "I'm fine. Just point the way."

She motioned toward the kitchen and swung ahead of him, knowing she needed more dinnerware. She stood at the counter, watching him unload the containers and trying to keep her reaction to a minimum. Finally she gave up and laughed.

"Chinese has a lot to offer." He lifted the boxes and listed the contents. "Egg rolls, wonton soup, fried rice, pepper steak, chicken with Chinese vegetables, almond cookies and fortune cookies."

Nina turned around to hide her grin as she drew out soup bowls and small plates. Not only from the amount of food but from the joy on his face. Today, Doug's quiet demeanor had blossomed, and she loved it. Her spirit lifted, observing his reaction to something as simple as setting out the multitude of cartons.

She placed the dishes on the table, and then returned for soup spoons and large serving spoons. Finally they gathered around the table, and as she opened her mouth to speak, Kimmy folded her hands and bowed her head while Doug followed. Closing her mouth, she waited and listened to Kimmy's little prayer.

"Come, Lord Jesus, be our guest and let these gifts to us be blessed. Amen."

Doug joined in the *amen*, and she sat in silence, wanting to say it, too, but it felt too strange. She had no idea if God wanted to hear an *amen* from someone who had drifted so far away from Him.

When she lifted her head, Doug's eyes were on her, a look of curiosity on his face. "Are you all right?"

This time she did bite the edge of her lip before managing to speak. "Thank you, Kimmy, for the prayer."

The child gave her a fleeting smile and plucked an egg roll from the container with her fork.

She and Doug chuckled, and the tension faded.

Digging into the excellent food, everyone was silent, even Kimmy, which was rare. Nina grinned to herself, realizing how the presence of a child had changed her life. The child and Doug. She drew in a breath, and Doug gave her another questioning look. She shrugged and monitored her emotional reaction to curb any more conversation.

Kimmy finished first and she asked to be excused. With Doug's approval, she skipped off to the living room, anxious to watch a children's program on TV. They continued in silence for a few moments until Nina stood and gathered the plates and silverware she and Kimmy had used. When she set them on the counter and turned, Doug grinned and laid his fork on his plate.

"I'd better stop or I'll burst."

She flashed him a silly grin. "I wondered." She waved her hand over the abundance left. "Now you can call in the neighbors."

"Leftovers. Did you forget?" He leaned back, his grin still there as if he had to force it.

She shook her head and reached to gather the rest of the dishes.

"Not so fast." He grasped the last small bag. "Dessert, but first…" He motioned for her to sit.

She sank into the chair, curious about his forced grin. "Something's wrong? Is it Roseanne?"

"No. And nothing's wrong. I wanted to tell you that last night after I left here I ran into Angie in front of her house."

Angie? She studied his face, her mind at a standstill.

"She mentioned the wedding, which is coming up fast, and told me you were coming without an escort and she extended an invitation, suggesting I invite you to go with me."

Unable to control her irritation, heat burned on her

cheeks. She shook her head. "I'm sorry, Doug. That's no way to be invited to a wedding, and I've already told her that going alone was fine with me, so please don't—"

"Nina, don't apologize. You know Angie. She likes to solve everyone's dilemmas. Apparently she wouldn't want to attend a wedding alone, and she's projecting that on you."

He was right. Angie wanted to fix everything. Even things that didn't need fixing. A burst of air escaped her lungs and she shook her head. "Let's start again, okay?"

He drew back, confusion on his face. "Okay."

The response rang as a question. "The more I thought about going alone I realized it wasn't the best idea, but I'm not seeing anyone right now..." She noticed his expression and grinned. "Naturally I see you, but I meant I'm not dating anyone." She gnawed her lip. "But today when you said you owed me one and said I could ask for anything...the wedding came to mind. I considered asking you to be my escort but I feared I wouldn't have the nerve. So I guess Angie at least opened the door to that."

The tension on his face was replaced by a smile. "She did, it seems. And to answer your question, I would be happy to be your escort. I haven't been to a wedding in years."

His response seemed too easy, yet her shoulders relaxed as she heard the positive tone of his voice. "What about Kimmy?"

His smile broadened. "Angie solved that situation, too. She has someone sitting with Carly and said the girls would have fun together."

"You are kidding." She rolled her eyes, hearing Angie's voice ring in her head.

"Nope. Problem solved." He lifted the smaller bag and set it in front of him. "Now dessert. But we'll have to call Kimmy. She loves fortune cookies."

With his call, Kimmy darted into the room and spotted the crescent treats. "Can I read mine?"

Doug handed her a cookie. She broke it open and tugged out the little slip of paper. She studied it. "'Learning is a tre…'" She held the paper toward Nina. "What's that word?"

"Treasure. Sound it out. Trea-sure."

Kimmy nodded. "'Learning is a treasure that will follow its…owner.' I don't understand."

When she hesitated, Nina eyed the paper. "It means that what you learn will be with you and follow you everywhere."

Kimmy crinkled her nose. "How can learning follow me?"

Nina tousled her hair. "Everything you learn is inside your head so where you go it goes."

She tittered. "My head holds everything."

"Right, my girl." Doug eyed Nina and flagged his little white flag of paper. "Mine says, 'Your home will find happiness.'" He gave her a wink. "That's something I can use."

"Me, too." She lifted the fortune cookie and snapped it open. When she eyed the few words, her chest contracted as the words swam in her head.

Doug cocked his head. "What does it say? We all read ours aloud."

She managed to grin and lifted the ribbon of paper. "'Look around. Your life is changing.'" When she looked at him, her pulse hitched. "Summer's nearly gone and autumn is closing in. Life is changing."

His eyes searched hers as a coy grin slipped to his lips. "Hmm? That's true, but it says your life not the seasons."

Heat crept up her neck. She didn't believe in fortunes. So why had her heart danced? Nothing made sense anymore.

Chapter Five

Doug leaned back against the kitchen chair and savored his coffee. Saturdays always cheered him. Kimmy, to his surprise, had settled on the sofa watching a kids' TV show. Though rare, he liked the moments when he didn't feel the need to entertain her. He'd be a poor father. His knowledge of kids sank in his mind like quicksand. From one day to the next, he tried to recall what necessities were essential for a little girl's needs. If she'd been a boy, he might have a better grasp. He gave five stars to women who seemed to be born with a maternal instinct.

Nina's image formed in his mind, and with her face in his thoughts, he steeled his determination to escort her to Angie's wedding. Though she was irked, an emotion he'd seen before, she admitted she'd planned to ask him. They had both needed the gumption to do it, and he was glad he'd been the one.

The jingle of his cell phone broke through his thoughts, and he grasped it from the table and clicked Talk.

"Are you busy?" Nina's sweet voice sailed from the line.

He eyed his coffee. "Not busy at all. Do you need help?"

"Not from you really, but I promised Kimmy she could help me plant the fall flowers I bought yesterday. Did she tell you?"

"No. She was too wound up about the pinecones and Christmas ornaments."

"I felt bad about that, Doug. She may not be with you at Christmas, but she really wants to make decorations."

Her comment sank into his chest, causing an ache. "I am anxious for Kimmy to be with Roseanne, but it's a change. I'll miss her. Even though life's more complicated with her here, I've begun to breathe it now. I hope you understand what I mean."

"I do. She's important to both of us. She's brought fun and excitement into my humdrum life."

He closed his eyes and pressed his lips together. "Kids are infectious, aren't they?"

Nina chuckled. "You make them sound like a disease."

"A disease of the heart." Burdened with emotion, he segued from his dilemma. "Kimmy's watching TV, but I'm sure she'd prefer to be outside with you. I'll let her know you're ready for her help."

"Thanks, but only if she wants to. Okay?"

"Sure thing." He ended the call and poured his cooling coffee into the sink. "Kimmy." He strode into the living room as she jumped up from the sofa.

"Are we going to do something?"

"You are." He grinned at her quizzical expression. "Nina's ready to plant flowers."

"Yeah." She clapped her hands but faltered as she looked down at her clothes. "Will I get dirty?"

"Maybe, but everything's washable. Even you."

She giggled as she ran to the door. "I'll see you later, Uncle Doug." She gave a little wave and headed outside.

He watched her through the window, skipping along the sidewalk as if on her way to a party.

Watching her go took him back to the days before Roseanne's accident when he lived a quiet undisturbed life. That time seemed empty now as he pictured his weeks—months—with Kimmy filling the house with giggles and noise. When she vanished beyond his view, loneliness washed over him.

Nina slipped her cell phone into her pocket and headed for the garage, but its ringtone caused her to dig it back out. She hit Talk.

"Nina, how are you, dear? You haven't called in ages."

Her mother rarely called. "Just busy. Is everything okay?"

"I'm fine, dear, and so is your stepdad."

Howard. No matter how hard she tried he had never gained her favor, but she'd made the best of it. The call had a purpose, she knew. "Glad to hear everyone's well." She retreated to the front of the house and pointed to the phone as Kimmy arrived. "Mom, I was getting ready to plant a few perennials so they'll bloom next year. I can't seem to find time during the week." Hoping her mother would get the hint. she waited for her goodbye.

"Flowers for your new house. How nice. And that's

somewhat why I'm calling. We thought we might come to visit for Thanksgiving. Wouldn't that be nice?"

Her eyes widened. Nice? Images of Thanksgiving with Doug had entered her thoughts, and hopefully with Kimmy. Now the idea dangled like a loose thread. Her chest tightened. "Yes, it would be nice. But isn't it a long drive and what about bad weather? The north has early snowfalls sometimes. Are you sure Thanksgiving's a good time?"

"We'll fly from Florida and rent a car. That would be easier, we thought."

"Rent a car. Yes, that's good idea."

Kimmy sidled closer. "Are you talking to Uncle Doug?" Her piping voice broke the quiet.

Nina shook her head. "My mother." She'd tried to whisper but it hadn't worked.

"Do you have company, dear?"

"Kimmy just came over to help me with the planting. She's seven and in the second grade."

"Seven? Why in the world are you entertaining a seven-year-old?"

"She entertains me, Mom." She gave Kimmy a wink. "Children like to learn things, and I'm teaching her how to plant flowers."

"Couldn't she learn that from her mother?"

Nina released a stream of air. "Her mother was in a serious accident and she's staying with her uncle, who's a neighbor."

Her mother offered a loud sigh. "I suppose it's none of my business."

That's right, Mom. She muzzled her thought. "Once you make plans about visiting, call and give me the details so I know when to expect you. Okay?"

"I'll call when I know."

Nina held her breath, knowing if she remained silent her mother might catch on.

"Okay, dear. We'll talk later then." Her mother added her goodbye and hung up.

With her mother's visit clinging to her thoughts, she caught her breath. Under normal circumstances, she would be happy for a short visit with her mother. One thing they'd both learned over the years was their personalities tended to clash, and absence didn't always make the heart grow fonder. "What did your mommy want?"

Nina grinned at her curious expression. "She wants to visit for Thanksgiving."

Kimmy smiled. "That will be fun. I hope my mommy can be with us on Thanksgiving, too. I hope she's better."

"I do, too, sweetheart." She wrapped her arm around Kimmy's shoulder. "Are you ready for planting?"

"I'm ready. Then I can tell Carly that I planted flowers, too."

"Maybe she'll see you when we put the ones in the front yard."

She nodded with abandon. "Okay, but what should I do?"

"Let me show you." She guided her to the garage and pushed the button to open the big double door. It slid up, and she steered Kimmy to the plants. "We'll set these out where we want to plant them first."

Kimmy grasped a large pot and waited by the door. Nina hoisted two into her arms and headed out to the front flower beds with Kimmy following. "We'll plant a coneflower on this side and the other over there."

Kimmy followed directions and placed the pot where she'd pointed. They added two more plants to the front and then moved to the back after she entered the garage and brought out two trowels, garden gloves, a hand cultivator and a bag of mulch.

In the backyard, she showed Kimmy how to use a trowel to dig the hole and the cultivator to loosen the soil. Once she placed the plant in the hole, Kimmy replaced the dirt and patted it down. Then Nina grabbed the mulch.

"What's that stuff for?" With her nose curled, Kimmy eyed the mixture of soil and compost.

"It insulates the flowers from the winter weather. It protects them."

Her expression changed with the information. "It's good to protect things."

"It is, Kimmy." Her heart constricted. Doug had become Kimmy's protector during the difficult time of her mother's accident. His generous nature and kindness stood out in her mind as a badge of honor. Doug tried to hide those attributes but he'd failed, and in Kimmy's eyes he was a hero. In her eyes, too.

With the planting completed in the back, she and Kimmy carried the gardening tools into the front yard to finish the four plants she'd set in the beds. Before the first plant was done, Nina sensed someone watching and she turned.

Doug stood back, a loving look on his face that sent her pulse skipping. "Spying on our handiwork?"

"Only curious." He ambled toward her and stood closer to Kimmy as pride glowed on his face. "You have a pretty good helper here, Nina."

"I do. She's a fast learner."

Kimmy gazed at her with her trowel poised in mid-air. "Tell Uncle Doug about your mommy."

Her grimace managed to become a grin. Mommy? Her mother had never been the mommy type. "My mother called a short time ago. She and my stepfather, Howard, want to visit me here for Thanksgiving. Mother wants to see the house and offer her opinion, I'm sure." The words were out before she could stop them.

Doug gave her a questioning look. "You've never mentioned your mother before."

"I was closer to my dad. My mother and I have a few personality clashes." She winced, unable to admit how much worse it seemed than a few disagreements.

"That can happen. And you have a stepfather."

Her chest tightened. "Daddy died about seven years ago. Mom didn't like living alone."

Curiosity remained on his face, but he didn't ask. Relief eased her nerves. "The good news is we're almost finished here."

"You are?" His spirit had brightened. "That's great, because I have an idea." He gave Kimmy a wink.

"What?" Kimmy paused on her final plant. "Is it fun?"

"I think so. Would you like to go to the Autumn Festival in Durand?"

Kimmy pushed the last pile of soil back into the hole and leaped up, forgetting about the mulch. "What's a festival?"

"They have contests for kids and pumpkin decorating. All kinds of things." He drew her into his arm. "I think it would be fun."

"Can Nina come, too?"

He lifted his gaze to her and grinned. "I'd love her to join us." He tousled Kimmy's hair, then shifted his gaze to Nina. "They have arts and crafts."

His eagerness made her chuckle. "Are you trying to tempt me?" His warm smile melted her.

"Naturally. We can stop at McCurdy Park on the way back and check out their Playscape." He refocused on Kimmy. "I don't think we've been there, have we?"

She shook her head.

"It has swings, slides, rock climbing and bridges for kids."

Kimmy bounced on her heels. "Can we go?"

"What do you say, Nina?"

His eyes captured hers, and she lost her voice for a moment. "Sounds…like fun. Right, Kimmy?"

Kimmy gave a vigorous nod.

Doug sidled to her. "Okay, when you're ready we'll leave."

"As soon as I add the mulch we're finished." She bent down and emptied some compost on the plant.

"While you finish there, I'll run home and let Kimmy get cleaned up. I'll be back to get you in a few minutes."

She eyed her dirty pants and dirt-streaked arms. "Make that twenty minutes." She rose and showed him her dirt-speckled skin.

"Half hour." He gave her a smile and turned toward home with Kimmy skipping beside him.

Doug eased into his recliner as Kimmy skipped off to wash and change. His mind turned to its new favor-

ite subject. Nina. His thoughts fluttered from trying
to guess her feelings for him to trying to decipher his
own. He liked her. Liked her a lot, but he had so much
on his plate with little to offer a woman.

Maybe worse was Nina's protected past life. She di-
vulged so little, even regarding her mother. What had
happened? He had learned nothing about her mother
except their personality differences, and he suspected
the problem was deeper than that. He saw it in her expression, but Nina monitored what she told him. Only
when she was willing to give could he weigh the possibility of something greater.

Yet no matter what his reservations told him, he still
admired her generosity and her open heart that welcomed Kimmy into her life while he dragged along
behind. He knew she'd been married once, so why no
children? Had her husband not wanted them? He had
no doubt Nina would welcome a child with her arms
and heart wide-open.

"Ready." Kimmy's excited voice entered the room
before she did.

When she came through the doorway, he was
pleased to see her face shiny clean and her clothes
ready for fun. She already had an eye for color. He
grinned, thinking of the times he'd struggled to match
pants and shirt or suit with a suitable tie.

He checked his watch. "We should give Nina a few
more minutes. Do you want a snack?"

"Can't we eat at the place we're going?" She ran her
tongue over her lips. "Like a hot dog?"

"What if they don't have food?"

She plunked her fists against her waist and leaned

forward, eye to eye. "Uncle Doug, who doesn't have food?"

He arched a brow. "Okay. We'll look for a hot dog." He drew her into his arms and she slipped onto his lap. "We could call your mom and see how she's doing. What do you say?"

"I say yes…but can we still go to the slides and other places?"

"For sure." He reached into his shirt pocket and pulled out his phone. Roseanne's phone rang and when he'd just about given up, he heard the click. "Roseanne?"

"Sorry, Doug, my doctor stopped in and was saying goodbye when the phone rang. I couldn't find it in the bedclothes." She chuckled. "Is everything okay?"

"That's what I called to ask you. Kimmy hasn't talked to you in a while so before we go out for the day, I thought we'd call. Here she is." He handed her the phone and watched her face light up when she heard her mother's voice.

"Mommy, are you better now?"

She listened, her questioning frown lessening with every word. "Really? Then I can see you sometimes."

His curiosity amplified the frown on his face. "Kimmy, let me talk before you hang up."

She nodded. "We're going to a place with contests for kids and all kinds of fun things and then to the swings and slides."

He waited until she reiterated all he'd said to her, and he hoped the festival was as much fun as she envisioned it. He kept his guard up, fearing she might forget and click off the conversation.

"Uncle Doug wants to talk, Mommy." She returned the phone with a broad smile. "Mommy has a surprise."

Being released? The possibility divided his emotions. "Roseanne, what's up?"

"They're moving me to a rehabilitation center close to home, Doug. When I can handle things without too much assistance, I'll finish any other therapy at home. It won't be long now, and I'll at least be close to you so I can see Kimmy more easily. You won't have to make those horribly long trips. I know that's been difficult."

"Great news. I wish you could see Kimmy's face. But I need to be honest. I'm going to miss her. The house will be too quiet when she returns home."

"Doug, I know you don't want to hear this, but you need to get serious about your life. You've put all your energy into your work and nothing into relationships. I hope my bad relationships haven't influenced you. I'd feel—"

"Roseanne, you know better than that. I was shy in high school. Mom and Dad had a relationship that seemed practical. I never saw much romance there, and I don't think most women want to get involved for companionship alone. I didn't think I had much more to offer."

"Don't use other people's lives to build your own, Doug. You've been such a great brother to me. You've always been there for me and now for Kimmy. I can't tell you how much I appreciate that, but life is wonderful when you have the right person. I'm still trying. You know that. Kimmy is the love of my life, but I also want some romance and intimacy. My sweet daughter can't provide that for me or for you."

"Thanks for your concern, Roseanne, but I'm a big

boy and I'm learning. In fact, I have to pick up Nina. She's going with us."

"That doesn't help if she's a friend of Kimmy's."

"She's my friend, too. Nina's a neighbor who has kindly watched Kimmy for me a few times, and yes, she's single. Divorced to be exact."

"Single. That's a step in the right direction, dear brother. Now I can breathe a little easier." She chuckled. "I'm doing well, Doug. Painful therapy and it's frustrating trying to get around, but I'm doing better. That's progress."

"It's great news, Roseanne. We have to get going, but lots of love from me and Kimmy."

Kimmy leaned into the phone. "I love you, Mommy."

He held the phone to her ear. "I love you with all my heart, Kimmy. It won't be long, sweetie."

"I know." She beamed and stepped away.

Doug ended the conversation, his spirit rising for Kimmy. He slipped the cell phone into his pocket, and they were on their way.

Kimmy pulled a hunk of cotton candy from the cone. Nina chuckled, watching the floss melt on her tongue. She knew that Kimmy ate healthy food with no qualms, so she muted her thoughts about the sugar.

"Want some?" Kimmy held the fluffy cone toward her.

"No, thank you. The hot dog filled me, and I smell popcorn coming from somewhere. Before we leave, I might get some of that." Free popcorn, cotton candy, coffee. A generous festival and a great idea to create community spirit.

Doug caught her arm. "Look over there." He pointed

to a man holding a chain saw. "The man is making things with that saw."

His eyes bright with interest, she and Kimmy followed him to the barricaded area. Amazed at the man's talent, she watched the chain saw artist create part of a bench with birds providing the legs on each side of the seat. Earlier they'd admired sidewalk chalk artists and laughed at the decorated pumpkin display.

She'd eyed the arts and crafts but couldn't decide on anything. Kimmy had also passed on the children's games. Other than watching a clown make balloon animals and having a small butterfly painted on her cheek, Kimmy had only watched.

Fearing the event had been a disappointment to her, she sidled closer to Doug. "Should we see if Kimmy would rather go to the Playscape?"

He gave her a wink and introduced the idea to Kimmy. Her rousing *let's go* made their decision.

Though she'd enjoyed spending time with both Kimmy and Doug, Nina's spirit had been dented by the news that Roseanne was being transferred closer to home and would be released soon. Her selfish attitude struck a bad chord, but she faced that life would change for her and Doug when Kimmy was gone. Kimmy had been the catalyst for much of their time together. The upcoming wedding might be the only event they would share alone. With Kimmy back with her mother, life would slip back into the occasional contact with neighbors and her work. Not much to say for that.

Doug had brought a new spirit to her life, one that caused her to anticipate the day. She looked forward to waking in the morning to see what the day held. But all of their activities had Kimmy as their focus. They would be at a loss without her.

Doug steered them away from the festival to his car, and they slipped in and headed back to Corunna and McCurdy Park, less than ten miles away. Doug parked as close as he could to the Playscape and Kimmy unsnapped her seat belt and darted across the grass before they closed their doors.

Nina grinned at Kimmy's exuberance. "This is more like it, I think."

He gave a nod. "I suspected she'd love this, but she wouldn't have gotten her sugar quota for the day without the cotton candy." He chuckled. "Hopefully she'll burn off the energy here."

She moved to his side and they followed Kimmy's path to the tower of play equipment. The late-summer sun spread across her shoulders, and she enjoyed it, knowing that soon a cold wind would replace the warm rays. The idea filtered through her mind. Life was like that, too.

Doug's arm shifted beside hers, brushing against her and warming her thoughts. When they were together, her emptiness seemed to be a thing of the past. Yet reality sat on her doorstep, waiting for the door to close and lock her inside again. Caught up in the moment, she took a step and stumbled. As she hurled forward, Doug caught her in his arms and drew her up as if she weighed nothing. With his arms around her, his eyes met hers. "Careful. Those sneaky sticks are out to get you."

She grinned, adhered to his gaze, her lungs begging for breath with his lips so close she could almost feel them on hers. She grasped her wits and dragged her eyes from his. "Thanks for the save."

"We Boy Scouts promise to be prepared."

"Were you really a Boy Scout?"

"No, but I had friends who were. Nothing wrong with helping a woman in distress." He ran his hand down her arm and wove his fingers through hers. "For safety." He lifted their knitted fingers. "Okay?"

"Thanks." She managed the comment, uncomfortable with her giddy feeling. Based on her reaction to hand-holding, she might drop over dead if he kissed her. Heat rose in her chest and she worked to keep it from cresting.

The ground evened out as they neared the Playscape, yet his fingers remained woven with hers. When they reached a bench, he motioned for her to sit. Through the slats of the play area, they could see Kimmy climb the tower and zoom down the tube slide to the ground. Without seeing them, she made her way back up the tower.

Doug slipped his arm along the back of the bench, his body close to hers. "Nina, I'm having a difficult time."

Her heart jumped with his confession.

"I am thrilled that Roseanne is being transferred closer, but I know what that means."

While wrangling her disappointment that she'd misconstrued his confession, she understood, having dealt with the same feelings. "It will be different, Doug. Quieter."

"Lonelier." He shook his head. "She's forced me to come out of my shell—a shell I don't totally understand, but one I've lived with—and I'm afraid I'll slide back into my reclusive world. Work, home and church. That's what it's been. Not much social life." He shook his head. "I don't want to be there again."

"You don't have to, Doug. No one put you there but you, and you have the power to live outside those narrow walls."

"I know."

His head lowered and he fell deep in thought, thought she didn't feel right to disturb.

Finally he looked up. "I know I should be in control, but my mind goes blank. Without Kimmy to stimulate action, it's easy to sit in a chair and stare at TV programs I don't care about or read a book that my heart isn't in."

"Maybe you're reading the wrong book." She hoped it sounded lighthearted, but he didn't laugh and she wanted to apologize. "Seriously, Doug. Look around. What do people do? Get involved in church activities. I'm sure they have programs that need volunteers. Most organizations do. Become a Big Brother. Have you thought about that?"

He shook his head. "I don't have much to offer kids. You see how I stumble around with Kimmy. If it weren't for you, I'd be telling her to read a book or do her puzzles, about the same as her mother does."

"That's not true. And since she's been here, you've discovered all kinds of good activities for kids. What about the train museum for a boy? Don't they let kids get inside during the train festival? And this Playscape. Boys would like this. Take a boy to a sporting event. Most kids would love that."

His eyes searched hers. "You have the ideas."

"So would you if you didn't doubt yourself." She

laid her hand on his. "Doug, you've set your mind on being a failure. I don't know why, and I'm not sure you know either, but it's not really who you are. I see your delight with Kimmy. Yes, she's your niece, but a boy who needs a male friend can be a delight, too. You can teach him how to catch a ball, how to play croquet or badminton. Those are things you can purchase in most toy stores. Or get yourself a dog. They can be the best company and they're faithful."

Her voice had betrayed her. From his expression, he'd caught her tone on the faithful comment, an emphasis she'd hoped to control. Her mind shot to Rema's surprise visit and the discussion they'd had on faithfulness.

"Uncle Doug, did you see me?" Kimmy's voice severed their silence.

"We saw you on the big slide." He nodded.

Kimmy's face made it clear she meant something else. "Not that. I walked on the swinging bridge and I climbed on the caterpillar." She pointed away from the wooden structure. "Over there."

Doug glanced at her, surprise on his face. "I didn't see you over there."

Nina hadn't seen a thing but Doug's expression as they talked. He shorted himself so much when it came to children. His confidence at work seemed opposite to his uncertainty with children. The discrepancy aroused questions, but those would have to wait.

Doug rose. "Are you ready to go?"

"If you come and see me on the caterpillar." She beckoned him to follow.

Nina stood and treaded along the path to the free-standing metal structure with the look of a crawling caterpillar, its back humped as it moved forward. Kimmy straddled the red metal tail and used the rungs to work her way up the high hump, then wiggled around to climb down the hump before she grasped the final rung to reach the insect's bright blue head and yellow antennae.

They applauded as she grinned and lifted her hand as if she'd conquered Mount Everest. "Good job, Kimmy." Doug reached her side and helped her jump from the metal structure.

Nina slipped her arm around Kimmy. "If I were littler, I'd climb it, too."

"You can do it." Kimmy's eyes brightened, and Nina, wishing she'd not offered the suggestion, shook her head.

"No. You're too good."

Perfect response. Kimmy gave an agreeing nod and skipped along beside them as they wended their way back to the car.

Nina's spirit lifted, then sank as Roseanne's news struck her again. One day Kimmy would be back with her mother, a wonderful gift really. But for Doug and her, it would change the course of their lives. Did it have to? Couldn't they continue to be friends and enjoy each other's company? Doug had made no overtures for anything beyond friendship. Even holding her hand earlier had been out of concern that she might fall again. That was all it had been.

The recollection of his firm grip revived the warm feeling she'd experienced, a sense of security she'd had only rarely in her life when she was young and her father took her places. The loss of a relationship with Doug would be another loss even greater than her divorce. Before marriage, Todd had seemed to be a kind man. He had a good job and had been generous, but the intimacy she'd expected from their marriage had faded quickly. It died after she'd lost the second child. Died as quickly as their marriage.

Doug faltered at the car and gave her a questioning look. She smiled back, unwilling to talk about Kimmy returning to her mother's home and what that meant to them. She would wait and see. That's all she could do.

Chapter Six

Doug stood in Roseanne's doorway while Kimmy stood beside him, studying her mother, who seemed to be asleep. Her transfer had occurred sooner than he expected, and he struggled with pangs of selfish sorrow. Soon Roseanne would be home. He'd always adored Kimmy, but since she'd been with him so long, he'd grown even fonder of her, far more than he anticipated.

Roseanne stirred and lifted her head. A smile parted her lips, and she opened her arms as Kimmy darted to her bedside. He stayed back, allowing mother and daughter to share the special moment. A month had passed since they had been together. Roseanne had been in pain and didn't want Kimmy to see her during that time. Though they had spoken on the phone, it could never replace being together.

When Roseanne noticed him, she beckoned him inside the room. "Why are you standing back like a stranger.?" She grinned, her arm wrapped around Kimmy as she leaned half-prone on the mattress, her feet dangling toward the floor.

He sauntered closer. "It's called bonding."

She tilted her head. "You're right." She shook her head. "As always, big brother."

"And don't forget it." He grasped the arm of the chair and moved it closer. Then he lifted Kimmy and set her on the edge of the bed. As soon as he did, she leaned her cheek against Roseanne's chest.

"I've had fun with Uncle Doug, Mommy, but I miss you, too." She turned her head to face her mom.

"I'm glad you're having fun. I would be sad if you had a terrible time." She petted Kimmy's cheek. "But I missed you, too."

"You were sick." Kimmy lifted her head and kissed her mother's cheek.

"Very, and you wouldn't have wanted to see me whining."

Kimmy giggled. "Did you really whine?"

"Sometimes." Her eyes shifted to his. "But Uncle Doug will only have to put up with you for a few more weeks. I want to be home by Christmas. Maybe sooner."

"Really?" Kimmy's eyes sparkled as brightly as her smile. "But can we go to see Uncle Doug before Christmas, because I want to make Christmas ornaments."

"Ornaments?" Roseanne drew her head back as if questioning. Kimmy giggled at her curiosity, and she rattled on about making the decorations.

His mind sailed back to Nina and the plans she'd made for the Christmas pinecones. His chest ached not only for his plans but for Nina, who had admitted that her life had been solitary, too, before she'd moved to Lilac Circle—perhaps since her husband left her.

Again the question haunted him. Why? Why had her marriage failed?

While Kimmy and Roseanne talked, he glanced around, looking for flowers or a stack of cards, anything that might have let Roseanne know she was missed. He didn't see much, but the drawer in her stand held get well cards. Flowers seemed a simple gift and they would last after he and Kimmy had gone.

"While you two talk—" he rose "—I'm going for a walk. I'll be back shortly."

Although Roseanne gave him a questioning look, he escaped. He hurried down to the lobby, found the gift store and headed for the floral arrangements behind the window. He spotted one in a white vase filled with colorful flowers in reds, yellow and orange shades. They reminded him of the trees beginning to color. Soon they would be in full autumn hues like fire. He purchased the flowers and a box of chocolate mints. Roseanne liked those.

When he returned, Kimmy had stretched out beside her, and the first thing he heard was something about Nina. He faltered, wishing he could stand outside the door and listen like an eavesdropper. Instead he strode in with the bouquet.

A smile lit Roseanne's face. "I wondered where you were sneaking to."

"Sneaking? I said I was going for a walk. I did." He set the flowers on her stand and placed the chocolate mints beside it. "Something for your sweet tooth."

"Doug, you remembered." She raised on her elbow and reached over to grab the box. Before taking her own, she offered one to him, which he declined, and one to Kimmy, bubbling with enthusiasm as she accepted it.

Roseanne popped one in her mouth and arched her

eyebrow. "Kimmy was telling me how much fun you both have with Nina."

He released a breath. "I'm not sure I would call it fun, but it's pleasant."

Kimmy rolled over and jammed her fist into her waist. "Uncle Doug, you do too have fun. You laugh a lot when Nina's with us, and you smile more than ever."

He managed not to wince at her honesty. "I'm being amiable."

"What?" Kimmy gave him one of her looks. "You're being fun and nice. You like Nina, don't you?"

"Yes, I like Nina." A lot, but he avoided admitting it even to himself. "She's very nice, and she really likes you, Kimmy."

"She really likes you, Uncle Doug. She told me."

He wanted to control his surprise, but he felt his jaw drop so it was too late. "I'd better stop going for walks. All kinds of things happen."

Roseanne shook her head. "Doug, I've said it over and over. Life is out there waiting to happen. Don't lose something or someone that could make a huge difference in your life."

Though Nina filled his thoughts, Kimmy also fit the description. He kept his mouth shut. "I'll heed your warning, sis."

Kimmy gave him a bigger frown, probably lost in the meaning of *heed*.

A sound behind him gave him pause. Before he turned, Roseanne acknowledged the visitor. "That time already?" She shook her head. "More therapy. It never ends."

"But it's what's needed for you to go home and be on your own again." He rose and shifted back his chair.

"Kimmy, I think our visit has to end so your mom can have her therapy."

Kimmy slipped from the bed. "I want you to get better, Mommy, so you try hard to walk and stuff, okay?"

Roseanne pulled her closer and kissed her. "Okay, and it won't be long. Since I'm closer, you can come and visit me again."

"I will. Uncle Doug said we can come more often."

"And bring Nina. I'd like to meet her."

"Okay!" She bounded from the bed her face beaming. "I'll tell her you want to meet her, okay?"

"Okay." Roseanne gave a wave as they moved out of the way for the empty wheelchair. With one more goodbye, he steered Kimmy into the corridor, longing to ask her how much she told Roseanne. Instead, he let well enough alone. Maybe later he could think of a subtle way to ask. Kimmy was too smart for her age.

A nippy breeze penetrated Nina's jacket as she treaded along the sidewalk to El's. She hadn't talked to him in a couple of weeks, and when she pulled the batch of cookies from the oven, he broke through her thoughts. She'd decided to make Snickerdoodles with the wonderful texture that cream of tartar seemed to add. She'd sneaked one herself.

Approaching El's home without him in the yard looked strange, but the weather had curtailed that. Indian summer had taken a vacation. El's car was in the driveway near the garage so she was reassured that he was home. She climbed the porch steps and rang the bell. In a moment he answered with a smile so bright it warmed her.

"How nice." He pushed open the door. "And I see

you're bearing a gift." His eyes twinkled as they did when he suspected she'd brought him a sweet treat.

She handed him the bag and followed him inside, but when she saw the dining room, her pulse skipped and she drew back. "Birdie." She moved forward, following El's beckoning. "How nice to see you."

She grinned, and seeing Birdie smile was a bigger surprise. "El and I are just visiting. It's too cold to do much outside."

Nina agreed and sank into the chair beside her.

"El, bring Nina a cup of coffee." Birdie turned to face her. "Or do you prefer tea?"

"Either is fine, but—"

"Coffee with cream. It's on the table." El ambled into the room carrying a mug, the steam rising, and a plate of the cookies. "Now, this is a nice addition, Birdie."

Birdie eyed the treat and accepted the plate. She took one and passed it to Nina.

"I already had one at home." Nina set the plate close to El, noticing some crumbs on his lips so she was assured he'd already tried them. "I was thinking about the weather on the way here. I hope it warms up for the wedding or at least it's a sunny day."

"No matter what the weather, Angie and Rick will have sunshine in their hearts." El gave her a wink.

"You're right." Her wedding had filled her mind and heart with joy and hope for an amazing future. But as marriage did sometimes, her sunshine turned to gloom.

"Angie said you were invited, too." He grasped another cookie and took a bite.

"Yes, I was surprised."

He frowned, and then seemed to understand. "New

to the neighborhood, but when Angie connects with someone, she's a faithful friend. I've noticed that. She's been good to me."

"Me, too." Birdie shook her head. "And I didn't deserve it."

El waved his hand through the air. "Birdie, everyone deserves friendship. You made a few mistakes, but now you let your personality break free from that negativity." He rested his hand on her shoulder. "When I told Angie you were my date for the wedding, she was happy. Really happy. I saw it on her face."

Nina guessed Angie had set that one up, too.

"You're not going alone, are you, Nina?" El's eyes glinted.

She suspected he already knew the answer, and she grinned. "You know I'm not."

"Last I heard you were going alone, but I'd hoped—"

"You hoped Angie's meddling would work, and it did."

His expression gave him away. "And I'm glad, Nina."

"Angie loves to play matchmaker, but I'd already considered asking Doug." Surprised at her admission, she swallowed and decided to hush up. She trusted El, but Birdie had been the street gossip, which still left her uncertain.

Birdie gave a nod. "You two have become good friends and I see that little girl—what's her name—is fond of you."

"Kimmy. I'm fond of her, too. She and Doug are visiting her mother today. She's been transferred to a rehabilitation facility that's much closer, and she should be home soon."

"In time for Christmas. That's wonderful." El faltered as a frown appeared. "But that means both you and Doug will miss her."

"Very much. I feel selfish that I want something to happen so Kimmy stays, and I feel terrible when it enters my mind."

"Oh, the Lord understands what emotions love can bring out of us, Nina. Don't fret. He forgives before we ask. God is love and He made us in His image."

Her admission lightened her, and her shoulders straightened. "Thank you, El. I forget so many things about God's blessings."

"We all fall short of God's commandments and desires for us. I'm sure that's why He gave us the forgiveness that comes through Jesus."

Forgiveness brought up another topic she'd had in mind when she brought the cookies over, but today she eyed Birdie and hesitated.

"Nina, you have something else on your mind, don't you?"

El's uncanny ability threw her off balance for a moment. "Speaking of forgiveness, I do have a situation that's troubling me." Though Birdie listened, she told him about her mother and stepfather's Thanksgiving visit. "It puts a damper on being thankful, El, and that shames me but it's true. Mother has always been critical. Even if something is nice, she adds a *but* to the sentence. It ruins the compliment or the noncommittal reaction to something."

"Are you thankful for things not related to your mother?" A look in his eyes signaled he'd cornered her.

"You know I am. I'm grateful for meeting my new neighbors and for people like you and Angie who brought me out of myself and into the warmth of new relationships."

"And what about Doug? And Kimmy?"

Her chest exploded with emotion. "Yes, I am very grateful for Doug's friendship and the joy of meeting Kimmy. She's changed my attitude and my life in a way." Her admission shone on her face like a neon advertisement.

"In what way, Nina?" El's forehead crinkled. "Did you have a bad attitude toward children?"

"No. Not at all. I can't—" Unable to go on, she swallowed her words and closed her eyes, willing away the tears that had come without warning.

"Dearest Nina, we are friends who care about you. Please let us help if we can, and if not us, the Lord has promised to take your burdens from you. 'My yoke is easy, and my burden is light.' Those are Jesus's words."

"I'm trying to remember those things, El. I'm trying, but sometimes…"

"Sometimes it's good to say it and then pack it away. You said that you can't—"

He lifted his brows, waiting for her to finish, but the words tangled in her head. When she could stand the silence no longer, she admitted what she could. "I've learned I can never have a child."

"*Never* is a powerful word, Nina."

"But it takes two people with strong love and healthy bodies to bring a child into the world, El, and I realized that Todd and I didn't have the gift of love, and then I—" The admission raked through her being.

"That was one relationship. What about another one? Two people whose love is strong and two people who think of a child as a bonus package of love from the Lord."

She bit her lip. "I never expected to find a relationship that strong, El, and even if I do, it doesn't change the fact that I'm physically unable to carry a child. I'm not sure that I will find a man who has enough love for that."

Though he shook his head, a faint smile curved El's mouth. "But you know a man like that, Nina."

Doug. El's expression gave the answer without question. "Yes, but I don't see our friendship heading in that direction."

Though Birdie had been silent throughout, she released a long sigh. "You're seeing with warped eyes, Nina. Take a fresh look. I never thought my life would change or I would find a person with patience enough to like me as a friend, but look at my life now. El is a man who knows how to bring the best out of people and to make them see that they have better inside. My life is different, and I see things differently. Maybe one day you will, too."

"Very wise, Birdie." El reached across the table and slipped his hand over hers. "I'm proud of you. You said that very well."

Nina hadn't expected to take much stock in anything Birdie said, but at the moment, her attitude had altered. Letting someone bring out the best in her could change how she saw things. Birdie had a point. But how did that happen? She needed to think about it, but she wanted to do that alone.

"Stop, Uncle Doug!"

Kimmy's voice ripped through Doug's thoughts with

a blast. He pulled to the edge of the road and stopped, his heart banging against his chest. "What's wrong? Are you sick?"

She gave him a look as if he was stupid. "No. I thought we would stop at Nina's?"

He shook his head instead of shaking hers. "Kimmy, you scared me nearly to death. Don't do that, okay? I thought something was wrong." He stared at his niece, realizing how her heart had wrapped around Nina's. "Can I park the car at home first?"

"Can I get out?"

"No. It will only take a minute." He'd refused her something, one of his rare moments, but she had to learn that life didn't revolve around her as much as he knew it had for some time. And it wasn't just him. Nina jumped at her commands, too.

Though a wonderful little girl, Kimmy's situation had motivated him and Nina to try to make her life better. She'd done well with her mom's illness, but he needed to get her back to real life. When she returned home to live with her mother again, she wouldn't be the center of attention. Her mother would be, since she still had many needs.

A sigh escaped from his depths. Even thinking about Kimmy leaving ripped through his heart.

He turned off the motor and looked into the backseat. "Now, was that so bad?"

Though she wore a frown, she shook her head and opened the passenger side. "I guess not."

Instead of responding, he remained quiet. He had to be patient with her. Life was changing, and Kimmy was old enough and smart enough to recognize it. As she rounded the car, he met her at the back and put his arm around her shoulders. Without a word, he guided her down the driveway to the sidewalk, heading for Nina's.

He noticed her head shift, and when he looked, she gave him a smile.

Tension lifted from his chest, but he knew the situation had to be addressed. "Are you sad about saying goodbye to your mom again?"

She shrugged. "I miss her, but…" She lowered her head as if counting cracks in the concrete sidewalk.

"But?"

"But I'll miss being here, too. Carly is my new friend and so is Nina. And you are the best uncle in the world."

Though he opened his mouth to speak, emotion lodged in his throat. He gulped down the sob and gave her shoulders a squeeze. "That was a sweet thing to say, Kimmy. You are the best niece in the world, too. I will miss seeing you every day, but I know your real home is with your mom."

"I know."

Her comment reached him as a whisper, and she, too, dealt with the emotion of change. Children also felt the pangs of sorrow and loneliness. As they walked up Nina's sidewalk, he spotted her at the window. She opened the door and held it wide as they entered.

"Did you have a good visit, Kimmy?"

From Nina's expression, she seemed to sense a mood swing in Kimmy, who usually skipped up her driveway. She gave Kimmy a hug and then drew back. "How about some lunch or—"

"We ate after we left the facility. Thanks, though." He gave her a smile and settled into the easy chair she motioned toward. "How was your day?"

"Good. I had a nice visit with El and Birdie. They seem to be quite a couple lately."

"Is that good?" He recalled hearing about the infamous Birdie when he first moved in.

She looked thoughtful a moment. "I think it is. She's not the same Birdie I met when I moved in. She's more positive. She listens, and when she talks, she has something worthwhile to offer rather than the street gossip or her misconstrued situations." She chuckled. "I think she likes herself now."

He loved hearing her voice lilt without the weight of worry.

"Kimmy, tell me about your visit." Nina drew Kimmy closer and eased her beside her on the sofa. "I bet your mom was happy to see you."

"She was, and you know what Uncle Doug did?"

He drew back, his heart in his throat.

Nina gave her a playful frown. "What?"

"He bought my mom a vase with flowers in it. They were pretty and my mom loved them."

Nina's frown vanished. "I'm sure she did. Every lady I know loves bouquets of flowers. They're bright and cheerful, and they say *I love you.*"

Kimmy giggled. "Flowers don't talk."

"No, but that's what they mean."

Kimmy appeared to toss that around in her head. "Then I would like flowers, too."

"We all do. It's a girl thing."

"And you know what else?" She leaned closer. "My mommy wants you to come and visit her."

Nina's head drew back. "She does. Why?"

She glanced at him, and all he could do was shrug.

He'd only caught the end of the conversation when he returned with the flowers.

Kimmy giggled again. "'Cuz I told her that Uncle Doug is happier when he's with you.'"

Her revelation struck him with the blow of a jack-hammer.

Nina glanced his way but without an ounce of surprise on her face, and then he knew. Kimmy had already revealed this to her. No wonder she dropped a barricade between them on occasion. Yet even that thought sent an ache through him. He'd hoped she, at least, enjoyed their friendship. Though needing to respond in some way, he searched his mind and came up empty. How could a person dissuade the honesty of a child?

Kimmy eyed him waiting for something.

He finally grasped a response. "Maybe you make me happy, Kimmy? Is that possible?"

She tittered, her head swaying like a bobblehead. "It's not the same. You look different with Nina. I see those looks on TV."

"You aren't watching adult programs with me, Kimmy."

"I know, but I do at home sometimes when Mom finally takes a break."

This time he became a bobblehead, unable to push away her comment without it bobbing back and making him look a fool. He eyed Nina, who had got quiet since Kimmy's declaration. "I admit I've enjoyed meeting a neighbor who is so kind and a lot of fun. So maybe I am happier."

Kimmy nodded her head. "See, I told you."

Changing the subject was the only way to go. "By

the way, I looked at the extended weather forecast. We're supposed to have another break in the weather. I think we'll have a sunny day for Angie's wedding. The temperature is supposed to be back in the midseventies. That should be nice."

"I hope you're right. I've been trying to think of something to wear, but I guess that's something only girls care about." Still beside her, Nina gave Kimmy a playful poke.

"Can I help you find a dress?" Her eyes brightened as she gazed at Nina.

"Not today since it's getting dark already, but maybe tomorrow. I need to find something soon or I'll have to go shopping."

Kimmy slipped forward on the sofa and clapped her hands. "We can go shopping. Yeah."

He shook his head. "Kimmy, she didn't say anything about *we*."

Her eyes filled with pleading turned to Nina. "Can I?"

"Maybe I own something already, sweetie. We'll see after we look." She turned an arched brow to him. "That's if your uncle Doug doesn't mind."

Angie had mentioned the darkness and she was right. He hadn't noticed. He rose. "If you have to go shopping and want to take this young lady with you, it's fine with me."

"Yeah." She stood and jigged around Nina. "I hope you have to shop."

From Nina's expression, he guessed she didn't, but Kimmy would deal with it.

"We'd better get home. Tomorrow is a school day,

and it's time for a young lady to take a bath and think about bedtime."

Kimmy looked around. "What young lady?" Then she giggled.

He slipped his arm around her shoulders. "Good night, Nina. Sleep well."

Kimmy slipped from his arm and hurried over to Nina, drew her down and kissed her cheek. "Good night. I'll see you tomorrow after school."

Doug drew in a deep breath. Tonight had been a revelation. He had no idea what Kimmy had been telling Nina or what she thought about it. He could only pray that Kimmy's prattle hadn't done any damage to the friendship they had cultivated. It still needed a lot of hoeing and maybe a few fresh seeds of hope.

Chapter Seven

Nina plopped on the edge of her mattress, her frustration tightening her shoulders. She had scoured her closet for something special to wear to the wedding and found nothing. Going alone to the wedding she wouldn't have cared, but she had sort of a date.

She caught her image in the vanity mirror and shook her head. Her sort-of-a-date thought had twisted her mouth to a pitiful grin. How could someone have a sort-of date? It either was one or it wasn't one. Since Angie had influenced the situation, she had a difficult time thinking of it as a normal date.

She threw her hands into the air and gave up. Date or no date, she had an escort and wanted to look nice. Doug was good-looking in jeans and a polo shirt. She could only imagine how striking he would be in a suit, his broad shoulders above a trim waist.

The thought rippled down her chest, making her too aware of the growing feelings she could no longer deny. Asking herself what she could do had become pointless. She'd read enough of the Bible to admit that the outcome was not totally in her hands.

She eyed the dark red dress she'd stretched across the chair and curled her nose. The dress didn't suit her, especially since she'd lost a few pounds after she'd moved to Lilac Circle. Life had become more active and filled with toting, flower planting and entertaining Kimmy. The experience had been good for her.

Kimmy would be there for a while longer, and since she could do nothing about her returning home, she'd recognized her useless worrying.

She rose and hung the dress back in the closet, admitting she needed a new dress. That would make Kimmy ecstatic. The image aroused her smile.

Grasping her cell phone, she wandered into the kitchen and sat at the table as she called Doug. When he answered, her pulse skipped as it did each time she heard his voice. "Tell Kimmy the shopping event is on."

"I'm glad to hear it since I heard about nothing else this morning before school. I'll drop her by when I pick her up from school."

"See you then, Doug."

He hung up after telling her he was dealing with a new client. She understood, having those situations, too. But thankfully so much of her work could be done at home that an episode of impatience was witnessed by no one.

She eyed the clock to validate she had time to put a dent in one more job before Doug dropped off Kimmy. She made a quick mug of her favorite tea and settled in front of the computer. With work her focus, time flew and before she knew it a door slammed outside and she suspected her shopping partner had arrived. She saved the work and rose.

When she reached the living room, she heard Kimmy's piping voice before they rang the bell. She opened the door, and Kimmy's beaming smile warmed her heart. "Come in a minute." When she pushed back the screen door, Kimmy sailed in with Doug in her wake.

Doug gave her one of these eye-roll looks. "Someone's excited."

"I noticed." She slipped her arm around Kimmy's shoulder. "I looked at all my dresses and didn't like any of them for the wedding so…guess who's going to be my helper."

Kimmy poked her finger into her chest. "Me."

"Right." She eyed Doug, waiting with a grin. "Are you coming, too?"

He chuckled. "Not unless you need a man's opinion, and I don't think you do."

"Right again." She managed a lighthearted smile, but part of her would love to spend more time with him. Obviously this trip wasn't an appropriate time. "I'll get your opinion on Saturday."

He nodded. "I can't wait."

She located her bag and returned. "Ready, Kimmy?"

She rushed to her side. "I'm ready."

Doug headed for the door with Kimmy on his heels, eagerness shining on her face. She locked the door and headed for her car. Doug followed and helped Kimmy buckle her seat belt, then closed her door and watched as she drove away.

When she reached downtown, Nina spotted a couple of consignment shops but decided to keep those for later. Instead she drove to a store she knew had numerous choices of women's evening wear. Kimmy jiggled in the backseat ready to make her escape, and when they finally reached the parking lot, she charged from the car and waited for Nina to round the car and meet her.

Inside, she headed for the women's department and then for the dresses. Kimmy began pointing to dresses before she could get a good look. "Hang on and let me find my size."

"But Uncle Doug said you would look pretty in purple and this one is purple, isn't it?"

Her chest knotted, and she tried to imagine how the conversation might have occurred between Kimmy and Doug. She shifted through the rack and pulled out a teal dress that she would have loved but the dress was too short and the neckline dipped too deep for her taste. She rejected a black dress that seemed too plain but spotted another one with a rounded neck, straight skirt with an embossed texture that added an interesting effect. She laid it over her arm and headed back to Kimmy's find.

The dress was indeed plum with a scoop neckline embellished with stones that glittered when the light hit them. A nice touch. The bodice and skirt were form-fitting in a flattering way and the skirt looked as if it would touch her knees. The sleeves were short, but she already owned a black bolero-style jacket she could wear if the room was cool. In the same rack she spotted a similar black dress that looked more practical and she could wear a strand of pearls, but then did she want to be practical?

"Nina, here's one." Kimmy tugged at another dress in a hunter green, fuller in the skirt but with a longer sleeve and a bit of ruche in the bodice.

She saw Kimmy's excitement, and since it was a

possibility, she selected that, too. "Okay, we have four dresses. I'll try them on. What do you say?"

"I say yes." Kimmy nestled close and followed her into a nearby dressing room. She settled on a bench and watched wide-eyed, as Nina tried on each dress, turning this way and that with Kimmy's oohs and aahs with each pose. After trying them all on, she tried to decide between the plain black and the plum color dress that Kimmy had spotted. She held up the two dresses. "Which do you like best?"

Kimmy stood and studied both dresses as if she were a high-fashion designer. "The black one is too plain."

This time she couldn't stifle her laugh. "That's what I thought. You have a good eye for dresses. You'll be a beauty when you grow up."

Her eyes widened. "I will?" Kimmy turned to look in the mirror and studied herself. "I guess I have to wait until I grow up."

"That'll come soon enough, sweetie."

She eyed the other three again, pressing her lips together and touching the material, then ran her finger over the sparkling stones. Nina managed to muzzle her chuckle. "I like the purple-colored one and not just 'cuz I picked it out. It's pretty and I like the color and Uncle Doug likes it, too. Buy the purple one."

Nina grinned, but she liked that one best, too, so Kimmy's opinion worked. She gathered the dresses, hung the three on the return rack and took Kimmy's hand as they headed back to the cashier. On the way, she spotted children's clothes, and as she drew closer, she saw a long-sleeved turquoise knit T-shirt with a rounded neckline and the word *cute* printed in block letters on the front. She grasped size seven and held it up to Kimmy. "Do you like this?"

"For you?" Her eyes sparkled.

"No, for you."

"I love it. It's so cute." Then she pointed to the block letters. "It says so right here."

"Then I think it's yours and you'll be cute in it."

"Uncle Doug will think you look beautiful in your new dress. I know he will."

Her mind snapped back to Kimmy's earlier admission. "Why do you know?"

Kimmy gave a big head shake. "'Cuz I asked him what color you would look pretty in."

"And he said purple?"

"First he said you looked pretty in everything."

Her eyes widened before she could stop them. "Really?"

Kimmy nodded again. "But then he said you would look pretty in purple because of your dark hair and lovely eyes." She hugged the T-shirt to her chest and turned away toward the checkout.

The words spiraled in Nina's head as she headed for the exit. Within minutes, she owned the dress, Kimmy had her gift and they were on their way back home. Though she enjoyed the time with Kimmy and buying the dress, she grew excited knowing she would see Doug soon. She couldn't wait until Saturday when he saw her dressed for a special occasion for the first time. She might even have her nails done.

The drive home took only minutes, and when she pulled in to Doug's, she slid out and turned toward the door, but as Kimmy ran ahead to the porch, she noticed she was carrying the shopping bag containing her dress. Then she recalled the package also held Kimmy's new top.

When Doug opened the door, Kimmy scurried in waving the bag. "Nina bought me a cute shirt." She giggled and dug into the bag until she came out with the purchase. "Look." She held it up.

Doug eyed Nina for a moment. "Did she ask you for—"

"Totally my idea. I thought it was darling."

Kimmy dropped the shirt into his hand, and he held it up again and fussed over it until she took it from him and ran to her room.

Nina gathered up the discarded sack and set it on a nearby chair. Before they could say a word, Kimmy trotted into the room.

"Nina, show Uncle Doug your new dress." She twirled to face Doug. "I helped find it and Nina loved it."

"You did?" He gave Nina a wink.

"Actually she did see it and showed me. I tried on four dresses and like this one the best."

Kimmy grasped the parcel. "Show him, Nina." She shoved it into Nina's hands.

"I'm ready for a viewing." Doug gave her a playful grin.

"You'll see it Saturday when I'm in it." She tilted her head waiting for Kimmy's challenge.

Doug gave a nod before looking at Kimmy. "I'm sure it will look better that way. Don't you, Kimmy?"

"Nina looks beautiful in it."

Doug gave Kimmy a smile and turned to Nina, his gaze capturing hers. "I'm sure she does. I'm looking forward to it." He tilted his head toward the sofa. "Won't you stay for a while?"

His expression drew her in, and mesmerized, she walked to the sofa and sank into the cushion. "Just for a few minutes. I'm sure you're hungry and ready for dinner. It's late."

"I planned on ordering a salad and pizza. How does that sound?"

Kimmy shouted a loud yes that sounded like a cheer. She skipped out of the room and Doug watched her for a moment. When she didn't return, he grinned. "Okay, now we can talk. Is pizza okay?"

Her stomach rumbled hearing him mention food. He gave an approving nod as if she had answered him. "Sounds great. Thanks."

"I'll call in a minute." He settled near her in his recliner. "I've been wanting to tell you something."

Her heart hit her throat, and she nearly choked. "Is something wrong?"

He gave her a vague grin. "Nothing like that." He drew in a breath and leaned forward, his hands folded on his knees. "When I mentioned that Angie suggested I be your escort for the wedding, I didn't lie but I twisted the facts a little."

"What do you mean you twisted the facts?" He looked uncomfortable, and though her curiosity screamed for an answer, she longed to soothe him.

"She mentioned the wedding and said she had a couple guests who couldn't make it and that she'd already finalized the head count, so would I like to attend." He paused, looking even more on edge, and studied her.

"And?" She could see there was more from his expression.

"I admitted that I would have loved being your date…escort. I knew you were going alone, and it seemed like a nice way to get to know…" He glanced again toward Kimmy's bedroom. "A nice way to get to know you better since we'd be alone."

"Alone at a wedding reception? I don't think so." She knew what he meant, but she needed to say something to break the tension.

He arched a brow. "Without seven-year-old ears listening."

She grinned. "I understand."

"So what I'm saying is after I said what I did, Angie jumped in and arranged the situation. Her comments gave me the courage to ask you. I'm sorry I didn't just admit it then, but—"

Seeing his discomfort, Nina rose and moved to the arm of his chair. "Doug." She looked into his eyes, her pulse thudding in her ears until it hindered her thoughts. "We are both careful with others. I know our reasons are different, and I don't know why you are as you are, but we are cautious when it comes to relationships. At least I sense that you are. You know I'm divorced. Getting involved, even dating, sends me a warning signal. I'm sorry I'm like that."

He shifted over to be on the couch and put his arm around her shoulder. "Do you mind? Are you comfortable?"

"This is nice." She had longed for him to be there, as senseless as it was.

Relief washed over his face. "I can't explain my problem exactly. It's a bundle of circumstances. I dated but never found anyone that I wanted to spend my life with. I wanted someone special. My sister got involved with that jerk, and their relationship was a disaster. And though my mom and dad had a comfortable relationship, it wasn't one full of fun and romance. I wanted more."

"Some marriages are like that, it seems."

"But is that the kind you want?" His eyes searched hers while his fingers brushed against her arm.

"My marriage became that kind, Doug. Sad but true. No, I didn't want that, but I finally gave up trying and felt a failure." She pressed her hand on his. "So what happened to your parents?"

"My dad was diagnosed with diabetes in his midforties and didn't follow the doctor's orders. He ate poorly and played games with this medication. He ended up losing a foot and then his leg and then the other. Life was hard for my mother, and I devoted myself to helping them. After Roseanne learned she was expecting and the jerk split, I did all I could to help her." He shrugged. "I guess that's been my life, living other people's and not worrying about my own. But I never resented it."

"You wouldn't. That's the kind of man you are. I admire you for being like that."

"You do?" His eyes filled with questions.

"I admire a lot of things about you, Doug." A rush of warmth traveled up her arms where his fingers lay, and she longed to tell him what held her back, but the words wouldn't form in her mouth. Losing his friendship, the closeness that she enjoyed, could end if she revealed her huge shortcoming as a woman. Doug deserved children.

Doug drew her closer, his eyes searching, his arms protecting her, and as his lips neared, she longed for the kiss to happen, and today she knew it would. As his lips touched hers, Kimmy's voice severed the moment.

"Look at my top." She strutted across the living room posing like a runway model. When she neared, she faltered, and her eyes narrowed as if what she saw finally sank in. "Uncle Doug, you're hugging Nina."

Her awareness caused them both to react. Nina rose while Doug laughed and remained seated. "I noticed."

Kimmy missed the humor, but Nina had to work to hold back her laughter.

She moved to Kimmy's side and slipped her arm around her. "We were talking about serious things."

"Mc?" Worry slipped to Kimmy's face.

"No, not you, sweetie. Uncle Doug was telling me why his father died. He would be your grandpa."

"I have a grandpa—Grandpa Bill."

"Grandpa Bill is my stepfather, honey. My birth father was in heaven before you were born." Doug beckoned her forward and slid her onto his lap. "He was sick and didn't take care himself even when Grandma told him he should, so he just got sicker and died."

"When I'm sick, I take medicine." She nestled against his chest.

"And look how healthy you are, plus you look really cute in your new top."

Concern flew from her face and changed to a smile. "That's 'cuz it says so right on the front."

Doug tousled her hair and slipped her feet to the floor. "If we're going to eat, I'd better make that call."

Kimmy skipped off again, and Nina relaxed, sensing Kimmy had forgotten what she had seen when she entered the room. But Nina couldn't forget her anticipation when Doug's lips touched hers. She could still taste the sweetness of his mouth on hers for that fleeting moment, and the one taste left her craving more.

Doug rang the doorbell. Since the near kiss, he could think of nothing else and anticipated seeing Nina in the new dress. He rarely wore a suit, not even for church, so tonight Nina would see him in his finery. He grinned at the silly thought.

The door opened, and his jaw dropped. Nina stood before him, striking in a plum-colored dress with glistening stones outlining the scooped neck. He stood outside mesmerized by what he saw. Her dark hair shone in the bit of sunlight still in the sky, and tonight she wore it loose and flowing around her shoulders. Her lips shimmered a shade of pink and her cheeks were bright with color. She had done something to her eyes, as if contoured in a dark color. Like a whirlpool, they drew him in.

"Are you okay?" She studied him as if confused.

"Tremendous. You look amazing." He released a ragged breath and made it through the doorway. "The dress is gorgeous. I love the color."

"Kimmy said you liked purple."

Heat warmed his cheeks. "That girl talks too much." He grinned. "But she's right. I knew you'd be stunning in a color like this, and I love the sparkling stones." He leaned closer spotting her earrings that looked like diamonds.

"If you're wondering, they're faux diamonds. Definitely not real."

"But they're still effective." His chest constricted as a thought barreled into his mind. He could picture a real diamond on her finger, and the vision rippled along his spine.

She gave him a grin while her eyes searched his. "You look very handsome, but I knew you would. I love the tie, and did you realize it has a deep purple shade, almost plum like my dress? Did Kimmy tell you the color?"

"No. That's one thing she didn't tell me." He eyed her again from head to toe. "I realize you'd never seen me dressed up. I hoped you would approve."

"Doug, I more than approve. I'm proud to be dating you tonight."

She tilted her head as if questioning if he'd heard her. He had. "I'm honored to be dating you, too." He stood back, eyeing her from head to toe, flooded by the amazing outcome of events. "Are you ready?"

"I just need my coat. It's in the closet."

She drew it out, and he helped her slip it on. As they headed for the car, a feeling overwhelmed him. Tonight he was a man dating a beautiful woman, and a good one too with love for others, especially for Kimmy. She would make an amazing wife and mother. The thought broke through the lock he'd put on his emotions for the past month when he realized how he felt. Freedom wrapped around him, freedom to hope and dream for a brighter future.

And a real kiss.

Nina spotted familiar faces as the wedding guests made their way into the church. The church had an arrangement of three stained glass windows depicting Christ, the colors brilliantly lit by the autumn sun. The rich oak wood in the chancel glowed, the focus on a wooden cross, and the lovely baskets of flowers in shades of purple and white. She spotted calla lilies, chrysanthemums and lavender with touches of white carnations.

She and Doug chose aisle seats on the bride's side near the middle of the church. She looked around and spotted a few people she knew. El, accompanied by Birdie, sat a few rows in front of them. She still smiled seeing those two together. El had a forgiving heart along with his strong faith.

Doug pointed to his watch, and she grinned, seeing the wedding should have begun a few minutes earlier. Her creative mind at work, she thought of those horrible runaway bride or vanished groom stories and was happy to know that neither Angie nor Rick were the types to escape their wedding. Flinching, she imagined her own fears triggered those terrible ideas.

She eyed Doug, looking so handsome she lost her breath. When he arrived at the house, he'd looked at her with an expression she'd never seen before, not in his eyes or any man's before him. Todd had proposed and kissed her, but now that she'd met Doug, she acknowledged the truth. Todd's idea of romance paled in the light of what she had already seen reflected in Doug.

The music began as Rick and two attendants entered through a doorway at the front. Doug turned toward her, a gentle look on his face, and shifted his hand to hers. The warmth rolled up her arm and settled in her chest. When she had opened herself to possibilities, faint ones, her reaction to his looks, his scent, his touch sent her on an amazing emotional journey. A journey with apprehension but one she longed for.

The bridesmaids came down the aisle in lavender gowns. Their flowers were cascades in white and shades of violet. Nina thought of her plum-colored gown and smiled to herself.

Doug squeezed her hand as if he understood her grin. He seemed to have an instinctive awareness of her. Sometimes that caused her to put up her barricade. But today nothing about him caused her concern, except the feeling she had when she looked into his eyes.

A fanfare began, and she turned, knowing Angie would be coming down the aisle. Instead the children made their timid way forward, coaxed by an adult as Carly sprinkled flower petals on the white runner and the boy carried an amethyst satin pillow.

Her emotions swelled as she heard the rustle of excitement behind her. People rose, and when she turned again to face the back, Angie had begun her approach to the altar and to Rick. Nina wiped tears from her eyes, remembering her own wedding wrapped in hope and expectations, all crumbled now and in a pile at her feet.

But today wasn't about her hurt. The day belonged to Angie and Rick, a couple she sensed would have a long and happy life together. She grinned at Angie as she passed, and Angie returned her smile, looking radiant. Her gown, embellished with tiny white flowers in the bodice, fell into graceful folds to her feet.

When she faced the altar again, Rick's face glowed with love and anticipation, and her heart rejoiced at the beauty of this day. Doug slipped his hand in hers again and when they were seated, he rested his arm behind her on the pew. The intimate coziness filled her emptiness, and she recognized the joy of having a partner to share the important things. She'd missed that so much in her life.

The vows began, and Doug leaned closer as he seemed to concentrate on the pastor's words, the same words that had captured her. "Do you promise to love her, comfort her, honor and keep her for better or worse, for richer or poorer, in sickness and health, and forsaking all others, be faithful only to her, for as long as you both shall live?" Rick's "I do" rang loud and sure, and the promise raced to her heart.

The words filled her mind and tangled in her heart. She knew Rick's abiding love would keep that promise, a promise Todd had uttered without thought. But a man of honor, a man who followed the Lord's commandments and His guidance would speak those words in truth. A man like Doug could do that. He could promise to keep a woman for better or worse, and he would mean it.

Shifting his arm from the pew back, Doug lowered it to her shoulders. His fingers brushed her arm and the warmth blanketed her with hope. *Lord, could this be?* She looked toward him, offering a reassuring grin. He drew her closer, and though an alert sounded in her mind, exhilaration overcame the warning.

The exchange of rings blurred in her head. So many images hung above her, all bringing pleasure and possibilities she'd longed for. A soloist sang, prayers were said, and soon Angie and Rick bounded down the aisle as man and wife. Nina's pulse skipped, watching joy radiate from Angie.

When the organ music rang out the end of the service, the wedding guests rose and filed toward the exit where Angie and Rick waited to greet them. As they inched along behind the others, Doug slipped his hand into hers, and she reveled in the comfort that spread through her.

Her eyes blurred with tears as they reached Angie and Rick. She gave them both a hug, and their warm welcome added to her growing assurance. Angie treated her like an old friend as she smiled and moved ahead with Doug to the parking lot to drive to the reception at the Comstock Inn.

Doug held the car door for her as she settled inside, and in moments, he joined her and slipped the key into the ignition but didn't turn it. Instead he turned toward her. "You were thinking about something during the wedding. Was it your own wedding years ago?"

He surprised her with his question, but the answer came with ease. "I did once, but only for a moment. I realized how sad it was and how I had misread so many things about Todd, I suppose in my eagerness to have a husband and begin my own life."

"I think that would be natural to have those thoughts." He reached over and touched her hand. "I've never been married but I realized the seriousness along with the happiness. Marriage is a life change and a powerful commitment. I think Angie and Rick are headed for many years of good things."

She grinned, hearing him nearly echo her own thoughts. "That was part of what I was thinking about. With the right person, the vows spoken at a wedding can be a path for people to follow. Supporting one another in sickness and heath, for better or worse. Those words spoke to me. With a failed marriage in my past, considering another hasn't been on my list of possibilities, but the vow brightened my hope. I suppose reading the Bible and understanding how faith impacts a relationship is another important part of the *I dos*. Todd didn't have a speck of faith and mine had gone by the wayside. A divorce is built on empty promises and vows with no glue to make them stick."

"But you see things differently now. Is that what I hear you say?" Hope seemed to glow on his face.

"Yes. I need to digest it and its meaning for me, but I believe when a couple speaks those words in agreement, marriage has God's stamp of approval and His powerful support." Her admission wove into the fibers of her being.

Doug squeezed her arm and turned the key. He backed out of the space and rolled through the church parking lot toward the inn. She remained quiet, filled with ideas slipping into her mind and heart. Possibilities blossomed like flowers in Angie's bouquet, bright and fresh. With the new awareness, would her life change? Would bolted doors open? Or would she only be disappointed again?

Chapter Eight

Doug watched guests spill into the Comstock Inn Grand Ballroom and wished he and Nina could escape for a while until the food was served. He'd forgotten to eat lunch since his mind was filled with Nina and his expectation of the evening. He'd been forward during the wedding, holding her hand, and his heart sang when she didn't pull away. Her acceptance escalated his hopes for the evening. Yet sitting at the table with El and Birdie and others he knew put a damper on his plan.

Though he wasn't as new to the town, he'd never been inside the inn, but he was always impressed with the redbrick building with its white bay windows along the upper floors that stretched along Main Street. He particularly admired the colonial front porch with white pillars, and he watched Nina's expression as they pulled in.

"This looks like a lovely place for a reception, especially with Angie's color scheme."

Doug couldn't stop his grin. Men often missed those details thinking about the overall cost of a large wedding. Besides, he had a difficult time focusing on anything but her. Tonight Nina glowed, her hair color and eyes enriched by the deep hue of her dress.

He half listened to Nina chatting with El and Birdie, his mind focused on his hopes for the evening. With her openness to his romantic overtures, he rehashed how far he wanted to push, and he hoped he knew when to back off. He respected Nina and would never go beyond the bounds of what was moral and good, but since the day their lips touched in the fleeting kiss, he'd yearned to make it happen again but this time without interruption.

His gaze drifted to the miniature silver picture frame that listed their names and the table number that Nina said was a gift for guests. He loved seeing their names listed together as a couple, and yet he'd made a joke and asked her which half of the frame was his. So much for a romantic nuance.

"This room is a fantasy in white and various shades of purple." Nina ran her hand over the white linen with centerpieces filled with purple flowers and bound in wide white ribbons surrounded by small candles around the center display. "Don't you think this is gorgeous, Birdie? Look at the choice of flowers—lilies, dahlias and lavender blossoms—and I love the chairs covered in white and tied with the chiffon ribbon. It's glorious."

Birdie nodded. "It's very nice."

El gave him a wink, and they both grinned, but he couldn't resist his admission. "This reception could have bought them a mansion instead of living in Angie's house."

El and Birdie chuckled, but when he saw Nina's expression, he wished he'd kept the comment to himself. The cost hung in his mind but he let it fade, concerned that it would taint his enjoyment of the special day. Maybe his attitude would change if he ever…when he married. He liked hearing the more positive attitude for once. His mother would love it.

The mother idea struck his thoughts. Nina had mentioned Thanksgiving with her mother but nothing more was said. The open-ended topic left him curious. His wedding attendance was limited, and he'd forgotten how close people were seated. This was not a time for intimate conversation. It gave him even more motivation to find a place to talk.

El pointed to the other side of the room. "Anyone else ready to investigate the appetizers?"

Doug's stomach growled, and he looked toward the hors d'oeuvres. "I'm ready. Nina, what do you say?" She rose, and they made their way across the room. A wide selection of hot and cold dishes enticed him to try a little of many things and as they headed back, he stopped at the bar to pick up a club soda with lemon and an iced tea for Nina.

Before they reached their seats, the wedding party had arrived, and they hurried back to their seats, bypassing neighbors he barely knew. Though he was cordial, he preferred to enjoy the appetizers while watching the wedding reception tradition of introducing the wedding party.

With his disinterest in chitchat, time dragged. Nina tried to lure him into the conversation and he added a few words, but he wasn't one for small talk, except when he was alone with Nina, and then nothing was small talk. He listened to the dinner music performed by a string quartet and was relieved when the dinner service began.

Following the first course of salad and rolls, the highlight arrived, prime rib and chicken. With others focused on the food, he focused on Nina. "This meal reminds me of Thanksgiving. You mentioned your mother coming to visit. Is that still the plan?"

She didn't respond for a moment, then wiped her lips with the napkin. "It's not my plan but it's still on as far as I know. My plans have to be altered, I suppose."

Curious, he hoped she would go into detail, but instead, she sliced off a small piece of prime rib. "You're disappointed?"

She nodded. "I'd thought about inviting you and Kimmy for dinner." She turned to him with disappointment in her eyes. "And if Roseanne is home, I would have been happy to include her, but now…"

"I would have enjoyed that." His chest weighted but no answer came. "Now it will be your mother and stepfather?"

"I suppose, and that not only frustrates me, but it makes me sad."

Her eyes searched his, but he felt at a loss to respond. But as the seconds ticked by, he asked the logical question. "Is there a reason you can't invite everyone? I'm happy to help with the meal, and—"

"Doug, it could end up being the worst Thanksgiving dinner of your life. My mom isn't easy to please, and it frustrates me. I don't want to spend the day defending myself in front of guests." She closed her eyes.

Sorry he'd chosen now to bring up the topic, he searched inside for a meaningful response. "I heard a tip once, and maybe you could try it. That is if you'd like to hear it."

Her eyes opened and she looked at him. "I'd like to hear anything that might work."

"No matter what she says, agree with her."

"Agree?" Her tone rose, and she caught herself and hushed.

"I know it sounds difficult but after you do it awhile it becomes easier."

Her brow wrinkled. "I'll think about that, Doug. It's an idea, if I can keep my mouth closed and do it." She gave him a grin. "My mouth doesn't like to be closed."

That made him chuckle. He loved knowing her traits so well.

Conversation rose around them as the meal ended, and he joined in as they discussed the good food. The dinner music had ended, the noise of the guests rose and a deejay was setting up in the same area. Soon, dancing would begin, and though it had been forever since he'd been on a dance floor, he suspected he could remember how. As so many said in that situation, it was like riding a bike.

Coffee and tea arrived, and soon the cake was cut and brought to the table. The dancing began with the traditional bride and groom dance followed by the wedding party, parents and all the folderol that went with a wedding. Nina's situation broke into his thoughts. What would she do for a wedding dance without parents she felt connected with? She had said she'd never marry again, but he sensed that would change, and he prayed he would be involved in that decision.

Having Kimmy in his care and Nina's positive approval had caused him to rethink his ability as a fa-

ther. Maybe he would be a good one despite his lack
of confidence.

The words encouraged him beyond his expectation.
He wanted to be a father, and in the past months, he
also wanted to be a husband.

"You're quiet."

He lifted his eyes to Nina's curious expression.
"Sorry, I was thinking about weddings and…"

"The cost." She gave him an arched-brow look.

"No, not this time. I was thinking about the joy of
it all." He gestured toward the dance floor. "Look at
Angie and Rick. Happiness is written all over their
faces."

She looked their way and smiled. "I've noticed. And
they are very confident, which is so nice to see. And
I think they'll have a great marriage…in sickness and
in health. That's important."

The added addendum jarred him. He could see from
her expression it had a meaning for her. Now he wondered if she had an illness and that's why she said
marriage was impossible. Possibilities spiraled in his
mind, but he only changed the subject. "And they're
both so wonderful with Carly—they will make tremendous parents."

"Absolutely."

"I've talked to you about my doubt of being a good
father. I don't like the feeling, but as I told you, I felt
inadequate. But the other day at work, one of the men
who just became a new father said something that made
an impact on me. He said that no one is prepared for
parenthood. It's learn as you go and different for everyone, but it's worth the effort and time. He put his
hand on my shoulder and said that the reward of a

child is far greater than the concern of whether or not I would be a good father." He held his breath watching her expression.

Her eyes lit. "He's a wise man, Doug. I've been telling you that you're wonderful with Kimmy, and if you'd made mistakes, you corrected them quickly. I've seen nothing but good things with you and Kimmy."

He slipped his hand over hers. "Thanks. I'm thinking I would like to be a father one day, even though I've said over and over I wouldn't."

"You need to be a father, Doug. You're one of the kindness, sweetest men I've ever met."

He loved hearing her say it, but her expression broke his heart. As the words left her, sadness slipped across her face. "Don't you want to have a child, Nina?"

"Yes, I do. Very much."

Her soft voice brushed past him, leaving him confused. Tony Bennett's voice filled the air, and instead of lingering in his thoughts, he drew her hand in his. "Would you like to dance? We can take advantage of this slow number."

Though she hesitated, she stood and followed him to the dance floor. When she stepped into his arms, warmth rushed through his body. Her thin frame lay in his arms and her sweet scent filled him with hope. The words of "The Way You Look Tonight" echoed his sentiments. Nina represented beauty without and within. Her heart opened to others and their needs. He'd seen that in his own life. And her love for Kimmy. How could she hesitate about having a child? It made no sense.

They moved in sync as if they'd danced together forever. Her breath brushed his cheek, and he longed to place his lips against her smooth skin. "You do look beautiful tonight, Nina."

Her head turned. "Thank you, and you're a handsome man, Doug."

The music ended, and she turned toward the table, but Etta James's voice filled the room, and she faltered. "Etta James. Do you mind? I love 'At Last.' It's such a meaningful song."

Mind? As the song said, he was in heaven. "Are you kidding? This is the best part of tonight."

She grinned. "Better than prime rib?"

"One hundred percent." He drew her closer this time, her head on his chest, her heart beating next to his. They glided across the floor, and when they were beside Angie and Rick, they smiled but he kept moving not wanting to break the rhythm of their movement or their hearts.

Exhilarated, his spirit soared as did his optimism. Despite her strange reaction to his question about having children, he hoped one day he would learn why. He'd learned too well that pushing Nina for answers caused her to raise a barricade between them. He couldn't take the chance. Instead, he would be as patient as he could instead of barreling forward like an express train.

Etta James's voice faded away, and he spotted El and Birdie making their way across the room. He motioned toward them. "If they're leaving we should say goodbye."

She agreed, and he slipped his hand into hers and crossed the room. When they caught up with them, Doug laid his hand on El's shoulder. "Are you leaving?"

El chuckled. "Birdie and I fade away by ten so we're

heading home. The food was good, and I even enjoyed some of the music."

Birdie nodded. "And we don't dance anymore." She gave El a sweet smile. "So nice to spend time with you both."

"Same here, Birdie." Nina gave her a hug, a sight he never expected to witness.

Before El said goodbye, he eased closer to Nina. "Drop by one of these days. I want to talk to you about something."

Her eyes widened, and while she grinned, her voice resounded with question. "I'd love to, El. I enjoy our conversations."

El gave her a nod and waved goodbye as he steered Birdie toward the exit.

Doug watched a second, and then slipped his hand back into Nina's. "We missed dessert. Look at that table full of sweets."

Nina patted her trim tummy. "I've had enough food. I couldn't eat the cake. I'll probably wish I had some later."

Doug eyed the cake table and the pile of slices wrapped in napkins and ready to be taken home. "I can solve that problem when you're ready."

She chuckled when she saw where he pointed. "I know you have Kimmy on your mind and it's getting late. I'm ready if you are."

"Let's grab some cake to go…plus a piece for Kimmy, and when we get home, I'll make coffee or tea, decaf if you prefer, and we might be ready for the treat."

She smiled and gave an agreeable nod. They said good-night to Angie and Rick before leaving and hurried to the parking lot. The weather had grown colder, and Nina had only carried a light dress coat for warmth.

He needed nothing. Being with her warmed him body and soul.

Nina leaned her head against the passenger seat headrest, the words to Etta James's "At Last" filling her thoughts. Out of nowhere, Doug descended on her life. Her move to Lilac Circle had been for convenience and a new beginning. She lived closer to her work and away from the old memories. And while that was her plan, she learned that memories faded but the incidents that nailed them into her mind lingered like black mold, inciting a kind of deep illness that warped her view of life.

But little by little Doug and Kimmy had been the medicine that had healed Nina's wounds. Though memories remained as a scar, the rawness had faded. But tonight, without realizing, Doug had pried open the wound again with his question about having children.

Hope crumbled with the reality of her situation. Yes, she wanted children. She had longed for children, but she'd failed twice and after that her husband moved into another bedroom and was only a paycheck in her life until he left her. She could never go through that again, and tonight Doug had let her know that he wanted children. Not that he would like to have them, but he really wanted them. The words were similar but different. The want leveled her hope and the possibilities she'd allowed to fill her mind.

Before she roused and forced away her sadness, Doug pulled in front of Angie's house. "Wait here. I'll run in for Kimmy, and then we'll go to my place. I'm sure she's ready for bed by now."

Though going home would be better for her, Doug had suggested they eat the cake at his place, and she hadn't objected. That would have been the right time. She sat in the car with the heater warming her legs while he hurried in, and in moments he appeared on the porch with Kimmy in his arms. She slid out and opened the back passenger door, and he placed the half-sleeping child onto the seat.

The cold prickled down her spine and she slipped back inside as Doug rounded the car. When he opened the driver's door, another slap of cold sailed past her. When they pulled into his driveway, Kimmy stepped out, her eyes drowsy, and hurried behind him to get inside.

Nina followed, and once in the living room, she sat on the sofa, waiting for Doug to return from helping Kimmy get into bed. She weighed her options, either go home or stay, and when Doug returned wearing a grin, his expression made her decision. He chuckled. "She'd fallen asleep a short time ago. I hated to wake her, but—"

"She'll be sleeping again in a moment. Maybe already."

"Coffee, tea or...?"

"Either is fine, but make it decaf. I want to sleep tonight." She rose, but he waved her back to her seat.

"I'll bring it in here. It's more comfortable."

While she waited, her mind returned to her thoughts. The struggle continued between her heart and her head. Reason told her to pull back and let the relationship be a friendly neighbor. Her heart swung miles in the other direction. Let go and let God be in charge.

Unexpected tears blurred her eyes, and she closed them to stem the stream. She brushed the back of her hands beneath her lashes and opened them again. Though she'd been reading the Bible and knew the Bible said the Lord was almighty and with Him nothing was impossible, how could God fix her problem?

God could do anything. His words echoed in her mind, but her doubt remained. It would take a miracle like the parting of the Red Sea or the total darkening of the sun at noon to reverse her infertility.

The sound of mugs clinking reached her, and her pulse skipped. Should she be open and tell him? The answer fell on her heart. She wasn't ready to end their relationship. Maybe the Lord had something up His sleeve or why would He have brought them together to face more disappointment?

"It's decaf coffee. Is that okay?" Doug headed toward her with a wooden tray and set it on a small side table. "And cake."

His boyish excitement lifted her spirit. "What's a wedding without cake?"

"Agreed." He handed her the mug and set the cake on the lamp table beside her. Then he shifted to a nearby chair and sat. "What is this cake?" He ran his tongue over his lips after taking the first bite.

She thought a moment. "White chocolate with a hint of raspberry. That's what I taste."

He nodded. "That's it. I tasted the raspberry but it was the white chocolate that threw me." He took another bite and gave her a wink.

The look rolled through her, and she watched him, unable to leave and yet unable to stay.

Finally he set down the plate and studied her a moment. "You said something at the wedding that made me curious."

Her memory ripped through the evening, fearing it was the statement she wanted to erase. She tried to look unconcerned while she held her breath. "I said a lot of things tonight."

"But this one made me wonder." He studied her serious expression.

It made no sense to delay the inevitable. "And what was that?"

"What you said about believing a great marriage happened when the couple believed in the vows, in sickness and in health." He shifted from his chair to the sofa and clasped her hand. "Nina, are you ill? Do you have cancer or MS or something that you think stops you from finding happiness in a marriage, because I don't think—"

"No, Doug. No. I don't have a terminal illness." Questions remained on his face. "I have nothing debilitating, nothing that will limit my life. I—"

"Nina, I'm so happy to hear that." He slipped his arm around her and drew her close, his eyes searching hers. "I could only think that you had a health issue so serious that you thought no one would love you. But that's not true, even if you were ill. Most people don't fall in love with good health or with perfect people. We... I fall in love with the person's heart and attributes. You are a beautiful person no matter what."

Tears pooled in her eyes, seeing his sincerity, and

though she'd tried to avoid the truth, Doug loved her. Tonight dissolved any doubt she'd had.

Doug brushed his finger beneath her eyes, wiping away the dampness, tears she couldn't hide. His arms drew her closer, so close her heartbeat reverberated against his chest. His lips lowered as her breath depleted. His mouth covered hers, tender and sweet, then the feeling grew to a depth she'd never experienced, as if their hearts and souls melded as one. An amazing sense of wholeness washed over her.

He drew back, his gentle look kissing her eyes and filling her with joy. *Tell him. Tell him now.* The voice echoed in her mind as fear crept in and cocooned the admission she'd longed to release. Unwilling to ruin the amazing moment, the kiss she'd longed for, she let her confession lie for now, but soon—very soon—she had to tell him the truth of her fear.

Doug drew his hand along her hair, his eyes capturing hers, until he lowered his lips to hers again.

Silence filled the room as she rested her head on his shoulder and prayed for courage.

Chapter Nine

Doug studied the documents piled on his desk, weighing his clients' options to purchase new properties. He had two good choices to present, but as their advisor, he wanted to suggest options.

The word *option* settled in his mind. He'd decided to open up to Nina, and though he hadn't fully proclaimed his feelings, he sensed that she knew. The kiss validated his hope that she had similar feelings. The next step was to break though the blockade she'd put up to her past or whatever it was that made her veer away from commitment again. He'd prayed often and hoped the Lord—

His cell phone jarred him from his thoughts, and he pulled the phone from his desktop. Roseanne. His stomach hitched seeing her name. He couldn't help worrying. After two rings, he hit the talk button. "Hi, sis. Are you okay?"

"I'm great. I came home yesterday, and—"

"Why didn't you tell me? I could have come over and—"

"Doug, I have to know I can take care of myself. I

knew you'd come, but then I wouldn't know how I'd do alone. But thanks for caring. You've already done more than anyone could ask."

"You're my sister. That's what family does." As the words left his mouth, Nina's family dangled in his mind.

"I'm ready for Kimmy to come home. I really miss her, and—"

"Are you sure, Roseanne? She'll add a lot of work to your life. Have you forgotten? I'm happy for her to stay until you're really up and stronger."

"Doug, I wouldn't ask for her back if I didn't think I could handle it. And she's seven. She can be a big help to me. I can't drive yet, but I can order food in and I have a connection with a grocery, which will deliver what I need. One of my neighbors will drop by and I'll have people come in to clean. Actually I often get help on that when my work becomes overwhelming."

"It sounds as if you've planned it well. Do you want to tell Kimmy yourself? She can call you when she gets home."

"Good idea. I'm sure she'll be thrilled."

He ended the call with her words ringing in his ears. Kimmy would be thrilled but he wouldn't. He'd miss her too much. Yet the experience had been validating and helped him know he was ready to be a dad to a little girl or boy. Even two or three children. He dropped the cell phone onto his desk and rubbed his temple. He had known the day would come, but he wasn't ready for it, especially so close to Christmas. And Nina would be disappointed without Kimmy there, he had no doubt.

The more he thought, the need to talk with Nina

compelled him to call her now and not wait. He hit her phone number and listened to the ring.

"Hi, Doug. Aren't you at work?"

"I am, but I wanted to call you. Roseanne is home already."

"She is? That seems fast."

He heard concern in her voice. "I'm not sure she's ready to be alone, but I couldn't say much to her. She's determined she'll be fine, and then…" His voice caught in his throat.

"Then…what?" Silence except for the sound of open air. "Don't tell me she wants Kimmy home already."

"That's it. I'm… I don't know, Nina. I have no right to Kimmy but she's been so much a part of my life the past months I already feel lost—and even more important, I'd like Roseanne to wait and see how she does on her own first. Don't you think—"

"You're right. It's too rushed."

Her voice softened, and he recognized the same loss he'd experienced. His chest ached with the vision of being home in an empty house with no child's voice piping questions or needs. He loved being needed and being loved. He… "I'm almost speechless, Nina. I've never felt this way before."

"I've known Kimmy a much shorter time than you, Doug, and the loss still hurts. Sure, you'll see her over the holidays, but… It's not the same, is it?"

"No. I'll tell her tonight, and I'm sure she'll be happy, so I'll try to be happy, too."

"Doug, I'll be over when you get home or you can come here. Rema's visiting now, but we can talk more then, okay?"

"I have to go anyway. I have a pile of work in front

of me and absolutely no desire to do anything…but the work goes on." He shook his head. "Thanks for understanding, and I'll see you later."

He ended the call, lowered the phone and placed it on the pile of documents and memos on his desk. Unable to concentrate, he caved against the chair back and drew in a breath, trying to digest his conversation with Roseanne. All he could do was tell Kimmy her mother wanted her back home, and then wait.

Waiting had become the bane of his life. He prayed one day the Lord would bless him with life moving forward.

When Nina returned to the living room, Rema watched from the sofa and scrutinized her with concern. "Is something wrong?"

She shrugged, hoping to cover her sadness. After she sank into the chair she had occupied earlier, she told her about Roseanne's hospital release.

Rema's expression relaxed. "Kimmy will be thrilled."

The comment pierced Nina's heart. "She will."

A frown returned to Rema's face. "But Doug isn't." Her frown deepened. "Neither are you."

"I am, I suppose. A child should be with her mom, but…from a selfish viewpoint, I'll miss her terribly. She's been a light in my life."

Rema's head tipped, her eyes searching Nina's face. "Doug's still here. Doesn't that help?"

A sense of guilt tore through her. Was it Kimmy who had captured her heart or…? She closed her eyes a moment trying to imagine life without him. "Doug makes it easier. We've become very good friends."

"Friends?" A faint grin curved Rema's lips.

"Good friends."

A laugh shot from Rema. "Are you trying to convince me or yourself?" She shook her head and rolled her eyes. "Nina, I would have to be blind to not see… even hear in your voice…how you really feel about Doug." She closed her eyes a moment. "Girl, you are in love."

Nina drew back, startled with the blunt comment. Did everyone interpret their relationship as love? She loved him, yes, but anything deeper than friendship…

"Frankly, I'm jealous, Nina. Trey's and my marriage was hopeless from the beginning, I fear."

"Why?"

"Because I saw things…suspected things, but refused to dig deeper. I closed my eyes and accepted his excuses for being late or having to travel for his work. After I looked back, once I realized he was having an affair—maybe more than one—I revisited those excuses. I should have used my brain, but…" She lowered her head and shook it. "I wanted to be married. All my friends had husbands and some with little ones, and I was envious. I felt as if I had the plague and couldn't get a husband."

Her heart weighted, hearing the truth of Rema's marriage. Situations like that were the kind she feared. How easy was it to be duped? How often did women or men allow their desire to marry hide the truth they were seeing but didn't want to admit? "I'm really sorry, Rema."

Her own failed marriage washed over her. She'd trusted him, never seeing the truth. Her husband was there for the better but not for the worse. "Sometimes,

Rema, we want to trust so badly that we twist the facts to make them fit our want and not our need."

Need. What did she need? Her mind swam in a sea of confused images. A good job. Hers was perfect. A cozy home. She had one. Faithful friends. She had new friends that she enjoyed. Someone to share her joys and sorrows? Someone to hold her when she cried? Someone to cuddle with at night?

If two lie down together, they will keep warm. But how can one keep warm alone?

The scripture floated through her mind on a wave of faith.

"You're right, Rema. I do love Doug, but sometimes I worry it's not in the plan. I've had one unsuccessful marriage, and I wonder if marriage again is meant to be."

"Why not?" Rema's eyes widened. "You were innocent. I tried to be a good wife. I did everything I could to make Trey happy. You didn't know me when I didn't do a thing. No classes, no friends, no job. He wanted me home. I hated my life, but I did it for him. Then I realized why he wanted that. If I stayed home, I wouldn't hear the rumors of his carousing."

A lump formed in Nina's throat, imagining a life controlled by another. Being under someone's thumb with no movement. No activities. No joy. Nothing. "God gave you a blessing, Rema. Yes, in a strange way, going against His Own Word, in a way. But I believe the Lord plans our steps despite the course we devised."

Her response knocked her cold. Chills rolled up her arms and down her back. Had she determined that she would never fall in love again and now the Lord was showing her otherwise?

"I'm not a big churchgoer, Nina, but I do have faith, and yes, I agree. Look at me now. I'm a person. An individual who is enjoying life. I take yoga and I've met a very nice man. He's not pushy. He's friendly and kind. He's invited me to stop for coffee after the class. I'm not looking for anything now. It's too soon, but it lets me know that maybe I'm a little bit appealing."

"Little bit? Rema, you're very pretty."

Rema grinned. "I fixed myself up a little. Got a nice haircut, bought cosmetics and learned how to use them." She chuckled. "That was another class I took. Can you believe? I found a night school class that teaches improving self-image."

Nina rose and gave Rema a hug. "You look lovely, and I'm glad you took the class. If we don't love ourselves, it's difficult for others to love us." She shook her head. "Except maybe our parents, and then that's not a guarantee."

Rema hugged her back. "You've become a good friend, Nina. Thank you. It's so nice to visit people and not think I'm like a termite appearing at their door and wanting to be friends. I always felt people were kind but standoffish. That's not a good feeling."

She nodded, unable to imagine having self-esteem that devastating.

"Now at least I can smile." She grinned. "But I need to go. I have dinner planned with a couple of women I met at the self-image class. It's fun to hear what's happening in their lives. I never wanted to be a glamorous model. I just didn't want to feel like a termite."

Nina shifted back while Rema's frank admission

lifted her spirits. "You amaze me, Rema. I can't even picture you in that way. It makes me realize we can create an image of ourselves, and then work to change it for the better."

"Positively." Rema pushed herself up from the sofa. "Thanks for the great talk, and I hope everything turns out for the best with Kimmy. I know it will be difficult when she's gone. Children can fill a life with love and noise. Both can be missed." She chuckled.

Nina walked her to the door, and after saying good-bye, she stood a moment digesting everything that had been said and what it meant. She'd heard herself say things that had new meaning the longer she thought about them.

She wandered to the kitchen, pulled out a diet pop and eased into a chair. What did the Lord have planned for her? Was He guiding her away from the images she had created for her life and changing her steps to His plan? A plan that included Doug?

A new weight struck her heart. Doug deserved children and she couldn't give him those with her issues. But with God all things were possible. Could it be? She loved Kimmy. Could she have a child one day? Lowering her head, tears spilled from her eyes and rolled down her cheeks, a few dripping to the table.

Changes. What needed to be done? Like an arrow, Thanksgiving shot into her thoughts. Maybe having company could soften her mother's negativity? No, not her mother. Shame rose like a dragon. She backed away from her thought. Anything could happen. She wasn't in charge. Things could change.

Her mental argument gave way to a solution. She

would host Thanksgiving dinner for Doug, Roseanne, Kimmy and her parents, God willing.

God willing times two. She needed assurance.

Doug observed the smile on Kimmy's face with a heavy heart. When her mother told her the news, he'd managed a contrived smile that must have resembled a grimace forced upward at the edges.

After her bubbling excitement, her expression faded. "But I won't be here for Christmas and the decorations. Nina said we could make acorns with ribbons and sparkles."

Despite his ache, a smile eased the tension in his face. "I think you mean pinecones."

She tittered and gave him a toothy grin. "One with the little ruffles all around."

A novel way to explain it. He was smiling now, inside and out. "That's right. The one with ruffles. But don't worry about that. Nina will make sure you get to make decorations with pinecones."

Her concern fell away, and she turned to look behind her. "Where's Nina?"

"She's home, but she said she'd come down to visit."

A deep frown inched to her face. "Is she mad at me?"

"Mad? Why in the world would she be mad?"

Her eyes lowered to the carpet. "'Cuz I'm not going to be here for Christmas."

"Am I mad?" He managed another grin and hoped it looked sincere.

"No, but... I'll miss you and Nina every day. I have fun living with you, Uncle Doug. You do things with me and take me to the park, and..."

Her lip trembled, and he opened his arms and drew her in. "Kimmy, you can come here whenever your mom agrees. We're not that far away that I can't pick you up at school and bring you here." His arms tightened around her for himself as much as for her. "We can still have fun and do things."

She brushed the tears from her eyes with the back of her hand. "Momma needs me to help her, but... Uncle Doug..."

His lungs constricted. "What, Kimmy? Are you worried?"

"I don't know how to do things, and maybe she needs me to—"

"Sweetheart, she doesn't want you to cook dinner and clean the house. Your mom just wants you there. She misses you." The words hit the air as they hit his heart. Roseanne did need her reassurance. She'd faced a life-and-death situation, and his hope was that she'd learned what was precious in her life. It wasn't giving her life to her work. Kimmy was her most precious gift, and he could only pray she realized it now.

Kimmy lifted her gaze, the concern gliding from her face. "I can be there. Are you sure that's all?"

"I'm sure." His prayer rose that Roseanne hadn't forgotten that Kimmy was only seven. "I want to take you someplace special before you go back home, so I'll check with your mom. How's that?"

"Where?"

Her eyes lit up brighter than he'd seen them since the conversation had begun. "It's a surprise."

"But—"

"No buts. You'll find out soon enough."

"Can Nina go, too?" She searched his face.

"Would I go to a fun place without Nina?"

Her head swung back and forth in a flurry. "It's more fun with Nina."

A chuckle rose from his throat. "I agree. She's terrific."

"And you like her a lot, don't you. A real lot."

His pulse skipped. If Kimmy read his feelings, who else realized how much he cared? Heat burned in his chest and climbed upward. "I do like her a lot...a real lot."

"I know. I think you love her, Uncle Doug. Do you think so?"

She'd cornered him. The longer he remained quiet the more she probed with her eyes. "I think I do, Kimmy. What do you think about that?"

"I think...yippee. I love her, too."

He released a deep breath as he watched her expressive face. Kids came up with too many truths at times. Honesty was on the tip of their tongues and sometimes it needed to be. He knew how he felt, but saying it made it real. Real and amazing.

A soft knock punctuated the moment, and he hurried to the door with Kimmy on his heels.

When he opened the door, Kimmy threw herself into Nina's arms. "Uncle Doug wants to take us to a surprise." She studied Nina's face as she tried to get inside with Kimmy clinging to her. "Do you know the surprise?"

Nina's questioning eyes captured his. "I don't. So it's a surprise for both of us." She grasped Kimmy's hand and they closed the distance. "What is it?"

"It's a surprise." He motioned for her to sit. "But not today. We'll go tomorrow in the late morning. It's supposed to be pleasant weather, but I have to make sure that's okay with Roseanne."

Her expression told him she understood. She wandered across the room and sank onto the sofa. "Do you want to hear my surprise?"

Kimmy plopped beside her. "You have a surprise, too?" Her intent gaze clung to Nina's.

Nina tousled her hair. "It won't be after I tell you." She lifted her eyes to his. "I've decided to have everyone for Thanksgiving if that works for Roseanne."

"My mom?" Kimmy's eyes widened. "Is my mom coming to your house for Thanksgiving?"

"I hope so, and you'll meet my mom then, too."

"Yours?" Her eyes widened more.

Nina grinned. "I have a mom and a dad, Kimmy, just like you." Her mouth snapped closed as if she realized Kimmy had no father, only a father she'd never known and one she thought had died.

She held her breath, waiting for Kimmy to ask a question or make a comment.

"I hope Mommy can come to Thanksgiving 'cuz otherwise we'll be home alone."

Doug's tense shoulders lowered, relieved she'd let the reference to a father pass without a thought. "We'll work out something, sweetheart. Don't worry."

She thought a moment, and then bounded from the sofa to his side. "Call Mom, and see if I can stay here until after the surprise."

He drew her into his arms and gave her a squeeze. "I'm sure she'll agree but I'll call so you don't worry." He sent her to sit with Nina, knowing he'd have to explain and went into the kitchen to call his sister, praying she would agree.

When he returned, he tried to keep his expression serious. "I talked with your mom."

Kimmy leaped from the sofa into his arms. "What did she say?"

"She said...yes!"

Kimmy shot from his arms, piping her happiness as she twirled around the room and dive-bombed onto the sofa beside Nina.

He and Nina roared while Kimmy sent them a smile that warmed his heart.

Chapter Ten

On Saturday afternoon, as Doug drove away from town, Nina watched the signs as they passed and wasn't surprised when they approached a large barn with a Country Corn Maze placard on the side. Cars dotted the parking lot, as it was late in the season, but the weather had allowed the maze to remain open until the first frost would end the fun-filled event.

Kimmy began to squirm behind her, her shoes kicking against the seat back as she leaned in every direction, trying to figure out where they were going. "This is a barn. Are we seeing animals?"

"Read the sign, Kimmy." Nina pointed to the red-and-white sign in the peak of the red barn.

She squinted through the side window. "What's a corn maze?"

Doug flashed her a grin. "Wait and see."

When the car stopped, Kimmy flung open the door and slipped out, but Nina wasn't far behind. "Kimmy, don't forget to watch for cars. This is a parking lot and cars might pull into this space. You know what could happen?"

She looked at the open door and frowned. "The car could hit Uncle Doug's car."

"Worse than that, it could hit you."

Her eyes widened. "I'll be careful next time."

Nina gave her a pat. "Good. I won't worry then."

Kimmy studied the huge corn patch. "What do we do here?"

"Have you ever worked on a puzzle?"

Kimmy nodded with questions in her eyes.

"A maze is sort of like that. You start down a path and try to find your way out the other end."

Kimmy's eyes lit up. "I have puzzles like that in a book. I try to draw a line to the end but I keep running into paths that stop."

"That's it. Same idea." As they followed Doug, she slipped her arm around Kimmy's shoulders, too aware that these special moments would soon end.

"Do they find us if we get lost?"

The concern in Kimmy's voice made Nina grin. "No, they give you clues along the way so we can get back. Anyway, your uncle Doug wouldn't let us get lost."

She agreed and skipped on ahead to slip in next to Doug. Nina stood back and watched the two, anticipating the loss they would feel when Kimmy was gone. Though he'd planned the special day for them, the corn maze couldn't stop the ache in her heart.

As she neared, she couldn't believe her eyes. "Angie, I had no idea you guys would be here."

Angie tilted her head toward Rick. "He wanted to come earlier but things got in the way so today he announced do or die we were coming to the corn maze.

His excuse was Carly had never been to one. But the truth is Rick's more excited than we are."

Nina chuckled, suspecting Doug edged out Kimmy and her, too. "This will be great for the girls."

"Carly whined on the way here about not having a friend along. She'll be happy now."

When Doug and Rick approached them with a map, they had already turned the maze into a contest with the loser paying for dinner.

She shook her head and grinned, forgetting how competitive men were at times. Angie caught on and gave her an "I understand" look. The group headed off to the entrance, and after deciding which path to follow, Rick darted ahead with Angie running along beside him. Carly begged Doug to let Kimmy be on their team, and he finally agreed, hurrying ahead to make sure the girls caught up.

Nina ambled along, assuming Doug would wait for her. When she turned the next bend and realized she had choices, she stopped and looked around, trying to guess which way they had gone.

Before she panicked, Doug returned, a grin plastered on his face. "I thought you'd followed me."

She raised her shoulders and let them drop. "No, I thought this was a fun outing and not a race to the finish."

From his expression, he got her point and slipped his hand into hers. "I've got you."

His warm hand pressed hers, and the heat rose up her arm and to her heart. After a few false turns and no sign of Rick and the others, they found one of the checkpoints. Doug picked up the paper punch and made a hole in the map.

"What's that for?"

"It's another contest. If you find all the checkpoints on your part of the maze, you turn it in. Later they'll do a draw for the large pumpkin." He chuckled. "You've always wanted one of those, haven't you?"

The expression on his face made her laugh, a feeling she'd learned to cherish. Thoughts of her past soared through her. Days that passed without laughter. There had been some pleasant days, but after the miscarriages. the darker days had overshadowed the bright ones.

Doug squeezed her hand again and heat rushed to her heart. When he stopped and looked at her, she lifted her free hand to touch her cheek for a flush, but it was cool. "Why are you looking at me like that?"

"Because you're beautiful."

Her breathing became shallow. "I'm what?" She shook her head. "If you said *beautiful*, you need to have your—"

He moved in front of her and captured her cheeks between his hands. "I have perfect vision. No need to have them checked. We see differently. I see a woman with a generous heart and a loving spirit. A woman with brown, glowing eyes and dark hair with highlights of sunshine." He brushed his hand along her hairline to the nape of her neck.

Chills ran down her back, but his eyes wrapped her in a kindled glow.

"Nina, I've been single all my life without any regrets until now."

A frown tugged at her face. "Why now? Because you've enjoyed Kimmy and now you want to have—"

"Because I've met you, and I feel whole for the first time in my life."

"Whole? I—I don't understand."

"You live alone, Nina, but once you lived with someone...when you were married. Doesn't life seem different now than it did when you had someone in your life?"

She had someone in her life. Doug...and Kimmy until she moved back home with her mother. "I had to adjust, but sometimes alone is better than together in misery."

"But I'm not in misery anymore. In the past year, I felt lonely at times, but mostly I didn't realize what I was missing. Now I do. I don't like the feeling of coming home from work to no one."

She drew in a breath, her chest tightening with an awareness she didn't recognize. Doug's expression, the way his eyes searched hers, the closeness of his face left her weak and longing for him to hold her close.

"Nina, I'll miss Kimmy. There's no doubt about that, but what I would miss even more is you if you walked away. Sometimes I fear that's what you will do."

Reality washed over her. "I'm not going anywhere, Doug. I enjoy your company too much. I care about you."

He lowered his hands to her shoulders and drew her closer. His tenderness spread through her, and when his lips lowered, she raised hers to meet him. All fears, all concerns sailed away on the breeze and the rustle of dried cornstalks became the music of her heart. His kiss deepened, and she yielded to feelings she had blocked. Today they soared, caught in the rush of longing and hope that had escaped her for too long.

Voices rippled over the dried stalks, and Kimmy's giggle crackled in her ears. Doug eased back and looked toward the sound. "I think we have visitors." He slipped his hand into hers as the girls darted around the corner.

"Where have you been?" Kimmy's fist rested on her waist but this time she looked concerned. "We waited for you."

Nina gathered her wits and managed a guilt-ridden smile she hoped Kimmy didn't recognize. "Maybe we were waiting for you."

Kimmy shook her head. "You got lost, didn't you?"

Lost in each other's arms, but that wasn't the answer she could give Kimmy. "No, we're just being slow."

"You're supposed to be fast and win the race." She flagged them forward.

Doug gave her an "I surrender" look.

Nina trotted off behind the girls, not caring who bought who dinner. She'd opened her heart and with that came a cavern of worries she would resolve. Doug needed to know the truth before he met her mother, who had never spent time with her without reminding her that she couldn't have children.

Doug deserved more than getting smacked that way. She'd opened her heart to him when they were alone, and now she had to not only open her heart but also her past.

The truth would set her free one way or another. She prayed it wasn't the other—being alone again without Doug.

But she had to take a chance.

Doug stood in Kimmy's bedroom, once again a guest room, and watched her pack the last of her belongings. He'd helped her assemble a boxful of toys and books she'd collected during her stay. His gaze swept the room, which looked empty already, exactly as he felt.

His reaction to Kimmy's return home was not only about his feelings. He was also concerned about the situation Kimmy was going home to. Roseanne seemed to think she was well enough to handle the bundle of energy he'd lived with—and loved—the past months. He had more than second thoughts.

Kimmy's move had drawn his mind from Nina and the amazing kiss in the corn maze. He longed to know where she stood with her feelings. If the kiss was the barometer, she cared as much as he did, but sometimes his instinct failed. Today he teetered with that concern.

Instinct about Kimmy's return home flailed in the same way. His emotions tangled with his own desire. Maybe he wasn't thinking about what was best for her and Roseanne.

"I think I have all my clothes, Uncle Doug." Kimmy scrutinized her luggage and turned to face him. Though excitement had bounced around her the night before, today when she began packing her eyes had a moist glow.

He strolled next to her as if to check the contents of her bag, but instead, he slipped his arm around her shoulders and gave her a hug. Her reaction startled him. "I don't feel good."

"What's wrong, sweetie?"

"My head hurts and my tummy is sick." She swung around and buried her face in his hip, tears flowing.

Doug crouched down and cuddled her in his arms, his own heart torn by her response to the hug. "Kimmy, you'll feel better when you get home. Making changes is hard for us, but I know you want to be with your mom, and I'm still going to see you a lot. And so is Nina."

"I want to help my mom, but I want to be here, too." She choked on the comment and sobs broke free.

Doug wasn't sure if she felt guilty balancing her two emotions or if it was the leaving itself that really made her so sad.

"Kimmy, I'll miss you, too. I've loved having you here, and if your mom decides you'd be better staying here a little longer, she'll let you come back. But I know she's so anxious to have you home. You're an angel, Kimmy, and I know you'll love being home once you've been there a couple of days."

She pulled her head up and nodded, but her expression revealed her struggle.

"Where's Nina? I thought she was going with us."

"She's on her way over."

He closed her suitcase, gave a last look at the room and slipped his arm around Kimmy's shoulders. "If you forget something, I'll bring it over for you. Okay?"

"Okay."

The doorbell rang, and Kimmy broke free of his arm and rushed to the door. When she saw Nina, she reached up and gave her a hug, and again tears rimmed her eyes.

Nina knelt beside her and talked so softly he couldn't make out the words. Kimmy clung to what she said as if her words were gold. When her tears faded, he carried the luggage out to the car.

In moments, Kimmy and Nina came from the house, deep in conversation, but this time, Kimmy had a faint smile on her lips. Doug grasped the image and prayed it would get him through the final steps of the trek to Roseanne's.

While Doug made coffee, Nina sat in the living room reliving the difficult goodbyes. Though Kimmy had whispered she was sick, her reaction when she saw her mother eased the pain of saying goodbye. Though Kimmy longed to be in two places at once, her mother's presence added a surety to her move back home.

She had clung to them during the goodbyes, but Doug promised to visit often and she guaranteed she'd make the Christmas pinecone ornaments with Kimmy. Those promises eased the difficult parting. But outside, tears had blurred her vision, too. She turned back to the doorway, where Kimmy watched them climb into the car. Nina had waved and blew a kiss and Kimmy returned it and eased the door closed. As they pulled away, she spotted Doug brushing away the emotion from his eyes. And now she sat in his living room, anticipating the silence.

Doug returned with two mugs of coffee, and she grasped one, warming her icy hands, too aware of where the conversation had to lead.

The corn maze had been her undoing. Doug's gentle touch, the vulnerable look in his eyes, the nearness of his lips to hers had broken the barrier of her full emotions. Love poured out in the kiss they'd shared, and she'd revealed herself to him. It was too late to put on the brakes. She'd driven full speed ahead, and now she had to face either walking away or telling the truth. At Thanksgiving dinner, she knew her mother would reveal the truth if Nina hadn't already. But how should she begin?

She took a sip of the hot coffee and fell into silence, her thoughts writhing with all she had to say.

"This is silly."

Doug's voice jarred her thoughts as tension thrashed through her. Did he suspect she had something to say? "What's silly?"

He gave her a hopeless look. "I'm a grown man and can't believe I'm acting like this." He ran his finger beneath his moist eyes.

"It's not silly, Doug. That little girl got under my skin, too, and I'm not calling it silly. I'm calling it love."

He eyed her as if surprised at her response, and yet he must have known how she felt.

"One day you'll have your own kids, Nina. Think how hard it must be to say goodbye when they strike out on their own."

His response smacked her chest and drained the air from her lungs. He'd opened the door to her admission, and now her mouth twitched with the jumbled words she needed to say. "I'm sure saying goodbye in any circumstance is difficult." The feeble response was all she could think of in the moment. She needed to organize her thoughts.

"As much as I worry about Roseanne hobbling around, I suppose I need to give her credit."

Her stomach knotted when he returned the subject back to Roseanne.

"I don't want to see her depending too much on Kimmy for things. I hope—"

"Doug, I understand your concern, but as we both agreed on our way home, you have to wait and see.

Don't you think Roseanne will admit if it's not working? If she needs too much help, she'll realize Kimmy's a handful. Getting her back and forth to school will be the biggest issue."

"She said another parent agreed to pick up Kimmy when she took her daughter to school. I hope that works as planned."

"You can pray that it works. Did you forget?"

He chuckled, and it was the first time that day he'd shown any lightheartedness.

Tension faded from his face, and her pulse raced, knowing she had to dampen his spirit again with the truth she had to reveal. She swallowed bile that rose to her throat and sent up a prayer.

"Doug…"

He studied her, a scowl revisiting his smooth brow, and his reaction wrenched her confidence.

"You said something a second ago that…that I need to talk with you about."

"What? What did I say? If I hurt your feelings or—"

"No. It's nothing like that. It's what I haven't said that's the problem, Doug. Something I don't tell anyone, but I must explain it to you because it's important."

His scowl deepened and he shifted closer and sank into a chair. "What's wrong, Nina? I can tell it's serious, and I—"

"Yes, it is serious because it's something I know is important to you. A few seconds ago, you said one day I would have children of my own, but…but that isn't going to happen, Doug."

His jaw dropped and his mouth opened as he took a deep breath. "What do you mean?"

Pressure weighted her chest and knotted her vocal

cords. She waited a moment to get control before she could bring her voice to life. "My marriage ended because of the situation."

"What situation, Nina. Just tell me." A desperate look filled his face and broke her heart.

"I had two miscarriages, Doug, and the doctor found a problem that will cause me never to carry a child to full term."

His face twisted from desperation to confusion. Silence hung between them, and nausea rose upward, plowing into the back of her throat. She fought back the sensation, praying one of her rare prayers for God's guidance. "I wanted children badly. As much as any woman who loves children, but it didn't happen. Do I blame God or do I blame something I've done or—"

"Nina, please. Blame no one. Life hands out joys and sorrows."

He quieted as if in thought and she feared talking, asking, knowing what had muted his voice. She had offered him a piece of news no man wanted to hear, not one who deserved to be a father and would be a good one.

After time passed, her love for him nudged her to offer an out to his dilemma. "Doug, I understand your confusion. Yes, I care about you with all my heart. I tried to lock my feelings inside and let you know that I was serious about never marrying, but I failed miserably. My actions were unfair to you. I loved your kisses and the corn maze undid me."

"I'd been undone before that, Nina. You're not to blame, and somehow I believe that the Lord moved us to these feelings. He opened my eyes to what I had been missing. You showed me what companionship is like. You opened my eyes to feelings I'd locked away. You're not alone with that ability to conceal things through avoidance. I'd dedicated my life to family and watched marriages falter and crumble. They held no interest for me."

She searched his face, seeing his heart shine in his eyes.

"And then came Kimmy. I adored her always. She's been the cutest child, creative and a bundle of charm. Spending time with her for these past weeks made me realize what marriage can be. It doesn't have to be a failure filled with problems. Love can heal everything, and I knew I would never marry unless I saw my marriage filled to the brim with love."

"But now a relationship with me is different. I cannot give you or any man the children that you long for. A marriage to me can't grow into a family. It's a couple, a childless couple. But you don't have to live with that, Doug."

Tears broke from her eyes and blurred her vision. Seeing him in a haze relieved her from seeing the disappointment in his face, the sadness in his eyes. "I'm sorry. I'm so sorry that I let it go too long without warning you."

Doug lifted his head, a new expression on his face. "No blame and no sorrys, Nina. First, it's not your fault. It's life. Many couples are childless and many by choice. Second, do you believe the words of one doctor? Did you have a second opinion? Will you explain what's wrong that you assume you can't carry a child through the nine months?"

The intimacy of her problem knotted in her throat, but she owed him details. "It's a chronic disease that can eventually result in more serious illnesses. It's hard to treat. After my first loss, I went on the medication. We were so sure but it happened again. The doctor believed that medication wasn't the answer. Even with surgery, having a child is far from guaranteed. Any treatment is close to hopeless."

He shook his head as if he could dislodge the problem from her body. "Nothing is hopeless. Second opinions, new medical treatments…in the medical field new discoveries are made daily."

Any response she could make seemed empty. She'd once had hope but it had left her three years earlier when Todd walked out and ended their marriage.

"But, Nina, if that's the problem that's holding you back from loving me I can live without my own children. Kimmy's my niece and I love her as deeply as I would a child of my own. Why would I feel any different with an adopted child? Love given has nothing to do with blood running through the veins. It has to do with what's in your heart."

His words touched her to the depth of her being, but her own needs struck her. "I would want to give my husband a child. A little person that's a blend of the husband and wife. I want—"

"Do you care what I want, Nina? Do my wants and hopes mean nothing to you? I'm being honest with you. Yes, I would love a child of my own, and you would, too, but what happens if I can't have children? That's a possibility. I would only have some guarantee with tests. Would you expect me to have them—or any man—before accepting his proposal?"

Her throat ached from holding back sobs. "No. Never, Doug. I wouldn't think of such a thing."

"Neither would I. So here's my request. Would you please visit another doctor for a second opinion or for new treatments? Don't accept never, Nina."

She looked away, and then raised her head. "After Thanksgiving. I'll give it thought."

"Nina, the outcome wouldn't change my feelings about you, not one iota, but you might have hope again, and I want that for you."

Tears broke free, and Doug drew her to his chest, holding her against his heart. She opened the floodgate and let the salty water flow down her cheeks and onto his sweater.

He swayed as a father might for his crying child, and she clung to him, wrapped in his care and concern. He'd never flinched at her confession. He'd been thoughtful but steady in his gaze. For once, she knew she could trust him fully. He meant what he said.

Now it was in her hands.

Chapter Eleven

Nina slipped on her jacket, grasped the container of cookies and headed down the street toward El's. Each time she read something in the Bible, her talk with El came to mind as did Doug's request for her to visit a new physician. This time she didn't need the cookies as an excuse, but he loved them and who didn't enjoy an appreciative fan?

When she pushed his bell, the door flew open, and she faced a young woman she'd never seen before. "Is El in? I'm a neighbor." She motioned toward her house and waited while the stranger gawked at her a moment before she turned and headed back inside, leaving the door open. "Gramps. Another of your lady friends is here."

Nina grinned, certain Birdie had hustled over seeing a woman she didn't know visit El.

El's chuckle reached her ears as he came through the archway. "Nina. I'm so glad you came." He pushed open the storm door and she entered. As she did, he eyed the container and his grin grew broader. "And you came bearing gifts."

"I hope you like them."

He accepted the container and gave her a playful look. "If they're sweet, you know I'll love them." He motioned for her to sit as he continued past her. "Ginger, can you come here a minute?"

"What?" She ambled in, a scowl growing on her face. "I'm busy."

He eyed her a moment, and Nina sensed he had sent up a prayer. "I hope you can spare a minute. I'd like you to meet one of my neighbors."

Ginger shrugged and looked at Nina. "Hi." She turned away.

Before she could leave, El touched her arm. "Ginger, this is Nina. She lives in the house at the corner."

"Okay."

Nina forced a pleasant look. "It's nice to meet you, Ginger. How long are you visiting?"

Her eyes shifted to El and back as if she were uncertain.

"Ginger will be staying here for a while." He arched an eyebrow and looked at her.

Ginger squirmed under El's gaze. "Right. It's here or jail."

Her blunt response threw Nina off balance. An appropriate response swirled through her head. "I'm sorry, Ginger, but you have a wonderful grandfather, so the choice was a good one."

Ginger pressed her lips together though a faint grin sneaked to the edge of her lips. "I suppose you're right." She turned to El. "Is this necessary, Gramps?"

He opened the container and offered her a cookie.

Ginger eyed the treats a moment, and then took one.

"I don't mean to be rude, but I know if I didn't tell you, Gramps would."

Another challenge. She sought a response and decided honesty was best. "Sometimes getting things out in the open is better than skirting the issue or lying. I've skirted the truth often, Ginger, and I want to tell you it's caused me more grief than I can explain."

Somehow what she said caught Ginger's attention. This time she gave up the battle and let her grin come through. "You sound like my grandpa. He says things like that."

"That's because it's true. I've spent my life hiding something about myself that'd kept me from moving forward and being happy."

Ginger backed up and dropped into an easy chair. "Really?"

"Really. In fact, that's part of the reason I dropped by today, hoping I'd catch El alone so I could talk with him about it."

"What's the other reason?" Ginger narrowed her eyes.

"The last time I saw him, he asked me to come over because he had something to talk about."

El chuckled and settled into his recliner. "I don't need to say much now, Nina. You've just opened the door to why I wanted to see you. I watched you and Doug together at Angie's wedding, and I recognized two people who were in love, and yet I could still see a kind of hesitation in your behavior. Something unsettled you. Only a faint hint of it, but I've seen it too often. It's like the day I gave you Margie's Bible."

"You gave her Grandma's Bible? Why?" Ginger's voice had an edge.

Nina's head jerked. "Ginger, if you'd like your grandmother's Bible, I'd be happy to give it to you. I've read so much of it and—"

"No." Ginger shook her head. "I was just surprised. Gramps always kept that Bible beside his bed. It was as if he kept a little of Grandma with him."

"That's true, Ginger." Nostalgia filled El's face. "But I've begun to heal, and I thought your grandma would like someone to read it who really needed to learn about Jesus."

"You weren't a Christian?" Ginger's jaw sagged.

"A very watery one at one time, but the water had dried up and so had I."

Ginger nodded as if she understood. "Gramps is right. I have a Bible. I just don't read it anymore. I fell for a guy with a dark past. I let him drag me down with him." She shook her head. "I hate talking about it."

Nina understood and resisted questions. Ginger would talk more when she was ready, just as she'd learned to do.

"Are you ready for this, El?"

"Sure am, but only if you're ready to talk with an old geezer like me."

"El, I've told you many times. A wise old geezer like you. You're filled with more wisdom than anyone I know."

He grinned, while she gritted her teeth, wanting to hold back the story she'd come to tell, and yet she could see it served even more purpose with Ginger there. She eased her back against the sofa cushion and drew in a breath. She started from the beginning and spilled the details into the space between them, one that had been silent except for her voice. "And then I met Doug, a man who God meant to be a tremendous father and a good husband. But, El, I am caught with my situation."

"You have a situation, but are you really caught in it?"

"Not as much as I was. I finally confessed what held me back from falling in love and being a wife."

"Doug didn't walk out on you, did he?" El tilted his head as he waited for her response.

"You know he didn't. But he asked me questions and made me think."

El leaned closer. "Questions?"

An ache grew in her chest. "He wanted to know how many doctors I'd talked with. I said one." She shook her head. "So he asked me to have a second opinion."

"And that's frightening, isn't it?"

She nodded, her gaze sweeping across Ginger's face, filled with her own pain.

Forcing her gaze from Ginger, she sorted through her thoughts. "Yes, but it made me act. I went online and researched. I learned some things that helped me to understand Doug's question. Medical advances happen daily, and doctors do make mistakes. My problem is very similar to another female issue, and that one has a new surgical procedure that helps, but…"

El's gaze grew tender. "But what if you get your hopes up, and your first doctor was correct."

She nodded, a ragged breath tearing from her lungs.

"But, Nina…" Ginger's voice shot past her. "What if your first doctor was wrong? What if you can have a child? What if you turn down love that would be wonderful just because of a what-if?"

"Smart girl, Ginger." Pride rose in El's voice. "Those are good questions. And here's another thought. My

Margie had some kind of female problem, and the doctor warned her that it was a good possibility she would never have a child."

"Really, Gramps?"

He gave Ginger a nod, and then shifted his gaze back to Nina. "She kept that a secret for a short time, but I sensed something was wrong. I didn't bug her. Margie wasn't one you wanted to bug."

Ginger chuckled. "Grandma liked life to run her way."

El gave Ginger a watch-what-you-say look. "One day, Margie told me, and I said I loved her for her and I reminded her the Lord was in charge. He would decide." He chuckled. "I was right. Within a year, Margie was expecting our first daughter, and a couple years later we had our second." He smacked his knees and rose. "See what I mean. We're not in charge."

"So I should trust that Doug is telling me the truth. He will still love me if I go through with another doctor and learn the same thing. No babies."

El's expression answered the question.

"That's what I thought, but I wanted validation, El. I value your opinion. Very much."

Ginger scooted to the edge of her seat. "So you'll get the second opinion?"

Nina nodded. "I've looked up a few doctors, and I'll call for an appointment as soon as I get past Thanksgiving."

El crossed to her side. "That's the best thing to do, Nina, and I'll pray the answer blesses you, no matter what it is."

"Me, too." Ginger nodded.

Ginger's offer startled her. "Thank you." Nina rose

and took a step toward the door. "Ginger, I'm happy to listen anytime, and, El, thank you so much."

He opened his arms, and she stepped in and accepted his hug. Outside she had a bounce to her step she hadn't had earlier. Her decision was made and El had validated it. The truth was what she needed. She would learn to live with it.

Nina opened the oven and basted the turkey, golden brown, the way she liked it. She eyed the wall clock, and her pulse skipped. Her mother and stepfather would arrive soon. She looked heavenward for the nth time and asked the Lord to help her deal with her mother's criticisms.

The potatoes boiled in the large kettle and she turned down the burner. She'd prepared well. The vegetable casserole was already baked and ready to slip into the microwave for a warm-up, and she'd done the same with her corn casserole, one of her favorites. She grinned, picturing Doug, who'd insisted he would take care of dessert.

Her cell phone's ringtone began, and she crossed to the table and grasped it. "Doug. Are you—"

"We're just leaving. Kimmy's still not feeling well, but Roseanne is pretty good. I guess it's a trade-off."

"Poor Kimmy. I thought once she'd adjusted to home she'd be okay."

"Me, too. I think she needs to see a doctor, but Roseanne can't take her so I'll suggest Roseanne make an appointment for next week. If she needs a ride, I'll take her."

"Good idea. My mother isn't here yet but I expect her anytime now. I'll see you soon." Their call ended and she returned to the last-minute details to burn off her anxiety.

As she closed the oven, a horn reverberated from the driveway. She hurried to the front, managing a pleasant expression. When she opened the door her mother had reached the porch with her stepfather on her heels. "Mother, you made it. How was the trip?"

"As good as can be expected." She stood a moment scanning the front of the house.

Nina nodded to Howard and waited to hear her mother's evaluation.

"I thought it would be bigger." Her mother arched a brow and grabbed the doorjamb as she made her way inside.

"It's big enough for me, Mom. One person doesn't use a lot of space."

"One person doesn't. Too bad. I think women should have a husband, but then I guess you have other ideas."

She squelched her rebuttal and avoided agreeing with her. The agree-with-her technique was meant to be used at selected times. It was the best way to stop an argument. "Have a seat. Dinner's in the oven. Would you like some coffee or tea?"

"What brand of coffee?"

Nina ignored her mother's expression. "I have a coffeemaker with individual cups. Would you like to see what I have?"

"Never mind. Give me something bold." She flashed a look at Howard. "He'll drink anything."

Howard's lengthy sigh whispered in the air. "Anything."

She returned to the kitchen, grateful for the break to regroup and pray for her patience. With the two coffee mugs in hand, she joined them and sank into a chair across from them. "How have you been?"

Her mother shrugged. "Nothing earthshaking. The question is how are you?"

"Good. Very good. In fact, I have some friends joining us for dinner. I hope you don't mind."

Her mother's eyes widened. "Friends? Why would you—"

"Because it's Thanksgiving, Mom, and I'm thankful for the friendship I have with Doug and his family."

"Doug?" She flashed a look at Howard again. "Who's this Doug?"

"A neighbor. I met him shortly after I moved here. They had an end-of-summer block party, and—"

"Block party? Goodness." She snorted. "This is a small town. I've never seen a block party in—"

"Big cities don't always have them, I suppose, but it was a wonderful way for me to meet my neighbors. I'm not a coffee klatch type person, but I know if I need help where I can go."

"Why do you need help, Nina? You've always been very independent. You don't listen to anyone's advice. For example, when you lost that first baby—"

Patience flew out the window and no technique could stop her. "Mother, that was four years ago. Do we have to relive that again?"

"I only meant—"

"I know what you meant." Nina forced her fists open. "You enjoy reminding me of—"

Noise at the door saved her from herself.

"They're here." She held up a finger and hurried across the room. "Come in. You're right on time." She gave Doug a look she hoped he understood.

He gave her a wink and shifted for Kimmy's entrance, but instead of her bounding inside, she walked in, a look on her face that caused Nina to be concerned. She bent over and pressed her cheek to the child's. "Are you feeling any better?"

Kimmy shook her head, and then noticed the company. Her eyes shifted to Nina's.

"This is my mother and stepfather, Kimmy." She eyed them again and gave a timid wave.

She'd never seen Kimmy that shy and her concern rose. She looked at Doug, holding the door open for Roseanne, and he only lifted a brow.

Roseanne swung in on crutches and Doug followed. With the three inside the door, she motioned toward her family. "Mother. Howard. These are my friends, Doug, his sister, Roseanne, who you can see is recuperating from leg injuries, and Roseanne's daughter, Kimmy."

She turned to them. "This is my mother, Alice, and my stepfather, Howard."

They exchanged greetings, though her mother and Howard sat without making an effort to stand to welcome them.

Doug faltered to a stop. "I forgot to bring in the dessert." He held up his index finger and retreated through the doorway.

Roseanne settled in an easy chair with an ottoman while Kimmy sat beside her on the floor. Before she could offer drinks, Doug returned carrying two pies and something in a paper bag. She took drink orders and followed Doug into the kitchen.

As soon as he set the pies on the counter, he turned and drew her into his arms. "You don't look happy."

She released a long breath. "It's tedious already,

but I'm doing okay. Hopefully with you here, she will soften up a bit."

"I'm sorry, Nina. You don't need any added stress in your life." He drew her closer, his lips lowering to her mouth.

Since she'd explained her inability to have children, each kiss became more precious, a validation that he hadn't abandoned her. His request entered her mind and her thoughtful talk with El. Ginger, of all people, had said something that touched her. What if the doctor was wrong? She'd convinced herself that never was reality. Never left out God's hand on her life.

"What can I do to help?"

Doug's voice drew her back and made her smile. His willingness to do anything came naturally to him, and she loved it. "How are you at carving turkeys?"

"A pro." He chuckled.

"I'll take that answer with a grain of salt...or even a grain of sage, but you'll do a better job than I will."

She opened the oven and he brought out the golden-brown bird and set it on a cutting board while she slipped the corn casserole inside to warm it. After she popped the veggie casserole into the microwave, she hurried back into the living room, hearing her mother ask questions about Roseanne's accident and the where-abouts of Roseanne's husband. She winced, seeing Roseanne's uneasiness as she said they had separated years earlier.

Grateful that her mother didn't ask more, she was even more grateful she'd interrupted the conversation. "We're finishing up in the kitchen. The food will be on the table in a few minutes."

"Can I help?" Kimmy rose from the floor and crossed to her.

"If you want to. Can you carry things to the table?"

Kimmy nodded, too quiet in comparison to her usual enthusiasm.

She set out the cranberry relish she'd made and a tray of relishes for Kimmy to carry into the dining room while she slipped the dinner rolls into the oven. The corn casserole had warmed, and the microwave beeped as the veggies were finished.

Doug filled a platter with turkey and she grabbed a masher and attacked the drained potatoes. Soon the food was ready and she invited everyone to the dining room table. Once everyone had gathered around, she shifted her attention to Kimmy. "Would you like to say the blessing?"

Kimmy nodded, and from her peripheral vision, she noted the shocked look on her mother's face. Everyone folded their hands except her mother and Howard as Kimmy began the prayer. "Come, Lord Jesus, be our guest and let these gifts to us be blessed. Amen."

Again Roseanne, Doug and she reiterated the amen though her mother and Howard continued to remain silent.

"This dining room is a bit small, wouldn't you say?"

Time for her technique. "Yes, it is for a large group, but we seem to fit just fine."

Her mother looked away and sliced a sliver from her turkey.

Though Roseanne had been quiet, she accidentally helped Nina's plight with her mother. "The turkey's excellent, Nina. It's moist and such a good flavor. Do you do something special?"

The questioned brightened Nina's day. "Nothing but baste it often."

"Well, it's delicious."

She grinned at Roseanne. "Thanks, but maybe it's Doug's carving."

Doug smiled at her and dug into the corn casserole. "Now, this is excellent."

Nina's spirits rose. Despite her mother's scrutinizing, hearing compliments relaxed her. She knew her mother wouldn't try her negativity on the company.

Kimmy only picked at her food, so unlike her, and Nina's concern deepened as she watched. When she asked to be excused, she beckoned to Kimmy to come to her and felt her cheeks and forehead. Heat penetrated her hand.

Roseanne noticed. "Does she have a fever?"

"I think so." Nina pulled her hands way. "I can take her temperature."

"I'm guessing it's the flu." Roseanne shrugged and, with a grimace, shifted her leg, obviously still in pain.

With the meal concluded—and enjoyed from everyone's comments—Nina suggested saving dessert for later. Doug and her mother rose and began to put away the food, so she sneaked off for a moment with Kimmy to take her temperature.

When she read the results, her concern turned to worry. The thermometer read a hundred and three degrees. She found Doug in the kitchen, and after she told him he said he would warn Roseanne.

Nina struggled to concentrate on the conversation, distracted by Kimmy's health. Her mother's acerbic comments lessened, and she fell into conversation with Doug about his work and Roseanne's situation. Nina was even more surprised to hear her mother talk about her father's illness and death. Since her mother said little about those days, hearing her speak in a positive light about her dad touched Nina's heart.

She placed her hand on Kimmy's forehead to check the heat again, and this time her mother noticed. "Nina, you seem to be preoccupied with Kimmy. It's such a shame you don't have children of your own."

Though the comment might have slipped by the others as a remark from a caring mother, Nina saw it as another way to belittle her. The dig bit into her self-esteem once again and dampened her spirit.

Doug leaned back and gave her an understanding look before addressing her mother. "You know some women enjoy waiting to have a family until the time is right. Who knows what the future holds for Nina? I know she could make an amazing mother. She has lots of love to give to a child. Ask Kimmy."

Kimmy nestled closer to her, lifting a faint smile.

Her mother's comment dropped to the floor while Kimmy's reaction sent her to the sky.

Nina watched her mother's eyes shift from Doug to Kimmy to her, and she said nothing. Doug had come to her aid and she loved him for that. Loved him for many things.

Despite being store-bought, the dessert was a hit—a pumpkin and a French silk pie. Each took a slice of their favorite and Doug tried both. He'd brought along a can of real whipped cream, and the pie and coffee finished off a successful meal.

Though Roseanne's focus turned to Kimmy, she began to look achy. Doug noticed the situation and rose. "I think I need to get this patient back home, and we can take a good look at this young lady." He scooped Kimmy into his arms, and despite her illness, she giggled. The sound delighted Nina, and even her mother made a kind comment.

After the others slipped out the door, Doug leaned in and squeezed her hand. "I'll see you later. I want to get them home, and I'm as worried as you are about Kimmy. I don't think this is the flu."

"I agree. I think Roseanne is beginning to realize Kimmy's sicker than she suspected."

From his expression, she knew he wanted to kiss her goodbye, but with her parents watching from the sofa, he winked and hurried to unlock the car.

When she closed the door, her mother gave her a questioning look. "Are you not telling me something?"

"Like what?" She kept her voice casual, not willing to open her heart.

"You know 'like what,' Nina." A frown edged her face and grew. "This man is more than a nice neighbor. You two have a connection. I watched you through the day with your little looks, and you love that girl, don't you?"

"Yes, Mom, I do. She's sweet and fun. Kimmy's a creative, wonderful child."

"But it's not his child, right?" Her frown eased to curiosity.

She nodded. "Right. She's his sister's but she's been alone for years raising Kimmy and Doug is always there for her. He'll make an amazing father."

Tension eased from her mother's face. "He would make a good husband, too. I hope you see that."

She gave an evasive nod.

"Does he know about your problem?" The lift of her voice communicated her assumption.

But Nina had a response ready. "Yes, he does."

"Really?" Her pitch arched somewhere between surprise and question. "And he understands."

"Doug cares about me for me, Mom. And though I believe he will handle it if I can't carry a child, he suggested I get a second opinion. Medical advances have been made since the last diagnosis."

Her mother lowered her head and shook it, leaving Nina to wonder what it meant.

"I appreciate his gallantry, but I'm not sure the reality has hit him yet. I don't want you to get your hopes up, Nina. The doctor seemed confident when he gave you the verdict. What if you go through more doctors and tests, and the first doctor was correct?"

Though her comment sounded negative, Nina witnessed true caring in her mother's eyes. She opened her mouth to respond but Howard's voice slipped in first and startled her.

"Alice, what happens if the doctor was wrong, and Nina could have a child? Isn't it worth the chance?"

At this moment, Nina loved her stepfather. "That's how I see it, too, Howard. I've avoided thinking about it, but I care greatly for Doug, and yes, Mom, I can see him as a wonderful husband. One who would stand by me no matter what. I want to give him a chance to have children with me."

"I agree. If you are willing to take the chance on being disappointed, then I support your decision. I would be a good grandmother, Nina, although I doubt if you agree."

"Mom, I don't know what I think. You and I have butted heads for a long time, and—"

"You were Daddy's little girl. I was your mother, and I suppose I was jealous."

Her eyes widened before she could digest what her mother had said. "I had no idea you felt that way, Mom. Lots of girls are Daddy's little—"

"I suppose their mothers are confident that they are good parents. I didn't have much of a role model, but I did the best I could. I know I failed in many ways. I wanted you to be perfect so people would know I raised a lovely daughter, but you couldn't hide your disdain for me, Nina. The more I sensed your feelings, the more I tried to build myself up by—"

"Finding faults with me." Her chest ached, controlling her emotion. "Mom, I didn't know. I never suspected. I thought you didn't like me or that I was a horrible disappointment. You talked about only my flaws, all negatives. I never knew you saw anything positive."

"My defense. I'm sorry about that. Howard noticed and finally said something and I analyzed my behavior. He was right."

"But when you arrived you…"

"I slipped into my old self. You know it's hard to break bad habits, Nina. But now that I have explained, I hope you can understand even if you can't forgive me."

She released a stream of air. "I can forgive you. Forgive you with all my heart." She opened her arms and her mother rose and hugged her for the first time in years.

"But let me bug you again. If you are thinking about this, what do you plan to do?"

"I'm going to find out all I can about my problem. I've already done some research and investigated a doctor. But this time I'll go with ammunition and this time maybe I can find an answer."

Her mother smiled. "And I'll keep my fingers crossed."

"Thank you, Mom. That means the world to me."

Doug plowed through paperwork in his office, grateful today he didn't have clients to see since he was distracted, waiting to hear about Kimmy.

After he'd taken Roseanne home and started to leave, she had asked him to stay for a while so he could help with Kimmy while she tried to make arrangements to see a doctor the next day. Roseanne dealt with an answering service, and a while later the doctor finally called. Doug watched her struggle through the conversation. Though Roseanne was grateful that the physician had returned her call, she appeared to struggle to keep an even tone while she begged him to see Kimmy the next day rather than take her to emergency.

Doug agreed. The wait would be forever on Thanksgiving Day and Kimmy had become nauseated and could keep nothing down. Waiting in an emergency room was no place for a sick child.

He offered to drive Roseanne to the appointment, but she called in the morning to say a friend had agreed to drive them to the doctor's office. And now he waited, his heart in his throat.

His distraction wasn't only Kimmy. Nina had been on his mind when Kimmy wasn't. He'd made a quick call to her the past evening to tell her where he was. He longed to talk with her about the Thanksgiving dinner experience, but there wasn't time. He'd left Roseanne's late and he'd been in a rush this morning. He'd wait to call until he had news. When his cell phone rang, he grabbed it, his pulse pummeling before he realized the caller was Nina.

"I thought you were Roseanne."

"You're upset. What happened last night?"

He filled her in as quickly as he could. "I'm now waiting for Roseanne to call. I don't know what's happening at this point."

"Please let me know and I'll be praying it's nothing serious."

He'd prayed, too, but he continued to worry. "I'll call you when I hear something."

After he disconnected, his mind shifted to Nina and her mother. He could understand why their relationship had been strained, and no matter what solution he considered, the situation had a hopeless feeling. Yet he knew better. Something could make a change, but he had yet to think of anything.

Forcing his mind back to his work, he managed to complete a plan of action for one of his clients, and outlined some financial steps for another who wanted to expand his business and his real estate.

When his ringtone jarred him again, he knew it was Roseanne. He hit the talk button and listened, his apprehension growing. "What does that mean? Isn't meningitis serious?"

"There's two kinds, according to the doctor, and the tests will tell us which."

Two kinds. Questions filled his mind but Roseanne's distress caused him to hold the questions for later. "What can I do to help?"

A sigh breathed across the phone. "I can't ask my friend to spend much more time here. She's taking us to the hospital for the tests, but she can't wait. I'll need a ride home, hopefully with Kimmy."

She choked and he recognized the beginning of her tears. "I'll get there as fast as I can. Where will you be?"

"Probably in the medical building for the blood work and X-rays, but maybe not since you'll be a while before getting here."

"I'm not waiting, Roseanne. I'll talk to my boss, and I'm sure he'll give me the rest of the day off. I'm not that far." They hung up and Doug hurried into his boss's office. His work could wait. He needed to be by Kimmy's side.

Nina sat in her home office and checked her watch again. She'd thought Doug would call earlier. Time had ticked by and she'd heard nothing. While waiting, she decided to do more research on the diagnosis that explained her inability to carry a child. Doug could be right. New treatments and information were found daily. She'd hoped that something could make a difference, but she'd found nothing specific that gave her hope.

When she clicked on another link, she came to the section on diagnosis. She scanned the options and spotted the test she'd had—laparoscopy. She read the article and words jumped out at her. The test was only 60 percent accurate. The doctor had never told her that.

Knowing internet facts could be wrong, she found another article, one from a reputable hospital, and she was certain the information would be accurate. Her heart skipped as she read. Only 45 to 67 percent of suspected lesions were confirmed as accurate. Twenty percent found that the positive finding in laparoscopy would be incorrect.

Her heart soared. Hope she'd given up on for years could be renewed. Maybe, just maybe, she was one of that 20 percent.

Overwhelmed by her findings, she rose from the computer and wandered into the kitchen. It was too early to eat, but her stomach had rebelled since she'd begun her wait. She searched the fridge and found a couple of apples in the fruit drawer. She withdrew the smaller one, cut it into pieces and headed to the living room. As soon as she popped a piece of apple in her mouth, her cell phone rang. She dug into her pants pocket.

"I got off work early to give Roseanne a hand. She'll need a ride home. They're at the hospital for some tests. The doctor thinks Kimmy has meningitis."

The diagnosis wrenched air from her lungs, and all thoughts of her research faded from her mind, filled by Kimmy's diagnosis. "That's serious, isn't it?"

"Roseanne said there are two kinds. The tests are supposed to determine which."

"Doug, is it okay if I go, too? I can't sit here. Can I meet you there?"

"Please, Nina. I know you love Kimmy. I'm not sure where she'll be and I don't know what will happen after the tests, but you can ask where she is at the information desk. That's what I'll have to do."

"See you soon. I'm on my way." She hit End and pulled her coat from the closet. Nothing could keep her from being there with Doug. Racked with concern, she headed for the door, then gathered her wits and returned to grab her purse before she darted to the car.

She drove to the end of Lilac Circle, turned right and then left onto Hickory Street and right onto King Street. Her heart hammered as she followed the highway and once she crossed Shiawassee, she knew she was almost there.

After parking, she made her way inside, located the first information desk and received directions to the waiting room where she hoped to see Doug. To her relief, he was there.

When she stepped into the room, he rose and she rushed into his arms, anxiety writhing through her body. "Have you heard anything?"

"Roseanne is with her. We're still waiting to hear the test results. They did blood work and X-rays. And Roseanne said they might do another test. It was PCR or something like that."

"What's that for?"

He shrugged. "Roseanne said the doctor suspects viral meningitis which is less serious, so they're checking for viruses to determine the best treatment. If it's not viral, it might be bacterial, and she'll need a spinal tap. That's more serious."

"No, Doug. Please, Lord, let it be viral only." She lowered her head, her mind spinning.

"I'm a knot of nerves, too. But I really feel for Roseanne. She's so scared and blaming herself."

Her head drew back. "Why? That doesn't make

sense. If anybody's to blame, it's you and me. We've been with her for months." The possibility devastated her. "But what did we do wrong?"

"Nina, no one's to blame. People get sick. Bacteria is everywhere and viruses fill the air. We can't fix that. Let's wait and see what the tests show."

He backed toward his chair and patted the one next to him. "Sit with me, and we'll wait. We can't do much else. I can go down to the room or you could, and see what Roseanne knows, but I think she would have told us if she knew anything more." She nodded, too anxious to think of anything better to do. She sank into the chair and leaned back her head as she drew in a breath.

"I ran out of the house so fast, I almost left my purse."

He chuckled and snapped his fingers. "We need a distraction. Tell me what happened after I left on Thanksgiving. How did it go with your mother?"

"Amazing. I was anxious to tell you, and then with all this I forgot." She related the change in her mother—and in herself. "I think it was a step forward, Doug. It's not perfect, I suppose, but we made strides. Now I understand partly what happened, but I can't picture my mother jealous of my dad. She always came across as confident in her actions. As if she were always right and the rest of the world was wrong."

"People sometimes do the opposite of what their real feelings dictate. It's a cover-up. If they can't fool themselves about their feelings, they can fool other people by their behavior. Have you ever seen a guilty person?"

She grinned. "Yes, and they do everything to hide their guilt. You're right."

"I'm guessing that's what your mother did. It would have been hard for her to admit she was jealous of her own husband."

"You're right." The idea worked through her mind, and she took one more step forward. "I need to find ways to develop a relationship with her. It's been at a standstill for so long."

"You'll think of something." His grin tingled down her spine. She sank into silence, her mind sorting through the past and clearing the cobwebs of confusion that she'd faced for too many years.

Doug slipped his hand into hers and gave it a squeeze. Feeling his nearness and his overpowering effect on her, she sank into a kind of peace. Learning there was a possibility her diagnosis could be wrong would stay buried for now. Kimmy's health was all-important, and she needed to learn more before she could be confident in the hope she'd felt. She would read more, and then act.

"Mr. Billings."

Doug jumped, hearing his name. He rose and headed to the desk. In a moment, he turned back to her. "Rose-anne said I can come to the room. The doctor is there."

He paused a moment and she knew what bothered him. "Doug, you go. I'll wait here and pray it's good news."

He gave her a questioning look until she rose and gave him a quick kiss. "I prefer to wait. You're family. I'm not." But oh how she wished she were.

He gave her another look before turning toward the door and hurrying out.

She folded her hands, her gaze clinging to the empty

doorway. Though prayer was still new for her, she'd been surprised how easily it came with each prayer. She bowed her head and prayed the Lord's blessing on Kimmy. That's all that mattered.

Chapter Twelve

Doug stood in the doorway, his chest aching. Kimmy looked so tiny, covered in hospital sheets and a blanket. She appeared to have drifted to sleep, and Roseanne's eyes were closed in prayer or she'd also fallen victim to exhaustion.

He crept into the room, but Roseanne's eyes flew open with a startled expression. "Sorry. I fell asleep, I guess. I'm as worn-out as an old rug."

"You should be, sis." He drew to her side and gave her a hug. "What did you hear from the doctor?"

She gazed at him as if part of her had remained in dreamland. Finally the glaze left. "He's still waiting on the last test, but he is quite certain she has viral meningitis, which, believe it or not, is good news."

"You mentioned it was less serious. Praise the Lord if he's right."

She nodded. "I'm torn, Doug. They want to keep her overnight to administer an antibiotic and keep her fever down until they're certain that it's a virus. They told me to leave and they would call if there's a problem, but I don't think I can. I don't want her to wake and be afraid when I'm not here."

"I know it's difficult to leave, but you need your rest. And you don't want to spend time in the hospital. If your immune system is compromised from the surgery and recovery, you could easily catch something here. It happens."

She gave him a grave look. "I know, and here's the worse news. Viral meningitis can be contagious. They'll know more when they get the test results back. Sometimes it's not."

"So that gives you greater reason to get home and rest. Would you feel better leaving after you talk with Kimmy? She is a smart girl and she will probably understand and give you permission to go home without being upset. Why don't you decide after you talk with her?"

She studied him a moment without responding. After drawing in a lengthy breath, she looked into his eyes. "I know you're right. Let me talk to her and I'll make a wiser decision then."

He could only nod in agreement to her idea. He looked into his own heart and realized how difficult it would be to go home and leave a little one in the hospital. "Nina's in the waiting room. I know she'd like to see Kimmy. Would you mind?"

"Not at all, bring her down. Maybe Kimmy will wake up soon and we can all see her."

He gave her shoulder a squeeze and slipped into the hallway, praying that his advice would come true. Kimmy wasn't a whiner or a child who needed reassurance. She had gumption for her age, and he sensed she would want her mother to go home. His thought became a prayer as he returned to the waiting room.

As soon as he stepped in, Nina's eyes met his and he beckoned her to follow him. She rose and met him outside the doorway. "How is she?"

"Sleeping, but I'm sure she'll wake up soon. They want Kimmy to stay overnight until they're sure about a few things." He gave her the details. "I'd like Roseanne to go home for the night so I'm hoping when she talks to Kimmy, she'll agree."

"I'm sure it would be hard to leave, but for her own health, that would be best."

He slipped his arm around her back as they finished the trek to Kimmy's room. When they stepped inside, he noticed Kimmy had turned on her side and seemed to be waking.

Her eyes widened. "Uncle Doug. Nina." She studied them a moment. "I had tests and now I have to stay overnight." She glanced at Roseanne. "I've never been in a hospital but they are nice. I like the nurses 'cuz they talk to me and make me laugh." She giggled. "And they brought me ice cream in a little cup."

He grinned. "Ice cream in a cup makes the hospital not such a bad place, doesn't it?"

She tittered again. "Mom?" Her grin faded. "But you can't stay here 'cuz there's only one bed." She patted the mattress. "And this one isn't big enough for you and me."

Roseanne gave him a glance before she responded. "No, I would have to sit in a chair."

Kimmy shook her head. "You can't sleep in a chair, and you need to rest too 'cuz of your leg."

"I know, but that means I would have to go home."

Kimmy thought that over a minute. "But I could call you on the phone if I had a problem."

"You could."

Doug leaned over and pointed to the bedside button. "Or you can press this and the nurse will talk to you or send someone to help you."

She eyed the button. "They will?" She studied it again. "Then I can stay here and you can go home, Mom. Okay?"

"Are you sure?" Roseanne reached past her outstretched leg and touched Kimmy's hand.

She nodded. "I'm sure. I'm seven and I'll be eight in a couple of months."

Doug lifted his brows. "I think it's more like four months."

"But I'm big now."

"You are, Kimmy. You're my big girl." Roseanne dropped back into the chair, her leg causing a grimace as she shifted.

"I think we should get going then. What do you say, Kimmy? It's almost bedtime."

"Okay. And maybe I'll get a snack and some more ice cream. That's what the nurse said."

Nina rounded the bed to the other side. "Then it must be true."

Kimmy opened her arms to Nina, and they hugged. Before she pulled away, Nina kissed her cheek. "Sleep well, sweetie, and we'll see you tomorrow."

"Tomorrow, and maybe I'll be better."

Roseanne opened her mouth, and then closed it, and Doug was relieved. It made no sense to concern Kimmy with possibilities until tests revealed the truth. Then they would all know. He gave Kimmy a big hug and he and Nina walked into the corridor to wait for Roseanne to say her goodbyes.

When they were out of earshot, he drew closer to Nina. "Everything is still hanging, but hopefully tomorrow the tests will give us good information, and I'm praying Kimmy will go home. This trek is too hard for Roseanne each day, and I know she'll want to be here all the time."

"Can't blame her, though." She eyed him. "You'd be the same kind of dad."

"Look who's talking? I can picture you having to be torn from the room if Kimmy was your child."

She eyed him a moment before a faint grin removed her serious expression. "You're right. I guess parents are often softies."

"Parents like you, definitely."

As the words left, he wished he'd been quiet, but instead of the usual frown or icy silence, for some reason, Nina's lips curved to a tiny grin. Something had made a difference. He hoped it had something to do with him.

Nina looked for Doug's car when she drove down Lilac Circle, but unless it was in the garage, he wasn't home. Still at work or Roseanne's or the hospital. She pulled into her driveway and entered through the back door.

Doug never called her home phone and he hadn't called her cell phone so she remained ignorant. Agitated by being unaware of Kimmy's diagnosis, she dropped her purse on a kitchen chair and eyed her home phone just in case. No blink to alert her to a message, so she dragged herself in her bedroom and slipped into a pair of pants and a sweater. At least she could be comfortable.

But comfort wasn't the answer. Though she longed to call Doug, she trusted him to call as soon as he knew anything. She brewed a mocha latte and wandered into the living room. After she set her mug down, she strode across the room and opened the door to check her mailbox. A couple of bills, two women's clothing catalogs and some advertisements. As she closed the door, Doug's car rolled down the street and stopped in front of her house. She tossed the mail on the nearest table and flung open the door. On the porch, the cold pierced her to the bone, but she waited for Doug to come up the walk. "What's happened? Good news or bad?"

"Both." He slipped his arm around her and steered her inside. "You'll be sick if you stand outside without a coat." His cold hand slipped into hers. "Let's sit. I need to let my head clear."

She sank onto the corner of the sofa, and he dropped into the closest chair.

"The bad part is Kimmy is contagious. It means washing her hands and our hands thoroughly. It's not likely we would catch it, and if we did, it would be a mild case probably without symptoms, but why take a chance."

Nina agreed. "And what's Kimmy's treatment?"

"Rest, lots of fluids and over-the-counter medication to reduce her fever."

Her concern remained. "Can Roseanne handle this?"

"She wants to try, but it's not wise. In her situation, she's likely to be more susceptible to the virus, and, naturally, using crutches and trying to take care of Kimmy doesn't make sense, either. But you know Roseanne. She's determined."

"And there's nothing you can do." She stopped her eye roll, but she'd noticed the attribute in his sister.

Doug tilted his head with a shake. "Time will prove us or Roseanne wrong. She's strong willed, and she'll have to be the one to admit she can't handle it. Or maybe she can."

"No matter, Doug, it's out of your hands or mine. We can pray everything works for the best."

"You're right."

She looked at him for the first time without focusing on Kimmy. He looked exhausted and cold. "You need something warm in your body. Coffee, tea, soup?"

He chuckled. "Chicken noodle for my health?"

"Whatever it takes. You looked chilled inside."

He nodded and rested his back against the chair. "Stress takes its toll. Kimmy's happy to be home, but rest is vital to her getting well quickly. I worry about Roseanne transporting glasses of water or juice to her. Unless she gets off those crutches, it's near to impossible. And I'm concerned about her healing, too. She's not supposed to put any weight on her legs yet, and I can see her doing anything to meet Kimmy's needs."

"Give her a day or two. That's all you can do." She rose. "I'll bring you something warm to drink." She left him resting against the chair back, and in the kitchen, she spotted a container of hot chocolate mix. She spooned powder into a mug and poured the hot water from her coffeemaker into it. The chocolate scent filled the air.

The aroma took her back to Christmas morning when she was a child. Her daddy would make pancakes, sausage and hot chocolate for breakfast after they'd opened her gifts from Santa. The memory warmed her even more after talking with her mother. All those wrinkles of bad memories had been smoothed, and they lay sweeter on her mind.

She carried in the cocoa and Doug accepted it with a smile. "Now, this is a treat." He took a sip and studied her. "You've become so much a part of my life, Nina, I have no idea how I lived all those years without you. Loneliness grows on a person I guess, and it's easier to withdraw even more than step out into the world. I suppose that's what I did. I concentrated on my family's needs and forgot that I might have a few of my own. I didn't see them. Now since you turned on the light, I can't live in the darkness anymore."

"You brightened my life, too, Doug. And my darkness was worse because I didn't even have the Lord to talk with or share my burdens. I lugged it all myself, thinking that I could carry the load. You and I know it's impossible. We might drag the baggage alone but it's difficult and miserable. It's self-defining. And I don't like that self anymore."

He rose from the chair and settled beside her. "I hate to bring this up, but I believe it's important to you. You're still carrying some baggage, Nina."

His look touched her heart and his meaning was clear. "I have been thinking, Doug. More than thinking. I've been doing some research, and I don't want to get my hopes up, but I'm closer to action than I've ever been."

His tender look melted her heart. He took the mug from her hand, set it on the nearby table and drew her into his arms. His eyes captured hers, and as he lowered his lips, the sweetness flowed through her body. His kiss strengthened and she yielded to it and a depth of love she'd never experienced. They had shared more in their months together than Todd had been willing to give—honesty, tenderness, joy and even heartbreaks— each the rhythms of life.

Doug eased back, his breath quick. "Nina, you've become an amazing part of my life. I'm so thankful that you're willing to think about seeing a physician. I promise you, I care about you without promise of children, but I believe you deserve a chance to know the truth. If another doctor agrees with the first diagnosis, I will never ask again, but you are entitled to another chance."

She lifted her hands to his cheeks, studied his eyes filled with assurance and touched his lips with hers. He drew her closer, blending their hearts as one with every beat. She trusted him. She believed in him. She longed to learn the truth.

On Friday, Doug arrived home with Kimmy and settled her into her old bedroom. Though it had taken three days, Roseanne finally admitted caring for Kimmy's needs was more than she could handle.

Kimmy had showed no qualms when he picked her up that morning. She'd kissed her mother's cheek and listed a set of rules for her mother's well-being. Doug had to control his laughter while Kimmy gave her orders with such authority.

Roseanne hugged him goodbye, and he promised to bring her home for a visit. As soon as she could get around without the crutches, Kimmy would return home for good this time. Her doctor had given Rose-anne hope that it could happen soon.

Since Nina had gone to work that morning, he wanted to surprise her. He'd been tempted to call her but had resisted. Instead, he kept his eye on her house, hoping he'd notice when she arrived home from the of-fice, which was often halfway through the day.

Though Kimmy's headache had eased with medica-tion, she still needed rest. After gazing down the block one more time, he filled a container with apple juice, snapped on the lid and carried it to her room.

Her eyes were closed, so he tiptoed in and set the juice on the nightstand before creeping toward the doorway.

"Where's Nina?"

Surprised, he turned toward her and moved to her bedside. "She's at work, but she'll be home soon and I'll call her." He lifted the plastic tumbler and slid in a straw. "Can you sit up and drink some juice? It's apple."

She didn't move for a moment, and then eased her-self up on the pillow and took a sip of the drink. "When will I be better, Uncle Doug?"

A serious expression played on her face, and his lungs pressed against his breastbone. "We'll see in an-other week. You should have more energy and be able to do a few things, but rest and fluids will get rid of the virus. When your symptoms are better, then we'll know you're on your way to recovery."

"It's going to be Christmas and I'll miss it." Her eyes rimmed with moisture.

He sank to the edge of her bed and slipped his arm around her. "You won't miss Christmas. You'll be bet-ter before that, I promise." He lifted a prayer that his promise didn't disappoint her. He could only guess from the physician's prognosis.

She took another sip, a larger one this time, and handed him the juice.

He set the container back on the stand and tucked her in before heading back to the window.

When he looked outside, he spotted Nina's car in the driveway. His pulse skipped as he pulled out his cell phone and hit her number. When he heard her voice, he managed to monitor his excitement. "I see you're home."

"What? Aren't you at work?"

"I had extra vacation days for working on that long project so I decided to take the day and give Rose-anne a hand."

"Doug, you're the best brother there is. That's not much of a vacation for you."

He grinned to himself, hanging on to the surprise with a death grip. "When you get a chance, come down. I want to show you something."

"What?"

"Come down and see."

She chuckled. "You must have bought yourself a Christmas gift. I'm changing my clothes and I'll be down soon."

He disconnected and paced, as time ticked past. He'd become as excited as a child waiting for Christmas, but a guilty one. Though he felt bad for Roseanne, his selfish side arose again. Despite his guilt, he knew it really was best.

Though he'd doubted his every step with Kimmy until Nina came along, now he realized that if he had been that bad, he wouldn't be so eager to have

Kimmy back. Maybe he hadn't done such a bad job. He'd missed the joy of having someone in his life that he had to stay one step ahead of.

Her giggles and excitement had wrapped around his heart. Another person to share his days, his hours. Nina fell in line with those changes, too. She'd slipped into the lonely niche in his heart and filled it with new life and new hope.

A knock jarred him from his thoughts and he hurried to the door to open it before she rang the bell. He hoped Kimmy wouldn't hear her arrive until she had rested.

When he swung open the door, she arched an eyebrow. "I'm curious, you know." She stepped inside. "I've never heard you so excited. I know you bought something new."

"Wrong. Nothing new and it was free."

A frown dashed across her face for a fleeting minute and ended when Kimmy's voice sailed into the room.

"Is Nina here?"

Her eyes widened, and she sped past him and vanished into the guest room. Their voices merged, both talking at one time. He stayed away for a moment to give them time, and then sauntered in to be part of the new situation.

When he came through the doorway, Nina looked at him with a grin. "We have our girl awhile longer."

"Am I your girl?" Kimmy's tired face brightened with a grin. "My mom can't carry my food and drinks even though she tried." A faint titter left her. "She tried to put a tray around her neck and it tipped over and everything spilled on the floor." She looked at them with a shrug. "I knew it wouldn't work, but she thought it would."

Doug strode across the room. "That shows you how much she wanted to have you with her."

"But I want Mom to get better. She would hurt her bones trying to do everything, and I like staying here. I told her I would come to visit when I felt better."

"Once you're rid of the headache and all the stiffness, and your fever's totally gone, then you can visit and even go back home."

She nodded with a look that said she had figured that out by herself.

Kimmy's gaze shifted to Nina. "Can we make ornaments while I'm here?"

Nina brushed her cheek. "As soon as you get rid of that fever, we will make them. How does that sound?"

"Good." She lowered her head to the pillow, wearing a content expression.

They stayed beside the bed until her eyelids drooped. Doug eased from the room, and Nina soon followed. "I know this is for the best, but I can't help but feel sorry for Roseanne's situation. She had been so hopeful."

Doug drew closer. "I don't think it will be that long, and meanwhile, she'll enjoy getting ready for Christmas here, and then I'll have to help her mom do something to make the house look like Christmas."

"We can help Roseanne."

He caught her meaning and drew her into his arms. "We can. I don't think I can manage without you."

She gave him a playful poke but her eyes said more.

His heart read her message, and he lowered his lips as she honored his kiss without restraint. Though he had questioned her feelings and understood her reservations about commitment, the message had changed. In the past weeks, the assurance had grown that Nina loved him, and her willingness to consider having a second doctor's opinion validated his confidence. Trying to imagine life without Nina had grown hopeless. One day she would be his wife. Yet despite his strong belief, he lifted his eyes heavenward and asked the Lord for His blessing.

Chapter Thirteen

"Kimmy, you'd better rest awhile. Doctor's order." She grimaced but did as Doug asked.

He looked at the clock. He'd called Nina's cell phone but she hadn't answered and that concerned him. She'd be anxious to hear how the visit to Roseanne's had gone, and he'd expected her to be clinging to her phone.

Since pacing hadn't accomplished anything, he slumped into his chair and sorted through all he and Roseanne had discussed. He knew the time would come again when Kimmy returned home, and he tried to be happy for that day.

His cell rang and he hit Talk. He opened his mouth to greet Nina and then stopped short when he heard his mother's voice.

"I haven't heard anything lately, Dougie. How's Kimmy? Roseanne? I hate to call in case they're sleeping. You know I worry."

"Sorry, Mom." He'd been neglectful recently. He wouldn't like to be neglected by his children either— if he ever had any. "They're both doing well. Kimmy should be released from the doctor's care next week.

It's just about Christmas vacation at her school, so I'll just get some of her work, and she'll go back after the New Year."

"That's good news. And Roseanne?"

"Off her crutches next week, and Kimmy will go home."

"Wonderful. We need to get over that way and—"

"You're coming here for Christmas dinner, aren't you?"

"We are. It's not that far off, is it?"

Doug grinned. "No, it's right around the corner. If it's too hard to make the trip, then just come for Christmas. You can spend the night here if you'd like."

"Wonderful. Maybe we'll do that."

The conversation ran on and finally, with the promise of seeing him soon, his mother hung up.

When he wandered into the bedroom to check on Kimmy the doorbell rang. This time he had no doubt. He hurried to the door and when he opened it, Nina grinned and stepped inside. "I've been anxious to hear how things went. I thought you might call."

"I did. More than once."

"You did?" She patted her pocket. "I went to El's and I forgot it. I'd been glued to it before I left."

He glanced behind him, making sure they were alone, and then brushed her lips with a kiss. "Kimmy's in bed for a while. I feared she would hear you and bound out here again."

She lowered her voice. "I'll be quiet. Tell me what happened."

He filled her in on Roseanne's health, and then told her what she didn't want to hear. "Since she'll be off the crutches next week naturally she wants—"

"Kimmy home."

He nodded.

"I can't blame her, Doug. I'd want the same."

"So would I. But if you want to do those pinecone ornaments, you'll need to fit them in this week."

"I planned to, and maybe we could get your tree decorated while she's here." She thought a moment. "I'll go home and bring over what we need to make the ornaments. Then if she gets tired, she'll be home. It's easier." She tilted her head in that direction. "I have a couple things to do, and then I'll come back."

When she looked at him a moment, he saw a sparkle in her eyes. Her lips touched his with a kiss he would never forget. When she eased back, he caught his breath, but before he could say a word, she hurried out the door, leaving him with a warm and wonderful memory.

While he waited, he pictured the few ornaments he'd packed away in the garage. If he put up a tree, and it sounded as if that was Nina's plan, he would need to do an inventory. But the most important part of a tree would be buying one. He grinned at his silliness.

He pulled out a recent newspaper and looked through the ads to see where Christmas trees were sold. His thoughts drifted, and he imagined what it would be like to shop for a tree with Nina at his side and a child or two, excited about selecting the tree. No artificial trees for him. He'd grown up in a live tree home. He wanted to continue that tradition.

"Uncle Doug?"

He laid the paper on the table and rose, wondering what Kimmy wanted. She had slipped off the blankets and sat on the edge of the mattress. "What's up, sweetie?"

"Can I get up? I'm tired of being in bed, and I feel better." Wrinkles formed between her brows and her mouth bent down at the edges.

Her pleading look caused his heart to twinge. "The doctor said you still need to rest."

"If I'm tired, I promise I'll rest. I could rest on the sofa, couldn't I?"

He looked down the hall toward the living room and guessed what had stirred her. "I suppose the sofa is as good as the bed for rest."

A grin replaced her imploring scowl. She slid on her bathrobe and slippers and hurried past him through the doorway. When she reached the living room, she came to a halt and turned to look at him. "Where's Nina?"

His suspicion had been validated. "She went home for a while."

"Home? But I thought—"

"She'll be back soon." He crossed to the sofa and patted the cushion. "You heard her."

She nodded. "But I really feel fine. I think the doctor is being too careful."

"Ah, so you have a medical degree?" He arched a brow, unable to hide his grin.

She giggled and shook her head. "But he is being careful."

"Yes, but that's because he wants you to get better without setbacks."

She ambled to the sofa, propped up the pillow and rested her head on it.

He grasped the newspaper ads and strode toward the

chair when he heard a faint knock on the door. Veering his direction, he opened it and beckoned Nina inside.

She took two steps in and chuckled. "I see the patient isn't into resting."

Kimmy peeked at her through half-open eyes. "I'm better, but the doctor doesn't know it."

"Is that right? Well, maybe then we can work on something I have in this bag."

Kimmy widened her eyes and rolled on her side. "What is it?"

Nina reached into the sack and pulled out two pinecones.

"Ornaments." Kimmy's voice rattled the windows. She pulled herself upward and slipped her feet to the floor. "Can I help?" She eyed him, her pleading expression returned. "Can I, Uncle Doug?"

"For a while." He turned to Nina, sending her a subtle grin. "Is the kitchen table best?"

She nodded. "It's safer there, but you'll want to cover it with newspaper. I have glue and glitter."

She made them sound like weapons, and he laughed. He clasped the stack of papers he'd been looking through and headed for the kitchen. By the time he'd protected the table, Kimmy had arrived and anchored herself to a chair. Nina opened the bag and emptied out numerous pinecones along with a bottle of glue and containers of red, green and gold glitter. She reached in again and pulled out a spool of red velvet ribbon.

He stood back listening to Nina explain the process and almost had the urge to give it a try himself. Instead, he contained his eagerness and watched. His heart lifted, seeing Kimmy's excitement as she painted glue along the pinecone scales, filled a plastic bag with glitter and shook it until the pinecone sparkled with gold.

"Now, let this dry while we do another." Nina brushed on the tacky glue and Kimmy selected another color—this time, red. When she pulled it out, she turned to Nina. "Can I drop it into the gold, too?"

Nina told her yes and spread out the pinecones across the table to dry. After Nina had emptied the bag of pinecones, she put a lid on the glue and poured the unused glitter into the containers. "This can dry for a few hours, and then I can hot glue the top and we can add ribbons or beads for decoration and for hangers." She leaned back. "What do you think, Kimmy?"

Her eyes sparkling with life, she opened them even wider. "I love to make these, Nina. Thank you. They will be pretty on the Christmas tree." As if struck by an idea, she turned to face him. "Uncle Doug, are you going to have a Christmas tree?"

"I am, but I have to buy it."

"Can I help?" Her enthusiasm nearly knocked her from the chair.

"I don't think so this year, Kimmy. I want to get it soon, but you can help hang the pinecones."

Her disappointment eased with his offer. "Okay, but I won't have any at home."

Nina slipped Kimmy's hand in hers. "We can divide these up and you can pick your favorite ones. How's that?"

"I love you, Nina." She opened her arms, and he swallowed, seeing tears in Nina's eyes.

"I love you, too." She leaned into Kimmy's embrace and his heart swelled.

Kimmy released Nina's neck and turned to him again. "When are you buying the tree?"

He shrugged. He'd envisioned Nina joining him, but someone had to stay behind to be with Kimmy. His enthusiasm waned, wishing he could find a solution, but none came. "I'll need someone to stay with you when I go so I'll have to work that out."

"I can stay with her." Nina's eyes captured his.

"I know, but—" He managed to keep his wish to himself. "I may take you up on that."

Kimmy was all for it, but he eased away. Maybe, he could... What?

The obvious answer was he could go alone. He hoped this would be the last time he picked out a Christmas tree alone. It was the kind of thing people did with their family, and he finally knew how much he wanted a family.

Chapter Fourteen

Snow drifted to the ground and tipped the tree limbs and evergreens as Nina left the doctor's office, unsure where things stood. He'd explained similarities in diagnosis causing miscarriages and infertility and he'd mentioned a growth. Though it had panicked her, he'd told her not to worry. She still didn't understand fully, but he sounded hopeful, with some reservations.

Maybe she should be hopeful, too, but she didn't need to hear his uncertainties. She had prayed for good news. He'd told her that good news was possible from the tests he'd scheduled for her.

Every moment of the exam and his comments brought Doug to mind. He needed to be a father. His life would be incomplete without that blessing. And though she badly wanted children, she had lived without the hope. She could handle it, but Doug? He claimed he could. Though he would try, she feared resentment would eventually destroy their relationship.

With her heart the weight of a wrecking ball, she brushed snow off her shoes and slipped into her car to head home, where Rema had volunteered to sit with

Kimmy. Rema had proven a good friend to her and Doug with her willingness to care for Kimmy when they had to be in the office. The responsibility of caring for Kimmy had given Nina a taste of motherhood. Amidst the difficulties, joy permeated every moment, whether good or bad. Her love for Kimmy had grown beyond her imagination, and proved that if she became a mother, her life would be full.

As she pulled into the driveway, her tires leaving an imprint in the deepening snow, her cell phone's ringtone sounded. She shifted to Park and pulled the phone from her bag. Doug's face smiled at her from the screen as she hit Talk. "Why am I so honored?" She smiled at the photo.

"I've arranged someone to sit with Kimmy tonight after dinner so we can pick out our trees. Does that work for you?"

The trees. She'd assumed he would buy his without her. "Who did you get?"

"Rema volunteered. She's been great, hasn't she?"

She winced. She'd been great far more than he knew. "She has, Doug.

"How's Kimmy doing?"

Caught again. "You'll never guess that I just pulled into the driveway. I had to run an errand and Rema's sitting with her."

"She is? Maybe asking her wasn't a good idea. I just talked to her a couple hours ago."

"I'll ask her again and call you if it's a problem."

He'd accepted her solution and they disconnected, but the call left her with a pile of guilt. An errand? A doctor's appointment might be called an errand, but it left her feeling dishonest.

Facing the possibility of a good or bad diagnosis burdened her, and until she knew one way or the other, she wanted to avoid a discussion. In her mind, talking about it would only create more stress and confusion. She leaned back, watching the flakes glide through the air and land on her windshield. When she could no longer see outside, she opened the door and stepped into the white carpet of cold, as icy as her spirit had become.

Lord, give me hope.

She trudged onto her porch, plastering a pleasant look on her face. Rema was too discerning. She captured the image of selecting a Christmas tree with Doug. Her heart lightened as she opened the door.

Bundled in her warmest jacket, scarf and gloves, Nina eyed the tree lot from Doug's car, the heater and seat warmer making her cozy. Outside the snow continued to drift and she glanced at her boots, hoping they were high enough to keep out the icy flakes.

He pulled into the lot and turned off the motor. "Ready?" He sent her a coy grin. "I chose a day we may be buried in a snowbank."

"Adventure is good." She stepped into the snow as the cold penetrated the leather.

Doug held out his hand, and she grasped it, following him into the rows of trees. In the dusk, the trees were lighted by strands of overhead lights reflecting off the diamond flakes resting on the branches. Douglas fir, balsam, blue spruce. They studied the trees, estimating height and structure for open spots to hang the ornaments.

Near the back of the lot, a tree caught her interest and when she slowed, Doug did the same.

"Now, that's a beauty." Doug shifted around the tree. "It's great on all sides. I can put it in the picture window with no problem."

She studied the branches, each growing smaller to the top of the tree with open spaces to hang the ornaments. "Perfect."

He gazed at her, snow landing on his lashes, and her pulse skipped.

She lifted her finger to brush away the flakes, but he captured it with a kiss that warmed her hand. "Doug, this is the best Christmas I've had in…forever."

He drew her closer, his foggy breath whispering past her. "It's mine, too, Nina."

The look in his eyes melted the ice chilling her body, and when his lips touched hers, it sent rays of sun to her heart. She yielded again to his kiss, longing for blessings to make her able to announce her love to the heavens.

The rustle of trees eased them apart as a man strode between branches. "Did you find what you were looking for?"

Their eyes met and the glow of love they'd experienced had been exactly what she was looking for.

Doug eased away and pointed to their selection. "What is this?"

"A good choice. The balsam fir is our most popular. Short needles and strong branches with spaces for different-size ornaments. It has a long life in your home and the strongest scent of any Christmas tree."

"We're convinced." Doug grinned. "We'll take this one."

The man dragged it away for them, but Doug faltered. "What about you? Did you want to pick out a tree?"

"I've thought about that, Doug, but I'm spending most of my time at your house, and I have a small artificial tree that I think will work for this year. But if you need ornaments, I have more than I need so I can share."

His questioning look faded. "If you're sure."

"Positive, and if you'd like to buy more lights or ornaments, we can make a quick stop on the way home."

"Maybe we will."

He slipped his hand into hers as they returned to the front of the lot. The overhead lights glittered in the snowdrifts like a fairyland of glitter and gleam, matching the glow of her heart.

Four days later, Doug carried the tree from the garage to the living room, set it into the tree stand and placed it in the center of the picture window. Kimmy bounced around the living room like the seven-year-old she'd been for the past months before her illness. When Kimmy had begun to recover, it bolstered everyone's holiday spirit. Kimmy's temperature was near normal, and though the doctor advised another week of rest and fluids, he'd given her permission to spend more time being active.

Doug had wrestled with his emotional attachment to her and had accepted that she would return home that evening after the tree trimming since her mother was now off her crutches. He was grateful that she could be there to help decorate and make the occasion special.

As soon as he'd strung the white lights, which had

been Nina's request, Kimmy darted to her room and carried in the box filled with glittery pinecones. "Can we put the ornaments on the tree now?"

Doug shook his head. "Can we wait for Nina? She'll be here soon, and then we can all enjoy the fun."

Though she thought a moment, she agreed that they should wait for Nina.

The wait was short. Nina arrived carrying a small box just as he'd finished fetching the new ornaments he and Nina had purchased and the box of older ones he'd used in years past.

She stomped snow from her feet onto the doormat and handed him the box. "Here's some more ornaments if you need them. I have plenty on my tree."

He accepted the box and put them beside the others while she removed her coat and hung it in the closet.

"Let's decorate." Kimmy had latched on to Nina and tugged her to the box of pinecone ornaments.

Nina gave her a hug. "Let's keep those for last so they get the best spots."

Kimmy's eyes brightened. "Okay." She gazed at the other boxes. "Which ones go on now?"

Doug shook his head and chuckled. "Let's get organized after we turn on some Christmas music and I make us some hot chocolate."

"Yummy." Kimmy skipped her way to the kitchen as Doug followed.

Nina stayed behind and soon he heard Christmas music drifting through the doorway. She appeared shortly after with a demure grin. "I love the TV station with music for the holiday season."

"Me, too." He slipped his arm around her shoulders as the teakettle whistled. He reached into the cabinet and pulled down the chocolate mix, spooned the powder into mugs and poured in the water. In moments the fragrance of chocolate filled the air, and they moved back into the living room with their drinks.

Moving around the tree to the strains of Christmas favorites, he and Nina wove gold garland through the branches, and they all selected ornaments to hang on the tree. Kimmy worked her way around the lower branches while he reached the tall ones, and Nina hung them wherever she found spaces.

When dusk turned to darkness, the tree became heavy with decorations. He snapped on the tree lights, and the room glowed as sunny as their spirits.

"Can we now?" Kimmy stood close to the tree, holding the smaller box of decorated pinecones.

Nina cozied up to her and looked into the box. "We have about twenty of them so let's put half aside for the tree at your mom's house. What do you say?"

A frown slipped to her face. "But what about your house?"

Her chest warmed. "But you made them, Kimmy."

"We made them." Without letting her respond, Kimmy counted out the ornaments in three piles but paused holding the last two. "I need one more."

"My tree is small so give Uncle Doug one more and your mom one more. That will make me very happy."

Her eyes widened. "It will?"

"It will." She drew Kimmy into her arms and gave her a bear hug.

With the decision made, the seven glittery pinecones were added to the open spots on the tree. When they were finished, Kimmy stood back and let out a piping squeal. "It's beautiful, Uncle Doug." Her eyes shifted. "And Nina's beautiful, too."

Doug moved to Nina's side and slipped his arm around her shoulders. "I agree, Kimmy. She's as pretty as the tree." Far prettier than the tree, but he wasn't sure Kimmy would understand.

On the way back from taking Kimmy home for good this time, Nina fell silent. She'd had her tests and would soon hear from the doctor so it was time to prepare Doug for the good or the bad diagnosis. She'd been hoping she'd get some speculation from the surgeon or the technicians, but they'd said nothing despite her questions. Her doctor would study the two tests and let her know the results.

Waiting unsettled her, but she prayed for patience and for her acceptance, whatever the outcome. Though Doug had been sincere in his statement that the result would not influence his feelings, she left the door open. She'd been hurt once before and she could be wounded again. This time could result in a deeper wound, since Doug had opened her heart and her mind to loving again and this love seemed deeper and stronger than her marriage had ever been.

"Are you okay?"

Doug's question jarred her thoughts. "I'm fine. It's difficult when things change."

He reached across the space and squeezed her hand. "It's not a forever goodbye. We'll see Kimmy often. But I agree that it's different now."

Tension eased when she heard his response. Naturally, he'd considered her statement a reference to

Kimmy's returning to her mother's home. It was for the best.

She initiated conversation about Christmas. They were attending a small neighborhood party to celebrate the holiday, and Christmas dinner when both of their families would meet. Her mother had called and probed her with questions about her relationship with Doug. She'd finally given in and admitted her feelings. "Finally," her mother had said with a puff of relief. "And what about your infertility?"

The question had knocked the wind from her until she found her breath. "We will deal with that when it happens. Doug knows the problem, and he seems to accept the possibility. I can only trust his word, Mom, and he's never broken it in the months I've known him."

She remained silent and Nina prepared herself for a biting remark. Instead her mother surprised her. "I would agree. He comes across as a very down-to-earth, honest man. At least, there is hope that he means what he says."

Her pulse tripped, then calmed.

"We look forward to meeting Doug's parents. I'm so glad you invited us, Nina."

"Thanks, Mom. It won't be long."

The conversation ended and she clicked off and released a lengthy sigh. The idea of their families spending time together made her nervous but worrying about it got her nowhere. Her mother had made amends and they now could look beyond the past, and Doug's family was not a threat.

By the time they'd exhausted their Christmas plans, Doug had pulled into his driveway. The glimmer of lights from the large front window lifted her spirits.

"The tree looks lovely, Doug, and look at the reflections on the snow outside. It's like white cotton fluffs littered with diamonds."

He sat a moment, looking through the window, and then turned to her. "It is lovely, but as I said to Kimmy earlier, Nina, you are far lovelier than diamond-littered snow or a falling star."

He leaned closer, and she turned her face to his, accepting his kiss. When he drew back, he touched her cheek. "Let's get inside before we freeze out here."

A whoosh of icy wind filled the car when he opened his door. She unhooked her seat belt and stepped outside, meeting him halfway. He grasped her arm to keep her from slipping on the frozen surface. When they entered the house, he took her coat and motioned toward the sofa. "I'll make something warm to drink. How about some mulled apple cider?"

"Sounds good." She sank into a chair facing the tree and wrapped herself in the warmth of his kiss and the cozy Christmas decor. Yet as she waited, the admission she had to make swept through her again.

Doug came into the room whistling "Jingle Bells," and she wished her heart could be as merry as the tune.

The scent of cinnamon and orange zest passed her chair as he set a mug of cider beside her. He settled nearby on the sofa, his gaze shifting from the glittering tree to her. "You've been too quiet, Nina, and I sensed the long discussion of Christmas Day was a cover-up for something that's bothering you. Are you worried about our parents being together? I think it will be fine. I—"

"No. That's not it, Doug." She pressed her lips together, knowing she'd made a mountain out of a tiny bump in the road. "I've been wanting to tell you something, but it's been difficult."

A frown struck his face. "Did you hear something? Did you see the doctor and—"

"Yes, I saw the doctor, but I have no news."

Doug patted the seat beside him on the sofa. "Sit with me, Nina."

She rose and settled beside him. "The doctor spotted a discrepancy in the first doctor's diagnosis and he scheduled me for two tests."

"When? When will—"

"Doug, I had them already, and I should know the prognosis soon, but—"

"You've gone through this alone? Without telling me? Nina, why? You know how much I care. Why wouldn't you let me support you in this? I'm the one who asked you to have a second opinion. I did it for you as much as for me. Naturally I hoped the second doctor would disagree with the original diagnosis." Doug touched her cheek and turned her face to his. "And that's what happened."

"But it's not a sure thing, Doug. The tests may prove that—"

"They may prove anything. The first doctor was right or…the first doctor was wrong. Nina, I'm willing to take the chance so you know for sure. You've changed your life, afraid of being left again. I've promised you that I will never go anywhere without you at my side no matter what prognosis we hear. I hoped you'd understood me and believed me."

"I trust you, Doug. I do, but—"

He nestled her in his arms. "But you're afraid to hear what they say. It's natural, Nina. You don't want to get your hopes sky-high to have them nose-dive to earth again. I understand. But we can pray that whichever we learn, we can accept it and move on. Children are wonderful gifts. Most everyone wants their own flesh and blood, but Kimmy wasn't your flesh and blood and you adored her. Can't you see that no matter what, you can have children in your life?"

Tears broke through the dam. Hearing the wise words come from him, the depth of his sincerity, had broken the floodgates. He cuddled her against him until she calmed, and then he peeked at her, puckered his lips and whistled "Jingle Bells."

How could she not adore a man who could bring her to laughter in the midst of tears? She loved him.

Chapter Fifteen

On Christmas Eve, Doug had longed to talk privately with Nina but the time got away from him. She'd been busy the day before preparing the house for her parents' visit. Though they had come to Owosso close to Thanksgiving and had planned to stay home for Christmas, something had changed their minds. Now both families would be together for Christmas, and this was the perfect time for him to tell Nina how he felt about her.

But his plan failed and now they were in the midst of a neighborhood party. The only time they would have together was later tonight. The past days' tension had created concern, but when he stopped at her house to walk with her to the party, her Christmas spirit had lifted higher than Santa's sleigh. She swept into his arms, a look on her face that had been nonexistent for a long time.

Longing to understand her change, he drew in a breath and filled two punch glasses with sparkling apple cider. As he headed back to Nina, she'd begun to talk with one of the party guests he'd never met. He didn't think Nina knew the man either, but somehow Angie knew everyone. She and Rick seemed to be the neighborhood friendship league. Though he felt guilty leaving his mother and stepfather behind, they were in good hands at Roseanne's and had encouraged him to enjoy the festivities.

As he maneuvered his way through the neighbors, El beckoned to him. Surprised to see Birdie nowhere in sight, he turned toward El, curious. "Where's your friend?"

El chuckled, the usual glint in his eyes. "Birdie'll be here soon. Her cousins invited her to their home for a visit, and she couldn't say no on Christmas Eve."

He nodded, though he was still curious about El's relationship with her. They'd become a twosome and the friendship, though unexpected by most everyone, made him happy. Companionship now meant more than Doug might have imagined a year ago. "Is your granddaughter here?"

His eyes lost their bright flicker as he gave a toss of his head. "She's over there somewhere in the corner. She didn't want to come, but I encouraged her. Finally she gave in, but I know it was against her wishes." For the first time, El had a hopeless expression.

"This is a new situation for her. Hopefully once she's here awhile, she'll change, El. We all know what to do."

"Pray. That's what I've been doing." He lowered his eyes a moment. "I've always been a proponent of prayer, and my heart aches when I face what I already know. Nothing is in my time. It's in the Lord's hands. I only wish she could find a friend. Someone closer to her age who would make her time with me more fun."

Doug's gaze drifted to the neighbor still with Nina

but now with the added audience of Rema. Doug made a subtle motion toward the man. "What about him. Do you know the man?"

"Met him once. I think his name is Craig. He must have inherited his grandfather's home or maybe he's just staying there to prepare it for sale." El shrugged but continued to study the man. "I'm not sure how old he is. Hard to tell. The younger ones all look like kids to me."

Doug laughed. "I suspect he's in his mid to late twenties."

"He's only a kid then." He chortled a moment. "Once a person's close to pushing up the daisies, everyone's a kid."

"Who's a kid?"

Birdie's voice sailed between them, giving Doug the opportunity to say hello and continue to Nina with the drinks.

Nina grinned when he slipped to her side. "Doug, this is Craig Dolinski. He lives on the turn at the end of the cul-de-sac."

"Gramps died and left the place to my dad. Since they moved to California, he offered me the house at the greatest discount I'll ever find so...you know what I did."

Doug patted his back. "Can't blame you. That was generous."

He agreed. "Mom and Dad don't need the money, and I'm just getting started."

Rema took over the conversation, and Nina eased closer, eyeing the threesome in conversation. "El looked rather serious when you were talking."

He told her El's concern, and Nina agreed with his

mention of Craig. "I think I'll sidle over there and invite her to join us. What do you think?"

He agreed, and she excused herself a moment while he joined in the conversation.

Minutes passed before Nina returned with Ginger at her side. The girl's sullen look remained, but a look of interest flashed in her eyes. "You must be Ginger." Doug extended his hand. She eyed it a moment before grasping it with a less-enthusiastic shake. "I'm Doug Billings. I live across the street. I know your grandfather very well."

She gave a halfhearted flinch of her shoulders. "Gramps knows everyone, I think."

Though she seemed disapproving, her eyes shifted to where her grandfather had settled now with Birdie. A tender look slipped to her face and thwarted her attempt to be hard and disinterested. Doug wondered what had happened to the young woman, and he prayed Ginger would heal in her own way. Without the deep frown, she was quite pretty.

Before he turned, he heard Nina introducing Rema and Craig to Ginger, and he noted that the young man's gaze connected to Ginger's for a telltale moment, and he hoped he'd been right. A friend her age might draw her back into the world again.

Ginger appeared to let down her guard and get involved in Craig and Rema's conversation. She even joined in the laughter.

When the conversation shifted to fun things to do in town, Nina gave him a poke. "I think that did the trick." She eased her head in their direction.

"We do good work."

She tucked her arm into his. "Should we stand here or be more social?"

He eyed the other neighbors around the room and suggested they meet a few more people. They worked the room, introducing themselves to neighbors they'd never formally met, and spent time with Angie and Rick, thrilled to hear a baby was on the way.

"What do you say we leave?" He monitored his tone, not wanting to put a damper on the party if she wanted to stay. But he had too many things on his mind to stay much longer.

"I'm ready. It's been a long day."

With a quick goodbye, they slipped on their coats and stepped outside. Winter filled the air. An icy breeze whisked at his back and penetrated his limbs. He clutched Nina's arm as they made their way along the shoveled sidewalks and across the street where the tree lights brightened the windows. The hope of time alone with Nina warmed his heart. Tonight would change his life one way or the other.

As they stepped inside, warmth greeted them. He hung Nina's jacket in the closet and motioned her into the living room as he slipped his beside hers. "How about a fire?"

"It's a good night for one." She sank onto the sofa, her face hinting of preoccupation.

He let it go and added kindling and piled a fresh log on top. When the match caught the sticks, he watched it a moment. Satisfied, he settled beside her. "You seem happier than usual. Are you pleased your parents came for Christmas after all?"

"It's nice to see them, especially with the beginning of a better relationship. That's like a wonderful gift."

"I'm sure it is." He studied her face, sensing something else distracted her. "What are they doing tonight?"

"They have some friends who live closer to East Lansing, and they decided tonight was a good time to see them. They're staying with the friends until morning. I gave them a key to the house in case I'm in church."

"That worked out well."

She nodded, a faint grin on her face. Though it had taken him a while, he suspected he had the answer to her distraction. He'd hinted at a special surprise for her at Christmas, and now he was positive she knew what it was. "Are you thinking about my surprise?"

Her lips curved upward, no longer able to hide her smile. "A little, but—"

"I knew that was it. It took a while but—"

"You're wrong."

He drew back, his pulse skipping from her abrupt response. "What do you mean?"

Her eyes captured his and a sparkle lit her face and gave her skin a rosy glow. "It's not your surprise. It's mine."

His heart skipped, constricting his lungs, and it took him a moment to speak. "Your surprise? I knew something had made you happy."

She nodded as a smile broke free.

"Tell me, Nina, before I burst. Did you hear the test results from your doct—"

"I did."

Tears swelled in her eyes but not tears of sadness. He knew they were tears of joy. "What? What did he say?"

"I have a small growth, not serious, but preventing a safe birth. A noninvasive procedure can change that, and then there's no reason I can't have a baby, the Lord willing."

He opened his arms, drawing her into his embrace, tears rimming his eyes with the same happiness he witnessed in her face. "I'm so relieved for you, Nina. I know that apprehension had overtaken your life but you're free now. Free to make decisions without the dread of disappointing another man."

He touched her cheek and eased her around to look in his eyes. "I told you before I would not let your problem stop me from wanting to spend my life with you, and I meant that."

He drew back his hand and slipped it into his pocket. "Earlier tonight, I came prepared with my surprise, before I knew about the doctor's call." He eased back, withdrawing the small blue velvet box from its hiding place. He held it in front of her and pressed it into her hand. "Nina, I'm asking you to be my wife. You are the love of my life, the air I breathe each day. You are the shining sun to me even in the cold of winter. I love your generosity, your honesty and your willingness to seek the truth. You trusted me and saw the new doctor. And you love children, Nina. I pray the Lord blesses us with children. If not, I pray we can agree to adopt a child who needs love and a home."

A sob broke from her throat, and she looked at him with a flood of tears that spoke of love. "I want to marry you more than anything else in my life, Doug. You helped me become the woman I never suspected was in me. You opened windows and doors. You taught me all the things you say you admire in me. You are everything I could ever want and more."

He opened the box, and she gazed at the diamond with clusters on each side, glinting in the light of the Christmas tree. The fire crackled and flames licked the burning log, warming the room as it warmed their spirits.

When he slipped the ring on her finger, Nina brushed his cheek and brought her hand to his neck, her lips greeting his with a new life and depth he had never known. His heart sang carols of love and peace, and a faint jingle in his chest made him smile. Tonight he had experienced the real meaning of jingle bells.

Nina's joy was heightened by the beauty of the Christmas Day worship service. Carols soared to the vaulted ceiling, the message rang with hope and peace, and her heart warmed at the sight of Doug, Roseanne, Kimmy and Doug's mother and stepfather side by side along the church pew. Another new experience Doug had given her.

Her ring glistened in the overhead lights circled with colorful glass. Wreaths and garland draped from arch to arch along the walls, and candles glowed in sconces. Today her world had opened. Fear had flown away and hope had sprung free from the depths of her being. As the service ended with the glorious carol "Joy to the World," the congregation rose and filed down the aisles, greeting one another with hugs and handshakes.

She'd attempted to keep her ring hand hidden from his parents until the announcement when they had all gathered. The scene created visions of congratulations and good wishes from his family, and she prayed from hers, as well. Still fearing an outburst from her mother, she worked to keep the anxiety at bay. If she had only learned one thing in her journey to faith, she'd learned that the Lord was in charge. She was but a reed in the wind.

A chill clung to the air, but the sun sent bright rays into the sky, which helped to dispel the gloom of winter. The news they would share later when her parents arrived would be the brightest moment of the day.

When they rolled onto Lilac Circle, her parents' car was parked in her driveway so Doug pulled in and she headed inside, promising to see them shortly. She knew that Doug's parents had already caught on that Doug and she had made a commitment to each other. Whether they knew anything else, she would learn later that day.

She hurried inside, keeping her hand covered with her coat or stuffed into a pocket. She joined them in the kitchen for coffee before suggesting they leave for Doug's.

"You went to church—is that right?" Her mother's eyes darkened with her question.

"It was beautiful, Mom." Instead of getting defensive, she shared the message, the carols and choir, and ended with the decor. "I was glad I attended."

"I suppose you were with Doug…and that little girl. What's her name?"

Nina gritted her teeth beneath her smile. "Doug and his family. Roseanne is off her crutches and doing well. Kimmy is back to normal. Their healing was a true gift to all of us."

Her mother studied her a moment. "I'm sure it was. That little Kimmy is a sweet child."

"She is, Mom. One day I hope to have a little girl

of my own." She swallowed, anticipating her mother's response.

"But...what are you saying, Nina?" Her mother pinned her with a look. "Are you telling me that—"

"I am, Mom. I saw a new doctor, and after the exam, he recommended a couple of new tests." She explained the findings and the anticipated solution, and as she talked, her mother's expression grew tender.

"That's amazing news, Nina." Tears inched from beneath her lashes, and she reached across the table to grasp her hand. "Did you hear that, Howard?"

"I'm sitting here, ain't I?"

"Aren't you." Her mother gave him a frown.

"Nina, that's the best gift you could have given me. I'm not a faith-filled woman as you are, but if anyone can bless you, it's God. I know that."

Nina's eyebrows arched with the double surprise. "Thank you, Mom. I'm pleased you're happy for me."

Her mother's gentle look and nod said more than words.

"Are you ready to walk down to Doug's? It's a short walk. Just five houses down."

"I think I can do that." She rose and Howard followed her through the kitchen doorway into the living room.

Nina grabbed her coat and led them down the street to Doug's. When they entered, the smell of ham hung on the air. She'd convinced him a turkey and stuffing was too much work, and he'd finally agreed on a ham. She'd helped prepare a few things in advance and delivered them before church, and since they'd returned from the Christmas service, his mother had taken charge in the kitchen.

Introductions took a few moments, but soon her mother had donned an apron and had joined in stirring and cutting, while Nina worked to keep her hand undercover and help as much as they would let her. Kimmy and Roseanne finished setting the table, and before too much time passed, they gathered around the dining room table.

"Let's have Christmas music?" Kimmy ran from the dining room and found the TV holidays carols they had listened to before. The background music heightened the spirit, and Doug held out his hands while others joined hand in hand. Even her mother and Howard caught on to the tradition and joined in.

Doug's gaze swept around the table. "I'm so pleased to have all of you here to join in the Christmas celebration, praising the Lord for His greatest gift, His Son, our Savior who came down from heaven to bring peace, joy, hope and salvation. Heavenly Father, we thank You for this wonderful day, for the presence of our families, and we thank You for Roseanne's and Kimmy's health. We ask You to bless this food, bless those around the table, and bless Nina's and my promise of love everlasting when we become man and wife. Amen."

The amen tangled in the surprised sounds coming from everyone at the table. "Nina." Roseanne's voice reached her. "I've been praying for this. I'm so happy."

"Thank you, Roseanne, and—"

"You could add me to the list." Her mother had risen and came to her chair, her arms opened.

Nina rose as Doug had done, and received the hugs, kisses and congratulations from everyone along with the surprise they expressed. She showed her ring, and Kimmy clung to her, gawking at the ring but most of all repeating her new litany. "You're my auntie Nina. You're my auntie Nina."

"I am, Kimmy, and I'm so happy I'll be your real auntie." They hugged and laughed as the others, still amazed, settled down again to enjoy the food.

Though she put food on her plate, Nina's appetite had vanished. Instead, she was filled with gratefulness for her wonderful news, and amazed that Doug had asked her to be his wife on Christmas Eve.

As the meal ended, Doug rose and picked up something from a cabinet sitting in the dining room. He walked around the table to Nina's seat and drew her up. When she stood beside him, he drew her closer and raised his hand above her head while everyone laughed.

"It's mistletoe, Nina." She looked at Roseanne, wearing a grin.

Everyone cheered and applauded as Doug gazed into her eyes. She raised herself to meet his lips, enjoying the blessing of commitment, hope for children of her own, and two families who rejoiced with them. Never in her life had she anticipated a day like this one.

But then with the Lord, all things were possible.

* * * * *

"I am so sorry," Daisy told Joe as they walked down the sidewalk together.

The sun had come out and it was warm. The kind of day that made her long for spring.

"I don't know that I need an apology," Joe told her. "But an explanation would be a good start."

She shook her head. "I saw you sitting with your family, and I knew how I'd feel. Ambushed."

"I could have handled it. Now I'm engaged." He tossed her a dimpled grin. "What am I supposed to tell them when I don't have a wedding?"

"I got tired of your smug attitude and left you at the altar?" she asked, half teasing. "Where are we walking to?"

"I'm not sure. I guess the park."

"The park it is," she told him.

Daisy smiled down at the stroller. Myra and Miriam belonged with their mother, Lindsey. Daisy got to love them for a short time and hoped that she'd made a difference.

"It'll be hard to let them go," Joe said.

"It will be," Daisy admitted. "I think they'll go home after New Year's."

"That's pretty soon."

"It is. We have a court date next week."

"I'm sorry," Joe said, reaching for her hand and giving it a light squeeze.

"None of that has anything to do with what I've done to your life. I've complicated things. I'm sorry. You can tell your parents I lost my mind for a few minutes. Tell them I have a horrible sense of humor and that we aren't even friends. Tell them I wanted to make your life difficult."

"Which one is true?" he asked.

"Maybe a combination," she answered. "I *do* have a horrible sense of humor. I *did* want to mess with you."

"And the part about us not being friends?"

"Honestly, I don't know what we are."

"I'll take friendship," he told her. "Don't worry, Daisy, I'm not holding you to this proposal."

She laughed and so did he.

"Good thing. The last thing I want is a real fiancé."

"I know I'm not the most handsome guy, but I'm a decent catch," he said.

She ignored the comment about his looks. The last thing she wanted to admit was that when he smiled, she forgot herself just a little.

Don't miss
The Rancher's Holiday Arrangement *by Brenda Minton,*
available November 2020 wherever
Love Inspired books and ebooks are sold.

LoveInspired.com

LOVE INSPIRED

INSPIRATIONAL ROMANCE

UPLIFTING STORIES OF FAITH, FORGIVENESS AND HOPE.

Join our social communities to connect with other readers who share your love!

Sign up for the Love Inspired newsletter at **LoveInspired.com** to be the first to find out about upcoming titles, special promotions and exclusive content.

CONNECT WITH US AT:

f Facebook.com/LoveInspiredBooks

Twitter.com/LoveInspiredBks

Facebook.com/groups/HarlequinConnection

Get 4 FREE REWARDS!

We'll send you 2 FREE Books plus 2 FREE Mystery Gifts.

Love Inspired books feature uplifting stories where faith helps guide you through life's challenges and discover the promise of a new beginning.

FREE Value Over $20